The Wolf Hunt

ALSO BY GILLIAN BRADSHAW

Island of Ghosts
The Sand-Reckoner
Cleopatra's Heir

The Wolf Hunt

GILLIAN BRADSHAW

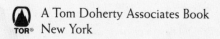

A Tom Doherty Associates Book
New York

THE WOLF HUNT

This book is printed on acid-free paper.

Book design by Jane Adele Regina

A Tor Book
Published by Tom Doherty Associates, LLC
175 Fifth Avenue
New York, NY 10010

www.tor.com

Tor® is a registered trademark of Tom Doherty Associates, LLC.

Library of Congress Cataloging-in-Publication Data

Bradshaw, Gillian.
    The wolf hunt / Gillian Bradshaw.
        p. cm.
    "A Tom Doherty Associates book."
    ISBN 0-312-87332-8 (hc)
    ISBN 0-312-87595-9 (pbk)
    1. France—History—Medieval period, 987–1515—Fiction. 2. Knights and knighthood—Fiction. 3. Brittany (France)—Fiction. I. Title.

PS3552.R235 W6 2001
813'.54—dc21   2001033825

First Hardcover Edition: August 2001
First Trade Paperback Edition: June 2002

Printed in the United States of America

0 9 8 7 6 5 4 3 2 1

The Wolf Hunt

fterward it seemed to Marie that she was born on the May afternoon when they told her that her brother was dead. Before that she had been cocooned in her own pretensions, a shapeless grub of a girl earnestly straining to be someone she was not. It was only when the fatal news destroyed all her dreams that she first emerged blinking into the real world.

She spent most of the day just as she'd spent a hundred others since her arrival at the priory, now nearly three years before—in copywork and in prayers. It was only after Nones, the midafternoon office, that she had the first hint of how everything would change. The prioress's serving girl hurried up to her as she was leaving the church and told her that the prioress wanted to see her.

"Me?" asked Marie with a mixture of puzzlement and dread. "Why?" She tried to remember if she'd actually spoken any of her many censorious thoughts about the prioress out loud. Prioress Constance was a worldly, aristocratic widow, and Marie, a passionate idealist of nineteen, had nothing but contempt for her.

"I wouldn't know, my lady," said the girl, unconcerned. "Some knights have arrived with a message, and my lady told me to tell you to go see her as soon as the office ended."

Marie's throat tightened with apprehension. Knights with a message that concerned her could only have come from her father, Lord Guillaume Penthièvre de Chalandrey, who was far away fighting on the crusade. Was he ill? Had he been awarded some honor by his overlord, the duke? Or—could he possibly have arranged for her to marry? For a moment she was standing in a cave at the back of her mind, smelling the stink that had filled the room at her mother's death: the scent of child-bed fever, of sex, of marriage. She didn't want to marry, ever; she wanted to become a holy saint instead. She crossed herself and hurried unhappily to answer the prioress's summons.

She did not have far to go: St. Michael's priory consisted of a large house with a single small courtyard adjoining the church. It was not, of course, a part of the monks' ancient abbey that crowned the hill; it was situated in the town that clung to the rock below. It enjoyed the abbey's protection, however, and the same secure position above the waters of St. Michael's Bay kept it safe from the constant raiding and turmoil that plagued the Breton March. The nuns were all respectable noblewomen, and they accepted only well-born girls as novices—a respecta-bility which had always frustrated Marie's ardent enthusiasm. The prioress's chambers were on the ground floor of the house. Even before she reached them she could hear Lady Constance's well-bred braying voice. It carried across the small cloister-court, punctuated by inaudible responses from the visitors. "No, no!" it exclaimed, just as Marie entered the dark porch. "She's a dear quiet girl, very modest and obedient; it's been a pleasure to have her here—do assure your lord of that! I'm sorry to summon her for such bad news, my lords, indeed I am, and I shall be very sorry to see her go."

Marie stopped dead, not listening for the still-inaudible reply. The oak door of the reception room before her was closed, while behind her the warm spring day continued smoothly in the sun. Bad news for her; so bad that she was expected to leave St. Michael's priory. She felt as though the threads that bound her heart to her mind had just been cut: she was aware that something had happened that would alter her life irrevo-cably, but it was an awareness without emotion. An onlooker inside her watched dispassionately to see what she, Marie Pen-thièvre of Chalandrey, would do in a crisis. The only conscious thought her mind shaped was a prayer: "Oh God, don't let my father be dead!"

She raised her hand and rapped upon the door.

The room was full of people. Lady Constance, a strong-featured woman of fifty, was sitting on the high-backed oak chair, dressed in one of the embroidered and bejeweled habits that drew scandalized fulminations from the abbey up the hill. Three knights were standing before her: they all turned to look at Marie as she came in, and with relief she realized that she didn't know any of them. Bad news from home would have had a familiar messenger. The knights were all young men and they all held cups of the priory's wine. Their conical helmets sat in a row on the prioress's table. Two of the men wore plain hauberks—knee-length leather coats stitched all over with iron rings—while the armor of the third was finer, forged of very small interlinked rings, with a gilded cross-harness on the breast. The hauberk sleeves, as was usual, reached only to his elbows, and one could see that the tunic beneath was dyed scarlet and trimmed with marten fur. He was evidently a man of some wealth, and she guessed he was the leader of the party. He was fair-haired and clean-shaven, a handsome man with wide blue eyes and even white teeth which he started to show her in a smile, before visibly remembering that he was bringing her bad news and looking solemn.

"Marie, my dear," said Constance gently, "thank you for coming so promptly. Child, you must strengthen yourself and trust in our Lord Jesus Christ. I'm afraid that these gentlemen have brought bad news for you."

Marie crossed her hands on her breast and bowed her head. Her heart was still cut off, but there was a sick taste at the back of her mouth. "Lord Jesus Christ have mercy," she said. "My lords, what is your news?"

It was the fair-haired man in the fine armor who told her. His name, he said, was Alain de Fougères; he and his companions had been sent by her father's overlord, the duke, to tell her that her brother Robert had been killed at the siege of Nicaea.

Marie had been braced for disaster, and its absence staggered her. She'd barely known her brother. He'd lived at the court of her father's overlord, Duke Robert of Normandy, since before she was born, serving the duke first as a page, then as a squire and a knight. He'd only returned to Chalandrey to bring home a silly wife who'd disliked Marie—and then he'd spent very little time there. She was shamefully aware that she felt a bitter jealousy toward him, the child her father loved, the heir all her world united to praise. But she'd prayed for him dutifully every day. He'd been a stout, cheerful man, fond of sweets and wine; she remembered him dancing the gavotte with his wife until his face was crimson. How could he be dead? She blinked at the fair-haired knight owlishly, and he looked back with an expression of dutiful solemnity. The silence lengthened. She realized that everyone expected her to say something, and, horribly embarrassed, she couldn't think what to say.

Into her numbed mind came one thought far too honest to be spoken aloud: if Robert were dead, their father would have to notice her at last. He never had, never, even though she tried to make herself modest and humble and pious, everything a gentlewoman should be; even though she had mastered the extraordinary accomplishment of learning to read. Marie's face went hot. It was wicked to be pleased at a brother's death. She pressed her crossed hands against her chest, feeling the heart pounding under the ridges of bone. One of the knights hurried over and set a stool down for her, and, dizzy with shame and embarrassment, she collapsed onto it with a thump.

Alain de Fougères coughed, with the air of a man who's completed an unpleasant preliminary and reached the point where he can do the business he intended. "Because of this sad loss of that good knight your brother," he said, "my lord the duke has sent us to escort you to his court."

"What?" asked Marie faintly, then, more sharply, "What do you mean?"

"With your father away you are the duke's ward," Alain said, as though he were explaining it to a child. "Now that you've lost the other members of your family, it's his business to provide for you."

Marie's face went even hotter. She knew the feudal law as well as he did. A man's overlord was always the guardian of his widow or orphans. But she was not an orphan and she didn't see —

Suddenly, she did see. Her brother had no children, so, under the marriage settlement he had made, his widow would not inherit from him. Marie herself was now the heiress to the manor of Chalandrey — and, as an heiress, valuable. An arranged marriage to an heiress was a fine reward for any knight a feudal overlord was pleased with. The sick taste swam back into her throat, and she felt herself begin to tremble. "My father provided for me already!" she exclaimed, too shrilly. "He sent me here."

"For your safety, child," said Lady Constance gently. "Your father arranged for you to stay here while he was on crusade, but he was very emphatic that you weren't to take vows without his permission. Now that your circumstances have changed, you should go to court."

Marie stared at her frantically, trapped, then whirled back to Alain de Fougères. "How could Duke Robert have sent you?" she demanded. "He's on the crusade with my father."

"I've come on the duke's authority," replied Alain. After a moment he added, "Duke Robert *has* left a steward, you know."

One of the other knights grinned. Marie looked from the grin back to Alain de Fougères, trying to fight off the horror and force her stunned mind into motion. She felt as though she had just missed something, something important. But it was impossible to think clearly. She was bound to obey her father's overlord. Bound to marry at his command some total stranger, probably a man much older than herself. Bound thereafter to regard her husband as her lord and master, to accept humbly whatever treatment he gave her — and most husbands beat their wives at least occasionally. Bound to lower her body, awkward and private and vulnerable, into the feverish, bloody filth of childbirth. Bound to lose herself utterly. Choking on a panic without outlet, she pressed her hands against her face and burst into tears.

She left Mont St. Michel that same afternoon. Lady Constance told her that it was best to keep busy. "You know that you must obey your lord as you would obey your father himself," she said. "And since you're bound to go, it's best if you go at once. It won't do any good to brood. I'm sure you'll be well looked after at the duke's court, and these gentlemen will treat you kindly on the way there. You go and pack."

It was the prioress's serving girl, though, who packed up the few belongings Marie had brought with her to the convent. Marie could only sit on the narrow bed, her hands folded in her lap, praying. She was still shaking, but now only partly from fear, and largely from shame. The onlooker within had watched to see how she would behave in a crisis. It had seen wicked thoughts, craven terrors, and childish bursts of tears. Of the firmness and faith that should have gone with that much-sought-after holiness, there had been no trace.

The sun was still well above the horizon when Marie climbed, dazed, onto the rawboned gray mare that had carried her to the priory three years before, and set out with the three knights.

Lady Constance had been right in one thing at least: the journey instantly wrested Marie's mind from her own concerns. Her mare Dahut was what her father had approvingly termed "a good horse": she was strong, fast, and enduring. She was also an iron-mouthed, bad-tempered bone-shaker, and for three years she had been used by a motley assortment of priory ser-vants, which had not improved her naturally contrary disposi-tion. Marie had learned to ride as a small child, but had not been on a horse since arriving at the priory, and Dahut kept her so busy that for some miles she had no time even to look back. She did notice, though, when they turned to cross the Couesnon River into Brittany. She could hardly fail to notice that.

For sixty years the Couesnon had formed the boundary be-tween the duchies of Normandy and Brittany. Though both nominally subject to the king of France, the two duchies were in fact virtually independent nations, and they were at war al-most as often as they were at peace. Many Breton families, however, had a foothold on both sides of the river. Brittany was poor and Normandy was rich: What could be more natural than that poor Bretons, second and third sons with no part in the family inheritance, should seek their fortunes in the north? And if they succeeded, what prevented the lords of small estates in Brittany from getting big ones elsewhere? The many branches of the Penthièvre family were the most eminent of all these allegiance-straddlers. Partly because of the glorious duplicity of more exalted Penthièvres, Marie's own, more modest branch of the family was absolute in its allegiance to Normandy. Guillaume Penthièvre's father had left the service of the duke of Brittany and sworn fealty to Duke William the Conqueror, and that loyalty, Guillaume declared proudly, could not be retracted again without loss of the family's honor. He boasted of never having crossed the Couesnon.

Marie dragged her mare to a stop in front of the low wooden bridge. Dahut snorted and laid her ears back, jerking her head against the reins and shifting her feet in resentment. The three knights stopped, too, and turned back to fall in beside her. Behind her lay the empty expanse of salt marsh, and beyond that the pinnacle of Mont St. Michel, already four miles away but looking close enough to touch. The river before them flowed brown and smooth, the current so gentle that it seemed not to be moving at all.

"My lady?" asked Alain de Fougères, speaking for all three, as usual. "Why have you stopped?"

Marie looked at him in confusion. "You're going the wrong way," she said—and winced inwardly at how timid and unsure of herself she sounded.

He hesitated, and one of the other knights looked at him in exasperation. Marie thought the exasperated man must be some kind of kin to his leader: they looked alike, though Alain's wide-featured good looks were exaggerated in his follower to a peculiar resemblance to a frog—a gap-toothed frog with sandy hair. The follower's name, she'd gathered, was Tiher. "Tell her the truth, Alain," he urged.

Alain hesitated a moment longer, then nodded. "Very well. Lady Marie, we're going to Rennes."

Marie stared. Rennes was the capital of one of the three great counties of Brittany. Again her heart was cut loose from her mind, and she felt unreal, as though this were happening to someone else. "You said we were going to Duke Robert's steward!" she protested.

"No," said Alain, looking enormously pleased with himself. "I said we were going to the court of the duke. Duke Hoel is presently at Rennes."

Duke Hoel of Brittany. Marie stared in incomprehension. Dahut seized her moment, jerked the reins out of Marie's hands, and sidled stiff-legged toward the lush grass at the side of the road. Marie hurriedly drove her heels in to start the horse back the way they'd come—but at this the bad-tempered mare laid her ears back and balked. Tiher was right beside her: he leaned over and caught her bridle, a gesture that might have been merely helpful but suddenly was not. With a froggy grin he looped the trailing reins over his own arm. This is an abduction, Marie thought in amazement. That was why I felt I was missing something. It wasn't that I was stupid; it was that they were deceiving me. Duke Hoel! Oh sweet Jesus, I should have thought! Of course the duke of Brittany would jump at a chance of getting hold of a fine rich manor like Chalandrey!

"You lied to me!" she exclaimed furiously to Alain.

"I didn't lie," answered Alain righteously. "I told you that I had been sent to escort you to the duke who is your rightful overlord. That's true."

"My rightful overlord is Robert of Normandy!" protested Marie. "You told me you'd come on the authority of Duke Robert's steward!"

Alain shook his head. "I never said that," he corrected her, smug at his own cleverness. "I said I'd come on the duke's authority, and that Duke Robert had appointed a steward—which he has. I never lied. You believed what you wanted to."

"You knew you were deceiving me!" Marie shouted, her face flushing with rage. "I was a fool, no doubt, to believe that you were a true and honorable knight, and to trust . . ."

She stopped. The one she'd trusted had been Lady Constance: she'd assumed Alain was honest, because the prioress had urged her to go with him. It was inconceivable that the prioress, with her love of pedigrees and her knowledge of all the noble families of the Breton March, could have been deceived about the allegiance of any knight. And Constance, Marie now remembered, was a Breton Penthièvre, half-sister to the duchess of Brittany. Constance had connived at this.

Marie had devoted herself to holiness and humility, but she came from a long line of knights famous for their ferocity in war. The discovery that she had been betrayed into the hands of her enemies jolted her into a cold rage. If her inner onlooker had still been regarding her behavior, it would have found her accepting her betrayal with far more steadiness than she had found for her difficult obedience. But her inner self was no longer playing the detached observer. It was calculating, with a fierce intensity, the best way to escape.

She bit off her protest to Alain. Too much noise, too fierce an opposition, and the knights might decide to tie her to her horse for the rest of the journey. She drew her white novice's wimple forward to veil her face, as though she were overcome by emotion, bent her head, and locked her hands, which were trembling with anger, together in her lap.

Alain protested indignantly that he *was* a true knight, and a loyal servant of the duke, but, getting no response, spurred his horse to clatter proudly over the bridge ahead of her. Tiher hesitated a moment, then tightened his grip on Dahut's reins and gave the mare a sharp slap on the rump to start her across the bridge. The third knight, Guyomard, fell in behind, and they rode on into Brittany in silence.

Tiher felt sorry for his captive. Her brother's death had clearly hit her very hard—he had been touched by the stricken silence with which she'd received the news—and it was, no doubt, cruel to take advantage of her in her grief. It was also fairly deplorable to trick a novice nun from a priory, even though the prioress had turned a blind eye to the deceit. The cause might be just—Tiher had no doubt that the duke of Brittany had a right to the manor of Chalandrey—but it was hard on the girl. And she was a pretty girl, too, he thought judiciously, watching the downcast profile. Marie had a strong, clear-featured face whose fashionably high forehead owed nothing to the artifices of plucking and shaving, and her eyes under the straight brown brows were a dark gray. The plain monastic dress, black gown and white veil, was unbecoming, it was true, but Tiher had no objection to imagining her without them. Nice wide shoulders, nice wide hips, very nice in between.

Marie glanced up, and Tiher grinned at her in what was intended to be reassurance. She looked back at her folded hands at once, and he gave a sigh of rueful resignation. He never got anywhere with pretty girls—not with well-born ones, anyway. He was not merely ugly, but landless. Landless knights didn't marry. How could you have a wife when you had no house for her to live in, and your bed was in your lord's hall along with a score or two of your comrades in arms? Even Alain—who was, as Marie had guessed, Tiher's cousin—was unlikely to marry, and he was the second son of a lord and not just an impoverished nephew. Still, Tiher liked women's company when he could get it.

"You'll come to no harm with us, Lady Marie," he told her. "Duke Hoel will treat you honorably."

She did not reply. Tiher sighed again, and they rode on in silence.

They traveled for nearly four hours that afternoon. The mare Dahut continued to misbehave, balking at streams, lunging at pastures, and occasionally kicking at Tiher's mount or trying to bite. Tiher cut a switch of willow and thrashed the horse each time she played up, but still found his arms aching from the mare's jerks at the bridle by the time they reached the abbey of Bonne Fontaine, where they were to stay the night. Marie by that time was pale with weariness, and she slumped painfully in the saddle. Her muscles had forgotten how to ride, and Dahut was not an easy goer. Nonetheless, when the abbot appeared at the gatehouse to greet them, she slid quickly off the horse and threw herself on her knees before him. "Help me, Father!" she cried loudly. "These men are abducting me. My father sent me to the priory of St. Michael, and they've stolen me away against my will!"

The abbot stared at her a moment, more in resignation than surprise. It was not unknown for knights to abduct pretty girls from convents. Then he looked accusingly at Tiher. A younger Tiher had once attended school at that same abbey, and he still thought of the abbot as able to fling God's thunderbolt at need. "It's the duke's orders, Father!" he protested hastily. "The lady is the heiress to Chalandrey, and Duke Hoel wanted her out of Mont St. Michel to keep her safe from the Normans."

The abbot's face cleared. He was a Breton of the March. He loathed the Normans, whose raids had often struck at his abbey's lands. He remembered nothing particularly reprehensible about Tiher, and he knew Alain de Fougères by sight. Alain's mother had been a great benefactress of the abbey. He had no doubts about whom to believe.

"You need have no fear, my daughter," he soothed. "Duke Hoel will see that you are well treated. And you must know, child, that whatever you've been told, Duke Hoel *is* your true overlord. In swearing fealty to a Norman, your father robbed Brittany of what was rightfully his."

Marie bit her tongue. It was clear that appeals would achieve nothing, and to persist in open opposition would only make her captivity harder to escape. She'd been ashamed of her tears and stunned stupidity at Mont St. Michel, but now she silently thanked God that she'd seemed such a fool. If they thought her weak and silly, they wouldn't expect her to do anything now but weep.

The abbot escorted them into the abbey guesthouse, where his servants prepared rooms for them: one room for the three knights, and one, next door but decently separate, for Marie. The knights took the precaution of closing the wooden shutter on the single window of Marie's room and barring it securely on the outside, and they locked the heavy door and kept the key. Marie sat down wearily on the bed and buried her face in her hands. Her limbs were still trembling from the ride, and she was so tired that she feared she would fall asleep where she sat. But she knew she must escape that night. Already they were twenty miles from Mont St. Michel, farther than she had ever gone on foot; after another day of riding the distance might prove too great for her. She didn't dare try to steal a horse. She had to go that night, or not at all. She must rest a little first, though, and eat to get her strength back. It would be best to leave in the early hours of the morning. She was used to waking before the dawn to say the office of Lauds, and she was confident that the deep-voiced abbey bell would rouse her as easily as the shrill jangler in the priory.

Now, how was she to get out? Marie heaved herself off the bed and carefully examined the room by the light of the single tallow candle the abbot's servants had left for her. The window shutter was not only firmly barred, but creaked at the merest touch: even if she could force it, it would be bound to make a lot of noise, and that would wake the knights next door. The walls of the room were thick mud and wattle upon a ground course of stone, the roof was tightly bound thatch, and beneath the rushes the floor was hard-packed clay. It might be possible to dig through one or another of them — but it would take hours of effort, and leave her too exhausted to go any distance.

That left the door. She went to it last. When she held her candle up she could see the bolt, slotted into a hole in the doorpost. Level with it, scraped into the wood of the post, was a small trench that must have been made by someone in the past opening the door with the bolt half in. Marie stared at that light scrape in the wood for a moment, her breath unsteady. She knew when she saw it that it was the way out, but it took a little time for her to understand how. Then, fumbling with excitement, she drew off her white wimple and jammed it in a wad between the bottom of the door and the stone threshhold, next to the hinges, where it would foul the door's swing invisibly.

A monastic servant came in a few minutes later, carrying a tray with a dish of pottage and a cup of wine for her supper, together with a ewer of water for washing, a basin, and a clean cloth. All three knights trailed behind him and stood in the doorway looking at her while the servant set his tray on the bed. Tiher was holding a candle, which made their shadows flap blackly about her room.

"Is there anything you require, Lady Marie?" asked Alain politely.

"Your absence," Marie returned coldly.

Alain looked offended, bowed stiffly, and left. Tiher gave her a froggy grin and followed, and the third knight, Guyomard, pulled the door shut behind the servant. The wadded-up wimple made it stiff, of course, so stiff that for a moment Marie stopped breathing, terrified that he'd look to see what was jamming it. But he didn't: he dragged it to, and through the thump of booted footsteps retreating, Marie just caught the click of the key turning in the lock. She leapt to her feet and rushed over. The bolt showed blackly in the crack between the door's edge and the frame, but it was impossible to see if it had stuck in the scraped-out trench or if it had gone securely into its socket. And she did not dare check, not yet. She leaned her head against the doorpost and prayed silently and passionately that the door was not locked. She thought of her father, camped before the walls of unimaginably distant Nicaea, grieving for Robert. *I will keep your honor safe,* she promised him inwardly. *I will never give your lands to your enemies. You will be proud of me, Father. You will be proud of me at last.*

Then she said three Paternosters to calm the thundering of her heart, and turned to wash before her supper.

When the bell rang for Lauds, Marie was up, three years of convent life taking her fumbling feet into waiting shoes even before she was fully awake. Then she stopped. Even in the complete darkness before cockcrow, the room was unfamiliar. This wasn't her little cell at St. Michael's; this was . . .

Remembrance brought a flood of almost unbearable excitement.

She made herself sit still, listening. The bell stopped; the rustle of feet died away across the court, and the opening phrases of the office, thin and slow with sleep, whispered from the chapel. Marie took a deep breath, rose to her feet, and groped her way through the total blackness to the door. There. Rough frame, smoother planking; latch. She let her hands slip down, over the latch, along the edge, then along the sill. There was her wimple, exactly where she'd left it. Her first eager tug didn't shift the cloth, and she had to force herself to work it out slowly, patiently shifting it back and forth until, suddenly, it came loose. The door gave a screech as it did and pulled toward her. Marie felt a jolt in her chest as though her heart had tried to descend a step that wasn't there, and she froze, crouching by the threshold. But still there was no sound but the distant whisper of the monks saying the office. She got to her feet, clutching the wimple in one sweaty hand.

"Christ and Saint Michael help me!" she whispered. She wrapped the wimple carefully around the door latch, then pulled hard.

The wimple muffled the noise a little, but still the bolt gave another screech as it dragged along the frame—and then the door was open. Marie rested her palm against the post for a moment, listening, over the thunder of blood in her ears, for some sound of alarm. Again she heard only prayers.

She stepped cautiously out into the corridor. Now she could hear something from the room where the three knights were sleeping—but it was only one of them snoring. They, of course, were not in the habit of rising for Lauds, and they'd slept through the bell. Marie tried to stifle the rush of triumph: she still had a long way to go. Closing the door of her room carefully behind her, she hurried along the corridor, pulling the wimple over her head and tucking her hair under it as she went.

The forecourt of the abbey was deserted. The outer gate was barred and bolted for the night, but only on the inside, to keep out intruders, and the gatekeeper was asleep in his lodge. Marie had no trouble unbolting it and slipping out.

The moon had set, and everything was dark and strange. The road was visible only as a gray open patch against the shapeless blackness of the land. The silence was so deep that it numbed the ears, and little sounds—the rustle of clothing, the clumping of feet, even the rasp of breath—resounded hollow and vast. The roadside weeds were heavy with dew. Marie stopped after a few steps and stood motionless, hearing again the rush of blood in her ears. For the first time, she felt afraid. She had never before been alone out of doors at night, and in the darkness, beyond the strip of cultivated land beside the road, lay the forest. She had seen it the afternoon before, a shadow on the hills, sometimes coming close to the road, sometimes fading into distance, but never completely out of sight. The forest of Broceliande, the mystery that filled the heart of the duchy of Brittany as deep as the sea. There were wolves there, and other savage animals; there were robbers more savage still—and there were other things more dangerous than either, things that fled with a laugh and a ringing of crystal bells into hollow hills, or smiled up at you from wells when you looked for your own reflection. Things that could steal away your shadow and drive you mad; demon things.

Marie was a Breton of the March, where one spoke French; the forest belonged to the older Brittany, which spoke a more ancient tongue. But she had heard the stories. The country people left certain trees alone, decked certain springs monthly with flowers, built bonfires annually on particular flattened stones, and left little offerings of bread and milk. The church condemned it all, but the peasants stubbornly persisted, and few village priests had the courage to tell them to stop. Even priests could suffer if "the Good People" were offended. And the heart of the Good People's land was the forest.

Marie swallowed, crossed herself, whispered a prayer to Saint Michael. She had escaped: she would not let fear of things unseen keep her a prisoner now. But she started toward Mont St. Michel along the road. The afternoon before she had planned to make her way back through the forest in order to baffle pursuit, but she could no more enter the forest's shadow in that moonless dark than she could grow wings. The road would be safe until dawn. And in the daylight, she told herself firmly, the forest will seem safer, too.

As she walked, the land gradually, almost imperceptibly regained its shape. A hill humped itself up, black against the east; a brook followed a dip under a shadow that became willows. Then the silence was broken: a cock crowed from a farmyard as she passed, and her heart skipped a beat with relief. It was well known that all evil things retreated to their dens at cockcrow. Soon a few hesitant birds chirruped uncertainly; others called back. All at once the whole dawn chorus—the thrush and the warbler, the robin and the lark—sang full-throated from every bush and hedge, and the rest of Marie's dark fears drifted away on their tide of song. The light grew and the fields turned green, dappled with the white and yellow of meadowsweet and buttercups. Rabbits bounded for their burrows as she approached; a vixen ran across her path in a streak of red. Two swans flew low overhead, their wings booming. As the eerie quiet of the night receded, Marie found herself grinning with pure joy and walking with great bounding steps. This was no dream, no fantasy of holiness: this was real. She'd escaped! The knights had thought she was dull, timid, easy to deceive— but they were the ones deceived, and she was on her way home.

She should get off the road before they came galloping after her. Marie half-ran, half-skipped to where a farm track led off to the left beside a brook. Along a field, over a ditch, through a pasture, and there, closer than she'd expected, was the forest. There was nothing sinister about it now that the sun was up. The trees were covered with the vivid green of May, fuller than early spring's leaves, brighter than summer's. The morning sun had brushed their tops with a light as rich and yellow as butter. There were bluebells flowering under the old oaks, and the undergrowth had been coppiced recently, the straight young wood cut to be used and the rest cleared, so that the flowers carpeted a space open and airy as a hall, dappled with sun. The farm track continued on under the trees. The fear she'd felt before now seemed ridiculous: Broceliande was a beautiful place. Happily, she followed the path onward.

It was easy going for a while, and she was free to imagine what she'd do when she got back to St. Michael's. She'd go straight to Lady Constance. "Lady Mother," she'd say, "those knights who came to fetch me — they weren't from Duke Robert at all." And Constance, pale with shock at Marie's reappearance, would whisper faintly, "No?" "No," Marie would say. "They were from a duke, certainly, but not Robert of Normandy. Hoel of Brittany had sent them to abduct me. He meant to marry me off to one of his own men and steal my father's lands. But I managed to escape. I thank God and Saint Michael, who saved me from having to turn traitor to my sworn overlord. I hate treachery above all things," she would say pointedly. "I'm astonished, Lady Mother, that you didn't realize who that Alain de Fougères was and who he served — you, who know the pedigree of every knightly family on the Breton March."

Some of Marie's happiness vanished. Constance had certainly known. What would she do when the novice she'd betrayed turned up again on her doorstep?

Marie bit her lip and told herself that Constance wouldn't be able to do anything. She wouldn't dare admit that she'd connived at the abduction of a young noblewoman entrusted to her care; she'd have to pretend that she, too, had been deceived. The priory was *safe*, she told herself. It had to be. There was no other refuge within reach. She pressed on.

The path grew narrower, and soon she left the area of coppiced woodland behind. The forest floor became a mixture of brambles and saplings where there was a gap in the canopy above, and bracken shoots and bluebells where there wasn't. Eventually Marie noticed another track which left her path to the right. It was rough and half-choked with brambles, but it led north, the direction she wanted. She kilted up her skirts out of the way of the trailing brambles, and turned right.

The going became much harder. Last year's leaves covered the ground, hiding the fallen branches, the stones, the dips in the path, so that she stumbled often; in the sunnier patches there were nettles and thorns. The effort made her painfully aware that she'd already walked a long way on an empty stomach. Her muscles were still stiff and sore from the previous day's riding, and she longed to lie down and rest. She reminded herself of how proud her father would be when he learned of her daring escape, straightened her shoulders, and continued on. She walked more slowly, though, and watched for some sign of a farm or cottage where she could buy food. The night before she had filled her purse with all the money that had been packed into her luggage: it should be more than enough to see her home.

Two hours later, she'd come upon no sign of human settlement. Since she left the road she'd seen nothing but the trees, with the light slipping through them in bewildering patterns; heard nothing but the cries of the birds, and the scolding of an occasional squirrel. Her path had long since vanished into the undergrowth, and she'd struggled on along a series of deer tracks which ran a little ways into the forest, then disappeared without warning. As the sun climbed higher the day became hot, and midges and mosquitoes rose whining from black muddy patches on the forest floor. She found herself thinking longingly of water—but she'd passed no water since the brook where she left the road. Her legs were scratched by brambles and stung by nettles, and her face and hands had been bitten by mosquitoes. She wondered if the knights would already have passed her along the road. If they had, it would be safe to return there. She didn't think she could endure much more of the forest.

She sat down beside the trunk of a fallen tree, to rest and to check her direction by the sun. For a few minutes, though, she was too exhausted even to move, and she simply sat, leaning her cheek against the tree's green bark. At last she crossed herself and said a prayer, then looked up at the sun, which scattered light unevenly through the shifting leaves above her. It was noon, and the shadows were short. She looked down at the shadow of the tree beside her—and realized that the angle

of the shadow was wrong. She'd been walking west, not north.
West, into the heart of the forest. Worse, she could not remember when she'd last checked her direction, and couldn't say how
deep into Broceliande she had come.

Her eyes stung, and sobs of panic pulled at her throat. The
forest had lured her in, beguiling her with bluebells, and then
closed in behind her. She felt an irrational certainty that something was waiting farther in among the shadows of the trees —
something animal and rank and monstrous. She would be
caught in the forest at night and then *it*, the thing in wait, would
have her.

She told herself angrily that she couldn't have come far out
of her way. She had not been walking fast: she couldn't be more
than two miles from the road. If she walked due east, she would
reach the road long before nightfall. There would be houses
there, and people, and food. Meanwhile, she should try to find
water. She would feel much better when she'd had a drink.

She sat up straight, set her teeth, pushed the heels of her
hands against her eyes, and recited two Aves and her favorite
prayer to Saint Michael. Then she climbed resolutely to her feet
and began pushing her way eastward through the thick undergrowth, ignoring the tempting tracks that led in any other direction, and hoping she'd soon find a stream.

After a mere ten minutes or so of struggling through the
bushes, she heard the sound of running water. A few seconds
later, she broke through a screen of saplings into a clearing
among the oak trees. A spring bubbled up into a deep green
pool, then ran off through a sward of impossibly green grass as
a little stream. Wood anemones, celandine, and the wild pansies
called heartsease grew beside it, and the stream was half-
covered with the shining white cups of water crowfoot. As she
came into the sun, she paused first because of the beauty of the
place — and then because of the wolf which lay on the grass
beside the pool.

Eagerness and misery were lost together in the icy jolt of
terror, and for an endless moment she stared into the animal's
face. She found afterward that all the details of it had impressed

themselves on her mind so perfectly that she could recall the whole picture simply by closing her eyes and remembering her fear. The wolf was sprawled on its side, its head up, as though Marie had woken it from sleep. Its coat was a dark gray, tipped with black at the tail and brushed with black along the back, but paling on the belly and legs almost to white; the muzzle and ears were masked with brown. The brown eyes were incongruously black rimmed, like a painted courtesan's at a fair; the mouth was open, black lips slack around gleaming white fangs, red tongue panting in the heat. It seemed enormous, staring at her with the grim confidence of a lord in his castle facing an offending serf. Marie remembered stories of the beasts: children disappearing in the forest, babies snatched from cradles, a pile of white bones and a few scraps of cloth all that anyone found of them. She wondered why she didn't scream.

The wolf moved first. It jumped to its feet, its hackles rising and its ears flattening. At once Marie, too, broke from her paralysis. She bent and grabbed the nearest branch. "Scat!" she shouted, swinging her stick so that it cut the air with a vicious hiss.

The wolf's mouth curled in an insolent doggy grin — and then it turned and loped off into the forest.

After a minute, Marie went forward and stood over the pool, nervously listening. There wasn't even a rustle in the undergrowth. The wolf had simply run away.

It was as frightened as I was, she told herself shakily. Humans hunt them more than they hunt us. She knelt down by the spring to drink.

The water was delicious, fresh and cold and sweet. She sat down on the grass when she'd finished drinking, pulled her shoes off, and soaked her sore feet and scratched legs. The water's touch seemed to take away all pain. A nightingale was singing from a tree nearby. Farther away a cuckoo called, and a woodpecker knocked intermittently: *ch-ch-chunk . . . chunk* and then a long pause, as though he were tired. The air was full of a heavy summer hum, a mixture of running water, insect songs, and the soft noise of leaves shifting in a breeze too light to be felt. Marie lay down in the sun and wriggled her toes. The weariness she'd struggled against for hours washed over her. She hadn't actually taken her rest, back at the fallen tree. She would take it now.

She didn't expect to fall asleep, not with the urgency she felt to get out of the forest, not after the encounter with the wolf. But the exhaustion she'd pushed back so determinedly drowned her, and within minutes her eyes had closed and she turned into the soft moss under the blanket of sun, and slept.

She dreamed, thinking she was awake. She lay on the moss in the sun, and saw the wolf coming back. Its mouth was still curled in the insolent grin, and its red tongue lolled. It slipped through the new shoots of bracken, and as it came it seemed to grow larger, heavier, more misshapen. Then it rose on its hind legs, and she saw that it was a man, a wolfish, savage man, naked except for long hair that covered his body like the bristles of a pig. His nails were curved yellow claws, and his teeth were fangs, bared in the same wolf's grin. His genitals were red and erect. Marie tried to cry out in horror, to run away, but she couldn't move. He came closer. Now the hair on his body had become rough hempen cloth, patched with hide, and he wore his wolf skin as a cloak and hood, its empty eye sockets staring above his own. He stood over her, still grinning, then turned and spoke to two others who had appeared beside him, his harsh voice framing words she could not understand.

Marie opened her eyes with a jolt, looked up wildly, and found that the man was there.

The nightmare horror of it was so great that for a moment she thought she would be sick. She couldn't move, and only stared up, round-eyed, white with terror.

The man laughed and said something to her. She still couldn't understand, but suddenly realized why: he was speaking in Breton. She recognized the language, though she couldn't speak it. In Chalandrey even the peasants spoke French.

The man said something else and offered her his hand to help her up.

Marie sat up, looking from the hand to the man, and then

to his two companions, who stood a little behind him, grinning, leaning against their short bows. They were all heavily bearded, rough-looking men, fairly young, dressed in the hemp tunics and hose patched with hide of her dream. The man before her did have a wolf-skin cloak, but it was an old, tatty one, badly cured. She swam back to reality, weak with relief. These men were nothing worse than woodcutters or swineherds, ordinary peasants going about their own business in the forest. She had glimpsed them while she drowsed, and the wolf-skin cloak had joined the wolf she'd seen in a nightmare. Then relief gave way to alarm: she had drowsed, but for how long?

She glanced around at the sky, and saw that the sun was low now, slanting through the trees; it was late in the afternoon, almost evening. She pulled her heels under her and jumped up, then wobbled uncertainly on her bare feet.

"I'm sorry, good man, I don't speak Breton," she told the man in the wolf skin. "But if you can help me out of the forest this evening, I'll be grateful."

One of the other woodsmen laughed and said something. Wolfskin shrugged and replied. He caught Marie's sleeve. *"Nan gallek,"* he said, and grinned again.

She understood that much: "No French." She pulled her arm away from him fastidiously—his hand and clothes were filthy. "I want to get out of the forest," she repeated slowly, then waved an arm at the trees around her, and pointed eastward. "Out of here. Broceliande forest—no, *nan.*" She fumbled at her belt for her purse. "Here," she said, taking a coin from it, "I'll pay you for your trouble."

Wolfskin whistled and took the coin. The one who'd laughed said something else—a joke, because they all laughed. To her horror, Wolfskin reached over and grabbed at the purse, which was fastened to the belt. Marie clasped her hand over it.

"No!" she exclaimed angrily. "Take me to Mont St. Michel first. At Mont St. Michel, yes, you can have any money I've got."

"Mont St. Michel!" repeated Joker. "Eee—*religieuse.*" He made another joke, which the other two found even funnier.

Wolfskin took Marie's hand and firmly pulled it off the purse. She protested angrily and slapped at his hand, and Joker slid behind her, grabbed one arm, then the other, and twisted them behind her back. The pain shocked her. Calmly, Wolfskin unfastened her belt, slid the purse off, and hefted it appreciatively in his hand.

"Thief!" shouted Marie in astonished outrage. Nothing that had ever happened to her before had prepared her for rough robbery by peasants in dirty hemp tunics. She struggled to free her arms, and Joker jerked them upward, stilling her with another spasm of pain. She stood still, blinking, choked by a white-hot fury of indignation. What would she do without money? How could she get home now?

The third woodsman held out his hands, and Wolfskin tipped the contents of the purse into them. Money-man hefted the coins, sorted them out, and made a comment: the amount. The other two grunted appreciatively. Joker nodded at Marie and made another joke. Wolfskin didn't laugh this time. He merely smiled, said something to Marie in a friendly tone, and pinched her cheek. His cheerfulness was even worse than his thieving, and Marie could do nothing more than glare wordlessly. Wolfskin said something more, then untied her wimple and pulled it off. He stroked her braided hair, traced the line of her jaw lingeringly down along her throat, and smiled. *"Kaer,"* he said, sounding almost affectionate.

It was only then that she realized she had worse to fear than robbery. She jerked backward in horrified disbelief, then gasped as the move twisted her arms. "No," she said, shaking her head wildly. *"Nan.* No, you don't understand; I'm a noblewoman, a lady novice—my family will pay a ransom for me!"

She realized as she spoke that, even if this were something that might have moved them, she didn't look like a lady. She was dressed for a convent, it was true, but the clothes were not so distinctive: any woman might wear a plain black gown and white wimple—and, for that matter, no particular vocation was needed to have a place in a monastery. The fact that her habit was good cloth wasn't very apparent now that it was covered with bark and moss scrapings and kilted up above bare feet. To these men she must appear simply a peasant girl, a monastic servant, perhaps, who'd run off on a private holiday and now wanted to go back to her employment. They'd found her alone in the forest. She plainly wasn't herding pigs or cutting wood or gathering herbs or engaged in any other honest occupation, and if three rough, healthy young men meet up with a wild, disreputable girl in a lonely place, what are they expected to do?

Wolfskin caught her head in both hands and kissed her eagerly. His breath stank, and his tongue was slimy. She remembered with the vividness of hallucination the scent of her mother's sickbed and the cold slime on the skin of her dead baby sister. As soon as his mouth pulled away from hers, she screamed as loudly as she could.

He was surprised. He slapped her, and said something angry and impatient. She screamed again, and he put his hand over her mouth. At this the fury she'd felt since he grabbed her purse boiled over: How *dare* this filthy peasant treat her like a whore? She straightened her arms as much as she could, threw herself backward, nearly knocking Joker over, and lashed out at Wolfskin with a bare heel. She caught him hard on the thigh, and he shouted, then slapped her again, so hard this time that her shoulder twisted almost out of its socket, and she screamed in pain. Wolfskin grabbed both shoulders and shook her, shouting into her face.

"No!" she screamed back, so furious that she had no room even for fear. "No! Even a stupid lout like you must understand *that* much French! You stinking brute! No! No!"

Money-man shoved past Wolfskin and tried to smother her shouts with another kiss. Marie bit his tongue as hard she could, and he jumped back, spitting blood. They all began to swear indignantly, as though she were deliberately teasing them, inciting them to lust by appearing in their path and now perversely refusing to satisfy them. Joker twisted her arms, and Money-man punched her in the stomach. There was nothing she could do to defend herself, and she sagged, retching. Wolf-

skin elbowed Money-man aside and grabbed her. He dug his
fingers into her buttocks and dragged her against him, moving
his hips back and forth. He started to grin again. She caught
her breath and screamed even harder, struggling to get away.
Joker shouted at her, angry and irritable. Stop fooling, his tone
said; get down to business. It all seemed unreal, a nightmare.
This was not something that could happen to her, a girl of good
family and enclosed life, a scholarly girl who wanted to be a
nun. "No!" she cried again, shaking her head desperately. She
kicked frantically at Joker's legs, trying to make him let go, but
Joker hooked a foot about her ankle, tripped her, and forced
her down onto her side on the grass. He said something else.
Money-man laughed at it. Wolfskin nodded, knelt over, and
began unfastening her gown with the same deliberation with
which he'd stolen her money. Money-man hauled the bottom
edge of the skirt up and sat on her legs, pinning her to the
ground, while the other two stopped twisting her arms long
enough to pull the gown off. She screamed again—"No! No!
No!" But the only result of her cries was that Wolfskin shoved
her wimple into her mouth to muffle them. Money-man pushed
her linen shift up to her waist, and Joker caught it and pulled
it over her head. It was tight, and he hadn't bothered with the
laces. When he dragged it up it caught on her chin and twisted
it back, and wrenched her arms in their tight linen sleeves above
her head. Legs and arms pinned, stripped like a rabbit being
skinned, half-suffocated, she heard, in anguished disbelief, the
three men laughing.

She did not see what happened next. She only felt Money-
man's callused hands dig convulsively into her thighs, then go
limp. Someone shouted in horror. Joker finally let go of her
arms. She tried to pull them protectively downward, couldn't,
rolled onto her side and tried again. Then a hand grabbed her
imprisoned elbow, linen and arm and hair together, and hauled
her to her feet. Wolfskin's voice shouted something; he dragged
her in front of himself and shook her. Marie flailed her free arm
in the air, and succeeded in shaking the sleeve down and the
folds of cloth off her face. She spat the gag out of her mouth.

Wolfskin immediately twisted the arm he held behind her back, which at least shook the other side of the shift down as well. He put something cold against her throat: she realized it was a knife.

She looked in front of her, and saw Money-man lying face-down on the grass with an arrow sticking from his back. She blinked at him stupidly. It made no sense; she couldn't see how it had happened. Beyond him there were only trees.

Wolfskin shouted again. This time, after a pause, a voice answered him from among the trees, as calm and deliberate as Wolfskin's stealing.

Wolfskin swore. He pulled Marie backward toward the other side of the clearing. At once there was a hiss, and an arrow buried itself in the turf just behind him. He stopped and shouted something. The unseen other answered in a few calm, unemotional sentences, instructions, perhaps, or conditions.

Wolfskin shouted a question.

There was silence.

Wolfskin shouted another question. Again, there was no answer. Abruptly, Wolfskin shoved Marie aside so violently that she fell. She pulled herself onto her knees and started to crawl toward the trees. Wolfskin ignored her. He took the bow off his back and flung it on the ground. Marie noticed Joker for the first time, lying on his side with an arrow in his eye. Wolfskin faced the invisible archer and flung his arms wide, shouting defiantly — challenging the other, Marie realized, daring him to stop striking from hiding like a coward, and come meet his adversary man to man. She reached the edge of the trees and collapsed, shaking.

There was another long silence — and then the other man walked out of the trees.

Wolfskin gave a cry of triumph. The other set down the bow he was carrying at the foot of an oak, dropped a quiver of arrows beside it, and walked unhurriedly toward Wolfskin, pulling his own long hunting knife from his belt as he came. He was clearly of a higher class than his opponent: he was dressed in the standard clothing of huntsmen and foresters, a tunic and hose of plain green wool, rather than cheap hemp. His face was partly hidden, both by the hood of his tunic and by a chaplet of leaves which he wore, as hunters did, for concealment: all that could be seen of it was a black beard, clipped close to the jaw, and a pair of level dark eyes. He was a bit shorter and slighter than Wolfskin, but somehow looked more dangerous. As he came nearer, he pulled the twist of oak leaves off and dropped it.

Wolfskin's first triumph gave way to a look of surprise, then, all at once, of fear. As the other stopped, facing him, he suddenly spat out a single word which Marie did not understand, but remembered afterward: *"Bisclavret!"*

The huntsman's eyes narrowed. Wolfskin gestured toward the trees and spat out something more. Huntsman replied sharply. He dropped into a fighting crouch, holding his knife in front of him. Wolfskin matched him, but he took a step back, and his eyes were flicking frantically about, searching for a way out.

Huntsman lunged forward with a furious savagery, knife weaving from side to side as though it had a murderous will of its own. Wolfskin flung himself desperately backward—then lunged forward again suddenly. Huntsman whirled sideways, blocked the blow, catching Wolfskin's arm on his own, and stabbed violently upward. But Wolfskin had rolled with the block, and even while Huntsman was stabbing, he was tearing at his own skin cloak. He ripped it loose and, with a shout, flung it over the other's head.

Marie screamed, leapt to her feet, and stumbled toward the pair with a desperate and confused intention of helping. Huntsman dropped to the ground and rolled sideways to escape the anticipated blow, tugging clinging leather off with one arm. Wolfskin, however, wasn't attacking: he was running away. Head lowered, one arm clasped to his side and the other working like a pump handle, he thundered into the forest and was gone.

Huntsman pulled the wolf-skin cloak off his head and sat up. He shouted something after his adversary, something angry and contemptuous. He got to his feet, bunched the cloak up, and hurled it at the ground. Then he stood staring in the direction Wolfskin had gone with an expression of grim consideration.

"Are you hurt?" Marie asked him, then remembered that he probably wouldn't understand.

He glanced at her in surprise. "You speak French?" he asked.

She didn't know what to say. After the monstrous things that had happened, the simple question seemed unanswerable. How could she say what language she spoke, when she felt that she had become foreign to herself? She shoved the bent index finger of her left hand sideways into her mouth and bit it, a habit from her early childhood, broken many years before. She started to shake again.

Huntsman looked at her with concern. "Are *you* hurt?" he asked.

She shook her head and sat down, still biting her finger. Agonizingly wrenched shoulders, bruised face, bruised stomach and thighs: no, she wasn't hurt. Not as much as she could have been, not nearly.

Huntsman glanced about, then went to where her gown lay on the grass beside the pond and picked it up. "Here," he said, bringing it over to her. "You have nothing to fear from me, sister. I won't harm you. Put this on, and we will go." His French had a strong, soft Breton lilt: otherwise it was faultless. He was quite young, no older than twenty-five, and the air of danger that had come with him out of the trees was gone now. "You should not have been here on your own," he told her seriously.

She burst into tears.

Huntsman stood over her awkwardly for a moment, then knelt down beside her. He draped the gown over her shoulders like a cape. "Sshh," he said gently. "I know you are a brave girl. Be brave for a little longer. We must get away from here. Éon has run off, but he will think it his duty to kill me, to revenge his companions. He may have another friend nearby, with a bow; we cannot stay here."

Marie wiped her eyes, still biting her finger. She wiped her nose and stood up. Huntsman nodded approvingly. Marie pulled the gown off her shoulders with trembling hands. Her hair had come loose in the struggle and hung in thick brown tangles over her shoulders. Again she felt as though she'd been transformed into somebody else—a fairy, maybe, standing here in a forest glade in the fading gold light, dressed only in her white shift, barefoot, her hair loose about her shoulders. She fumbled the black woolen gown over her head and looked around for the wimple.

"We . . . we should hurry?" she asked Huntsman.

He nodded.

She saw the wimple, lying on the grass beside Joker's body, and went over to pick it up. Joker's face stared up at her sightlessly, one eye glazed, one bloody ruin. Numbly she bent and picked up the wimple. It was damp from its use as a gag and stained with blood: it slipped from her trembling fingers. She picked it up again, took it over to the pond, and rinsed it in the cool water. She knew that she must hurry—but she couldn't. She knelt, looking down at her reflection. The face was still her own, though it was blotched with bruises and there was blood on her chin. From her cut lip, or from Money-man's tongue? She started to shake uncontrollably again. She closed her eyes and said a Paternoster. Then she drank some of the water, splashed her hot face, wiped it with the scrap of linen, rinsed the wimple again, wrung it out, and pulled it over her head. Underneath it, her hair was still loose, but even if there had been time to braid it, she doubted that her hands were steady enough. When she tried to climb back to her feet, she found that her legs were unsteady, too.

"I . . . I don't know that I *can* hurry," she told Huntsman. "I haven't had anything to eat all day, and I'm not used to walking . . ."

This did not seem to worry Huntsman. While Marie was washing he'd dragged the two corpses to the very edge of the clearing and arranged them on their backs; her information merely made him take a wallet of supplies from one of the dead men. He picked up Money-man's purse as well, but didn't loot the bodies more than that, except to select some arrows from the quivers. Then he took the rest of the arrows, together with the three bows, propped them against a fallen tree, and broke them with a few smashing blows of his heel. With the same rapid deliberation he picked up the twist of oak leaves he'd worn when he first came into the clearing. He went over to the spring and dropped it in the water, muttering something, then tossed the purse in after it.

Marie swallowed. Even in her shocked state, she understood the gesture. It was *that* sort of spring. This place was sacred to the Fair Ones, and Huntsman was apologizing to them for staining it with blood. It occurred to her that most of the money in the purse must be hers — but after what the Huntsman had just done for her, she had no intention of asking him to fish it out.

Huntsman took the selected arrows back to his own quiver, still in its place under the oak tree, and slid them in. He picked up bow and quiver, and nodded his head in the direction he'd come from. "We will go this way," he told Marie, handing her the wallet of supplies. "You can eat as we walk." She nodded, though she no longer had any idea what direction it was.

Huntsman hesitated another moment, glancing back at the clearing. Then he turned to Marie again. "I . . . do not wish to pry," he said. "But . . . would the person you were meeting in the forest still be anywhere nearby? Because if so, he may be in danger."

Marie stared in confusion, then realized that Huntsman had made the same assumption as Wolfskin: that she'd come to the forest to meet a lover. "I wasn't meeting anyone in the forest!" she declared angrily, her face going hot. "I was lost."

"Oh," said Huntsman, surprised. "Forgive me." He set out into the shadows under the trees.

There was bread in the wallet, a coarse black bread full of grit and bran; it had a strange bitter edge to it that made her teeth ache, and she suspected that its baker had eked out his flour with acorns, but she ate it hungrily. Huntsman didn't share the bread with her, but walked with his bow in his hands and an arrow on the string, glancing from side to side. It was dusk now, and the forest was dim and mysterious, gray tree trunks melting into the gray light, leaves whispering to one another. After a little while they reached a grass-covered track, and Huntsman turned onto it. An owl hooted, and Marie jumped.

"Do you really think that Wolfskin is following us?" she asked nervously.

"Wolfskin?" repeated Huntsman. "Do you mean Éon?"

"Was that his name?"

"Yes," said Huntsman seriously. "I suppose he would not have told it to you."

Marie wanted to giggle hysterically. She bit her finger again. "We weren't introduced, no. You seem to know him."

Huntsman shrugged. "I have encountered him before. But I would have guessed his name even if I hadn't. He is a very notorious robber."

"What!"

"Haven't you heard of him? Éon of Moncontour?"

"No."

"Ah. Well, he has been a terror to the people for a year and a half now, but he moves about from place to place, and those the duke sends to catch him can never find him. I am sorry, by Saint Main, that he got away. I should have shot him from the trees."

"And . . . and you *do* think he's found some more of his followers, and is coming after us?"

"No," said Huntsman confidently. "I think he's run off. I wounded him in the fight and I broke his bow. He is afraid of me anyway: most likely he'll be far away by now. But he had three men, not two, in his company last autumn. Probably the third died during the winter, but perhaps he was simply somewhere else when the others attacked you. If that was so, he could have armed himself again, and they could be tracking us. He will feel obliged to kill me if he can."

Marie was quiet for a moment. She remembered his considering look when the robber ran off, and she suspected that if she hadn't been there, he would have followed at once. And if she wasn't here now, battered and exhausted and needing help, he would follow still. It wasn't wise to leave a wounded wolf alive, free to attack you another day. "Thank you for saving me," she said at last. "I . . . that is, I come from a good family. We can reward you richly for what you've done for me."

He glanced at her sideways. "You are from a good family?" he asked, surprised again. "What . . ." He stopped.

What were you doing alone in the forest? Marie finished for him silently. That was a question she didn't want to answer, not before she was safely back at St. Michael's. Huntsman's French was very good, surprisingly good, but it was still plain that it was his second language. A Breton-speaking Breton was almost certainly a servant of the duke of Brittany, either directly or through one of his vassals. From Huntsman's reference to the duke a moment before, Marie suspected he was one of the duke's own foresters. He certainly seemed skilled and brave enough for it. At any rate, if he knew that she was escaping from Duke Hoel, he'd turn from rescuer to captor in an instant. She wondered why he hadn't asked his question aloud. Probably because he still believed she'd gone to meet a lover and didn't want to pry.

"I am of good family," she repeated instead. "The Penthièvres of Chalandrey. My name is Marie."

He stopped short at that and stared at her hard.

"We're only a cadet branch of the clan," she told him, unsettled by the look of disbelief. "I'm a novice at St. Michael's priory. That's in the town of Mont St. Michel, under the protection of the abbey. I . . . I was on my way back there, but I stupidly left the road to . . . to avoid meeting someone, and I got lost in the forest. If you can bring me back there I'll pay you whatever you like."

He stared a moment longer, then seemed to decide that she was telling the truth. Even in the dusk she noticed his smile, a quick lift of one side of the mouth while the other side remained serious, and a tilt of the angled eyebrows. She found that she knew that his eyes were a light brown; she must have seen that at the spring, but been too shocked still to register it.

"So I have rescued a Penthièvre, a kinswoman of the duchess!" he exclaimed. "Indeed! I have done better than I knew. But you should not make such promises to strange men."

"You said I had nothing to fear from you," she replied.

"Nor have you. Well, I can bring you to a lodge belonging to a daughter house of the abbey of Mont St. Michel. There will be brothers there who can escort you home."

Marie bit her lip. "I'd prefer . . . not to go back to the convent by the public road. Couldn't you . . . ?"

"I am sure the brothers at the lodge know ways to reach Mont St. Michel that don't follow the public road." He began walking again.

Marie hurried to catch up with him. It was growing very dark now, and she tripped over a grass tussock and fell. Huntsman turned back and helped her up.

"Hold onto my belt, Lady Marie," he told her. "The ground is uneven."

She slipped her fingers over the belt and walked behind him. Through the loop of leather she could feel the muscles of his back shifting. He picked his way through the night so surefootedly that she wondered if he could see in the dark. If she echoed his movements, she walked without stumbling. A dreamlike peace slipped over her. She had been caught in the forest by night, and she had met the thing that lay in wait for her, but it was tamed, and there was no more fear. The darkness and the trees had no power to terrify her, for she was joined to them, linked by the strap of leather over her fingertips. Body and soul, which for her had always been at odds, moved together through the night: two ends of the same yoke; two fish turning as one in the silk current of a stream. She realized suddenly that she didn't want to go back to St. Michael's with any anonymous brother from a lodge. Without Huntsman, her shocked mind whispered to her, everything will dissolve into horror and chaos once again.

"You couldn't go to St. Michael's with me yourself?" she asked. "I'd reward you well."

"I am sorry, Lady Marie. I have important business in Rennes."

She bit her lip. Her eyes stung. She told herself severely that this was nothing more than shock and exhaustion, and in the morning, everything would seem different. She found her own severity carried no conviction. She wanted Huntsman to stay beside her.

He would not. "Well," she said, after another long silence, "come to Mont St. Michel when you can then, and I'll reward you."

He made a small noise of amusement. "I am not a man that needs to be paid," he told her. "I, too, am of good family, Lady Marie. I hold the manor of Talensac, and some lands near Comper and Paimpont. My name is Tiarnán."

"Oh!" exclaimed Marie. "You're a knight?"

He nodded; she could feel the movement down his back, though the darkness made it invisible.

"Oh!" she said again, feeling her face grow hot. "I'm sorry."

"Why?"

"I . . . I thought you were a forester. I offered you money."

"So you did. And had I been a forester, I would have been pleased to take it. What else were you to think, meeting a man on foot and dressed in a plain green tunic? Everyone looks the same in hunting clothes. Just as a lay sister or servant, which I took you for, looks the same as a lady nun. . . . Here. We have reached our destination."

There was a stink of pigs and a smell of wood smoke. A dog began barking madly. Huntsman — Tiarnán — stopped and stood still. "Salud!" he shouted and, after a moment, there was an answering shout, and then a light ahead, coming from an open door.

"Where are we?" Marie asked.

"At the lodge of some pig keepers, near the crossroads of Dol," said Tiarnán, beginning to walk forward again. A man was standing in the door, holding a branch of kindling for a torch in one hand, and a dog's collar in the other. Tiarnán's face appeared again from the darkness as they moved toward him; he gave her the sideways glance and the half-smile. "They are lay brothers of Bonne Fontaine abbey, Lady Marie," he told her. "A night spent here will do no damage to your reputation."

lain de Fougères pulled his helmet off, ran his fingers through his sweat-damp yellow hair, and turned in the saddle to scan the land around them. The fields lay flat and open under the noonday sun; Mont St. Michel at their backs stood out as a blue silhouette, twelve miles away and showing clearer than the nearest church tower. The hills in front of them were dark, however, already shadowed by the fringe of the forest. They'd reached the end of the coastal plain and were nearly halfway back to the abbey of Bonne Fontaine — and they had found no trace of the woman they were searching for.

Alain turned an imploring gaze on his cousin Tiher. "Where is she?" he demanded, in a voice far more tearful than suited a noble knight.

Tiher shrugged. Alain had asked that question at least thirty times in the past day and a half, and Tiher was tired of it.

Alain groaned. "She must have left the road," he said. "We would have caught up with her by now if she were on the road."

Tiher shrugged again. This phrase, too, had been repeated — not so often as the first, but that was only because Alain hadn't used it until the previous afternoon. Until they'd galloped all the way back to Mont St. Michel and been thrown out of St. Michael's convent by a shocked and outraged prioress, he'd clung to the belief that Marie was just in front of them. To Tiher it had been obvious before they were halfway that she couldn't be. She didn't have a horse, and no noblewoman would have the stamina to stay ahead of them on foot. *Obviously* she'd left the road — and if she'd gone into the forest, God knew what might have happened to her. If Tiher had been in charge of this party, he would have . . .

It was no use thinking of that. Alain or his elder brother would always be in charge of any party Tiher was in. Lord Juhel of Fougères would be affronted if a mere child of his sister commanded his sons.

"Perhaps the brothers of Bonne Fontaine have some news of her," Guyomard put in earnestly. When Marie's disappearance was discovered, the abbot had sent men to search for her throughout the countryside. "They may even have found her already!"

Alain looked at him eagerly. "I pray God they have!" he said passionately, and crossed himself.

Tiher snorted — not at the sentiment, but at Alain's acceptance of it from Guyomard. It had been Guyomard who locked the door of Marie's room at Bonne Fontaine, and Alain had blamed him for the escape. Alain never liked to blame himself, and it was easier to blame Guyomard than Tiher: Guyomard was not a relative. Lord Juhel could dismiss him from his service, and if he were dismissed, where would he go? All the way to Mont St. Michel and halfway back again, in and out of every hut and village along the way, Guyomard had humbly told Alain what Alain wanted to hear. Now, at last, it seemed that Alain wanted that comfort so badly that he was willing to forgive his dependent to get it. He'd had no sympathy whatever from his cousin. It was plain to Tiher that the girl would have found a way to get free of them whoever turned the key. If she could vanish from a locked room, then clearly a locked room wasn't enough to hold her. They should have kept watch, slept before her door, shackled her, even — but they hadn't thought it necessary. They were all to blame — but Alain most of all. He was in charge. Juhel de Fougères might take it out on Guyomard, but Duke Hoel would hold Alain responsible. And rightly so!

Tiher stirred and said spitefully, "If the brothers of Bonne Fontaine have found Lady Marie, *how* will they have found her? Alive or dead?"

Alain winced and wiped his face. He fumbled his helmet back over his head and did up the chin strap. They rode on in silence, and Tiher regretted his words — not because they'd hurt Alain, but because he'd voiced a thought they'd all had which had previously remained unspoken, and which he now wished were unspoken still. The first news the abbot had given them after Marie disappeared was that the robber Éon of Moncontour was known to be in the area: a poor cleric had been robbed near the crossroads of Dol not three days before. Marie Penthièvre might indeed be found dead in the forest, and that would be a disgrace for all of them. If it was deplorable to have tricked a novice away from her convent with the connivance of her ab-bess, it was far, far worse to lose her along the way, so that she ended up robbed, raped, and murdered in the forest. There was nobody who would not blame them for that. The prioress of St. Michael's had blamed them already. Of course, Lady Con-stance was just as eager to escape blame as anyone; she'd pre-tended that she hadn't known who they were before, that she'd believed they'd come from Duke Robert, that she, at any rate, had acted entirely as she should. But blame would stick to her, nevertheless. Credit is slippery, and hard for even one man to hold onto, but blame, sticky as honey, goes everywhere: it would stick to all of them.

He thought of her by candlelight, sitting on the bed in the room at Bonne Fontaine before they locked her in: pale with exhaustion but resolute, her disheveled hair in shadowy wisps about her face. A pretty girl, and brave, too. He felt a strange pang at heart, a mixture of pity and guilt.

"I pray their news is better," he said, suddenly as earnest as Guyomard. "I will buy Saint Michael a hundred candles for his church at Dol if the girl is found alive." And he crossed himself.

He was to comment afterward that Saint Michael, being an archangel, moved fast. A rider appeared in the distance; when he saw them, he spurred his horse to a canter, and as he drew nearer they saw that he was a monk. They all stopped together, instinctively trying to prolong the moment of hope. The monk cantered on until he drew his mount to a stop in front of them.

"Lord Alain de Fougères?" he said expectantly, for his eyes had already scanned and recognized the white hart emblem on the shield slung behind Alain's saddle.

Alain nodded. "Have you come from the abbey of Bonne Fontaine?" he asked, his voice pitched high with anxiety.

"Indeed, my lord. I'm Brother Samson; the lord abbot sent me to find you. My lord, the lady you were searching for has been found safe and well!"

Alain clapped his hands. "Thank God!" he cried passionately. "Thank God and all his saints!"

"Thank God and Saint Michael!" whispered Tiher, with a sense of release huger even than he had expected. He would not have to carry about with him for the rest of his life the knowledge that he had helped kill Marie Penthièvre.

"She was brought to a lodge belonging to our own house last night," Brother Samson went on happily. "There are two lay brothers there every summer, keeping pigs in the forest. The brothers didn't know that the lady had been lost, but this morning when the lord abbot's messenger came to tell them to search for her, he found her there eating her breakfast!"

"Thank God!" Alain repeated, beaming.

Guyomard crossed himself and thanked his patron saints.

"Where is she now?" asked Tiher, grinning, though mentally he was wincing at the cost of a hundred candles.

"On her way to Bonne Fontaine. The pig keepers were told to bring her there as soon as the horse for her arrived. The lady is exhausted from wandering in the forest, you see, and can't walk any distance, so the lord abbot's messenger ordered one of our tenant farmers to send a horse from his farm, which is not far from the lodge."

"I hope the pig keepers keep tight hold on the horse's reins, then," said Tiher. "Otherwise, the lady will gallop off to St. Michael's with the beast, and they'll look as foolish as we did."

"The knight who found her can manage the horse," said Brother Samson.

"A knight?" asked Alain sharply, his smile vanishing. "A knight found her? Who?"

"I don't know, my lord," Brother Samson replied, cheerfully oblivious to the devastation just wreaked upon Alain's career. "What the lord abbot asked me to tell you was that the lady was safe and well: a knight who was hunting in the forest found her and brought her to our pig keepers last night for safe keeping, and she is on her way to Bonne Fontaine. If we ride back to the abbey now, we may meet them on the road."

Alain was scowling as they started on. If another knight had rescued their charge, it would be impossible for Alain to present Marie's escape as a minor complication in an otherwise successful mission. The other knight would point up their failures just by being there, and claim a share of credit from the duke — credit which Alain could ill afford to share. He badly wanted to ingratiate himself with Duke Hoel, and this had seemed the perfect opportunity to do so. The duke had resented the loss of Chalandrey for years, and had leapt at the chance to get it back without fighting a war. The actual business of extracting the heiress from her convent in an impregnable Norman fortress, however, had threatened to be difficult. Alain had been the ideal person to lead the delicate mission. The de Fougères clan had several members in the service of Normandy: Alain could appear as Robert's envoy without arousing suspicion. He had done his part at the priory faultlessly. And now it had all gone wrong.

Tiher gave a sigh that mingled exasperation and pity, and his irritation with his cousin melted away. He knew well enough why Alain wanted to please the duke. Alain had hoped that the duke's good influence might help him win over the father of the girl with whom he was passionately and hopelessly in love.

Tiher watched Alain's back ahead of him, the gilding on the fine armor dusty from the past few days' hard riding, the head in its conical helmet bowed. You poor fool, he thought. Your father barely tolerates the thought of you taking a wife. Hervé of Comper is never going to let you marry his daughter just because the duke says a few good words for you, not when your rival has a rich manor. As for the duke, no matter how pleased he is with you over this, he'll never like you as well as he does your rival. Stop fighting your fate, Alain: the horse that kicks over the traces gets whipped.

But Tiher could never bring himself to say such things out loud. At times it seemed to him craven to trot quietly in the harness like a good cart horse, and he admired his cousin's ability to go on hoping for the impossible. Besides, Eline of Comper was beautiful enough to turn any man's head.

Alain apparently found his own reflections too painful to endure alone: he slowed his horse until it walked beside Tiher's, and fixed his cousin with his wide blue eyes. He had done it a thousand times as they grew up together: "Tiher, help me with this; Tiher, did you know? Oh, Tiher, what shall I do!" It had always been Tiher he turned to, never his own elder brother, and certainly never that harsh and fearsome man, his father. Tiher had always listened patiently, given advice, tried to sort out whatever muddle Alain had gotten himself into this time. There were only a few months between them, but Tiher felt himself much older, with the elder brother's privilege of wisdom. As they grew to adulthood, Alain's appeals had become less frequent and Tiher's advice more ironic: in the world's eyes, Alain had to be the superior. The underlying relationship between them, though, never changed. "Tiher," Alain whispered anxiously now, "when Brother Samson said *a* knight who was hunting in the forest found the Penthièvre girl—do you think he really meant *one* knight, hunting alone?"

"Alain, Brother Samson doesn't know anything about it!" Tiher replied. "You heard him! He's just a messenger. You ought to be glad. Think what the duke would have said if we'd arrived in Rennes without the girl—or worse, with her body!"

Alain chewed his upper lip wretchedly.

"What difference does it make, anyway?" demanded Tiher.

"If it was only one knight, hunting alone, and on foot . . ."

"Why would he be on foot?"

"Well, he was, wasn't he? They wouldn't have had to send a horse from a farm for the girl if he wasn't. She could have used his."

Tiher's heart sank on Alain's behalf as he realized it was true.

For a knight to go about alone on foot was rare in the extreme. Tiher knew of only one knight in Brittany who regularly did so. If Alain was right, the horse that had kicked the traces was indeed about to get a whipping from Fate. "You're being ridiculous!" he declared loudly. "For all we or Brother Samson knows, a whole hunting party with thirty couple of hounds found the girl, carried her to the pig keepers, and rode off again sounding the *rechace!*"

"I'll wager my best hawk against yours that it was one knight," snapped Alain. "One who goes hunting alone on foot. My rival."

They were both silent a moment. "Tiarnán can't beat you in a game where he isn't even playing," said Tiher.

"Are you taking the bet?"

"I don't bet. I certainly don't bet my one and only hawk. Oh, cheer up! Whatever happens, the girl's safe, and so are we. If it is Tiarnán who found her, perhaps he'll fall in love with her and leave Eline free for you."

Alain brightened visibly. "Do you think he might?"

Tiher shrugged. "Put it this way: she's the heiress to Chalandrey, and Eline has a dowry of fifty marks and a few acres. I would've thought anyone could fall in love with Lady Marie. I certainly could."

"Could you?" Alain asked, looking at his ugly cousin in surprise.

"Most certainly," replied Tiher. Resignedly, he admitted to himself that he already had, a little. A hundred candles to Saint Michael! Sheer stupidity: gray-eyed heiresses were not for landless knights. A hundred candles at a silver penny the pound!

They did meet up with Lady Marie Penthièvre of Chalandrey on the road to Bonne Fontaine. About three miles from the abbey they saw a party traveling slowly along the road ahead of them. When they urged their tired horses faster, the group ahead resolved itself into a woman in a white wimple and black gown on a horse, flanked by three men: two brown monks and one in the stained green of a huntsman. Even before they'd caught up, Tiher saw that the man in green was indeed Tiarnán of Talensac. He knew him from court, and even from the back the clothes and the light step were distinctive. He glanced at his cousin, and saw that the scowl was back.

His amusement vanished when they drew level with the party, and Marie turned in the saddle to fix them with her cool gray eyes. Her face was purple with bruises, and she was holding one arm against her side as though she'd injured it. The look on her face was one of profound sadness.

"Mother of God, Lady Marie!" he exclaimed, for once forgetting both his subordinate position and his manners and bursting in before Alain. "What happened to you?"

Marie looked at him wearily and didn't answer. She couldn't trust her voice. After everything, to be handed back to her abductors like a runaway serf! There they were, the same wall of metal she'd faced two days before. Heavy, round-faced, anxious Guyomard; ugly Tiher; and Alain, with his polished good looks changed only by a two-day growth of stubble on his previously smooth chin. He was scowling furiously, though the other two simply looked shocked. She was sick of them, sick of inheritance and captivity and escapes. She wished she were someone else, a simple peasant whom nobody would bother about. She let her eyes drop away from them to Tiarnán, who was holding the bridle of the farm horse she'd been loaned. He held it so that she couldn't escape, she knew: from the moment the abbot's messenger had told him what she'd really been doing in the forest, his one aim had been to return her to her captors. But for her he still seemed apart from the whole sordid business. He was standing back on his heels, looking at the knights with a blank, wary expression, as though he was no more pleased to see them than she was.

"She was attacked by robbers," one of the brown-robed lay brothers said excitedly. He'd confided this piece of drama to everyone they met. "By God's mercy, Lord Tiarnán heard her screams, and arrived in time to save her from great dishonor."

Marie wished she could fall off the horse and sink under the earth. Everything she'd tried to do had gone wrong. She'd botched her escape, and now she'd become a thing to gawp at, a distressed maiden saved from the unspeakable. She tugged her wimple forward angrily to try to hide some of the bruises.

Alain, predictably, gave Tiarnán a look of thunderous resentment.

"God prosper you, Alain de Fougères," said Tiarnán politely. "And you, Tiher. And Guyomard."

Tiher shook his head admiringly. He liked the straight-faced subtlety of the other's rebuke, typical of the man. "God prosper you, Tiarnán of Talensac," he replied. "And thank you. We've been at our wits' end worrying over Lady Marie, and, it seems, worrying with good cause. We were in charge of her, and we'd have been disgraced if any harm came to her. What happened?"

Tiarnán glanced at Marie, who now stared with bowed head at her saddle. "The lady went into the forest to avoid being caught on the road. Éon of Moncontour found her at Lady Nimuë's Well, about two and a half miles due south of Châtellier, and behaved as one might expect. But she fought him off with great spirit, screaming for help, and I happened to be in the area and heard her. She has bruises and a twisted shoulder, no worse."

"What happened to Éon?" asked Alain.

"Got away," said Tiarnán impassively.

"Lord Tiarnán shot two of his companions," Marie put in, lifting her head again suddenly. He had no business making it sound as though the robbers had simply run off without a struggle. What he had done had been heroic, and he should have the credit for it. Perhaps he was trying to spare her reputation, but he had no business paying for hers with his own. "I think he would have shot Éon, too, but Éon put a knife at my throat, and threatened to kill me, so Lord Tiarnán agreed to fight him with a knife. While they were fighting the robber threw his cloak over Tiarnán's head and ran away, the coward." She looked at Tiarnán angrily.

Tiarnán's eyes were amused. "I agreed to fight him because he called me a coward," he corrected her gently. "Perhaps you did not understand us, as we spoke in Breton. He threatened you because he thought I must be a lover you'd come to meet, and when I told him I was no such thing, he let you go."

Marie bowed her head again, blinking rapidly. No, he was no such thing. The wish that he were could not yet form in her, but the resentment because he was not bubbled up within, hurting by its very unaccountability. "Oh," she said quietly. "No, I didn't understand what you were saying."

Alain was blinking, too. Not only had he lost the girl he was supposed to be guarding, but his rival had found her in deadly danger and saved her. He had hoped to please the duke, and instead his rival was going to be exalted at his own expense. It was so unfair as to be grotesque. In a tone of childish spite he demanded, "What were you doing near Nimuë's Well? It's in one of the duke's forests. Did he give you permission to hunt it?"

Mistake, thought Tiher. Petty accusations of poaching only make you look a bad loser. And everyone knows Tiarnán's a great favorite at court, and probably has permission to hunt wherever he likes. Poor Alain!

"I was looking for that big stag we lost last Holy Rood Day," Tiarnán replied. He was, as usual, perfectly straight-faced and serious, but Tiher had caught the gleam of those quick eyes: Tiarnán knew why Alain had spoken as he had. "I thought I'd see if he was still in the same part of the forest. The duke could have good sport with him when the season opens."

At this Tiher stared in concern. To track game a man needed a dog. Tiarnán owned a very famous tracking dog which, as everyone at court knew, he'd once refused to sell to the duke himself for fifteen marks of silver. "What happened to your dog?" Tiher asked. "I hope the robbers didn't kill that brindled lymer bitch of yours?"

"Left her at home," said Tiarnán tersely. "In heat." He let go of the horse's bridle and wiped his hands on his stained green tunic. "My lords, since you're here to take charge of Lady Marie's escort, I'll leave you. I meant to go home to Talensac this morning."

At this both Alain and Marie suddenly sat up straight, Alain in hope and Marie in dismay.

"You're not coming with us to Rennes?" asked Alain, with unseemly eagerness.

"No. Why should I stand in your light?"

"You said you had business in Rennes," Marie said accusingly.

"And I have," replied Tiarnán. "But I am not going to court dressed like this. I need to go home and change first. I will see you in Rennes, Lady Marie."

She put her hand to her mouth and bit the side of her finger, pulled it away again. She tried to imagine Tiarnán at court, dressed in scarlet and ermine. It was like losing her last foothold on a steep cliff. He was part of the sordid business after all: she had no allies, and nothing could prevent her from being engulfed. There were scores of ways to force a woman into marriage, beginning with stern lectures and continuing through starvation to beating and rape. She was tired already. She did not know how much she could endure. "Why did you bother to help me?" she cried bitterly to Tiarnán. "Why save me from Éon, and then betray me? If Éon had raped me at least he would have left me alone afterward. God have mercy! I'd be better off dead than married to my father's enemy!"

Tiarnán caught her stirrup. "No one is going to harm you, Lady," he promised her, entirely serious. "I will stand surety for that myself."

"I will not consent to marry any servant of Brittany!" declared Marie fiercely. Her father had declared that their honor depended on never changing their allegiance again. Marie would not lose the family's honor. No, never. "Are you saying that Hoel will accept that? After all the trouble he's gone to, to fetch me?"

"Yes," said Tiarnán evenly. When she stared in disbelief, he went on, "Duke Hoel is a better man than Duke Robert. He will suggest husbands suited to you, but if you refuse them, no one will force you. That would be contrary to the laws of the Church, which the duke honors. Besides, you are his wife's

kinswoman, and sacrosanct. I am his liege man, and I know
him."

She looked into his reserved dark face and believed him. In
offering to stand surety, he was promising to guarantee her
safety personally—if need be by fighting anyone who threatened her. He would not make that offer unless he was certain
it wouldn't set him against his own liege lord. A large part of
her sick weariness fell away, and she realized how deeply she
had dreaded the struggle. "If I tell Duke Hoel that I won't
marry any of his men, will he let me go home?" Marie asked
hesitantly, hoarse with relief and flushing under the bruises.

Tiarnán shook his head. "He will keep you at his court and
hope that you change your mind."

"But he won't force me to marry against my will? You'll stand
surety for that?"

"My hand on it," he said solemnly, offering the hand to her.

Marie took it in both of hers, sealing the compact before
witnesses. It was a narrow sinewy hand, stained with grass, and
she could feel the strength in it. It pressed her fingers lightly
and her face went hot. She could feel the tears stinging her
eyes. Something else was stinging in her heart. "Thank you,"
she said unsteadily. "I'll call on you if you're wrong."

"You won't need to." Tiarnán withdrew his hand and glanced
round at the company again. His eyes hesitated a moment on
Alain, and his self-possession wavered. "Alain de Fougères . . ."
he began, and paused awkwardly.

"You expect me to trumpet your part in this to the duke?"
asked Alain sourly.

Tiarnán shook his head. "No. But my business in Rennes is
to inform my liege lord that I am to marry the daughter of
Hervé of Comper."

Alain went white and stared wordlessly. He clutched his
horse's reins so hard that the animal snorted and laid its ears
back, fidgeting unhappily with the bit. Tiarnán looked back
impassively; only his eyes glinted again. Triumph? wondered
Tiher. No—pity.

"A pleasant journey then, all," said Tiarnán, starting off across the verge of the road in the direction of the forest. "I will see you in Rennes in a few days."

"I wish you joy!" said Tiher, remembering his manners this time.

Tiarnán paused, and when he glanced back his whole face was transfigured with one of his rare full smiles. "I think I have it," he replied, and strode on.

Alain, and Marie, sat quite still, watching him until he was out of sight. Then Alain clapped his heels to his horse's sides and set off down the road at full gallop, head bowed, not looking back.

Tiher watched him go with sincere pity. Alain had loved Eline of Comper for years, and for a few months it had seemed that he might even succeed in sweeping away every obstacle between them by the simple force of his passion: he'd even wrung a grudging permission to marry from his father. Then Tiarnán had taken an interest in the girl. The outcome had been inevitable from that moment — but Alain had gone on hoping against hope, until now. Tiher sighed, leaned over, and took Marie's reins. "We'd better get back to Bonne Fontaine, Lady Marie," he said. "It's late in the afternoon, and I'm sure you need rest."

Marie nodded and twisted her fingers in the farm horse's mane. She had not been able to react to what had just been said; there had been too many things she had not known for her to grasp it all at once. They rode in silence while she tried to piece it together. Tiarnán was going to marry a daughter of a lord of Comper. That was a sting which she felt even through everything else. But why shouldn't he marry? *She* couldn't marry him; he was Duke Hoel's loyal liege man, and an enemy of her house. Treacherous! she told the sting in her heart. Wanton! What about your family's honor? *And* you know almost nothing about him. The reason you've fallen in love is because he rescued you. You *can't.*

She wrestled with the hurt, which resisted, like an angry dog trying to cling to a disputed bone. Tiarnán is going to marry the daughter of the lord of Comper, she repeated to herself firmly. It's already arranged. He barely noticed *you*. Why should he, when he's just betrothed himself to someone else? And when Alain de Fougères heard it, he went white, and rode off in a rage.

She looked up at Tiher, riding beside her with her reins looped over his wrist. "Did Lord Alain wish to marry this woman who's betrothed to Lord Tiarnán?" she asked, too tired to care if her curiosity was blatant.

Tiher looked back at her approvingly. "You have the meat of it," he said. "And I'm afraid he's going to make the rest of this journey a perfect purgatory. He never can suffer in silence, and suffer he most undoubtedly will." One of the rewards he gave himself for his role as Alain's advisor and confidant was the right to make cutting remarks about his cousin.

Marie studied her companion a moment. He still looked like a frog, but there was something likeable about that sardonic grin. He was being pleasant to her, as well. She hadn't really noticed him when they first rode from Mont St. Michel; Alain had done most of the talking, and was more noticeable anyway, with his good looks and his expensive and fashionable clothes. "Is she very beautiful?" she asked.

"Of course," replied Tiher. He noticed the curiosity, but was not surprised by it. If a similar drama had been played out before him, he would have been full of questions, too — and he welcomed the chance to get Marie talking. "Alain wouldn't be in love with her otherwise. He wouldn't love a girl for her wits, not being overly well endowed with the commodity himself. Eline of Comper; incomparable Eline. She sings very sweetly, can play the lute and the viol, and dances as lightly as a leaf on the wind. She and Alain make a very pretty couple. But she has two elder brothers and a pair of sisters, so she's not going to bring her husband enough dowry for a noble to live on. My Uncle Juhel, Alain's father, isn't breaking up the estate for Alain's sake: he has an allowance for life, but that's all. They didn't really have anything to marry on. Talensac may not be as big or as grand as Fougères, but it's a very pretty manor and Tiarnán's been sole lord of it since he came of age. Poor Alain never had a chance."

Marie rode in silence for a minute, mulling that over. She'd heard similar stories all her life, and thought nothing of them. All marriage had been a foreign country to her. Now the private sting in her heart had showed her the unsuspected valley of pain that Alain would have to plod through. "What did . . . Lady Eline . . . think of it?" she asked at last.

"I imagine she agreed with her father," said Tiher. "She'd be a fool to do anything else. One can't ask a maiden about such matters, of course — saving your presence, Lady." Tiher grinned.

She scanned his face intently. "And what do you think? That your cousin was a fool to hope for anything else, because land matters more than love?"

He shrugged. It was impossible to explain how he respected Alain most when Alain was at his most perverse. "I think that love's a plant that likes rich soil," he said instead. "And if it still survives on poor sandy heathland, who'd want their loved one to scratch for a living? No, get good soil first, and if you cultivate it properly, you can grow what you like on it." He grinned again. "I've no land at all myself, incidentally."

"Lord Tiarnán, though, from what you say, is marrying for love."

"So he is, lucky man. But he can afford it. Not many young men are their own masters and free to choose. The rest of us make do with what scrapings of happiness we can find."

She bit her curled finger, and he felt suddenly weightless with gladness. Lord, I'd like to kiss her, he thought. But it's a whole slice of happiness even without. A beautiful May evening, the hedgerows white, my horse under me, and a pretty girl listening to me talk about love.

"You're lucky yourself now," he told Marie. "If what Tiarnán said is true — and I'm sure it is — the duke will let you pick your own husband, and you, too, will have the luxury of marrying for love."

"I won't marry any of the duke's men," said Marie flatly. "My father owes fealty to Duke Robert, and only to him. I won't betray my family's honor." Repeating it aloud was a relief: it seemed to confirm that she still was what she'd always thought herself, and not fundamentally altered by this sting in the heart.

Tiher's eyebrows rose. "I don't see how you can think that. Your grandfather served Brittany until he decided that it would be more profitable to follow the Normans. You'd be restoring your family's honor, not betraying it."

"I'm not responsible for what my grandfather did," replied Marie. "If everyone went back to their ancestors' original loyalties, we'd all pay fealty to the emperor of the Greeks. My father is Duke Robert's man, so for me to take any other overlord is treachery. I won't do it."

Tiher only laughed. He didn't want to argue. "I wish your grandfather had felt the same way. Tell me, how did you manage to escape from Bonne Fontaine through a locked door? We couldn't work it out."

Marie looked at him severely. But she knew already that she was not going to try to escape again. She was too drained — and Tiarnán had stood surety for her safety. "I jammed the door with my wimple so that it wouldn't shut properly," she told Tiher.

He laughed again. "I swear by all the saints, I'm grateful to Tiarnán, despite what he's done to my cousin, and even though it's cost me sixteen silver pennies."

She stared at him, frowning. He relished the way her forehead crinkled. *Before we reach Rennes castle*, he promised silently, *I will make you laugh. If that's all the happiness I can scrape from this journey, it will satisfy me.*

"I vowed a hundred candles to Saint Michael if you were found safe," he explained. "Well, it's sixteen silver pennies well spent."

"Saint Michael is a very great saint, and very powerful against evil," replied Marie seriously, and crossed herself.

"Amen," said Tiher happily. "And being an archangel, he moves fast."

When they arrived at Bonne Fontaine a little while later, they discovered that the party had lost its leader. Alain de Fougères, having galloped off, was not to be found in the monastery. Tiher was torn between exasperation and alarm. He had a very good idea where Alain had gone, and he thought it an expedition fit for a lunatic. If Alain failed in his probable aim, he'd have to come back to the duke's court disgraced by abandoning his mission, and he'd have enraged his father for nothing. But if he succeeded, he'd be even worse off: he'd have to go and seek his fortune outside Brittany, living on whatever he could get as a mercenary and supporting his wife on the scrapings of his lord's table — if, that is, he didn't get himself killed during the elopement. For elopement was almost certainly what Alain had in mind, and Eline's approved lover was unlikely to accept it quietly. Tiarnán of Talensac was not the man Tiher would choose for an enemy. He might be peaceable enough off the battlefield, but Tiher had watched him practice arms: an onslaught of appalling ferocity, concentrated to the precision of an embroiderer's needle, that left a trail of splintered spears and smashed shields in its wake. Tiher was not surprised that hardened robbers turned and ran when confronted with it; Alain was certainly no match for it. Any friend of Alain could only hope that his expedition would fail.

Tiher reassured himself that failure did seem the most likely outcome. Hervé of Comper would hardly welcome Alain to his manor house, and it was to be hoped that Lady Eline had more sense than to defy her father's wishes and run off with a man who couldn't support her — even if she did prefer him to Tiarnán, which was by no means as clear to Tiher as it seemed to be to Alain. And whatever had happened or would happen to Alain, there was nothing Tiher could do about it. The most he could do would be to make excuses for his cousin when the party arrived in Rennes without him. In the meantime, Tiher meant to scrape what happiness he could from the remainder of the journey.

It was an easy day's ride from Bonne Fontaine to Rennes, a pleasant trip through field and woodland on another golden spring day. Even the mare Dahut was forced to go quietly, for Tiher tied her on short reins between his horse and Guyomard's. They arrived at the city at evening. Rennes had been given a wall in ancient times, and the Roman stones enclosed it still, held up here and there by a more recent tower or gate. For long centuries the medieval city had huddled within a fraction of the space enclosed by its ancient walls, but now it had filled them again—filled them to overflowing, for the first few inns and bake houses had spread beyond the city gates and onto the road. The evening fires had been lit, and the haze of wood smoke that rose above the thatched roofs was illumined by the setting sun, so that the city seemed to float in a golden cloud. Marie had never visited a city, and for all her dread of captivity and determination to yield nothing to her captors, she found her heart beating hard with excitement. An unknown world lay before her, waiting to be explored.

The city gate had not yet been closed for the night, and the three riders clopped through. The street beyond was far removed from the golden illusion that had cloaked it: unpaved, deeply rutted, stinking of raw sewage, it meandered between rows of mud-and-wattle houses. Chickens pecked among the rubbish in the street, bobbing casually out of the way as the horses went by, and pigs penned between the houses looked over the fences and grunted. A furze bush hung above one door showed that that particular hovel was an inn; a few shops advertised their status by samples of their merchandise dangling from posts: here a pair of shoes, there a broom, over there a set of spoons carved from horn. Then the main street swung right—and there, far sooner than Marie had expected, towered the castle of Rennes.

It was a new castle, and its walls were of stone, rather than old-fashioned wood—though it was plain at a glance that it followed the traditional pattern, with a tall keep upon an artificial mound, or motte, and an enclosure, or bailey, surrounded by a curtain wall. Tiher turned left and began riding about the outside of the dry ditch that ringed the curtain wall. Marie turned in the saddle, watching the walls of the keep which showed clear above, hazed in the golden smoke. A great red banner flapped in the last of the sunset at the very height of the tower to declare that the duke was in residence.

"What's the duke like?" she asked Tiher. They had been talking easily all day, and she was beginning to forget he was an enemy.

Tiher gave her question some thought. "Do you like dogs?" he asked as they rounded a bend and came within sight of the castle gate.

"I like some dogs," said Marie, wondering if there was a connection.

"And that's well said, for there are as many different sorts of dogs as there are of men, and one might find correspondences between the two. Greyhounds, for example, are noble and swift and lovely—like yourself, my lady! Alaunts and brachets and lymers, which must be brave and wise to hunt a lord's quarry and to pull it down, might be compared to knights. And then there are fawning spaniels and mastiffs, to attend on a lord and to guard him."

"And the lord in this allegory of yours, the duke—he is a lion?" asked Marie, smiling at the conceit.

"No," said Tiher with satisfaction. "Duke Hoel is a terrier. But a very noble one."

Marie laughed, and Tiher grinned widely. He'd made her laugh before Rennes castle, just—even if it was partly from nervousness. A beautiful laugh, too, soft and gurgling. He did like a woman who laughed.

They clopped up to the castle drawbridge, and Tiher hailed the guard to let them through.

Inside the bailey, the horses were taken off to the stables by servants. The cooking fires were smoking in the kitchens built against the inside of the stone wall, and there was a smell of roasting meat. Tiher and Guyomard escorted Marie up the stone stairway into the keep; even before they'd passed the great double doors, a wave of noise rolled out over them, and a redoubled scent of food. It was dusk now, and in the guard-room torches were being lit and put into brackets on the wall. The guards greeted Tiher cheerfully and asked where Alain was; "Take too long to explain!" Tiher replied, and, with his spurs clinking oddly on the stone floor, he swept Marie on up another short stairway and into the Great Hall.

The hall filled the whole first floor of the keep. Its wooden floor was strewn with rushes, and it, too, had been lit by torches. Tables were spread out in the torchlight, and a great company was sitting down to supper. The crowd talking noisily along the benches was overwhelmingly masculine. Only at the high table at the far end of the hall were there any women: the lower hall held knights of the duke's household and garrison, priests, monks, visiting officials — all men. All wealthy, too: everywhere the red light fell it gleamed, here on a silver dish, there on the hilt of a sword, there on a jeweled finger or throat. Rich silks and brilliantly dyed woolens filled the shadows with gold, midnight blue, and deep crimson. Even the dogs that sprawled beneath the tables had collars that glittered when they stirred. Marie felt herself plainer, humbler, and dirtier with each step she took.

Tiher threaded his way through the tables toward the far end of the hall, where the high table sat raised up on a dais of wood. The people on the benches stopped their conversations as he passed, and by the time he had reached the high table, the hall was silent. Marie, following behind him, had to force herself to keep her head up. Under the weight of those curious male stares she wanted to sink through the floor.

Tiher stopped just before the middle of the dais and dropped to one knee with a jingle of armor. "God prosper you, my lord!" he said. "Here is the lady Marie Penthièvre de Chalandrey, whose company you requested."

Marie made herself lift her eyes to the man seated in the middle of the high table. Hoel, Count of Cornouaille, Count of Nantes, and, by virtue of his marriage, Count of Rennes and Duke of Brittany, was short, balding, and somewhere between fifty and sixty. Above his elaborate fur-trimmed tunic his face was round and red, and his eyes bulged slightly. His brow was furrowed in anger.

"What happened to your cousin?" he demanded in a high-pitched yap.

Good Lord, thought Marie, he *is* like a terrier.

"Hoel!" exclaimed the lady who sat beside the duke. She was a stout woman of about forty-five, dressed with extreme elegance and wearing a great quantity of jewels. "The poor girl is standing there like a lost lamb. Greet her before you sort out the de Fougères." She smiled at Marie. The smile and the hard clear lines of her face were peculiarly familiar to Marie, but she couldn't immediately think where from. Then she realized that this must be Havoise, Duchess of Brittany, half-sister of Prioress Constance—and a Penthièvre of the old stock that had continued to rule Brittany, though its branches ramified among the nobility of Normandy and England. Marie had seen the same long bones in her own mirror.

"You're very welcome here, my dear," said the duchess.

Marie took a deep breath. She would not be put off from what she meant to do because her gown was shabby or because the duchess condescended to be gracious. "I am not here of my own will," she declared in a clear proud ringing voice that could be heard in the far corners of the hall. "I was brought away from my convent by treachery and deceit, and kept from returning to it by force. My father owes no allegiance to Brittany, and I will never betray his house and lands to any man living. By God and my immortal soul"—Marie crossed herself defiantly—"I had rather die defending my honor than live deprived of it."

There was a moment of thunderous silence. Marie could hear the blood ringing in her ears, and the crackle of the torches about the walls.

Then Duke Hoel snorted. "She's true blood of yours, all right," he said to the duchess.

"Of course she is," replied Havoise placidly. "My father's half-brother's second son's granddaughter. We worked it out, remember? Child," she said to Marie, "Chalandrey is a fief pertaining to the duchy of Brittany, and not the private possession of your house. Your grandfather held it from my father. He had no right whatsoever to give it to Normandy: it wasn't his to give. My husband is your true and rightful overlord, and was fully within his rights to bring you here."

"I say he is not," Marie replied deliberately, though her breath was coming hard and her stomach was tight with fear. "And I say further that I will not marry any servant of my father's enemies. And Tiarnán of Talensac, a knight in your service, my lord duke, has gone surety for me that no one will force me."

"What does Tiarnán have to do with this?" asked Hoel in confusion.

Havoise frowned suddenly, staring hard at Marie's face. Between the red torchlight, the white wimple, and Marie's transcendent defiance, her bruises had not previously been noticed. "Hoel," the duchess said urgently now, "the girl's been beaten."

Then there was uproar, fury, and confusion, and Duke Hoel bounded yapping in to attack again the question of what had happened to Alain de Fougères. The whole story had to come out, and Marie was swept off by the duchess to have her bruises poulticed with borage leaves, while Tiher was given a lecture on his cousin's stupidity. The duke informed him that it was lunacy to allow any Penthièvre anywhere on any occasion any opportunity whatever to attack or escape, because any fool knew she was sure to take it; that one does not under any circumstances permit harm to come to a kinswoman of the duchess when she is under one's protection; and, finally, that a man entrusted with a mission from his overlord who runs off on the road leaving it half complete deserved to be pinned against the castle wall and used for jousting practice.

"Now I know how a rat feels," Tiher said later, "when the terrier has him by the neck."

iarnán reached Talensac in the morning two days after
parting from Marie on the road to Rennes. He would
have been there the evening before, but he'd decided to
go see his confessor first. The confessor was a hermit, and lived
alone at a tiny chapel in the depths of the forest, some fifteen
miles southwest of the manor. Going there added at least five
hours to the journey, but Tiarnán didn't mind. An extra five
hours walking in the forest in May was not an imposition but
a thing to cherish.

He loved the forest. What to Marie was one vast shadow of
mystery was to him a clear and precisely defined patchwork of
places intimately known and perfectly distinct. There were peat
bogs choked with alder, and mature woodlands of beech and
oak; there were acres of pine scrub and there were high barren
heaths which poked out of the trees like sows' backs from their
wallows. There were the wells and mounds sacred to the Fair
Ones; there were little tumble-down chapels built long ago by
saints; there were black squalid huts where old peasant women
sold curses or love charms to visitors who crept guiltily to the
door. Every area, even the wildest, had a complicated web of
owners and users. The days when Broceliande covered all Brittany were already long past: there was not one forest but many,
islands of wilderness in a sea of cultivated lands, some joined
by tenuous strands of green that snaked across the cleared
fields, others standing alone. There were ducal hunting preserves and noble hunting preserves; so-and-so had the right to
collect wood in one section of the forest, while someone else's
pigs foraged there for acorns and someone else again made
charcoal. Tiarnán knew each part, and would no more have

confused them than a man would mistake the rooms in his own house. He loved Broceliande in all its moods, from bitter winter to balmy summer, from brutal storm to dreaming sun. It was loveliest of all, though, in May, with the air fresh and the earth sweet with flowers, and the animals in the shadows guarding their young. Tiarnán walked beneath the branches with a quick light stride, taking deep breaths of the silken air. Among all the delights, though, he remained wary. Broceliande might be lovely, but itself recognized no love, and it held among its leaves a thousand forms of death. The robber Éon was merely one more thing to watch out for, no worse than the boar's tusk or the thousand sucking mouths of the peat bog.

It was still early in the morning when he arrived at the boundary of his own land. The manor of Talensac included some twenty square miles of woodland, all adjoining neighboring sections of forest, but Tiarnán knew almost to the moment when he had crossed onto his own domain. In his own woodland he relaxed his wariness enough to start singing aloud a song that had been running through his mind for some days. It was a common song that the Breton peasants sang in the field: he didn't like court music.

> "Gladly, gladly would I go
> if I knew my love was there;
> gladly, gladly I would make
> my arm a pillow for her hair.
>
> "Oh, the great long road I had to walk
> and the steep, steep slope to climb. . . ."

Tiarnán stopped singing: he'd been off-key, as usual. He sighed, snapped off a bramble shoot and began to chew it, then guiltily spat it out again. His confessor, Judicaël, had told him to fast in penance for killing the two robbers at Nimuë's Well. It was a grave sin, Judicaël had said, to snatch away two lives without warning. Perhaps it was true that the two dead men were themselves murderers and had been engaged in a violent crime, perhaps it was true that to give a warning might have endangered both their victim and Tiarnán himself — but two human lives were two human lives, ended bloodily and with no chance of repentance. If Tiarnán wished to keep his own soul alive, he would fast, and reflect upon the value of human life and his own arrogance in presuming to destroy it.

Tiarnán was fasting, but most of his reflections were upon the value of Eline of Comper. He had killed men before, fighting in the duke's wars. The two robbers lay very lightly on his conscience, and he regretted principally that he hadn't killed three of them. He actively hoped to meet Éon again and finish the man. He had arranged for the monks of Bonne Fontaine to bury the two dead men, and he'd paid for a funeral Mass and prayers for them, but that had been more to pacify Judicaël than out of concern for their souls. He'd known that Judicaël would be annoyed with him, and he had been resigned to the hermit's fierce lecture and stern penances. In a way he'd even been glad to have a couple of murders to confess. It had at least distracted Judicaël's attention from the news of his betrothal. To be sure, the hermit didn't reckon that a sin — but he did think it a mistake.

> "Gladly, gladly would I go,
>   if I knew my love was there . . ."

Eline's image danced in Tiarnán's mind, and he walked on through the woods smiling. She was beautiful, yes, but that wasn't the whole of why he loved her. She had an unself-conscious joy about her, as though life were a new silk gown she'd just been given. Everything delighted her; everything in her was fresh and new and at one with itself.

> "Oh, the great long road I had to walk
>   and the steep, steep slope to climb.
>   I could not sit to take my rest
>   for the thought of that love of mine.

> "She's sweeter than the blackbird's song
> or the nightingale on the willow tree,
> sweeter than the dew on the flowering rose,
> and sweetest of all is her kiss for me."

And it was all arranged; she would marry him. Soon. It was no more than courtesy to inform Duke Hoel before he set the date.

Hoel was the actual owner of the fief of Talensac; Tiarnán only "held" it. His father, grandfather, and great-grandfather had held it before him, and his sons would hold it in turn, God willing, but only after they had sworn homage to the duke. Once that oath was sworn, however, the duke could not take the fief away, unless the oath was broken. In that age the feudal contract was still a fluid thing, many of its details yet to be determined. But the principals were firmly understood. Tiarnán would fight for the duke when called upon, would obey all lawful orders, would offer counsel if required—and from courtesy would advise the duke of important events such as his marriage. In return he held the manor and everything belonging to it.

As he came out of the forest onto the main road and into the sight of his fields, he paused for a moment, as he always did, with a small involuntary jerk of the shoulders as though he were pulling the place around them like a cloak. The fields sloped away from him down to a small brook which meandered northward; from the heart of the dell poked the rickety wooden tower of the village church. Thatched houses, tiny in the distance, straggled along the road, some of them trailing plumes of smoke from cooking fires up into the clean morning air. On the far side of the brook, tall on its mound and ringed with a protective palisade, stood Tiarnán's manor house. The mill was out of sight upstream around a bend in the brook, but Tiarnán didn't need to see it to know it was there. Talensac was safe and well. When he started walking again, it was with the firm tread of contentment. Home. He had been born here, and he took his name from it: it was part of him. He had walked some sixty-odd miles over the previous two days, and he was tired—comfortably tired—and now he looked forward happily to resting in his own house.

The first house in the village belonged to Glevian the blacksmith. There was a well there, since forging iron needed water, and Tiarnán paused to get a drink. He heaved the wooden cover off and let down the bucket that stood always ready beside it. While he was hauling it up again, the woman of the house, who'd heard the thump of the well cover being moved, came out, wiping her hands on her apron.

"Greetings, Machtiern," she said, seeing Tiarnán.

Talensac called its lord by the old title "machtiern." This was not strictly accurate: machtierns had been officials responsible for justice in Breton villages, and had been replaced by feudal lords. The village called him "machtiern" anyway.

"Greetings, Judith, Conwal's daughter," replied Tiarnán, saluting her with the bucket before drinking from it.

Judith remained in her doorway, still nervously wiping her hands on her apron. Tiarnán finished drinking, set the bucket down, and hauled the cover back over the well. "It's a hot day for the season," said Judith brightly.

Tiarnán nodded, wondering what had happened during the six days he'd been away to make her hover like this. She was plainly aching to tell him something. "Has all been well in the village?" he asked helpfully.

Relieved, Judith threw her hands up. "Oh, Machtiern, my brother Justin—"

"What's he done now?" asked Tiarnán resignedly, his sense of well-being slipping away.

Judith's brother Justin—called Justin Braz, Little Justin, because he was enormous—was the village troublemaker. A big-boned sprawling young man with a shock of sandy hair and a broken nose, he had a habit of picking fights in alehouses and chasing unsuitable girls. In this latest incident he'd apparently combined the two, scandalously taking the sister of a freeman from the neighboring village of Montfort into an alehouse, and then brawling with her indignant brother. The brother had a broken jaw and collarbone, and the alehouse keeper, who'd tried to intervene, had bruises, two smashed ale kegs, and a broken window shutter. The bailiff of the lord of Montfort had come to Talensac to complain, and Justin had been put in the stocks.

"But it wasn't his fault," insisted Justin's sister, with more loyalty than conviction. "It was the other fellow started the fight."

"There never was a fight with Justin in it that wasn't started by Justin," replied Tiarnán. "So Kenmarcoc put him in the stocks, then?" Kenmarcoc was Tiarnán's bailiff, in charge of the manor in his absence.

"Yes, Machtiern," said Judith, giving up the argument for her brother's innocence, in which she believed no more than did her lord. "Yesterday afternoon, that was. And the bailiff of Montfort wants him to be flogged. And he says he must pay for the damage to the alehouse, and a fine as well."

Tiarnán sighed. People weren't flogged in Talensac. There wasn't even a whipping post to chain them to. Petty offenses, like moving boundary stones or taking other people's firewood, were punished with fines and the stocks; a poacher or a thief might be beaten round the churchyard with hazel rods, and then fined and shoved in the stocks. On the other hand, the lord of Montfort was a powerful man with a number of manors under his lordship, and he would not stand for his property and peasants being damaged. If he was seriously annoyed, he might send a party of men to Talensac to seize Justin and do the flogging themselves. Private wars between manors had started for less. Tiarnán wished furiously that Justin would learn to behave himself. "Well, run up to the lis and fetch Kenmarcoc," he ordered.

Judith gathered up her skirts and ran down the muddy road to find Kenmarcoc at the manor house, which the village called "the lis," and Tiarnán followed her at his usual quick walk. Glevian the blacksmith, who'd been working in the kitchen garden, trailed belatedly out after him, and several men who'd seen

Tiarnán arriving while they worked in the fields followed, interested to see what he'd do. Women who'd been spinning in the open doorways of the low mud-and-wattle houses, or working in the kitchen or garden, hurried to join them. Several children came running, calling out to Tiarnán that Justin Braz was in the stocks for smashing up an alehouse at Montfort. "I know," Tiarnán called back, but didn't pause until he reached the center of the village, the green space before the church where the stocks stood. From there the road crossed the brook on a low wooden bridge and went on by the gates of the lis.

Justin Braz was sitting on an upturned bucket, hands and feet locked securely in the stocks. He had a spectacular black eye, and a split lip which had filled his sandy beard with dried blood, but that would be from the fight in the alehouse. While it was traditional to throw things at people in the stocks, no one ever threw anything at Justin's face, because he'd be able to see who'd done it. His Talensac enemies paid tribute to his strength and ferocity by hurling their mud and slops over his back. He looked sullenly at Tiarnán and at the gathering crowd of villagers.

Tiarnán went to one of the willow trees by the brook and cut off a switch as thick as his thumb with his hunting knife. Looking impassively at Justin, he began to strip it of bark and leaves. Though Tiarnán had been born in the manor house, he had spent much of his childhood in the village. His aristocratic parents had both died in his infancy, and he had been cared for by a series of peasant nurses, overseen by the parish priest. This homely upbringing had ended when he was eight and sent off to the ducal court as a page, but he still felt in many things like a Talensac peasant. He did not need to be told that the village was offended with Justin but reluctant to bow to the wishes of the bailiff of Montfort.

Justin cleared his throat, unsettled by his lord's dark look. "So, Machtiern," he said. "You're back."

"Yes," replied Tiarnán evenly, still peeling off willow bark. "And I find you here, it seems."

"It wasn't my fault there was a fight," said Justin defensively.

"I just took the girl to the alehouse for a bit of fun. Her brother didn't need to make such a fuss about it."

There was a derisive snort from the assembled listeners. Respectable girls did not go to alehouses, and any brother who found a sister in one and didn't make a fuss as good as admitted that his sister was a whore.

"Justin," said Tiarnán deliberately, "you are a drunkard and a brawler and a disgrace to the village. Will you have it said in Montfort that Talensac people are whoremongers?"

The people of Talensac murmured their agreement; some of the elders nodded approval.

"You can't make any whores in Montfort," said Justin resentfully. "The girls are all whores already. Machtiern, you can't blame me for fighting. I'm a fighting man. I've fought well for you, as none knows better than yourself."

This was perfectly true. When Tiarnán was summoned to the duke's wars, he brought with him a band of able-bodied young men from his estate, armed with spears and slings and whatever weapons they could find. Justin had fought like a tiger for Tiarnán and the duke. On the other hand, he fought like that all the time.

"Alehouses," said Tiarnán disdainfully, "are no place for battles."

"I went to the alehouse for a little joy," Justin answered defiantly. "A man can't always be grubbing in the fields. And *I* can't afford to disappear into the forest for three days out of every seven."

At this there was an abrupt hush among the audience. Talensac's machtiern was indeed away that often, and the village had many theories about what he did while he was gone, of which the notion that he simply went hunting was by far the least interesting. It was, however, insolent and improper in the extreme for a peasant to mention it to the lord's face, and even Justin felt that he had gone too far. He raked up his defiance, though, and made no attempt to retract his words.

Tiarnán stepped up to the stocks and leaned over them, looking at Justin ironically. He tapped the wooden frame with the end of his switch of willow. "It is you who are here, Justin Braz," he said gently, and everyone relaxed again.

Tiarnán's brown and white tracking dog, Mirre, came bounding across the bridge from the lis, and ran, tail wagging, to press her nose into her master's hand. The bailiff Kenmarcoc was hurrying down the hill after her, along with Justin's sister and a crowd of people from the manor house. Kenmarcoc was a dark, horse-faced man with bad teeth. He was a priest, and held the office of chaplain as well as that of bailiff, though he had no pretensions to holiness. He had originally come to Talensac to manage the estate for the duke when Tiarnán's father died, but he had married a local girl—in those days no one dreamed of imposing clerical celibacy on the Breton secular clergy. When Tiarnán succeeded to the estate, he had invited Kenmarcoc to remain as bailiff. He liked and trusted the clerk.

"Greetings, my lord!" Kenmarcoc called, before he'd even crossed the bridge. Without waiting to be greeted in return, he panted out the history of Justin Braz, the alehouse, and the girl from Montfort, adding the information that the man with the broken collarbone wouldn't be able to work for a month, and that the ale and window shutter had been worth two sous.

"So five sous would cover the cost of the damage, and pay the man's wages till he's better?" asked Tiarnán.

"Yes, my lord," said Kenmarcoc disapprovingly, "but the bailiff of Montfort—bad luck to him!—is asking for ten. Also, he says that Justin must be punished."

"I've been punished!" complained Justin loudly. "I've a crick in my back like a dagger, my legs have gone numb, my hair's full of muck, and I had no sleep last night, sitting here locked up in my own stink. Let me out, Kenmarcoc!"

"The stocks can punish you for the window shutter," snapped Kenmarcoc, "but not for the man's collarbone, or his sister's honor."

"She never had any of that, that I could find," muttered Justin, "and she gave me every opportunity to look." A woman in the crowd called out, "Shameless!"

Tiarnán caught Kenmarcoc's eye and jerked his head at the

stocks. The bailiff sighed, took the key to the stocks from the ring at his belt, and unlocked them, top and bottom. Justin rose unsteadily to his feet, helped by his brother-in-law the blacksmith and his good friend and drinking companion Rinan. He stamped his numbed feet against the mud of the brookside, shook his arms, stretched his aching back, and looked warily at Tiarnán. He suspected that his punishment wasn't over yet — and he was right.

"Take your tunic off," Tiarnán ordered, tapping the willow switch significantly against his palm.

Justin groaned, but heaved off his muck-smeared hemp tunic and turned to face his lord, with a look half-indignant and half-imploring. His bare chest was impressively muscled, burned pink across the shoulders from fieldwork in the first heat of the year. He stood a head taller than Tiarnán.

Tiarnán put his switch down, pulled off his own green tunic — he had a linen shirt beneath it — then picked up the switch again and pointed with it to the gates of the churchyard twenty feet away. "There's sanctuary," he said. Justin looked, began to turn — and Tiarnán fell on him like a hawk on a rabbit. The whip of willow came down with a hiss and landed with a crack and a gasp. Then Justin was running, with Tiarnán beside him, whipping savagely.

A minute later it was over, and Justin was on the other side of the churchyard gate, clinging to it with both hands and breathing in great sobbing gasps. His back and shoulders were covered with bloody welts. Tiarnán brought the reddened switch down for the last time, harmlessly on the fence, then snapped it deliberately in two and walked back to the stocks. His breath was coming fast, and the hand that had done the whipping stung: he knew, without pride or shame, that he had done a proper job. "You may tell the bailiff of my lord of Montfort," he told Kenmarcoc, "that Justin has been whipped."

He did not glance round, but he felt something go through the assembly, like a ruffling of feathers among a flock of birds settling after an alarm. The contentment which the whipping had disturbed in him flowed back. He'd got the balance right.

Montfort would accept the whipping, but Talensac knew that a switch of willow, however fiercely wielded, was not the same as a whip of metal-tipped leather, and a running victim different from one chained ignominiously to a post. Justin had got neither more nor less than the village thought he deserved, and what the village thought mattered enormously to Tiarnán. He would never admit as much — after all, he was a lord, and needed to consult no one about what he did on his own estate — but without Talensac's approval he would have felt stripped of all authority. He tossed the bits of willow into the brook and continued, "Justin will pay for the ale and the window, but I will pay the rest of the fine myself."

Justin lifted his battered head. "I don't need charity from you, Machtiern!" he declared proudly.

"You don't deserve it, either," answered Tiarnán, "but I will pay it anyway, so that the manor can be quit of all debts when I come to marry, as I soon shall."

The crowd went "Ahhh!" and "God's blessing on your wedding, Machtiern! May it bring you joy!" Nobody asked whom he was marrying; they'd been waiting for the announcement for weeks. Tiarnán nodded curtly to the congratulations, picked up his tunic and slung it over his shoulder, and went off across the bridge and up the hill to his own house with his dog trotting happily at his heels.

Justin let go of the churchyard gate, staggered over to the brook, and began to wash the blood off himself as the crowd dispersed. His sister came over to help him. "That was a cruel beating," she said sympathetically, dipping a corner of her apron in the brook and wiping at the weals with it.

"Be quiet!" snarled her brother, wincing. "Find my tunic, if you want to be helpful." He plunged his muddy head into the running water.

Judith fetched the tunic and began rinsing it out in the brook. Justin leaned back on his heels and held his arms out in front of himself: the outraged muscles were trembling. "I take Christ to witness, the man has an arm on him like iron," he said. "Christ, that hurt!"

"I didn't think he'd do it," said his friend Rinan. "Not for the bailiff of Montfort."

Justin gave him a look of deep contempt. "You think our machtiern would do that for a black-dog-shit bailiff of Montfort?" he demanded. "What do you think he cares for the bailiff of Montfort — or the lord of Montfort, for that matter? Isn't he the finest fighting man in Brittany? Haven't I seen him sink a sword through a man's helmet a hand's breadth into his skull? A man like that's not scared of some bare-faced jackass from Montfort. He whipped me because *he* wanted to, and he's the only one with any rights in the matter."

Rinan was taken aback. "I only meant . . ." he began.

"You don't know what you mean," scoffed Justin. "Montfort couldn't tell our machtiern to catch fleas."

He would not say more than that, because he was ashamed to feel grateful to a man who'd just beaten him. Yet he did feel grateful. Justin had all his life had a horror of being helpless. His recurrent nightmare was of being tangled in a net, or pinned to the ground, and watching impotently as some deadly thing advanced on him. When he'd heard what the bailiff of Montfort was demanding, he'd been sick with a fear he was too proud to show. It wasn't the prospect of pain that frightened him — fights hurt, too, and he liked those — but the thought of having to endure it helplessly. Faced with a whipping post, he might even have broken and begged for mercy, God forbid. "There's sanctuary," Tiarnán had said, and then the pain was in his power: he could end it by reaching the gate.

Judith snorted and tossed her brother his soaking tunic. "Do you only think well of men who can beat you?" she asked.

"I don't think well of men I can beat myself," Justin answered with joyfully intact pride.

On that same sunny morning, Eline of Comper was sitting on her bed and looking at herself in her silver mirror. It was a big mirror, all of eight inches across, and she could see her shoulders as well as her face in it. She was checking whether

her new wimple was straight. How beautiful it was! She turned her head from side to side, admiring the effect from all angles, then set down the mirror and took the wimple off to admire it some more. It was forget-me-not blue, embroidered with tiny golden flowers along the edges, and it was pure silk. Tiarnán had given it to her, a present for their betrothal.

Eline clutched the wimple in both hands and dropped backward onto the bed, pressing the silken scrap against her heart and beaming at the ceiling. She was seventeen years old, and she was going to be married. She closed her eyes to relish it better: it still seemed too wonderful to be true. She couldn't bring her husband much property, but that didn't matter: he loved her, and she would be his lady. Lady of a manor, and wife to the finest knight in Brittany!

Eline was Hervé of Comper's youngest child, the cherished baby of a large family. Her two elder sisters had married years before; her brothers both had wives who were busily filling Comper manor house with children. Her father made a pet of her, his last and loveliest chick. She loved him dearly, but she'd sometimes feared that he'd never let her marry, that she'd go on sharing this tiny room with her cousin and her nieces, attending her father, helping to look after the house, until she was an old woman of twenty and had to be married off quickly out of very shame. And now she was betrothed to Tiarnán.

It was a better match than anyone else in the family had made. Hervé came from an undistinguished knightly line, and his modest estate labored to support all his offspring and relatives in a fashion fitting to nobles. Tiarnán not only had Talensac—a profitable manor, and only an afternoon's ride from Comper—but he had Duke Hoel's favor, too. Everyone had heard how the duke had once declared he would rather have one other knight like Tiarnán than a whole troop of common soldiers. Those who had an overlord's favor could expect to see their holdings grow. How wonderful, how glorious, that such a man should want to marry her!

Eline sat up again and kissed the wimple, then set it down on the bed beside her and looked back in the mirror. Her hair wasn't straight: that was why she'd felt that the wimple was crooked. She'd been practicing pinning it up like a married woman, instead of leaving it loose or in braids like a girl. She'd have to learn to do it! She smiled at the thought, and her face, reflected in the polished silver, smiled radiantly back. The sight of it made her even happier. It was a beautiful face. Was it sinful to be proud of that? Surely not. It couldn't be sinful to be glad that you could please people. Her father said it made him smile just to look at her, and Tiarnán watched her with a delight in his eyes that made her want to sing. Beauty was the gift she had for him, the real return for Talensac, and she was glad that she had it to give. She smiled again at her reflection: pink lips, fair skin, small straight nose, vivid blue-violet, black-lashed eyes, high forehead—a husband would be proud of that, certainly? She would swish about the duke's court in a blue silk gown, and all the courtiers would whisper to one another, "That's Lord Tiarnán's wife!"; she'd do him credit. She'd shaved her forehead to make it look even higher, and plucked her eyebrows because they were too straight, but there was nothing wrong with that. Her hair, normally out of sight under the veil, was beautiful, too, white blond and shining. She untied the ends of her braids and began to undo them. When she was lady of Talensac, she'd have a maid to do her hair for her. She'd choose one of her husband's serfs, a pretty girl, of course, younger than her, thirteen maybe, and she'd bring her into the household and teach her how she liked things done. Aunt Godildis said that was the way to do it, to train them young; if they'd had another mistress they always thought the way she'd done things was better.

Eline fetched her comb from the box on the shared dressing table, and, as she combed her hair out, she imagined that she was talking to the maid. "That's right," she'd say. "Part it in the middle, and comb it all out straight first." "Oh, my lady, how fine it is! Like gossamer!" "Careful, clumsy!" (as the comb stuck in a tangle) "You're pulling it." "I'm sorry, my lady; is that better? How beautiful you are! And how lovely it is here in the manor house. I'm so glad you chose me as your maid."

Eline beamed at her reflection again, surrounded now by her shining hair. She was sure she would love her maid. She would treat her like a younger sister, and when they went to court . . .

There was a noise at the window, and she turned to see Alain de Fougères sitting astride the frame.

Eline's jaw dropped and she sat frozen for a moment. She decided afterward that she should have screamed, but it didn't occur to her to scream for Alain. She'd known him since she was fifteen, when they'd met in the cathedral of Rennes at the Feast of Saint Peter. He'd come to Comper often, after that, and her father hadn't actually discouraged him — not until Tiarnán turned suitor, too. She'd never before been alone with him, of course; no unmarried girl of quality would ever be private with a man.

Alain put his finger to his lips and dropped into the room. He looked haggard and exhausted and he had several days' growth of stubble on his chin. The sleeves of his fine red tunic were thick with dirt, and over it he had one of the padded jerkins customarily worn under armor.

"What are you doing here?" demanded Eline in an undignified squeak.

"I came to see you," said Alain. "I had to. I've just heard that you're going to marry Tiarnán. Sweet Eline, you can't want to."

Eline got off the bed on the opposite side and stared across it. "How did you get in?" she asked. "Does Father know you're here?"

He shook his head. He had, in fact, told Hervé's gatekeeper — a simple old man who tended to trust anyone he knew — that he wanted to see the lord of the manor. Then he had slipped round the back of the house and climbed a trellis to reach Eline's room. But all this sounded undignified, and he didn't mention it. "Eline," he said instead, "I had to see you. I'm supposed to be in Rennes now. I was on a mission for the duke. But when I heard that you were going to marry Tiarnán, I couldn't bear it. I left my followers and the girl I was supposed to be escorting, left them on the road, and came straight here.

Why should we let them separate us? You know how I adore you. If I have you, I don't care what else happens to me. Come away with me now!"

He moved toward her, and Eline backed away rapidly. "You stay away from me!" she hissed at him. "Go away now, or I'll scream."

He stopped and stared in bewilderment. She couldn't help thinking how handsome he was, even in this state, so fair and wide-shouldered and blue-eyed, better-looking than Tiarnán — but she suppressed the disloyal thought at once. "What made you think I'd go away with you?" she asked him angrily.

"I love you," he replied, speaking straight from the heart. "I want to marry you."

"So does Tiarnán. What made you think I'd prefer you to him?"

He looked at her in stunned disbelief. His passion had possessed him so completely that he couldn't believe that it wasn't returned. "Eline!" he cried in distress.

"Oh, I like you, Alain," she admitted, relenting a little, remembering how a year before he'd ridden with her family to church, and on the way sung one of the troubadour songs the Duke of Aquitaine had written for his lady, a new kind of song, hot from the forge of a new kind of feeling. She'd known he'd sung it for her. "If it weren't for Tiarnán, I'd be happy to marry you," she conceded. "But he's a better man than you are, and everybody knows it."

"Because he owns *land*!" Alain exclaimed in a whisper strangled by contempt. "Worshipful land! You sound like my cousin Tiher! What do we care about land? Doesn't love matter more?" He'd held this conversation many times in his head, and she'd agreed with him there so often that he'd almost forgotten it was something he'd never dared to say in front of her father.

"Why shouldn't I be the lady of a manor?" demanded Eline, then blushed, because it sounded mercenary. "And everybody knows how brave Tiarnán is, and how skilled at arms. He killed Robert of Bellême's brother Geoffroy in single combat:

everyone's heard that. *And* he's wealthy and young and hand-some, *and* he loves me dearly. How *could* you believe I'd be willing to run off with you?"

"He will never love you as much as I do," Alain said flatly, falling back on the basic axiom from which all his imaginary arguments had depended. "Nobody could love you as much as I do, least of all Tiarnán. He's a cold, dark devil. All he really cares about is killing. I've seen him fight: he's a madman. People think well of him because all the men he's killed so far have been the duke's enemies, but he spills blood like a weasel in a henhouse. If there are no men for him to kill, he kills animals. I met him while I was going to Rennes; that's how I learned he was going to marry you. He'd been hunting—on foot, in that old green peasanty tunic and hood, all by himself without even a dog! Like a *serf*! He arranged to marry *you,* and then he went *hunting*! Didn't stay with you, didn't go straight to court to tell everyone the good news, just walked off into the forest alone." Alain caught his breath, then rushed on inconsistently, "But he goes off by himself a lot; everyone knows that. Three days out of a week, sometimes more. Hunting, he says. Alone, always alone. No one can come with him. He leaves his horse. He never takes a hawk. When I saw him, he'd left his dog. How could he hunt without a dog? Where is he *really* going, do you think? Hunting? Or to some woman's bed?"

"You be quiet!" shrieked Eline furiously. "You're just jealous. Get out. Out!"

There was a sound of footsteps running upstairs beyond the door.

"Eline!" Alain pleaded desperately. "Come with me!"

"Out!" screamed Eline. She jumped over the bed and shoved him toward the window. "If you're not out of the manor by the time my father learns you were here, he'll have you in the stocks, I know he will. Out!"

Alain half-jumped, half-fell out the window, and slid down the trellis to the ground. It was a rose trellis, and when he landed, his face and hands were torn by the thorns. He stood a moment in agony, staring up at the window above and listening to the voices, one questioning, one replying scornfully. Then he turned and broke into a stumbling run.

He was halfway back to the fortified manor gate before he realized that he'd left his mail shirt, sword, and helmet in a heap under an apple tree, where he'd taken them off to climb the trellis. He almost went back for them—then thought of the stocks and ran on to the gate. Fortunately, the old gatekeeper hadn't yet learned that he shouldn't have come in, and let him out.

Alain collected the horse he'd left tethered outside the gate and rode away from Comper at a gallop. As soon as he was clear of the village, he allowed the tired animal to slow down, and buried his face against its neck, helpless with tears.

He fled blindly all through the afternoon, and by nightfall had reached the town of Montfort, fourteen miles east of Comper. There was an inn there as well as an alehouse, and he stopped for the night. When he rose next morning, he wasn't sure which way to ride. He ought to retrieve his sword and his armor. Armor was valuable. It would take a year's rents from a small village to pay for what he'd left under the apple tree. But it seemed very likely that Eline was right, and if he were caught in Comper just now he'd find himself in the stocks. Stocks, public beatings, and similar humiliations were ordinarily reserved for the peasantry, and Alain couldn't bear the thought of them: the indignity, the inevitable subsequent ridicule! If Eline had said, "Father will kill you," he would have been far more likely to dare going back.

It would be better to go to Fougères first, then, and send a page to collect the armor. Though Hervé of Comper probably wouldn't give it back without a ransom. Alain would have to go to his father, Juhel, for the money—and explain to him where he'd been and what he'd done. He groaned out loud at the thought.

Perhaps he'd better go to Rennes first. Tiher would be worried about him. But then he'd have to face the duke and explain why he'd abandoned his mission; explain, too, how Tiarnán had rescued the girl he was supposed to be in charge of. He groaned again.

Everything had conspired against him, and in return for his faithful love he received only humiliation on all sides. He shouldn't have galloped off to Comper in the first place. But Eline *might* have agreed to come away with him, and if she had, nothing else would have mattered.

In the end, he saddled his horse and rode east from Montfort very slowly, hoping that he'd think of something else to do before he arrived in Rennes. The only thing that occurred to him was to pass by both Rennes and Fougères and go join the crusade. The idea appealed to him: exiled for love, he'd either die nobly saving the holy places from the Turks or come back a hero! But there were practical difficulties with that plan, too. The last news of the Christian armies was that they were besieging Antioch, and Antioch was a very, very long way away. It would take a lot of money to reach it, and he knew his father wouldn't give him any. Besides—the most relentless of his problems revolved back upon him like a wheel—he didn't have his arms.

He was riding with his head bowed, so intent on wondering how he could steal secretly into Comper and retrieve his weapons that he didn't hear the hoofbeats behind him, until they slowed. Then he looked up and found Tiarnán riding beside him.

iarnán had left Talensac that morning in an anxious and irritable frame of mind. This was in part simply because he was hungry: he was still religiously fasting in penance for the two robbers. For the term of the penance he could eat nothing but bread and salt, and drink nothing but water. If he made a short pilgrimage or two—to Saint Samson's shrine at Dol, for example, and Saint Mailon's at St. Malo—and if he gave alms to the poor, he could reduce the term of penance, but not elim-

inate it. It was of course possible to put penances off indefinitely — they could be done even after death, in Purgatory — but
Tiarnán wanted to marry in a state of grace, with all past sins
atoned for. Therefore, he was hungry.

The penances assigned by Judicaël the Hermit were, for the
age, strict. A generation before most priests would have given
similar penances for like offenses, but the new era was laxer:
many confessors wouldn't have considered the killing of a couple of robbers to be a sin at all. But it never crossed Tiarnán's
mind to look for an easier absolution. He shared the general
Talensac opinion that Father Judicaël was a very holy man, an
unacknowledged saint, but that was the least of his reasons for
loyalty. Before going to his hermitage, Judicaël had been the
Talensac parish priest. When Tiarnán was orphaned, it had
been Judicaël who supervised his care. He had taught the boy
his prayers and his letters, and had carried him on his shoulders
out into the fringes of the forest, and pointed out to him the
plants and the animals, telling him their names and their habits.
His was the standard by which everything had inevitably been
measured, and no absolution from anyone else could count. And
that was another reason for Tiarnán to be anxious: Judicaël
thought he shouldn't marry Eline. The hermit had been unhappy about the match from the moment it was first proposed.
"She will not understand you, and you will not understand her,"
he'd said. "You will do each other harm. From what you say,
there is another man who loved her first, a man who may be
better suited to her. If she loves him, is it right to interfere?"

The hermit's authority was such that his pupil had been dissuaded — for a little while. But Eline's father had invited him
back to Comper, and there his wishes overcame his scruples.
He told himself that Judicaël had never met Eline and couldn't
judge what she would understand. For his part Tiarnán loved
her: Love would give him understanding. He'd been happy with
this argument for a while, but now, in the irritability of hunger,
doubts were creeping in. He loved Eline, but did she love him?
He knew perfectly well that he had been preferred by Hervé

only because he was lord of a manor. Was Eline really being forced into marriage with him when she preferred Alain de Fougères?

He was thinking about Alain de Fougères as he set out for the court that morning. Alain was a proper knight, nobly born and gently reared. He was handsome. He could sing all the new songs from the south, and sing them in key, accompanying himself upon the lute. He could dance; he could play chess. His clothes were always in the latest style: *he* would never be found on foot in an old green tunic. He never seemed to feel any need to do anything unbecoming to a knight: there was no taint of the peasant in *him*. And he obviously sincerely loved Eline. The more Tiarnán thought about his rival, the more uneasy he became.

Tiarnán was painfully aware of his own inadequacies — his peasant upbringing, his simple tastes, his lack of sophistication and polish, of *gentillesse* and courtesy. When he first went to court as an eight-year-old page, his failings had been rammed down his throat. Judicaël's teaching had not included table manners, etiquette, heraldry, falconry, dancing, or a dozen similar matters of which, he had discovered, no one who called himself noble should be ignorant. Some of the older pages had taken it upon themselves to correct this uncouth Breton peasant, and had done so so persistently, and with such brutal inventiveness, that for a while he had prayed for death. Then he'd learned to fight. He still fought in the way he'd learned then, with the frenzied savagery of a child goaded beyond endurance. He had a man's control of the rage now: he could place his weapons accurately even in the heat of it, and he could summon it up at will. It was effective, and he knew that people were afraid of him because of it. That satisfied him — to fight well was the chief glory of a knight, the thing that brought him honor from his overlord and respect from his peers. But it was a brutal skill, and faced with a rival like Alain, he wished for grace, for breeding, for everything he lacked that might be pleasing to Eline.

When he first noticed Alain riding slowly ahead of him, he

thought that his reflections must have printed Alain's image on a stranger. But as he drew nearer and the identification became increasingly certain, incredulity gave way to a rising tide of fury. This was his usual road from Talensac, but Alain would only use it if he were coming from Comper. Alain, like those older pages long ago, was trying to make a fool of him. Alain, like those pages, would regret it. He rode up behind Alain in a tense silence, then slowed his horse and looked angrily into the other's eyes.

To Alain, after the first shock, it seemed inevitable that he should meet Tiarnán. Fortune's wheel was sweeping Alain down to the depths of wretchedness, so naturally it had brought his rival up to gloat over him. There was even a bitter satisfaction in the contrast between them. Last time they'd met, Alain had been splendidly armed, riding a spirited bay charger, while Tiarnán had been plainly dressed and on foot. Now love had transformed them both. Alain was haggard and unshaven, scratched by thorns, disarmed, dressed in a dirty tunic and trousers and a padded jerkin, and his horse was drooping and dejected after days of hard riding—while Tiarnán was splendid for the court. A painter might have drawn them in miniature to illuminate a poem on good and bad fortune in love.

Tiarnán was indeed splendid. Since inheriting Talensac, he had never gone to court without making every effort to silence the nonexistent heirs to those scornful pages. The stained green hunting tunic had been replaced by one dyed magnificently scarlet, with a collar and hem worked in gold brocade, and a red cloak trimmed with ermine, worn loose because of the heat. The sheath of the sword at his side was chased gold. A goshawk in a crested hood perched on one white-gloved hand, and the fine chestnut stallion he rode was caparisoned in crimson. For once he looked every inch a knight. Some four or five servants and attendants rode behind him, leading mules for the baggage. The face he turned to Alain was as guarded as usual, but there was something wicked and dangerous about his eyes.

"What do you want?" Alain demanded belligerently.

"I am surprised to see you here, Alain of Fougères," Tiarnán replied quietly. Fighting was a matter of blows, not words. "I thought you would be in Rennes." He spoke in Breton, not in the French he'd used out of courtesy at their last meeting. Alain himself spoke the French of the Breton March, but the other language was often used at Hoel's court, and he was reasonably fluent in it.

"I'm not," replied Alain, trying to sound casual.

"So I see."

"Tiher is taking Lady Marie to Rennes. If you're on your way to Rennes, there's your road. You'll excuse me, but I don't relish your company just at present."

Tiarnán made no response to this. He kept his horse beside Alain's, staring in an expressionless way that set Alain's teeth on edge. The pupils of his eyes had contracted, and the very blankness of his face made the concentrated anger of those eyes more alarming. "You should not leave unfinished a task your liege lord has given you," he said at last, very quietly. "And you should not pay court to other men's ladies when their backs are turned."

"She was mine before she was yours!" snapped Alain. His hand moved to where the hilt of his sword should have been, and grabbed the empty air.

Tiarnán eyes had followed the movement. "Where's your sword?" he demanded.

Cold, dark devil, Alain thought, glaring. But there was a sick lump in the pit of his stomach. One thing he hadn't thought of when he galloped off to Comper was that he might have to fight Tiarnán because of it. Not that it would have made any difference, he told himself; the son of a lord of Fougères wouldn't turn coward for any man—but he should have thought of it. After all, any peasant would fight a man who'd been seeing his woman behind his back, and Tiarnán was a knight.

As he'd told Eline, he had seen Tiarnán fight, at weapons' practice and tilting matches, and he knew that the man's deadly reputation was merited. He himself was only a very common-place swordsman. But he could not, in honor, back down. "My sword is at Comper," he told Tiarnán, trying to keep the fear out of his voice. "And my armor. I . . . can't get them myself just now, but if you like, you can send one of your men to fetch them."

There was a moment's silence as Tiarnán digested this. Then the brown eyes became less deadly. "Why can't you fetch them yourself?" he asked.

Alain went red. "Never mind," he said. "Hervé would give them to you."

Tiarnán continued to stare at him, this time taking in the scratches, the dirt, the armor not just taken off and packed in the bag behind the saddle, as he'd assumed before, but actually missing, the general air of dejection. Slowly the whole truth became apparent to him, and his anger and anxiety began to dissolve away. "You took them off to climb the trellis, didn't you?" he said. "That's where you got those scratches. And you left in a great hurry, and didn't have time to put them on again, and don't dare go back for them. But Hervé didn't catch you; you wouldn't be here if he had. You were riding along as mournful as an owl in molt, and don't relish my company at present. Eline herself sent you away, didn't she?"

Alain thought he had never in his life hated anyone as perfectly as he hated Tiarnán at that moment. The lump of fear was gone, swallowed up by utter loathing. He'd be glad to fight the man. He might even win. Someone had to teach the bastard a lesson sometime.

Alain's wordless glare was all the confirmation Tiarnán needed. Eline did not love Alain. His heart began to sing again, and the rest of his anger with his rival vanished. It was understandable that Alain should love Eline, but she did not love him back—poor devil! *She* had chosen Tiarnán.

Tiarnán made no open display of his delight, however. Another thing he'd learned from the bullying pages was never to show his real feelings. Happiness and pain alike had invited punishment. So he merely smiled a composed one-sided smile, and turned to one of his servants. "Donoal," he said, "ride to Comper. Give Lord Hervé my greetings, and ask him for Lord

Alain's sword and armor, which were left there . . . yesterday, Lord Alain?—yesterday. Tell him that I beg him, as a particular favor, to give them back to Lord Alain. Do you want them sent to Rennes, my lord? Or to Fougères?"

Alain swallowed. The lump was back. "Where would you prefer to fight?" he asked, trying to sound as though it didn't matter to him.

"I don't want to fight," replied Tiarnán contentedly. "I have two corpses to do penance for already this week. And why should I fight you? You've done me a service. I didn't know whether Eline cared for me, or whether she was just following her father's choice out of duty. You have many noble qualities that I lack, Lord Alain—don't think I haven't felt that. I didn't know which of us she'd choose, until you put it to the test. Allow me the victor's privilege of disposing of the armor of a noble opponent. Do you want it sent to Fougères or to Rennes?"

Alain wanted to tell him to take it to hell, but couldn't quite bring himself to say so. He was glad he didn't have to fight the man, but he wondered if he ought to refuse to accept his armor back. His father would be furious with him for losing it. Best-quality chain mail! Months of work for the blacksmith! You left it under a tree? Mother of God! And the sword I bought you in Tours for twenty marks? You idiot!

It would be much easier to face his father if he at least had his armor safe.

"Send it to Rennes," he muttered.

Tiarnán nodded and relayed the instruction to the servant, and the servant galloped off. Alain watched him go, then looked bleakly back at Tiarnán.

"Fortune's wheel never stops turning, you know," he said. "If it's brought me down, it will bring me up again one day. And you're riding the heights now, but that only means you've nowhere to go but down."

"I don't believe things are that simple," replied Tiarnán equably. "Most fortunes are mixed most of the time." He gave his lopsided smile. "And Fortune's been kind to you, for all your harsh words about her. You got into Comper and out again, and you're getting your armor back. If you ever try anything similar at Talensac, I promise you now, you will not be so lucky."

Alain set his teeth furiously and reined in his horse. This time Tiarnán gave him a nod and another complacent half-smile of acknowledgment, and rode on. Alain watched him until he was out of sight. Eline could never really love a cold, dangerous man like that, he told himself. A man like that wouldn't know how to be kind to her. After a few months he'd neglect her, go off on his hunting trips and leave her alone in his manor house, with no one but the servants to talk to. If she complained, he'd become angry. He might even beat her. A vivid memory from the jousting field leapt to his mind: Tiarnán flinging himself from his horse to fall on a knight he'd just downed, bringing the wooden practice sword down again and again so furiously that the sword broke and the other man was left stunned, blood streaming from his nose. A man like Tiarnán might do anything.

Alain's spirits began to rise again. He wouldn't listen to Tiarnán's threats. He'd let Eline know, somehow, that whatever had happened he was still her faithful lover, and if she ever wanted him, he would be there. All he had to do was wait.

Tiher was sitting in the Great Hall of the duke's palace that night when Alain came in. He'd been cleaning his mail shirt, but he dropped the armor with a jingle, jumped up, and ran over to him.

"Alain!" he cried, grabbing his cousin by the shoulders. "Thank God. For a while I thought you might have been chopped into small pieces by Tiarnán of Talensac."

Alain grunted, though he found the greeting comforting. Tiher was a prickly fellow, not given to sympathetic cousinly embraces, and this warmth from him seemed an acknowledgment of the seriousness of what Alain had undergone.

"You look awful," said Tiher, holding Alain by the elbow and guiding him to the bench where he himself had been sitting. "Here, come sit down; do you need something to drink?

Servant! A cup of wine for my cousin. — Lord Christ, Alain, you were a fool to go to Comper!"

"I had to," said Alain, and felt a secret satisfaction at his own daring. Looked at rightly, slipping into a stronghold and snatching a private conversation with his beloved under her father's very nose, and then boldly facing her approved lover on the road afterward, was a heroic thing to have done. He at once launched into a glorified account of it. Of the meeting on the road, he said only that his rival had asked for the privilege of returning the armor of a noble opponent.

"That was very magnanimous of him," broke in Tiher. "But I suppose you can afford to be magnanimous when your lady has thrown your rival out the window with her own fair hands."

Alain gaped at his cousin indignantly.

"Look, Alain," Tiher went on, brushing heroism aside, "I've made all the excuses for you that I could think of, and the duchess, who has a soft spot for lovers, has put in a few good words as well. When we turned up and they noticed that Lady Marie had been roughly handled, and you weren't there, there was uproar like a melee of hounds around a kill and —"

"Do you think I care about that?" demanded Alain. "I've lost the one thing in the world I most desired; what difference does it make that the duke's annoyed?"

Tiher rolled his eyes heavenward and crossed himself. "Jesus, Mary, and Joseph!" he exclaimed. "*I* wouldn't want to explain to your father that his overlord has dismissed you for disobedience and neglect of duty, but if you want to, by all means go!"

Alain gaped again. The servant came up with the cup of wine, and he took it numbly. "The duke couldn't really dismiss me, could he?" he asked.

Tiher shook his head in amazement at his cousin's simplicity. Of course, Alain had no great experience of the ducal court. He'd done his service as a page at Chateaubriant, the castle of one of his father's friends. Tiher had joined him there, as a squire, after his spell at the monastic school. Nobody at Chateaubriant would have dreamed of dismissing the son of the lord of Fougères. And after Chateaubriant there'd been different manors belonging to the castle of Fougères, months at Fougères itself — it had only been in the last year or two that he and Alain had spent any time at court. Alain still didn't seem to have grasped that the second son of a Marcher lord was not a person of much consequence outside his father's domain.

"The duke is perfectly entitled to send you packing," he told Alain. "You were in charge of bringing Lady Marie here, and you ran off and left her on the road. And cousin, he was angry. . . ." He told Alain of the duke's furious lecture. "And it doesn't make it any better," he finished, "that what you did instead was to try to steal away the betrothed of one of the duke's favorites. But, as I was saying, I put the best gloss on it I could, and I think the duke will pardon you. I made excuses for you, the duchess interceded for you, and when Tiarnán came in this afternoon he behaved very handsomely. He told us he'd met you on the road near Montfort, looking mournful as an owl because the Lady Eline had thrown you out the window, and that you'd be along as soon as you could, but that your horse was worn out with lover's errands and had to come slowly. Hoel was tickled by that; he laughed over it with the duchess. As soon as you've finished that wine, you'd better go and apologize to him. Tell him that you were confident that, after her ordeal, Lady Marie wasn't going to try to escape again; that you thought he wouldn't mind if you left me to escort her on the last stage of the journey; and that you were mad with love and despair. I think he'll give you a ready hearing and a free pardon."

Alain took a swallow of wine. "Tiarnán came in this afternoon?" he asked unhappily. "So the duke's been told that he's going to marry Eline?"

"What did you expect? Hoel had heard as much from us already — I had to explain why you weren't here — and he was a bit disappointed, but he congratulated Tiarnán and suggested they use the cathedral at Rennes for the wedding."

"Hoel was disappointed?" Alain asked suspiciously. "Why?"

Tiher shrugged. He was fairly certain that Hoel had hoped

Tiarnán would marry Marie Penthièvre and secure Chalandrey to Brittany. It was clear enough that if anyone in Brittany was going to be acceptable to Marie, it would be Tiarnán. She'd been singing his praises loudly to the duke and duchess, and had listened to their opinion of him with glowing eyes. Well, that was only fair: he'd saved her. But it was also perfectly clear that Tiarnán had no interest whatever in the girl he'd rescued, and had, indeed, almost forgotten her. When he'd arrived in Rennes he'd been surprised when the duke and duchess thanked him for his services to the duchess's kinswoman — "What? Oh, you mean Lady Marie" — and had gone straight on to talk about his forthcoming marriage. Marie herself had come into the Great Hall while he was talking, and he'd paused only to greet her politely and ask her how she was, before returning to the arrangements for the wedding. Marie had stood watching him for a little, then gone silently back upstairs to the duchess's apartments. And as soon as the announcement and the arrangements were concluded, Tiarnán had left the court without even waiting for the evening meal. He was doing penance, he'd said, so as to be free to take the sacrament at the wedding Mass, and was no fit company for a noble court; he would return in a month for the wedding.

Tiher had been relieved to discover that Marie's rescuer had so little interest in the rescued, though he was offended on Marie's behalf: a lady like that deserved more attention! But there was absolutely no point in telling any of this to Alain, who at the moment had ears for nothing but his own grief.

"Hoel would prefer a man of proven loyalty to marry land," he said instead. "Tiarnán could have had an heiress from him for the asking any time. But of course, the duke didn't want to offend Tiarnán, or Hervé, and he had no reason to interfere with their arrangement, so he blessed it. The marriage will take place at Rennes cathedral on Midsummer Day." It was a mark of the duke's esteem for Tiarnán that the wedding would be arranged by the court at the cathedral; a minor nobleman would normally marry at home.

Alain blinked miserably as he took in this further sign of his rival's honor and his own wretched disgrace. He put the wine down and pressed his head into his hands.

Lord, he's wallowing in it, thought Tiher. "I'm very relieved you've turned up unharmed," he said aloud. "I didn't know what I was going to say to your father. My God, man, you were a fool! Eline couldn't legally marry you even if she wanted to: she's under her father's authority. And Hervé was entitled to do pretty much what he wanted with you, finding you in his own manor—and, it seems, in his daughter's bedroom! As for Tiarnán, he's the last man in Brittany I'd want to fight. You've been very lucky to come out of this so lightly."

"Lucky?" asked Alain wretchedly. "To lose my lady, and then have to crawl to the duke with apologies for trying to get her back? I won't count myself lucky unless Tiarnán breaks his neck."

Tiher raised his eyebrows. Tiarnán's magnanimity had been squandered in vain. But he supposed there was no point to magnanimity if you didn't squander it. "There are other ladies in this world, thank God," he remarked neutrally.

"None as lovely as Eline," replied Alain.

Tiher shrugged. "I don't know. It's said they're all lovely in the dark. And, to speak plainly, there are some I prefer to Eline in clear daylight."

At this Alain picked his head up in genuine shock and astonishment. I have blasphemed, Tiher observed. Mary the mother of God couldn't be preferred to Eline. "There's Lady Marie, for instance," he said, unable to resist a bit of goading.

"Her!" exclaimed Alain in disgust. "How can you compare her to Eline? It's like comparing a swan to . . . to a thieving magpie!"

"The magpie is a brave bird, cousin. You'll find all the court agreed in praising her. When she came in here, she declared straight out that she would marry no servant of her father's enemy, and that she would rather die defending her honor than live deprived of it. She looked as gallant as Count Roland defending the pass, but much prettier. Now Duke Hoel has said that she may marry whichever of his knights she pleases, provided the man is noble, loyal to himself, and willing. And, of course, we've all declared our great willingness, all those of us that aren't married already, and some of those that are looked as though they wished they weren't. But she's refused us all, and announced to the world that Tiarnán is standing surety that no one will force her—though she never needed any protection from him, of course. It's a sad comment on the way they do things in Normandy that she thought *our* duke would let someone force her. Duchess Havoise has made her a lady-in-waiting. They're cousins of some kind, of course."

Alain had no interest in any branch of the Penthièvre clan. He drained his wine and dropped the cup on the table. "The court can praise any silly magpie it pleases," he said contemptuously. "I won't."

"Good," returned Tiher. "All the more chance for us."

Alain stared. "You really do admire that Penthièvre girl!" he exclaimed in surprise.

"Oh, yes," said Tiher warmly. "Without hope, cousin, without the least hope. But I intend to enjoy myself admiring. It's good sport. You go apologize to the duke. If your armor arrives, I'll see to it."

IV

*B*y midsummer the lovely weather that had gilded the end of May was only a dim memory. June started with rain and continued with more of it. At Rennes the castle moat was no longer a dry ditch, but a slippery bank leading to a deep puddle full of rubbish and drowned grass; streams ran through the streets of the town, washing their filth into the brown and swollen Vilaine River.

The wedding party from Comper set out at dawn on the nineteenth, and had a miserable journey to the court. The roads were deep with mud, and the cart of baggage got stuck twelve times, and had to be levered out with branches broken from the trees. When they at last arrived in Rennes, late in the afternoon, Lord Hervé left the servants at the castle stables to see to the exhausted horses, and hurried his equally exhausted daughter across the muddy outer bailey and up the stone steps to the keep. There he learned that Duke Hoel was in the kennels, inspecting his hounds. After a brief discussion in the guardroom, Hervé went off to greet his overlord, leaving the duke's butler to escort Eline to the Duchess Havoise, who was sitting with her ladies in the solar, the dayroom above the Great Hall.

The duchess and her attendants had been weaving, spinning, embroidering clothing, and, of course, talking. It seemed to Marie, sitting and listening to them as she so often did, that no one in Rennes ever stopped talking. The court was an exhausting and exhilarating labyrinth of voices: every evening she lay down weary but hopeful, thinking she'd grasped one of its patterns; every morning she woke up to find the pattern changed, a new voice added, another turning to the maze. People were always coming and going. The duke's family and officials, the servants, and some thirty of the household knights remained at the court all the time, but the rest of the faces changed with dizzying speed—knights supplying their overlord with their due of military service for the year, arriving, paying their respects, going off on postings or staying with the garrison; tenants and stewards of the ducal estates coming with reports and going with instructions; barons suing for a favor or complaining of their neighbors' depredations; bishops and abbots arranging benefices, arriving in a cloud of servants and leaving in a procession of clerks. To Marie, accustomed to small communities where the appearance of a stranger was an event, it was breathtaking. And all these people talked constantly. Even the language they talked in shifted all the time: a conversation could begin in Breton, end in French, and be Latin in the middle. Nearly everyone spoke both the vernacular tongues, and most of the officials were fluent in the learned one as well. The duke preferred to speak Breton—he was from Quimper, deep in Breton-speaking western Brittany—so most of the knights did the same. Marie had asked one of the duchess's ladies to teach her the language. She could get by on her own French tongue, though: the duchess, born and bred in the March city of Rennes, spoke French by preference, and her attendants naturally followed their lady's lead. When Eline entered the solar, it resounded to a lilting Breton French discussion of, naturally enough, the rain. Her arrival, cloaked and dripping, simply provided the conversation with more fuel.

"By Saint Anne, child, you're drenched!" exclaimed the duchess.

Marie had tried to dislike Havoise, but had utterly failed to do so. The duchess was strong-willed, domineering but good-humored, sentimental, sly, and surprisingly coarse; she had bad legs, a poor digestion, an omnivorous interest in other people, and a tremendous zest for life. She was kind, too: Marie would not quickly forget the poultice of borage leaves her first night in Rennes, or the way the duchess had fussed to find her new gowns, declaring indignantly that it was absolute nonsense for

Marie to be afraid: nobody was going to harm *her* cousin. It had been impossible even to refuse the gowns: "Child, you cannot, *cannot* wear that black thing at court. I forbid it." Since, apart from "that black thing," all Marie had were some old gowns from Chalandrey that no longer fit her, she'd had to accept the duchess's charity, though she'd taken only the plainest of the dresses offered her. Pressed between the firmness and the kindness, she found herself giving the duchess her oath that she would not try to escape from her gentle captivity again — not unless she was being forced into marriage.

"Take that wet cloak off," Havoise now ordered Eline. "Sybille, go fetch the girl a blanket. I don't know when I've seen such foul weather for June."

"If it keeps coming down like this," said Sybille, who was the wife of the duke's stable master, and Havoise's greatest confidante, "they'll have to cancel the opening hunt of the stag season. Lord, what the men will say to that! — There aren't any blankets in the chest here, my lady."

"Go fetch one off a bed!" ordered Havoise. "And you, Corentin" — to the butler — "have some mulled wine sent up for the girl. And — why not? — some for the rest of us as well." He bowed and went.

"I'll fetch my blanket," said Marie, and went to get it.

When she came back with it, Eline had been seated in Sybille's chair next to the duchess, and Sybille was on the chest, with Eline's wet cloak and damp wimple beside her. Eline had curled her cold feet up into the chair, leaving her muddy slippers in the rushes. Rain-sprinkled, fragile, fair, and radiant, she shone in the rain-dimmed solar like white violets in a dark wood. Marie looked at her with relief. She had hoped that Eline would prove extraordinarily beautiful. Her heart still clung to its habit of stinging when she thought of Tiarnán, despite all attempts to point out to it the absurdity of this behavior. If Eline was extraordinary, there was no reason to be ashamed of herself in comparison. Marie draped the blanket carefully around the slim shoulders, and Eline looked up at her with a sweet smile of thanks.

"I hope the sun shines for your wedding, Lady Eline," said the duchess. "But meanwhile, be very welcome here. The castle is crowded just now, I'm afraid, and you'll have to share a bed until your wedding."

"After it, too," put in Sybille slyly. The duchess had no doubt anticipated the joke, but she laughed at it heartily. Eline went pink.

Visitors might have to share a bed at any castle, but at Rennes more often than at most. There was never enough furniture for the private apartments. The court of Brittany, like most noble courts of the time, did not stay in one place, but moved about among the duke's various residences — Nantes, Rennes, Quimper, Ploërmel, and a number of lesser places. This spread the burden of providing for it over a larger number of estates, and it also helped to keep the castles sweet. (After a few months with the whole court in residence, the overburdened ditches and middens about any building reeked overpoweringly, for there were no proper sewers.) When the court moved away from the smell, it took some of the furniture with it in a great baggage train, but most was left behind in the empty rooms, guarded by the castle's regular garrison. Rennes was so new that it hadn't accumulated much furniture of its own. The very stone it was built from was sharp-edged and shining; even the ceiling of the Great Hall was bright, not yet blackened by decades of smoke. Inside, its walls were still mostly bare, the few tapestries and curtains hanging among yards of blank stone. The partitions used to divide up the rooms were designed for smaller residences, and never stretched all the way to the walls. If you went to the solar you had to remember to take a stool with you, or else you sat on the floor, or on the chest like Sybille.

"Lady Eline can share with me," said Marie, "if she likes."

Eline smiled at her again, this time with a touch of confusion. "Have we met, Lady . . . ?"

"Marie. We haven't met, but your husband-to-be did me a great service, and I'd like to repay it in any way I can."

"Oh!" exclaimed Eline, and jumped smiling to her feet.

"*You're* Marie Penthièvre! I've heard so much about you." Inwardly, she, too, was relieved. She hadn't been able to help feeling jealous and anxious about the runaway heiress Tiarnán had rescued, especially when one of her brothers told her that the whole court was in love with the unknown. But it seemed there had been nothing to worry about. Marie was ordinarily pretty, no more, dressed simply in a plain blue-gray gown, and old to be still unmarried. Eline liked the way she had referred to "your husband-to-be" in such a frank and friendly way. There was no danger here. "I'd be delighted to share with you," she said.

"That's settled, then," said the duchess with satisfaction. "You two will have the most enviable bed in the castle."

She didn't have to wait long for the expected response. "Because," Sybille said instantly, "every young nobleman in Rennes is longing to share it with one or the other of them."

The duchess laughed, the other ladies giggled, and Eline went pink again. Marie just smiled and sat down in her own place at the big loom, picking up the shuttle. Jokes like that had disconcerted her at first, but she was used to them now. Hoel had said that she might marry any of his loyal knights who was willing, and his loyal knights had seen it as a challenge, a glorious contest to win her heart and the manor of Chalandrey. They surrounded her constantly with a bantering, joking, exuberant celebration of a fiery new fashion from the south: courtly love. This was a new game with carefully defined rules: the beloved might have more than one lover, but the lover only one beloved; lovers should be apprehensive, and turn pale in their beloved's presence; nothing was too much to ask for love, but anything taken against the beloved's wishes was without relish. Brittany was enjoying a peaceful summer, and the young men, mostly landless lesser nobles, had plenty of time and energy to spare. The courtly love of their songs was usually directed to a married lady, a lord's lady, lofty and unattainable. An unmarried lady who had a lord's permission to choose whatever knight she pleased and confer a manor on him—that was a gift from God. The knights revelled in the sport of it. And Marie, after a few weeks of complete bewilderment, was beginning to revel, too. She had never thought that there could be so much pleasure in just living. The Marie who had arrived at Rennes a few weeks ago already seemed to her clumsy and naive.

The door of the solar opened once more, and one of the court pages, a boy of nine, appeared with a huge flagon of steaming wine carried carefully in both hands. Behind him came a handful of knights from the household guard; Tiher was one of them. Marie smiled and began to concentrate on her weaving.

"Greetings to the company!" said Tiher. "I thought young Howen needed some help to carry the cups. May we join you, ladies?"

"By all means," said the duchess. "It's a gray, grim day, and we need to brighten it. Hand the cups round."

When Tiher and another knight, Morvan, both tried to give Marie a cup at the same time, her hands were busy at the loom and she was able to nod for them to set them down by her feet, which saved choosing. Morvan, disappointed, put the cup he held down beside her, doing his best to look pale and apprehensive, but Tiher grinned, sat down next to the loom, and drank from his himself. "So," he said, surveying the room, "half the wedding party has arrived! Good health to you, Lady Eline. I'm sure my cousin Alain would be rushing to greet you, but he's back in Fougères, cherishing a broken heart." (Sent back by the duke, and told to sulk in private till the wedding was over, Tiher recalled—but there was no need to mention that to Eline.) "When is the bridegroom coming?" he said instead.

Eline was flustered by the reference to Alain but recovered quickly. "Tiarnán should arrive tomorrow," she said. "He told my father he'd be here then. But I'm not supposed to see him until the day after." At the thought that the day after was her wedding day, she smiled. Tiher grinned back, and she stopped smiling. Odd that he was ugly when Alain was so handsome. Even odder that that was so, but they still looked so much alike.

"I suppose that your bridegroom is still busy today, rushing about his manor, seeing everything made ready for his bride," said Havoise, indulging her sentimental side.

"I'd wager he's gone hunting," said Sybille.

Eline looked abruptly uncomfortable and anxious, and Tiher laughed. "Your wager's won, Lady Sybille. Tiarnán is undoubtedly tramping about the forest in the pouring rain, looking for that big stag he hunted with the duke last Holy Rood Day. The season opens on his wedding day. I wonder if he regrets the date."

"Tch!" said the duchess. "I'm sure the young man feels he must do something to keep himself busy. And I'm sure his servants were pushing him to go. Any normal servant would want the master out of the manor at a time like this."

"I wish he hadn't gone," Eline said plaintively. "Or, at least, I wish he'd take someone with him. I don't like to think of him wandering about in the woods alone. They say that that robber Éon of Moncontour has sworn to kill him."

At this there was an uncomfortable pause, a faltering of the room's good humor. Tiher looked quickly across to Marie.

"I heard that Écon robbed a parish priest in Ploërmel last week," said Morvan. "Broke into the house when the man was asleep, tied up the owner, and looted it."

"I am very sorry to hear that," said Marie quietly. She stared at her hands, now motionless on the loom, thinking, again, that if it had not been for her and her need for protection, Tiarnán could have killed Éon when they met. Then the parish priest in Ploërmel would be unmolested, and Tiarnán could wander about the forest without danger.

"This Éon is a most marvelous fellow," said Tiher lightly, though inwardly he was cursing Eline and Morvan for reminding Marie of her ordeal. "He roams about the forest like a wolf, outcast and outlawed, with every man's hand against him; he steals bread from houses at night and sleeps in thickets. When he last met Lord Tiarnán, he ran off in a great hurry. Yet he's able to tell someone or other that he means to kill the lord of a manor and get the tale believed. It seems to me that he never swore vengeance at all. How could he even spread the news of his intentions, let alone carry them out? He doesn't dare speak to anyone but his victims."

"Ah, that's not true," said Havoise. "There are peasants who help him. If there weren't, he would have been caught by now."

"Why would anyone help a creature like that?" asked Eline in disgust.

"Because he's a serf who dares to rob priests and landowners," replied the duchess drily. "Other serfs admire that, even when he robs them, too."

"He killed the bailiff of my lord of Moncontour," put in another of the ladies suddenly. She was the wife of a vassal of the lord of Moncontour, Marie remembered. Her husband was temporarily attached to the garrison at Rennes, performing military service on behalf of his liege lord. The liege lord was called Raoul, another of the Penthièvre clan, and the knight was called Branoc, but Marie had to struggle to remember the lady's name — Ducocan, she recalled at last.

There were exclamations of horror and disgust from the other ladies. "I'd heard he was a runaway serf from Moncontour," said Havoise, "but not that he'd killed the bailiff. How did he manage to do a thing like that?"

Ducocan hesitated. Daughter of a wealthy peasant, she'd been too shy to speak in front of the duchess before. Now she had a good story to tell, though, and it seemed that no one else had heard it. Storytelling was an entertainment shared by all classes, as eagerly welcomed in a lord's hall as in a peasant's hut, and her ignorance of courtly manners didn't need to impede her.

"Listen, then," began Ducocan, and her voice slipped into the distinctive rhythm of the storyteller, reshaping a story of recent brutal events into the pattern of the old tales. "This Éon was a serf in Tredaniel, a manor belonging to Lord Raoul, not far from his castle of Moncontour. A small village, it is, and surrounded by the forest: may God preserve it from evil! Éon fell in love with another serf in the same village, a pretty girl, and he wished to marry her. So he went to Lord Raoul's bailiff and asked for the lord's permission. Now, the bailiff was a man called Ritgen mab Encar, a hard man and a greedy one. He wanted a bribe before he'd agree to get the lord's permission for the wedding. Éon of course had no money, so instead he agreed to do ten days' worth of work on Ritgen's own land. Since he worked all day on the lord's land, he could not do ten days' work in ten days' space, for he had to do the work in the evenings, or at night when the moon shone. So he went and worked the soil late and early for Ritgen, and while he worked, Ritgen went to see the girl. Probably he'd thought to ask for extra work from her as well, but when he saw her, she was fair as the flower of the apple tree and sweet as its fruit. The black devil came into his heart and he demanded to sleep with her. Twice she refused, and a third time, but he was the lord's bailiff, and she was a serf. He vowed to bring suffering on her, and on her family, and upon Éon, her sweetheart, and at last she gave in. Now, Ritgen was a married man already, and couldn't bring her to his house, while her hut she shared with her parents and her brothers and sister. So he took her to Éon's hut, which was empty while he worked on the bailiff's land. So Éon labored in the bailiff's fields, and the bailiff tilled Éon's in Éon's bed. And all the village knew of this, but nobody told Éon, because he was known to be a bold man, and they feared what he might do if he learned of it.

"But one evening some busybody went to Éon and told him to put out the fire in his hut. He dropped his hoe and ran home, and there he found Ritgen and the girl, lying together in his own bed. He seized the man by the hair, dragged him out into the yard, and thrashed him till he howled for mercy, but no mercy did he get from Éon. He didn't stop the beating until the neighbors came and dragged him off, and half the village it took to do it. He was a very strong man.

"After that, of course, Ritgen took his bruises to the lord, and the lord defended his bailiff, as is only natural, though he reprimanded Ritgen privately for provoking trouble. Éon was flogged and put in the stocks for striking the bailiff, and flogged again when he came out of them, and at last sent back to the fields in leg irons. But that wasn't enough for Ritgen. He kept finding fault with Éon, and provoking him to get him punished, and Éon was in the stocks as often as he was out of them. The other villagers hated Ritgen on Éon's account, and did what they could to help him, especially the girl, who would creep up to the stocks at night and give her sweetheart food and drink. When Ritgen saw it, and knew how he himself was condemned by all Tredaniel, he told the lord that the girl was disturbing the village and it would be better if she were sent elsewhere. So Lord Raoul arranged a marriage for her with a serf in Plémy—my village, may God keep it well!—which lies to the north of Tredaniel, some three miles away. I know the man he chose for her, a steady, reliable young widower. It was a good match. But when Ritgen told her of the match they had made for her, she said she would not go, nor would she heed him at all, nor would she marry anyone but Éon. And she would not be moved from her denial, not for the stocks nor for all the threats Ritgen could utter. So Ritgen went to the lord and told him that a serf was refusing to obey his orders, and asked for men to shift her by force. Lord Raoul sent two men at arms, and they dragged the girl screaming and crying from her house, and bound her and put her on a horse. But when Éon heard her cries he came from the fields as fast as the irons would let him, and he struck one of the men so hard with his fist that he broke his nose and knocked him to the ground. At that Ritgen and the other man fell on him, and beat him senseless. Then they took him back to the bailiff's house and locked him up in the shed. They meant to charge him before the lord the next day, and ask for him to be castrated. That was what Ritgen really wanted.

"But that night, Éon escaped. The leg irons were found outside the shed, where Éon had dropped them after using them to lever open the door. He went into the bailiff's house, and there he found Ritgen, sleeping beside his wife. He strangled the man with his bare hands. Ritgen's wife woke while he was doing it, and tried to drag him off, but she had no more chance of moving him than of carrying off the church tower; Éon had the man by the throat and didn't let him go until he was dead. Then he ran off. Lord Raoul sent men after him, but they never found him, and he has lived since as a robber in the woods.

Because of his strength and his cunning, other runaways and criminals accept him as their leader."

Ducocan paused, then went on, lowering her voice, "Everyone in Moncontour can vouch for that part of the story. But there's another story they tell about Éon, which many people believe. They say that one time after he had been flogged, he was working in a field beside the forest in his leg irons, alone just as the day was ending. A stranger in a green cloak came out of the forest and said to him, 'Why do you disturb us, bringing iron so near to the forest? What have you done to be shackled like that?' Éon very bitterly told the man all that had happened to him. Then the stranger gave Éon a cloak made from the skin of a wolf. 'Wear this,' he said, 'and it will shelter you well.' Éon took the cloak, and as soon as he did, the stranger vanished. And they say that the man was one of the Fair Ones, for they fear the touch of cold iron. And they say that when Éon accepted the cloak, he became a *bisclavret*. That was the reason why he was able to break loose from his shackles, and kill the bailiff, and escape all those who have pursued him, then and ever since."

Marie stirred uncomfortably. "What is a *bisclavret*?" she asked in a whisper, not only because Ducocan had whispered, but because she remembered the word, and with it the shadow of the shock she had been suffering when she heard it.

Ducocan crossed herself. "A *bisclavret* is . . . I do not know the French word, Lady Marie."

"A werewolf," said Havoise. She used a normal speaking voice, rather than a whisper, and everyone jumped.

"A wolf that feeds on human flesh?" asked Marie. "I should think that's a good description of any robber."

"No, no," said Ducocan. "Not that." She lowered her voice again. "A *bisclavret* is a man who can take the shape of a wolf. They say such creatures have superhuman strength and can destroy all who oppose them."

Marie stared. She felt something cold run along her skin, like the air stirred by an animal moving past in the darkness. "But I dreamed that!" she exclaimed. "In the forest! There was a wolf there at the spring before I met Éon, and I dreamed that it became a man. When I woke Éon was standing over me in a wolf-skin cloak."

Ducocan exclaimed in Breton and crossed herself again. "Christ between us and evil!" said the duchess, and she crossed herself as well.

"You met a wolf in the forest, on top of everything else?" asked Tiher. "You never mentioned that before."

"I hardly thought about it, after Éon," returned Marie. But she remembered the wolf clearly now, the black-rimmed eyes and the fangs and the lolling tongue. She shivered. "I waved a stick at it, and it ran off."

Tiher silently cursed Branoc's superstitious wife and her ghost story. She should have thought how disturbing her tale might be to someone who'd been threatened by Éon. He did his best to drive the shadow away. "Naturally it ran off," he said firmly. "Wolves are cowards at heart. When they're hunted they won't even turn at bay, but simply run until the dogs pull them down. They're shyer of human company than the most timid doe — like robbers, even this Éon. Lord Branoc's wife has told us a fine tale of him, but in the end I think it makes me pity the fellow more than fear him. Taken all in all, he's nothing but a serf who was pushed too far, snapped, killed the man responsible, and ran. Faced by Tiarnán, he ran again. I suspect all the poor brute wants is to be left alone."

"But if the tale they tell is true," said Ducocan seriously, "it's clear why Éon would have run away at Lady Nimuë's Well. He wouldn't wish to offend the lady who owns it."

Even Marie understood that. The lady Nimuë, who gave her name to the spring, figured in many stories — and she was not a human lady. Marie had not forgotten how Tiarnán had cast his chaplet of oak leaves and Éon's stolen money into the spring. A creature that owed a supernatural power to the Fair Ones would have to be even more cautious about offending them.

Ordinarily, Marie would have scoffed at a story like Ducocan's. But she could not scoff away the terror of her own dream. She had woken and found it true, and she couldn't shake a sense that its truth ran on, like an underground river, beneath the solid ground of everyday events. Tiarnán had made a fearful enemy. She remembered Éon shouting something about a *bisclavret*, and waving toward the forest—had he been threatening Tiarnán, promising him that though he couldn't fight there, by the well, he would hunt him down? Tiarnán had seemed very certain that the robber would try to kill him sometime. She sat at the loom without moving, still staring at the shuttle in her frozen hands.

Tiher, looking at her, inwardly consigned Ducocan to a deeper pit in hell. He glanced at Eline, who was wide-eyed and pale with fright. He cast about for a way to reassure them, and discovered, with satisfaction, that he had the means comfortably within his grasp. He didn't even have to lie. "*If* the tale they tell *is* true?" he asked disparagingly. "Surely that should be *if* it *were* true? Your condition is what the grammarians call contrary to fact, Lady Ducocan! But if it were true, then Éon would be a *bisclavret* no longer, because he left his wolf-skin cloak at Lady Nimuë's Well." Marie, to his relief, looked up. "I heard about it from the brothers of Bonne Fontaine," he went on, talking directly to her now and ignoring the others. "They went to the well to collect the bodies of the robbers Lord Tiarnán killed, because he'd asked them to arrange the burial. They found the corpses lying there undisturbed under the trees and the wolf-skin cloak sitting by itself in the sunshine. One of the brothers brought it back to use as a rug, but he ended up burning it because it had so many fleas. It seems to me that Éon's magical wolf skin was nothing more than a mangy old winter coat, so worthless he never even bothered to return to collect it. He never came back to cover his companions' bodies, either. He was too frightened. And I doubt it was Lady Nimuë he was afraid of. He doesn't seem to have given any thought to her when he attacked you, sweet lady. No, he was afraid that a knight would kill him if he didn't get out of the area as fast as his feet would take him."

Havoise, who'd abandoned her own half-serious fears when she realized that two of her companions needed comforting, laughed. "I'm sure you're right, Lord Tiher," she said. "You don't need to fret, Lady Eline. Your bridegroom will arrive to-morrow, perfectly safe."

Eline did not obviously fret during the evening meal, but when the household was going to bed, Marie found her leaning against the wall of the solar, looking out the narrow window toward the forest. The late midsummer dusk was slowly smoth-ering the last dim gray light, and the rain was still pouring down.

"Shall I show you our bed, Lady Eline?" asked Marie.

Eline sniffed and wiped her nose. Marie came and stood be-side her. The room was dark, since at this time of year no one bothered with a candle. But the faint light from the window was enough to show that Eline was crying.

After a moment's awkward hesitation, Marie put her hand on the other's shoulder. "What is the matter?" she asked gently, knowing the answer.

Eline sniffed again. "I don't like to think of Tiarnán out there now, all alone. Sitting there in some shelter with the rain pour-ing down—and maybe that horrible creature Éon roaming about in the darkness. It would be so terrible if he didn't come tomorrow, if I was here, waiting for him, and waiting, and he never came. I wish he wouldn't go hunting so much!"

"Has he always done it?" asked Marie, not knowing what else to say.

Eline rubbed her eyes. "I suppose so."

She'd heard of Tiarnán's reputation as a huntsman even be-fore she met him. One of Talensac's forests lay near Comper's, and whenever her father and brothers had discussed setting up a hunt, someone would always say, "Lord Tiarnán of Talensac says that there's a fine stag"—or a boar, or so many fine hinds— "in such-and-such a place." And then everyone else would say, "Oh? We'll look for it, then." When she did meet Tiarnán, it was because a boar he was hunting had gone onto her father's land. It had been just after Christmas: a single horseman had come galloping up to Comper in the snow, and the rider had leapt down before the door and come into the hall in a swirl of white, greeting her father and telling him there was a great boar to be had if he'd come hunt it now. Hervé had been up on his horse in a minute, with all the other men in the household after him, and they joined up with the hunting party from Talensac, chased the boar until dusk, and killed it. Then they'd all come back to Comper together, to sit by the fire and drink and talk the hunt over. She had noticed Tiarnán even before someone told her which one he was: the rider who'd come first and alone, he sat among the others, lean and dark, smiling occasionally but saying very little. But when she sang for the company, a song about hunting in the forest, he'd looked at her and a light had come into his eyes. Yes, she knew that he'd always gone hunting.

"Oh, I suppose I don't mind hunting," she said now to Marie. "But I wish he wouldn't go hunting alone! It's . . . it's ignoble and undignified. People say stupid things about it." What Alain had said had lain uneasily in her mind for some time.

"I think he loves it most alone," said Marie.

Eline stared in surprise. "Why do you say that?" she asked suspiciously.

Marie wasn't sure, and didn't answer at once. She remembered, vividly, how Tiarnán had walked in the darkness of the forest, confidently, like a man in his own house; she remembered the sense of being linked to something vast and alive.

"He wouldn't go alone so often if he didn't love it," she said at last.

"I wish he wouldn't do it *now*," said Eline. "Do you think that horrible creature Éon really might kill him? You've seen him."

Marie hesitated again. She was afraid of "that horrible creature" herself, but she felt that Eline needed comfort. "I'm sure Tiher was telling the truth about the wolf skin," she replied. "That story of Ducocan's was just something somebody invented to explain how a serf could kill a lord's bailiff and escape. And Tiarnán wasn't afraid of Éon when they met, but Éon was afraid of him. Frightened as I was myself, I could see that. Tiarnán was concerned to get out of the clearing, where we could have been shot from cover, but he wasn't worried about meeting Éon on his own. If Éon shouted some threats, then or later, it may have been because he hoped it would make Tiarnán stay away from him. It can't be easy for a runaway serf to face a knight."

"Especially a knight like Tiarnán." Eline was cheering up a little. Then she frowned. "How did he know who Tiarnán was?"

"He recognized him. Tiarnán said they'd encountered each other before."

"Did he? He never told me that. But I suppose there are many things he's never told me. He doesn't talk a lot."

"Then I wish you joy in learning over many years all the many things he's never told you."

Eline smiled. "That's a sweet wish, Lady Marie. Thank you." She sighed and straightened her wimple. "I'm tired."

"Then let me show you to your bed."

The bed was in the room next to the ducal bedchamber, a large room separated into smaller ones by the too-short partitions. They felt their way in the dark. The space next to their own was occupied by some of the pages, and they could hear the soft, quick breathing of the sleeping children, and, further and fainter, the endless drumming of rain upon the roof. They stripped down to their shifts, and lay down together on the low pallet.

"You're very kind, Marie," Eline said, smoothing the sheets in the darkness. "May I ask you something?"

"If you wish."

"They say that all the knights in the duke's garrison want to marry you. Do you know which one you'll choose?"

Marie sighed, and resignedly repeated her standard defense. "I'm not going to marry anyone without my father's blessing. And my father, I'm sure, won't bless any servant of Duke Hoel."

"But I thought . . . that is, I'd heard you tried to escape on the way to Rennes, of course, but you seem so much at home here I thought you must have been won over by our duke."

Marie was silent for a moment. "I swore an oath to the duchess that I wouldn't try to escape unless I were being forced into a marriage," she admitted. "And everyone here has been very kind, and treated me like a guest . . . or better" — she felt her face growing hot — "so I suppose I do feel at home. But my loyalties haven't changed."

She wondered as she said it if it were completely true. Her resolve not to betray her family's loyalties hadn't changed, but it was hard to prevent new loyalties growing up beside them. She liked Duke Hoel — a noble terrier indeed, bounding, bois-terous, straightforward, fond of laughter and hunting. She liked the sly, sentimental duchess, who made her and all the world welcome. And she liked the young knights of the garrison who treated her "better" than a guest: she liked their praise and their jokes and their attention. It shamed her, how much she liked it. The girl she'd been at Chalandrey, the would-be saint of St. Michael's, seemed a heavy, dull creature beside the woman that Rennes had made of her.

"I was brought here because of Chalandrey," she reminded herself aloud. "Not because of anything I am, except its heir-ess." She could almost feel it about her in the darkness, as though she were lying alone in her own bed in the room where her mother had died. The house; the step that creaked on the stair; the hedge of hyssop in the kitchen garden; the weathered posts in the palisade that secured the manor house; the village and the fields running down to the river. Chalandrey's river was the Couesnon. That, she thought, was why the duke was taking so much trouble over it. It lay on the border, in the middle of the path along which the Normans would ride to attack Brit-tany. If the duke had it, he might build a castle there, to com-plete the line that protected the March: Chateaubriant, La Guerche, Vitré, Fougères — Chalandrey. The lord of a castle, a castellan, was superior to a knight who governed a mere manor, even a fortified one. Naturally the young knights of the garrison were eager for it. "But Chalandrey's overlord is Duke Robert of Normandy," Marie finished resolutely, "and to steal it from him would be base treachery on my part."

"But Chalandrey is a Penthièvre manor," said Eline, just as everyone else had.

"I've argued this with everyone in Rennes," said Marie

impatiently. "I can't help what other people did in the past. Maybe my grandfather was wrong to turn to the Normans, but that doesn't mean I can turn back without dishonor. Loyalty begins where you find yourself. No. I'll simply keep refusing to marry, and eventually people will believe that I mean it. And one day my father and Duke Robert will return from the crusade, and then, I think, Duke Hoel will let me go back to the convent — particularly if I promise to stay there, and give all my father's lands to St. Michael."

"You really *want* to be a nun?" Eline asked in surprise. "Why?"

Marie was glad of the darkness that hid her face. She had wanted to be a nun once. That wish was now a thing of the past.

"I wanted to be a nun," she said instead, hoping that Eline wouldn't notice the change of tense. "I . . . I wanted to take up arms against the devil, and defend the world by the power of prayer."

That wish now seemed nothing but arrogance, folly, and hypocrisy. She had flattered herself that she was one of a spiritual elite, that it didn't matter that she wasn't beautiful or accomplished, or that her father and brother scarcely knew she was alive. Now that she had praise and attention, she'd found that she was not so spiritual after all, and the world did look nearly as worthless and evil as it had.

"That's very noble," said Eline, much impressed. "I've never wanted to do anything but marry a lord and have children."

"I'm not very noble," returned Marie guiltily. "I think I'd want exactly what you do, if I could have it honestly."

Eline suddenly put her arms around Marie, as she would have done to one of her own sisters, and hugged her. "I pray you can!" she exclaimed. "When I go to pray before my wedding, I'll ask Saint Agnes and the blessed Mother of God to find you a husband that both your father and the duke will accept. I think everyone should be as happy as I am now."

V

The rain slackened the next morning and stopped altogether in the afternoon. The whole court went out into the bailey of the castle to enjoy the watery sunlight. The duke and duchess strolled out hand in hand, with the lords and ladies after them, and the castle servants, stopping their work, came out with their masters and breathed the fresh air. Marie found herself walking beside Eline. Everything shone with wetness; the sleek stone walls flung back gold reflections of the afternoon sun, and the grass seemed to be lit up from within like the horn shield of a lantern.

To escape the mud, the party of nobles climbed up onto the battlements of the great curtain wall and looked out over the city of Rennes. The cathedral, its front gleaming in the light, towered over the damp huddle of thatched houses beside the brown stream of the Vilaine. A few evening cooking fires had been built up, and clouds of smoke, thick and blue with moisture, colored the clean air in patches, dark against the brighter blue of the sky. A party of about a dozen horsemen was circling the moat toward the castle gate. Their horses, and their own cloaks and boots, were spattered with mud, but they'd thrown back their hoods to drink in the sun.

Marie noticed Eline tensing with hope at the sight of riders. As they drew nearer, it was possible to make out that the leader was dark-haired and bearded, and rode a chestnut warhorse. Eline relaxed, and her face lit with a smile as radiant as the afternoon. Her bridegroom had arrived on time. Marie felt the sting twist in her own heart.

When the knight was almost at the gate, Duke Hoel shouted

a greeting in Breton, and Tiarnán looked up, smiled, and shouted back.

Tiarnán was termed Duke Hoel's man. The description was a commonplace one, and could mean merely that he held his lands directly from the duke, without owing homage to any intermediate count or baron. In Tiarnán's case, however, the phrase carried its full weight: it was to Hoel that he gave his full loyalty and his unhesitating obedience. This was by no means inevitable. Tiarnán's feelings toward the previous duke of Brittany, Duchess Havoise's brother Conan II, could never have been so warm. Duke Conan had still been in his teens when Tiarnán first arrived at court, and had had friends among the young squires and pages who were Tiarnán's tormentors; he had been, like the worst of them, an exuberantly elegant French-speaking Breton of the March. Tiarnán had known that as a vassal he must be loyal to his overlord, but he had regarded their respective positions with nothing more than a detached acquiescence. The one Breton baron he'd really liked had been Duke Conan's brother-in-law Hoel. Hoel had no pretensions to courtly sophistication. He said what he meant, and the meaning was usually good-natured and the saying done in Breton. In war he was fierce and tenacious, and in peace he loved hunting. When he realized that the young squire Tiarnán shared this passion, he'd taken him along on a number of expeditions to the forest, and listened to his opinion on the beasts of the chase. Those were the only pleasant memories Tiarnán had from his time at Conan's court: the days hunting, with the dogs baying and Hoel blowing his horn, and the nights after, with the company sitting under the trees by a campfire, laughing over tall stories. Everything else from that time was grief and violence.

Duke Conan had died in battle, shockingly young and still unmarried. The title passed to Hoel, and Tiarnán's official loyalties were no longer at odds with his private ones. It was said that a knight should love his liege lord as a son loves his father; Tiarnán had never known his father, but he loved Duke Hoel.

As soon as his horse had trotted over the drawbridge he jumped down, leaving his attendants to catch the reins, and ran up the gatehouse steps two at a time. He knelt in front of the duke and kissed his hand, and when he rose again Hoel embraced him and slapped him on the back. "So you're here," said Hoel in Breton. "Finished your penances and ready to be wed?"

"Indeed, my lord," replied Tiarnán, smiling. When the duke had offered him the cathedral at Rennes for the wedding, he had secretly wanted to refuse. He was aware that Hoel was doing him honor, but he would have preferred to be in Talensac, among his own people. Now, however, he was reconciled to the distinction, and pleased at least that the duke would be present.

They spoke together for a few minutes very cheerfully, about the journey, the weather, the prospect for a hunt; then Hoel slapped his liege man on the shoulder and sent him off to greet the duchess.

"God bless you, Tiarnán!" exclaimed Havoise in French, holding her own hand out. Tiarnán bowed low over it and kissed it; he'd always had the same liking for the duchess as for her husband. "You're late arriving. The lady Eline was afraid you'd miss your wedding!"

His eyes skimmed for a moment to the crowd of ladies beyond the duchess, and found there the blue silk wimple they'd looked for. He had expected it, but his heart lifted with a rush, and he turned back to the duchess smiling. "Never while I live," he replied. "If the roads had been better I would have been here earlier." Again his eyes searched eagerly among the ladies, and this time found Eline's radiant face, and there rested.

> She's sweeter than the blackbird's song
> or the nightingale on the willow tree,
> sweeter than the dew on the flowering rose,
> and sweetest of all is her kiss for me.

"Ah, it's been foul weather," agreed the duchess. "But you seem to have brought the sun with you. Have you brought that brindled lymer bitch of yours as well? Hoel has great plans for a stag hunt the day after the wedding, and he swears by that dog of yours."

Tiarnán tore his eyes away from Eline and glanced down at the party of his attendants, just inside the castle gate. "There is Mirre," he said, and pointed. The dog was waiting at the foot of the stone stairs that led to the battlements. She would never climb steps anywhere, because she wasn't allowed to at Talensac.

Noble hunting parties did not simply go out into the forest and chase whatever they could find. A suitably grand quarry was always located for them beforehand by a professional huntsman with a good tracking dog, or lymer. Tiarnán, however, generally played the huntsman's part himself, with Mirre, though it meant getting up before dawn. "The duke's huntsman will have to take her out this time, though," he told the duchess.

"A fine bridegroom you'd be if you did it yourself!" exclaimed Havoise, and wheezed with laughter. "You have other game on your mind than deer. You'll be lucky to be up by Terce!"

Tiarnán expected a good deal of this sort of raillery at court. It was one reason why he had not been eager to marry there. He smiled politely. The duchess grinned back at him, then all at once embraced him, kissing him on both cheeks. "I'm glad for you, my dear, very glad," she said with a tenderness that took him aback. "But you shouldn't be standing there, staring at your bride the day before the wedding! Off with you, *eom ∂e'i*! Go stable your horse."

Tiarnán saluted the rest of the company with a wave and a lopsided smile, and went back down the steps to collect his horse. Mirre fell in at his heel, her brown and white tail wagging. Havoise looked after him affectionately, then turned to Eline.

"My dear," she said, "you're as lucky as you're lovely. I'm sure you and he will be very happy."

Eline was pale with excitement for the rest of the evening, and at supper in the Great Hall she ate almost nothing. The rest of the court seemed to catch her restlessness. The hall had a bright, breathless feeling, as though the next day would be a major feast, and not just a lesser nobleman's wedding. Hervé

of Comper joined his prospective son-in-law at the table set
apart for the young knights, and soon the roars of laughter from
that group interrupted the quieter conversations of the other
tables. Tiarnán sat composed in the middle of it, enduring the
sallies good-humoredly, but doing nothing to encourage them.
Marie found her eyes drawn to him again and again. It seemed
to her that in the middle of the swirl of noise he had a private
stillness. She had been wrong to think that he would be different at court than he had been in the forest.

The ladies left the hall early, when the long midsummer evening was still bright. Havoise ordered the servants to prepare
a bath for the bride in her own bedroom, and to sprinkle the
water with rose petals. While the great wooden tub was being
filled from steaming kettles carried in from the kitchens, all the
ladies crowded round to admire the new gown which Eline
would wear for the wedding. It was of blue Arras cloth, with
the newly fashionable long sleeves that came over the wrist
clear to the middle of the hand, and the neck and cuffs were
embroidered with tiny pearls. When Eline had finished bathing
she put it on, not bothering with her old shift first. She danced
about the duchess's room like a child, stamping and whirling,
her body showing white and supple where the blue gown tied
at the sides and her wet hair flying. The ladies clapped. Laughing, Eline curtseyed to the duchess.

"Beautiful, my dear," said Havoise affectionately. "But now
you must go to bed and get some sleep."

"Because tomorrow night you'll get none!" supplied Sybille,
and she and the duchess laughed.

The ladies began to disperse, going off to join their husbands
in whatever partitioned space they'd been allotted. Marie
started off with Eline, but the duchess called her back.

"The bathwater's still hot," said Havoise. "Why don't you use
it, Marie? One maiden's bath will do for another, and I had a
bath only the week before last; I don't want one now."

Marie was slightly puzzled, but it seemed a shame to waste
hot water. She thanked the duchess and began to untie the
fastenings of the blue-gray gown. Sybille was the last of the

duchess's ladies left in the room, and she was waiting impatiently at the door. Havoise nodded to her, and Marie and the duchess were alone.

Havoise picked up a handful of rose petals from the basket the servants had left and dropped them a few at a time into the lukewarm water. The long, slow dusk was deepening at last, and after all the noise and excitement, the castle was calm. In silence Marie stripped off her shift and stepped into the waist-high tub. She knelt on the rough bottom and began to unfasten the braids of her hair.

"So Tiarnán will be married tomorrow," said the duchess reflectively. "Oh, it makes me feel old. I remember him coming to court for the first time, riding behind the Talensac parish priest on an old farm nag—sixteen years ago, that would be? No, seventeen. I was not so very young even then. He was a scrawny, frail little thing, innocent entirely of any noble education, and he didn't speak a word of French. And look at him now! The finest knight in Brittany, so they say."

"So they say?" asked Marie, smiling and running her fingers through her hair.

Havoise laughed. "Ah, I'm not to cast doubt on your champion! But they say the same thing of two or three others now, they've said it of others before them, and they'll say it of others still in time to come. They even said it once of my poor brother—God give rest to his soul—though I think they wouldn't have done if he hadn't been duke. Tiarnán deserves it more than most. He's a deadly fighter and a peaceful neighbor, and what more does the world ask of a knight? I always liked him. God knows why, because I was a giddy, noisy young woman, and he was a silent child and a serious young man, but I did. I feel almost like a mother to him. And now he's to be married! Well, as I said, they should be happy. She's a lovely girl, and good-hearted. She never will understand him, but I suppose that doesn't matter so very much."

Marie did not know how to respond to this. She ducked her head under the surface of the tub and shook out her hair in the soft, rose-scented water. "She loves him," she said when she came up again. "Surely she will understand him, too, because of that?"

Havoise snorted. "Eline doesn't love Tiarnán. She'll do her best to be a good wife, and she may love him one day, but now . . . now she's just excited at the idea of being married to a famous knight and becoming lady of a manor. She's an uncomplicated creature. Talk to her awhile and you'll know what she thinks of everything. Tiarnán is another matter. There's deeper water there than I can fathom, and I've known him a long time. Does he love her, or is it just an excitement of the blood? I can't say."

Marie's heart began its stubborn tussle with her once again. She collected a handful of the soft tallow and wood-ash soap and rubbed it over her head. "It isn't just blood," she said firmly. "She is all open charm like bright sunshine. That enchants him—because he has dark places, deep waters, in his own soul."

Havoise regarded her for a long minute, then looked down and stirred the rose-sprinkled water of the bath. "Now, how do you know that?" she asked.

Marie felt her skin go hot. She could not know that. She barely knew Tiarnán. She ducked under the water to avoid answering, and rinsed the soap out of her hair. When she came up, the duchess was looking at her.

"I could wish, Marie my dear," Havoise said softly, "that it was you he were marrying. And I think that if he were the man asking, you would not give that modest little smile of yours and refuse, as you do with all the others."

"Why do you say that?" asked Marie, a touch more sharply than was courteous. "I'm certainly grateful to Tiarnán for saving me, but I'm not wicked or stupid enough to indulge in love for a man who's marrying someone else tomorrow."

Havoise gave her a look as shrewd as it was affectionate. "I was watching you while I spoke of him. You can always tell how a young girl feels about a man by watching her when he's spoken of—particularly when she's undressed." The duchess wheezed, then resumed quickly, "But don't be angry, my dear. I know you're honest, and I'm sure you haven't indulged anything; I'm the indulgent one. I've been indulging my curiosity tonight. I have lived at court all my life, and there is nothing that fascinates me so much as people. Simply watching them, simply observing the dance. I've known Tiarnán, and liked him better than most, ever since he was a child—and, come to that, you're a complicated one, too. But don't worry; I know it's Eline he's dancing with, and you're determined to sit by the wall. I mean no harm. You must forgive the impertinent curiosity of those older than yourself."

Marie climbed out of the tub and wrapped herself in Eline's damp towel. "I have no choice but to forgive the impertinent curiosity of a duchess," she said bitterly. She had kept private the sting in her heart, and now she felt ashamed and exposed.

But Havoise only chuckled. "Yes. It's good sport, being a duchess."

At that, despite her anger, Marie had to smile.

Marie dreamed that she was walking down a narrow path in the forest. The birds chirruped uneasily above her head, and the leaves whispered. She came to a clearing and found a long mound there among the trees. Red poppies grew in the green grasses that covered it, with wild hemlock and the purple-flowered bush called woody nightshade or bittersweet. At the end of the mound stood two tall gray stones, fixed in the earth with a space between them—like a door frame leading only to green turf. Marie walked up to them and leaned upon one with her hand, and at its cold touch she understood suddenly that it was indeed a door, and that beyond it lay something fearful or wonderful which would have changed her life forever, but that she had come too late, or too early, and the door was shut. She cried out in protest and turned away. A wolf was sitting under the trees behind her, watching her, and she looked back into the black-rimmed eyes without fear.

She woke and found that it was morning. Beside her Eline, who'd tossed restlessly much of the night, was peacefully still. Marie rolled over and lay motionless, staring up at the apse of the ceiling. There was a strange numbness in her heart. She felt no jealousy toward Eline: to be jealous, she would have to have had a place the other woman had usurped, and she knew she had never had any place with Tiarnán at all. Instead the dream feeling of having missed something of overwhelming importance was like thick fog over everything.

She sighed, got up, crossed herself, and knelt to say the short version of the morning office. Eline woke while she was still praying, and at once knelt beside her and joined in the Paternoster and the amens. When they came to the last amen, she beamed at Marie.

"Thank you, Lady Marie," she said happily. "I think that must be the best start I could make to my wedding day, don't you?"

Marie smiled back weakly. There was no need to make any reply. Eline was already on her feet and hurrying toward the clean shift and the new blue gown hanging over the clothes chest, ready for her.

Most of the morning passed in a blur. Marie rode down from the castle to the cathedral, along with most of the rest of the court, for the celebration of the wedding, in the porch, followed by Mass in the cathedral itself. She found afterward that she could remember almost nothing of the service, not even the looks on the faces of the participants; all that stuck in her mind was Sybille whispering comments to the duchess, and the duchess laughing.

When they had returned to the castle, however, Tiher came over to hold her horse while she dismounted, and she looked down into his froggy face, which was grinning at some joke he'd made that she had not even heard, and realized that she must discipline herself or become a spectacle to the whole court. She forced herself to smile back, slide down from the saddle, and take the hand he offered to steady her. "It's a fine day for a feast," she said at random, because she hadn't even noticed whether the sun was shining or not, but as soon as she had spoken, she saw that it really was a fine day.

"I pray it stays fair tomorrow for the hunt!" replied Tiher.

"I've never been on a stag hunt," Marie told him.

"Haven't you? Then you must come tomorrow. You can ride behind me."

Morvan of Hennebont appeared at her other elbow. "You don't want to ride on that nag of Tiher's," he said. "It has a backbone like a sheep hurdle and a gait like a striding cockerel. My horse is a pacing palfrey, and as smooth to ride as a boat on a millpond. You can ride with me, Lady Marie."

"If I come, I'll ride my own horse," said Marie, smiling. "She needs exercise."

They both began to urge her to come, and she walked into the Great Hall to a lively description of the joys of stag hunting, full of double meanings enough to make the duchess roar.

Duke Hoel had ordered a grand formal feast—like the cathedral wedding, a mark of respect for one of his favorite knights—and the customary order of rank in the seating was observed more strictly than usual. The important guests were at the high table with the duke and duchess, the others carefully arranged at tables graded by their distance from the lord's dais. Marie, as a lady-in-waiting and a kinswoman of the duchess, found herself at the high table, next to the bishop of Rennes and just down from the bridegroom, who had the place of honor to the right of the duchess; Tiher and Morvan, as landless knights, were at the seventh table at the far end of the hall. Both men, however, escorted her all the way to the dais.

"Some say the stag should be hunted with nets," Tiher was saying as they reached the high table, "but I say the poor creature's entangled enough as it is. When he hears the music of the horns and the baying of the hounds and finds himself the chosen one—why, if it were not for the bone God has given him in his heart, he would die for fear at the very wonder of it."

"What's that?" asked Duke Hoel, looking over from his place at the middle of the table.

"Lady Marie was thinking of coming to hunt the stag," said Tiher.

"Ah!" exclaimed Hoel, beaming. "Excellent! Lady Marie could hunt a unicorn, let alone a stag."

"Maybe I will," said Marie. "I don't like to think of causing such terror to a poor stag."

"Oh, but it would be a delicious terror!" protested Tiher. "With a huntswoman such as yourself."

Havoise wheezed. "Why should a stag care who sticks a sword in it, eh?" she asked, and shooed Tiher and Morvan off. They went, now making rather obvious jokes about the probability of each other's sticking his sword into anything, and Hoel and the duchess sat down. The rest of the company copied them, and the feast began.

There were olives of beef, and chicken stuffed with eggs and onions; there were sausages and veal pasties; there were great joints of lamb, and pork roast upon a fire of rosemary; there was marrow-bone pie and a flan of cream cheese. No game animals were served, apart from birds, because the season for boar and hind was long over and the stag season only just begun. There was a dish of pigeons stewed in cider, though, and one of young heron, and a plate of blackbirds glazed in honey, and at the end of the first course a roast swan was brought in with a blast of trumpets, draped in its own snowy feathers. The duke's officials, splendidly dressed, with white napkins draped across their shoulders, served the high table from dishes of silver, and the butler Corentin and the pages poured out cup after cup of the white wine of the Loire and the red of Bordeaux. The sun shone in at the high windows, and the hall was full of laughter. The conversation, having begun on hunting, continued very happily on the same subject.

"I'll have my huntsman borrow that lymer bitch of yours this evening," Duke Hoel said to Tiarnán. "Where is she?"

Tiarnán smiled and nodded at the space under the table, and there, sure enough, Mirre's jowly face and huge drooping ears poked up from under the cloth. She wagged her tail at being noticed, and Duke Hoel laughed.

"I didn't see her come in! Here, Mirre!" He tossed the dog

a piece of heron gristle, which she snapped up. "The finest hound in the world," Hoel confided to the bishop, Guillaume de la Guerche. "A man might pay a pound of gold and not get one as good. We'll see what she can sniff out for us tomorrow, eh?"

Tiarnán patted Mirre, and she licked his hand. "There's a very fine stag of sixteen tines in the forest near Châtellier," he told the duke. "I think it's the same beast we lost last Holy Rood Day."

"Too far," replied the duke. "I shouldn't need to say that to you! I can't imagine you'll want to stay out from home tomorrow night, and we don't want to drag the ladies farther than a day's outing. There are harts of ten tines in the forest of Rennes. We could ride out and have the meeting at Gaudrier in the middle of the morning, chase the deer, and be back home before the dusk."

"But why couldn't we take the ladies to Châtellier?" asked Tiarnán. "Most of this company could fit into the castle there, and we could bring pavilions for the rest. It's fair weather." He imagined being with Eline in a pavilion in the forest—the high-summer forest, with its thick leaves and its rich green smell; imagined lying with her, with the clear midsummer moonlight shining on her fair hair and her white skin. A shiver of delight crossed his own skin. He looked at her where she sat banded with sunlight on the duke's right, her hair virginally loose over her shoulders and crowned with roses.

Havoise laughed. "But does Eline want to spend the first days of her marriage camping in a wood?" she asked, and Eline blushed pink as the roses in her hair.

"Don't you?" asked Tiarnán in surprise.

Eline had once camped overnight on one of her father's hunting expeditions. She thought of the black mysterious trees, the mosquitoes, and the strange noises in the dark. "When we leave Rennes," she said in a small, hesitant voice, "I'd rather go straight back to Talensac with you, Tiarnán. To make it home."

"Oh," said Tiarnán, disappointed, and Havoise laughed again.

"She's been fretting over your hunting trips as it is," she told him. "Terrified that something might happen to you, her darling."

"I was afraid of that robber Éon of Moncontour," supplied Eline. "They say that he's sworn to kill you. And Lord Branoc's wife was telling us the most horrible story about him."

"What, how he killed the lord of Moncontour's bailiff?" asked Tiarnán with his lopsided smile. He had more or less decided to go hunting for Éon as soon as he had time to spare. But he'd seen no reason to mention this to anyone. The announcement would come more aptly when the man was dead.

"There was a story that he was a bisclavret," said Eline. "I was frightened."

Tiarnán's smile vanished. "That is foolishness," he snapped impatiently. "He is no such thing."

"Tch!" said the duchess, while Eline blinked at this first experience of husbandly rebukes. "How could she help it?"

"You don't need to be frightened," Tiarnán said, instantly regretting that he'd spoken harshly to his wife on their wedding day. "I'm sure the story you heard is untrue, my white heart, but even if it wasn't, why should it worry you? I am not afraid of Éon or of a wolf, so why should I fear the two of them together?"

The duke laughed. "Well said! But anyone would be afraid of a real werewolf."

"Why?" insisted Tiarnán. "There's no harm in wolves. They never kill except to eat or fight unless they're cornered. If they see an enemy, they always prefer to run away from him. They're gentler beasts than they're given credit for. A boar is far more dangerous, as anyone who's hunted knows. As for Éon, I fought him at Lady Nimuë's Well and I had the better of him. He has no extraordinary strength. If he's going to cause my lady wife to fret every time I'm late home hunting, I am doubly sorry that I didn't kill him when I met him — though I might have had to postpone the wedding if I had."

"Postpone the wedding, for killing a robber?" asked Duke Hoel. "Why on earth would you have had to do that?"

"I've only just completed the penances I was given for the two robbers I did kill," replied Tiarnán seriously. "If I'd had another death on my soul, I wouldn't have been able to get it all done in time."

Bishop Guillaume put down his glazed blackbird, daintily wiped his fingers on his trencher bread, and looked at Tiarnán with professional interest. "How much penance did your confessor give you for killing these two robbers?" he asked.

"Thirty days for each man," said Tiarnán. "I gave alms, and made two pilgrimages, and reduced it."

"A very strict confessor!" exclaimed the bishop approvingly. "That's the proper old way, indeed. As my father always said, if you make the penance light, men will think the sin slight. He used to hand out forty days' penance for each man that was killed in a battle, even if he himself had blessed the standard."

"I'm glad all churchmen aren't so severe," Hoel smiled, "or I'd be hard put to get men to fight for me."

The bishop shook his head solemnly. "My lord duke, you know very well that our mother the Church has struggled to check the bloodthirstiness of knights and failed. Whatever bans or immunities we urge mean nothing to a nobleman with a sword in his hand. And now the Holy Church herself has started a very dangerous trend, I think, with this new fashion of giving a nobleman an indulgence to go fight, and saying that not only does he commit no sin in killing, but even the penances he might have earned before are all remitted. I don't think the Holy Father should ever have begun it, even though it was for the holy cause of the crusade. These new movements in the Church, this turning against all the old ways . . . I don't know where it will lead."

Marie found she could anticipate Sybille's whisper. "It will lead to no more de la Guerche bishops of Rennes." The family had passed the episcopacy of Rennes down from father to son for almost a century, and Guillaume was known to deplore the specific "turning against old ways" of the new strictness in canon law that enforced a ban on clerical marriage. She met the duchess's eyes, and Havoise grinned.

"So, who is this strict confessor of yours?" the bishop asked Tiarnán, catching his breath after his sermon.

"Judicaël the Hermit," said Tiarnán, his eyes glinting with a suppressed triumph.

He was glad to have caught the bishop expressing admiration for the hermit. The authorities of the Church were uncomfortable with such individual, unregulated sanctity. It implied criticism of the Church: it smelled of heresy. Tiarnán was sensitive to his confessor's reputation, and eager to defend it.

Bishop Guillaume became less approving as he understood whose strictness he'd just praised. "What?" he asked sharply. "The one that lives at St. Mailon's Chapel? I've had complaints about him. It's said he blesses bonfires."

Bonfires might be an innocent way to dispose of garden rubbish, but they were also lit by standing stones and ancient trees to honor the Fair Ones. The church called the practice demon worship and a grave danger to the souls of those that engaged in it, and a churchman who condoned it could find himself before an episcopal court, charged with heresy. Tiarnán rushed instantly to his confessor's defense. "Father Judicaël is a very holy man," he said indignantly. "If he does bless bonfires, it is only innocent ones, and only to show that they are innocent. If priests have complained, they will not have been neighbors of his, but people from villages farther away who have heard a tale distorted in the telling. All his neighbors honor him."

"That's so," put in Hervé of Comper, nodding vigorously, and Eline added, "He's a very holy man, my lord bishop." Comper was one of the parishes which Judicaël's fame had reached. The authorities of the Church might not like hermits, but laypeople admired them immensely. Their presence in the forest was like a reassuring light in a frightening expanse of darkness; the mysterious and dangerous things that dwelt in the wilderness would be held back by their prayers.

Guillaume relented and picked up his blackbird again. "I hope that's so!" he said. "Tales do become distorted in the telling."

But he was clearly still unhappy about Judicaël the hermit.

Marie, who'd listened intently to everything, was surprised to find that she could have guessed that Tiarnán would choose a hermit for his confessor. Of course he would walk miles through the forest to some tiny chapel among the trees, and sit at the feet of the old man who lived there, humbly accepting his strict penances. Strange that she knew things like that, when she knew so little of him. It was as though in that walk from Nimuë's Well, the stuff he was made of had seeped into her through the touch of her fingers on his back.

Fanciful nonsense, she told herself irritably, rinsing roast swan off her fingers in the silver dish of rosewater provided for the purpose. No one could learn another's mind that way.

But she could not check the feeling that she did know him, down at some level where the mind didn't reach. It was as though what she had undergone at the well had stripped the skin off her own soul and left it tender to the lightest of impressions, and now Tiarnán's nature was printed on it more accurately than she could consciously grasp.

The feast went on for the rest of the day, and Marie did her best to enjoy it. The tables were pushed to the wall after the meal, and the duke called in minstrels and jugglers to amuse the company. Then there were musicians who played on the shawm, the viole, and the tambourine, and there was dancing. Marie was surrounded by young men offering to dance with her, and she accepted each of them in turn. She danced until she was flushed, sweating, and out of breath, and then she sat down between two of her suitors and had a drink of water. Midsummer dusk at last began to shadow the room, and the servants went about setting rushlights in the iron braces on the walls. Marie watched the light spreading slowly about the hall, and suddenly found herself staring at the bride and groom. They were standing under one of the lights, their hands joined before them. Eline's hair fell in a shining cloud about a face flushed and smiling. Her crown of roses was slipping from her head, and she looked up at her new husband with brilliant eyes. Tiarnán's dark face, looking back, was solemn with joy, and his hands held hers as though she were a swallow that might fly away. At that sight, the sting in Marie's heart slid out at last, leaving only an ache of relief. *O God*, she prayed silently, *let them keep forever the happiness that they have now.*

Then she remembered how her mother had died—the first time that tormenting image had inflicted itself on her since she came to Rennes. For once the memory brought with it no horror, no passionate disgust—only grief, and a still resignation. That was the risk women ran when they married. Perhaps Eline would never know that suffering—but even if it came to her in the end, it could not infect her now. The light might cast shadows, but in itself shone clear.

Marie suddenly felt in full the happiness she had pretended all day. In the cave at the back of her mind, her mother lay buried at last, resting quietly after the haunting years. *Requiem aeternam dona ea Domine, et lux perpetua luceat ea.* Marie was free to turn from the grave and love.

A little while later it was time for the ladies to leave the hall and escort the bride up the stairs to the bedroom which had been allotted to the newlyweds for the night. Eline was pink and giggling, from the excitement and the dancing more than the wine, and when she reached the room she went back and forth across the rushes in a capriole step, then collapsed on the bed, laughing. "Oh!" she cried. "Oh, nobody ever had a better wedding! Oh, what a wonderful day!"

"I'm sure it will be nothing compared to the night," said Havoise, and kissed her on the forehead before leaving her to await the perfection of her joy.

alensac, like its lord, was sensible of the honor of the cathedral wedding in Rennes, and, like its lord, would have preferred the marriage to be celebrated at home. Cheated of the ceremonies, however, the village still managed celebrations. The day after the duke's stag hunt, Tiarnán took his bride home, and found another feast prepared for him.

When the wedding party rode through the gates of Talensac manor house, it was to see trestle tables, laden with food, set up all around the enclosure between the house itself and the lodge, with planks arranged on shocks of straw for seating. An ox was roasting over the fire that burned merrily in the middle of the yard, and the front wall of the house was almost obscured by the kegs of ale and barrels of cider waiting there. The manor house servants had been sweating in the kitchens to prepare everything from the moment Tiarnán set off for Rennes, and when the newlyweds started back to Talensac one of their attendants had ridden ahead to tell those at home to light the fire.

Though nothing had been said, Tiarnán had been expecting it—which was just as well, as it was being done at his expense. Any peasant would provide food, drink, and dancing to all the villagers at his wedding, so naturally the lord had to provide more of them. He swept Eline off her horse and whisked her up to the manor house, where Kenmarcoc presented her with the keys to the manor, then whisked her back down to the manor gates. The villagers had by then assembled outside the lodge, dressed in their best and ready for dancing, some clutching pipes and tabors and drums. Tiarnán let them in and he and Eline led the first dance.

The party went on for three days, to the great satisfaction of the villagers. Mountains of food and rivers of drink were poured out, and the dancing went on each night until the moon was high.

Justin Braz missed most of the third day. He got into a fight with the father and uncle of a girl he'd been pestering, and ended up in the stocks. His friend Rinan came and sat with him in the evening, and gave him swigs of wine from a flask he'd filled from one of the barrels up the hill. The sun went down and the moon came up, half-shrouded in cloud; from the manor house the music floated down to them, slow now, the pipes faint but the drums carrying low and steady like the heartbeat of the world.

"What do you think of the machtiern's lady?" Rinan asked his friend.

Justin swilled his mouthful of wine thoughtfully about his tongue, then swallowed. "Well, she's a fair lady," he conceded. "I wouldn't mind keeping a lady like that, if I were a lord."

"Nor I," agreed Rinan warmly. "She's whiter than the lily, and sweeter than the song of the harp."

"She's a fair lady," Justin repeated approvingly. "Mind you, she's lucky to be lady of Talensac. Comper's no very fine place, for all I've seen or heard tell of it."

"And that's true, too," said Rinan, and put the wine flask to his friend's lips before taking another drink himself.

They were both silent for a few minutes, listening to the music and watching a cloud drift across the face of the moon, and then Justin said very quietly, "I wonder what she will do when the machtiern goes off alone to the forest."

Rinan stirred uneasily in the cloudy moonlight, glancing around as though the forest might be listening. "Will he, do you think?" he asked, dropping his voice to a whisper. "Now that he has a wife?"

"I think he will," replied Justin. "A man like the machtiern will never let a woman govern him. I think he will, and I wonder what she'll do then."

Rinan considered for a minute, then shrugged. "Get used to it, I suppose," he said.

Eline enjoyed being a married woman—at first. She had loved the grand court feast at Rennes; she loved the country celebrations at Talensac even more. She liked the Talensac people—honest, good-hearted, simple people, she thought, basking in their goodwill; how devoted they were to Tiarnán! She was disappointed only in her maid. Kenmarcoc offered his eldest daughter for the position, and of course the offer could not be refused without offending him. Driken was a sad substitute for the pretty, admiring young serf Eline had daydreamed about: she had an outspoken mind of her own, and she was fourteen, thin, dark, and horse-faced like her father. If her teeth were better than his, her spots were much worse. But Eline did her best to like the girl anyway. There was no need to waste time regretting one thing when she had so much else to delight her. Her husband, for instance: she came to revel in the sheer tender worshipfulness with which he touched her every night, and the ardor, and the joy. Her aunt Godildis had told her that a woman never went to the marriage bed except with shame and suffering: she decided very quickly that Uncle Marrec must be even more of a boor than she'd thought.

When the feasting was over, Eline joyfully set out to fulfill her new role as lady of the manor. This was a complicated task. The manor house brewed its own ale and made its own wine for everyday use; it baked bread, made butter and cheese, smoked and salted the meat and fish produced by the estates, and stored the produce of field and orchard. Woolen cloth was produced from the fleeces of the manor's sheep, linen and hempen from flax and hemp grown on the domain lands. Dyes were manufactured from any readily available source—broom, woad, oak galls, mulberries. Hides from all the animals slaughtered on the estate were scraped and soaked to get them ready for the tanner in Montfort; hooves and horns, and sometimes bones as well, were cleaned and sold to the craftsmen who used them. Wood from the forest was seasoned, either for the fire or for the use of the manor carpenter. Candles of tallow and beeswax were made, and simple medicines prepared from herbs grown in the kitchen garden. All of this was done in addition to the usual business of feeding and clothing a household that, with servants, numbered more than thirty people — to say nothing of dogs, cows, sheep, horses, and pigs. The management of the lands and stock was principally the concern of the bailiff, Kenmarcoc, but it was the task of the lady of the manor to provision the household and allot "housework" to the servants. Eline rushed into her new position with glee, tripped headlong over a raft of unforeseen details, and was gently picked up and set on her feet again by Kenmarcoc's wife, Lanthildis, who'd managed the manor house for so many years that she was able to continue her job unruffled, even when "assisted" by the ignorant enthusiasm of her new mistress.

When Eline had been in Talensac a week or two, and had had time to get to know the house and the servants, Tiarnán agreed to invite her family and some of the neighboring lords and ladies to the manor. For her that was the best time of all. It was intoxicating to be able to greet all her friends and family as the lady of Talensac, to assign them their places in the manor hall, and tell the servants to bring food and drink. On the evening after the last guests left, Eline still glowed with sleepy delight at the wonder of it, until Tiarnán tousled her hair and took her up to bed to give her something more to wonder at.

The uneasiness began a little after that. When the guests were gone and the first novelty of marriage had worn off, Tiarnán grew restless. He had no business at the court that summer, there were no wars to call him from home — but he seemed unable to settle at the manor. He threw himself into work on his estate: he went through all the accounts with Kenmarcoc; called the village elders together and settled two or three old boundary disputes; arranged for all the outstanding repairs to his mill, manor house, barns, and sheepfolds. He set up a quintain and targets, and practiced with his weapons, splintering wooden swords and practice spears by the dozen, teaching his warhorse new moves until he and it both were sweating and weary. But despite this furious activity, two or three times a day he would go out of the house and down to the manor gate, then return empty-handed, as though he'd forgotten what he'd set out to do. Each day's end found him more tense and dissatisfied. He went hunting a couple of times, leaving at cockcrow with Mirre and returning in the afternoon. But even when he'd been lucky with the catch it didn't seem to please him. He suggested once to Eline that she come with him, but she was afraid to leave the manor house in the dark, and hated the thought of wandering about the forest on foot. She suggested instead another hunting party with a neighbor, but he said— though with a smile—that they'd had a lot of company recently and needed peace.

None of this really worried Eline. She was sorry to see her husband so unsettled, but she supposed it was just the aftermath of the wedding. She'd heard that married men sometimes regretted the freedom of their bachelor days, and she did her best to make it up to him.

Then one evening near the end of July she found him standing in the doorway of the manor house, looking up at the waxing moon. He was so still and silent that it seemed unnatural, and she felt a stab of fear that he was hurt or ill. She hurried up behind him and put her hand on his shoulder. He started violently and whirled about, and his eyes were so strange that she jumped back. Afterward it gave her a peculiar constriction in the stomach to think of them. They stood a moment, each looking at the other as though they'd never met—and then Tiarnán announced abruptly, "I'm going hunting tomorrow." After a moment, he added in a more normal tone, with his one-sided smile, "I need time to myself, my heart." And the next day he was up before dawn and away.

He was gone for three days.

Eline was unconcerned the first day, anxious the second, and desperate the third. She thought of the robber lurking in the woods, and couldn't help the worry that choked her. There was another thing that tormented her, too, a thing that seemed small at first but gradually loomed larger and larger in her mind, until it almost blotted out even the worry: he hadn't taken his dog.

The dog had wanted to go with her master: she padded unhappily about the house, pricking her ears up every time the door opened, waiting each hour for his return. Why? Why not take her? The senselessness of it wore a sore place in Eline's thoughts, like a pebble in a shoe eating the foot with blisters.

The servants were no help. They assured her calmly that the master was often away for this long, it was nothing unusual, she might be certain he'd be back. "You'll get used to it, my lady," they told her placidly. But they spoke, she thought, with a peculiarly knowing air, and she caught glances exchanged between them when they thought she wasn't looking. Pitying glances. Why pity her? When she demanded to know where Tiarnán had gone, the answer was always the same, "Hunting, my lady," but the knowing eyes met over her head.

She began to feel, for the first time since arriving in Talensac, how much she was an outsider. The servants and villagers were pleased with her, because she was young and pretty, but Tiarnán was the machtiern — *their* machtiern, Talensac born and heir to generations of Talensac's rulers. His prestige at court gratified them, but at heart they believed it was only his due, and natural enough for the lord of the finest of all villages. They loved and valued him as they loved and valued themselves. She was nothing. They wouldn't even tell her the truth. She remembered again and again what Alain had asked her at Comper: *How could he hunt without a dog? Where is he really going, do you think? Hunting? Or to some woman's bed?*

Why else would the servants pity her?

By the third night of Tiarnán's absence, she was too tense and wretched even to sleep, and sat on the stairs in her shift, braiding and unbraiding her hair, with Mirre at her feet. It was almost midnight when Mirre picked her head up, whined, and ran to the door; there was a quick rap from outside, one of the servants unbolted the door, and Tiarnán strode in, dusty, happy, and relaxed. He patted the dog, slapped the servant on the shoulder, and crossed the hall to the stairs — then stopped in astonishment.

"Eline!" he said, running up the stairs and catching her

hands. "What are you doing up at this time of night? Aren't you well?"

"I was worried about you," she told him, and burst into tears.

But it was no use. He was gentle with her, kissing her hands and face, carrying her up to bed and making love very tenderly, but he could not understand *why* she'd been worried. References to Éon of Moncontour simply annoyed him, and now that he was back she was ashamed to mention her other worry. He told her that he saw no reason to be afraid of a robber; it was silly for her to fret over that.

"He might shoot you from hiding!" Eline protested tearfully.

"He won't go about shooting every huntsman he meets," Tiarnán replied, growing exasperated, "and if he got close enough to recognize me, I'd see him. He's not worth one tear from you, my heart, let alone these floods."

No, he wouldn't stop his solitary hunting expeditions for fear of Éon, nor, it seemed, because they worried his new wife. A couple of weeks later he was gone again—and a couple of weeks after that he was off once more.

By the afternoon of the third day of this third absence, Eline felt that she couldn't bear it anymore. She walked out of Talensac manor house and slammed the main door behind her. Outside, the courtyard within its encircling wall was almost empty, dry and baking in the heat of August. Mailon the carpenter, who was planing a rafter for one of the barn repairs, glanced up at the door's hollow boom, then hurriedly concentrated again on his work. Eline noticed the hurry, and it made her even more angry. He knew, all the servants knew, that she was angry—but they would ignore it as much as they could. Pity the new mistress is so upset, they'd say among themselves; but leave her be, she'll get over it. She'll get used to it. But she hadn't got over it, and she wasn't used to it *now*.

Angrily, Eline looked about the empty yard. The manor house was a square wooden tower, raised above the yard on an artificial mound that was not quite a castle motte, and surrounded by a wooden palisade and ditch that were not quite a bailey. A number of outbuildings ran around the inside of the palisade — stables, kennels, workshop, storehouse, dairy, kitchens. There was a garden behind the manor house, as there had been at Comper, and the whole enclosure was guarded by the gatehouse lodge. The gate was open most of the time, and in the morning and evening the yard was busy, peasants from the village mingling with the servants of the house. Now there was only Mailon the carpenter, pretending he hadn't seen her.

Eline hesitated, then marched across the yard. She was going to ask questions until she *made* someone answer her. She couldn't stand the sore place in her thoughts any longer; it made her whole mind limp. "Mailon," she demanded, "where's my husband?"

Reluctantly, Mailon set down his plane and straightened his back. He had stripped to the waist for the work, and had been working so hard, in his attempt to ignore her, that his brown torso glistened with sweat. "Hunting, my lady," he said without meeting her eyes.

"Then why hasn't he taken Mirre?" cried Eline furiously. "How can he hunt without a dog?"

"I don't know, my lady," mumbled Mailon, still without meeting her eyes. "He'll be back soon, though."

Eline crossed her arms and hugged herself with rage. "Where's Kenmarcoc?" she demanded.

"Oh, he's at the old barn," said Mailon, relieved at finding a question he could answer. "Seeing about the clay for the new threshing floor." After a moment, he added, more reluctantly, "Can I be of help to you, my lady?"

Eline bit her lip. "Yes," she said. "Take a horse and go fetch Kenmarcoc. I want to talk to him."

"Eh, Lady. Is it so urgent?" asked Mailon with a glance at his interrupted work.

"Don't argue with me!" snapped Eline. "Just do as I say!" She turned on her heel and stalked back to the house. Without looking back, she was aware of Mailon shaking his head, then shrugging and picking up his tunic. ("A pity the new mistress is so upset. But she'll get over it.") Again Eline slammed the manor house door behind her.

The manor hall took up the whole of the ground floor of the house, an immense room, dimly lit by narrow windows near its high ceiling. It was the main room of the house in more than just size: the household ate there, did much of its work there, and most of the servants slept there. Kenmarcoc and his family had partitioned off the far end for their private quarters. The floor was of packed clay, strewn with rushes. A stone fireplace filled the center of the room; the floors above it were pierced to allow passage for the smoke, and a single shaft of light fell from the smoke hole in the roof down onto the morning's ashes. Three long tables of dark oak were arranged around it in a horseshoe facing the door, flanked by oak benches, with the chair reserved for the master of the house standing proud at the center of the middle table. The walls were hung with tapestry hunting scenes of dogs pursuing and baying a stag, and a wooden stairway to the upper floors climbed past them on one side of the room. Driken and Lanthildis were sitting beneath this, working at their looms.

Eline slammed herself down at her own loom and grabbed the shuttle like a dagger. The two others exchanged pitying looks, and her temper snapped completely: she screamed at them shrilly to get out and leave her alone. Driken flushed angrily, but her mother simply slid her shuttle into the loom, gathered up her daughter, and went off to do something else.

Eline tried to weave, but she was so tense that she kept moving the heddles in the wrong order and making mistakes. By the time Kenmarcoc arrived, more than an hour later, she was in tears from frustration.

The bailiff knocked politely on the manor door but let himself in without waiting for a response. "You wanted to see me, my lady?" he asked, coming into the hall. Privately he was cursing the girl for dragging him away from his work. It was understandable that she was upset by her husband's absences, but did she need to proclaim the fact to the whole manor?

Eline shoved the shuttle into the loom's web and turned away from it with relief. She reminded herself that she was the lady of the manor and had the right to give orders to her husband's bailiff. "Kenmarcoc," she said hotly, "where's my husband?"

"Out hunting, my lady," replied Kenmarcoc patiently. He sat down at the nearest table and picked an early apple from a bowl.

"Out hunting?" asked Eline. "Without Mirre?"

Kenmarcoc took a bite of the apple. Eline looked away distastefully: she'd been brought up to believe that apples eaten raw caused wind. "He often goes out without the dog," the clerk said with his mouth full.

"I know he does! I've seen him do it three times now. But why? He never brings back any game. Where does he *really* go?"

"He says he goes hunting, my lady," Kenmarcoc replied through a mouthful of apple. "Why would he lie?"

Eline bit her lip again. "Because he's seeing another woman," she said in a trembling voice. She forgot that she was supposed to be behaving like the lady of the manor, and she gazed at Kenmarcoc pleadingly, her immense blue-violet eyes brimming over with tears. "Please, Kenmarcoc, tell me the truth!"

Kenmarcoc's resentment vanished. The girl was so young, after all—not much older than his own daughter. Tiarnán's absences were peculiar, and his explanation for them inadequate: any wife would be worried by them. He dropped his apple and went to pat her on the back. "Put that thought out of your pretty head!" he told her. "He's had no eyes for any woman but you since first he met you. Why else would he have married you? You mustn't let anyone worry you. Nobody in Talensac knows where he goes when he's away, but there's no reason to think he isn't just hunting. And he's gone off to the forest less in the past two months than in all the time I've known him. For my part, I think the hunting is just an excuse. He's simply a man who needs time on his own. If he had the dog he'd have to feed her and look after her, and he doesn't want the bother of it."

"What do you mean, nobody knows where he goes?" Eline asked in confusion. She scanned the bailiff's face suspiciously: for once there was no evasion, no look of superior knowledge.

Kenmarcoc saw that he'd said more than he meant to. He was uncomfortably quiet for a moment. "Well," he admitted finally, "the truth is, he never tells anyone where he's going or lets anyone come with him, so busybodies invent nonsense about it."

"I don't believe you. Somebody must know. He must tell *you*."

"He doesn't," replied Kenmarcoc even more reluctantly, "and I have asked."

"But what if you need to reach him about something?"

"My lady, I take Christ to witness, I don't know where he is. I did press him once just as he was going, when there was some business coming up that I knew I'd need to consult him on, but he didn't reply. I pressed harder, and maybe got a bit too familiar, and he whipped round and hit me across the face, and told me he wouldn't be questioned by his own servants. There's no point in asking; he won't answer."

Eline stared. At the heart of her anger had been the sense that everybody knew where Tiarnán really was — everybody except her. But there was no doubting that Kenmarcoc was telling the truth. Talensac had been living with a mystery for years, and the knowing looks were founded on nothing more than surmise.

"You don't need to worry, my lady," Kenmarcoc told her with a patently false heartiness. "I'm sure he does nothing but look for game. As for never bringing it back — why, he'd be poaching if he did. He walks miles, and not just on his own land: he'll say he saw such-and-such a boar near Carhaix, and such-and-such a stag by Redon. You must know yourself that anyone who wants to organize a hunt consults him. He wouldn't know as much as he does about the beasts of the chase if he spent all that time with some woman, now, would he? Don't pay any attention to the silly stories they tell in the village."

"What silly stories?" asked Eline, more and more horrified.

Kenmarcoc again hesitated uncomfortably, then nerved himself and said, "Well, I suppose it's better you hear from me than from someone who believes in the nonsense. Some of the villagers say he goes into the hollow hills, some that he meets with the lady of a well or standing stone. You know peasants: they're fond of marvelous tales."

Eline remembered, with the same constriction of the stomach, the look in Tiarnán's eyes the night before he went hunting. A fey, wild look; a look of enchantment. She believed absolutely in the Fair Ones. They were as much a part of the land she lived in as the forest itself. Most Breton peasants could claim to have heard their music, and every village had a tale of an encounter with them that had happened in living memory.

Kenmarcoc rumbled on, trying to reassure her. Eventually he patted her on the shoulder and went off again to see to the threshing floor, leaving her alone with her thoughts.

Eline went to bed early that night and lay sleepless. The moon, just past full, shone crisscross through the wicker shutters of the window, dappling the room with gray and black. In the garden the crickets sang, and the scent of the roses filled the night air. It was like Comper—but it wasn't Comper, and suddenly Eline wished desperately that it were, that she were home, where everything was simple and familiar and she knew what to believe about people. The man she'd married had a secret, and any attempt to probe it was met with silence or anger.

She could not believe that he was only hunting. If he were doing no more than that, why not tell Kenmarcoc? Why not bring the dog? No, either Alain was right and he had a mistress somewhere—or something even worse had snared him, something bird-voiced and inhuman. She remembered stories of the Fair Ones, who dwelt in the shadow country within the hollow hills. A girl once had loved a man who was on his way to meet her, when he came upon the Fair Ones dancing in the moonlight. She waited for him on the hill, but he did not come. Year after year, she went up the hill to their trysting place, until she grew old, and died, and was buried there. And then, long after she was gone, he did come back, thinking that he had danced for just a single night. But instead of his sweetheart waiting, he found her grave, grown over with the long grass. Then he lay down upon it weeping, and when he touched the earth, he crumbled away to dust. Eline rolled over on her side and chewed the pillowcase, crying.

When Tiarnán came back, again about midnight, she was still awake. She lay still, listening, as he came quietly into the room. He stood over the bed a minute, looking down at her, then sat down and began taking off his clothes. When he was naked he slid under the covers beside her. His body was still cold from the night, and he smelled of trees. He kissed her cheek, and stroked her hair so lightly that she knew he thought she was still asleep and didn't want to wake her. At that gentleness, she began to cry again.

"Eline!" he said in surprise. "You're awake?"

"Yes," she sniffed.

Tiarnán had returned from the forest feeling clean and light and happily tired. He had walked through the sleeping village with a sense of enormous contentment: he was coming home, not just to the place he loved, but to a beautiful young wife. When he'd reached the manor house and found it asleep, with no pale, unhappy girl waiting for him on the stairs, his contentment had grown. She was starting to get used to his absences; soon they wouldn't worry her at all, and she'd accept them as quietly as everyone else did. When he'd gone into the bedroom and saw her lying there crisscrossed with the moonlight, something inside him opened like clouds after the rain. He had all that a man could wish for: the shadows he had just left, and this lovely shining creature before him. For a moment he had been unable to move for joy.

And now it seemed she was awake, and still unhappy. He was very sorry for her distress, though he could not see the point of it. He put his arms around her and kissed her, tasting the salt of her tears. "What's the matter, my heart?" he asked tenderly. "You're not still fretting over Éon of Moncontour?"

"I want to ask you something," she said, "but they told me that it's no use, you won't answer, you'll just get angry. So I don't dare ask. I'm all alone here, and I couldn't bear it if you were angry with me."

"My dearest love! I could never be angry with you. There's

nothing you could ask me that I wouldn't give. Ask away."

She put her arms around him. The muscles in his back and shoulders were smooth under her hands, and when she touched his hair she felt the twist it made just above the nape of the neck, the drake's tail that never would lie flat. He was real and solid and no less loving than the night he had married her. There was no reason to be afraid. He loved her, and he would tell her what the secret was, and then they would both laugh over all her silly fears. "Tiarnán!" She sighed, relaxing and kissing the edge of his collarbone. "Then tell me, where have you been the last three days?"

At once he went still. He should have foreseen that she would ask him about that. It had been a mistake, he realized too late, to make such a sweeping promise. "I've been in the forest, hunting," he told her, hoping that this would do.

The repetition of the same empty phrase she'd heard from everyone else, when she'd hoped he'd make everything simple again, was a bitter disappointment. She turned away from him, curled up on her side, and burst into tears.

"Eline!" he protested helplessly. "Don't cry. There's no reason to cry."

"But you're not telling me the truth!" she sobbed. "You go away, and you won't tell anybody where. And you don't take Mirre. If all you're doing is hunting, why don't you take Mirre?"

"What else would I be doing except hunting?" he asked.

The feeble evasion failed as miserably as it deserved. "Alain de Fougères said you go to see a woman," wept Eline.

He was utterly lost for what to say. Anger with Alain de Fougères, indignation at the slander, and pity for Eline's distress all struggled to his tongue, but stopped there. Servants and villagers had had no choice but to accept whatever answer he gave them. Servants and villagers weren't married to him. At last he pulled Eline's heaving shoulders against himself, kissed her ear, and swore to her that there was no woman in the world for him but her.

It was effective enough to turn her around into his arms. But

the tears didn't stop: she merely wept onto his shoulder instead
of the pillowcase. "Then why do you go?" she demanded brokenly. "You're away so much! And Kenmarcoc says you used
to go away even more. And he says that the only time he
pressed you on it, you hit him. I've never seen you hit any of
the servants, let alone Kenmarcoc. And you know I fret over
that robber, and I'm frightened, but you still go away and leave
me all alone. . . ."

He tried to soothe her with gentle touches and soft words,
but she only cried harder. The intensity of her unhappiness
distressed him: he had never wanted to cause her grief. It
crossed his mind to tell her some reassuring lie, but lying was
foreign to his nature.

"Eline, Eline," he pleaded instead. "Why should you cry like
this? Whatever do you think I've been doing? I've told you,
there's no other woman."

She looked miserably up into his face. "Oh, Tiarnán!" she
gulped. "Promise me you don't . . . that it's nothing to do with . . .
with the Fair Ones."

The question jolted him; it touched painfully near things he
had locked away, treasures that played no part in the life of
manor or court, and could be taken out and handled in the
forest alone. "Why do you ask that?" he demanded, with an
edge in his voice.

"They say in the village that you go to the hollow hills, or to
see the lady of a well," Eline whispered, shaken out of tears at
last.

He hadn't known that they said that, and the fact that they
did filled him with indignant astonishment. They had been speculating about him. It seemed a gross intrusion on his privacy.
"It is utterly, damnably false!" he declared. "No one has ever
said such a thing to my face; if he had, I would teach him better
than to tell lies. Who told you this?"

"Nobody," whispered Eline, taken aback, and beginning to
be relieved. He was so indignant that it could not be true. "Kenmarcoc said it's what they say in the village, and he told me not
to pay any attention. But people will say all sorts of stupid

things when there's a mystery! And I don't know what to think. I can't bear it. Please, tell me the truth!"

Tiarnán was silent. Somehow, without his admitting that he did more than hunt, the thing he kept for the forest had pressed itself between them. He knew, guiltily, that he was wrong to pretend that it did not exist. Foolish, too, when its existence was so clearly understood that even the villagers had been speculating about it. But how could he tell Eline? He felt instinctively that it would be wrong to try to pin it down with words, particularly here, in a place to which it was alien.

Eline's glimmer of hope faded. She buried her face in her arms and began to cry again. He wouldn't tell her; he didn't really love her.

"Dearest heart, don't cry!" Tiarnán urged gently. "What you're asking . . . I *can't* tell you that."

"But why?" Eline demanded, lifting her head again and staring at him, trying hard to stop crying. "Why?"

He answered without thinking and with fatal honesty. "I'm afraid that if I tell you, I'll lose your love, and perhaps my own self as well."

He knew as soon as he'd spoken that he should have stayed silent. The words were too stark: *if I tell you, I'll lose your love.* Did he believe the thing he could not tell her was so terrible that it would make her hate him? If that were so, he must have been wrong to marry her. Any peasant who sold an ox that gored, and concealed the fact from the buyer, would be forced to pay back the money. A knight who had a vicious habit and who nonetheless took an innocent girl as a wife must be far more guilty. She had had another suitor, one untouched by dark secrets: a man who truly loved her would either have told her the truth or have given her up.

He did not feel that his secret was terrible, only that it was something she would not understand. It was a thing so strange and so private that he did not really understand it himself. But there was no comfort there. Father Judicaël had told him that she would not understand it, and that she and he would do each other harm. In answer he had told himself that anything could be understood through love. But now he found that he was afraid to risk being wrong.

She had been perfectly happy with him before she suspected the secret's existence; surely when she forgot about it, she would be happy again? It was not something that would ever intrude on the manor house or her life in it.

But she was so wretched now, and he longed so to comfort her. And would she forget it? Wouldn't his silence now cast a long shadow over their life together, poisoning her thoughts with suspicion of him?

Eline had gasped with shock at his terrible words, and rolled over again with her back to him. Now she was smothering her sobs in her tear-soaked pillowcase. He felt an immense pity for her, so young and beautiful and vulnerable. She was his wife, after all, with more claim upon him than any other creature. She had sworn at their wedding to love and honor him. Why should he believe that she would perjure herself? Wasn't it cowardly on his part to keep silent, and insulting to her not to trust? The secret was such a harmless thing. He had never hurt anyone by it. Surely, she would understand it after all, since she loved him? Surely it was better that she knew it than suspect him of demon worship or adultery?

"My thousand times dear," whispered Tiarnán, putting a hand on her shoulder. "Don't cry. I'll tell you, if you want to know so badly."

"Oh!" she exclaimed, rolling back and hugging him at last. She was damp with tears, soft-limbed and passionate, and the touch of her body went through him like a note of music. "Oh, I knew you loved me!" she said, kissing him. "And I promise you, I'll love you whatever it is. But I can't bear not knowing."

She leaned her head against his shoulder, quiet now. All the stormy tears she had shed over the day and night left her now with a feeling of immense calm, safely harbored in her husband's arms. Whatever it is, she thought, God will give me strength for it. And another of the stories about the Fair Ones hovered at the back of her mind: the tale of a girl whose brave tenacity saved her lover from the snares of the Queen of Fairyland and brought him safely home. Perhaps she would be the one to save Tiarnán from whatever trap the forest had laid for his soul.

Tiarnán was silent for a long time. He meant to tell her, but all the words he could find for his secret seemed false, ugly, and frightening. The reality was different, innocent and exhilarating: How could he cage it in language Eline would not be afraid of?

At last Eline stirred in his arms, and stroked his beard, whispering for him to go on.

"Years ago," Tiarnán began very slowly — and the sudden awareness that he really was about to expose himself clogged the words with dread. He had to stop and breathe before he could go on. "When I was sixteen. Duke Hoel had just taken up the dukedom, and there were celebrations at court. We all went hunting."

He was trapped in another entangling silence. He remembered the time well. Duke Conan had died in an armed expedition against the duchy of Anjou, and his men had been left stranded and disorganized. When Hoel had received the news, he had gathered together all the fighting men at the court, taking even the young squires and the old men, and had ridden frantically to extricate the survivors. It had been Tiarnán's first battle, and he had bloodily distinguished himself in it. Hoel had knighted him on the field of battle with a sword still red from the struggle, and allowed him to do homage for his father's lands. For Tiarnán the act of homage had meant he was no longer a ward of the duke, with an estate administered by ducal officials, but a lord in his own right. It had meant respect, reputation — but most of all it had meant that he could leave the court and go back to Talensac. He had been eager to go home, longing for the court celebrations to end, but, at the same time, he had been unsure of himself. Eight years at court; eight years struggling to learn sophistication; eight years of grief and the violence that left a bitter taste in his mouth even when it brought him honor — how could he go home after that? And then had come the hunt, and what happened in it.

Eline kissed him. "We gave chase to a stag," Tiarnán continued finally. "I and a few others were waiting with a relay of dogs to set on the deer when it ran past. When we heard the horns nearby, we uncoupled the hounds, and they ran baying into the woods. We galloped after them. I heard the horns off to my right, but my dog Ravault was baying to the left, so I turned to follow his cry and lost the others. I rode after Ravault until the sound of the horns faded, and then I realized that he'd started some other quarry and was pursuing it alone. But I saw no reason to stop for that. I would never have caught up with the main hunt in time for the kill, so I thought I might as well follow my dog, and see what he'd found for me. I preferred being on my own, even then."

Tiarnán stopped again. This time Eline lay motionless in his arms, sensing that he stepped in darkness toward the secret itself. "The dog led me to a mound guarded by standing stones," Tiarnán said at last, "and there I found him, struggling with a wolf. Even as I rode up, the wolf caught Ravault by the throat. I jumped down from my horse and hurried to kill the wolf with my sword, but by the time I'd done so, it was already too late, and the dog, too, was dead." He remembered the dog, a brown alaunt with the heavy jaws and rangy body of the breed, but with an unpedigreed mongrel grin and a constantly flapping tail. He had scratched the dead hound's ears and pressed his face against its still-warm side, before scraping out a hollow for it in the earth of the forest, and covering it with turf he had cut from the mound with his hunting knife. It had been dusk by the time he'd finished, and was beginning to rain. The dead wolf had lain gray and sodden between the two standing stones, and he had noticed for the first time how the turf he'd cut away from the mound looked like a door into the hill. A hollow hill, marked by the stones as a gateway to the domain of the Fair Ones. Perhaps he had realized then. He had never been sure whether he had known what he was doing, going to that place of ancient and capricious power and doing there what he had done. Perhaps he had realized; perhaps it really had been done as ignorantly as it had seemed at the time.

"My horse was foundered from the chase," he told Eline, "and I was very weary and grieved for the dog. It was too late to go anywhere that night. I unsaddled the horse and tethered it and tended it, and I made a camp for myself between the standing stones, because they gave me shelter from the rain. I skinned the wolf and pegged its hide above me for a tent, and I rolled myself in my cloak and went to sleep."

Again he stopped. He remembered waking, and finding that the moon was up and everything had changed. It had been like coming out of a thick fog into clear air. Every sense was so alive that it seemed that before they must have been swathed in wool. He had heard the voles squeaking in the grass and the bats in the air; he had smelled the rain, skidding away into the east with the clouds, and smelled the forest, too, all the richness of it, alive—he had never understood before how much it was alive, how each breath of its air tingled with a thousand messages. He'd got to his feet and found himself tangled in his own clothes. His thoughts had grown strange and wordless and unclear: he struggled with his own tunic and hose, tore at them with his teeth, and got free. And then he had rolled on the wet grass in the moonlight, and it was so sweet that nothing in all the world could match it. It was as though every hunt he had undertaken, he had been hunting for this; each beast he had chased, it had been to capture this. The bitterness of violence, the shame and anger of the past, the worries for the future— they were all gone, swallowed in that great moonlit now of night and rain. Experience became pure, innocent, and overpowering.

Eline picked up her head and looked into his face. The moonlight crossed it with shadows, but his eyes, in a patch of light, were the bright alien eyes of a wild animal. "What happened?" she whispered, feeling the sick constriction of her stomach.

"When I woke . . ." he said, fumbling with words that failed, that never could communicate that enormous wordless experience, "the wolf skin . . . I . . . was inside it."

"What do you mean?" she demanded, this time in horror.

"I had taken the shape of a wolf."

They were both silent for a long time. Tiarnán was warm now in Eline's arms, but she felt as though she were made of ice. She imagined the arms that encircled her sprouting hair and becoming the legs of a wolf, and the face changing to fangs under the strange eyes. She began to shiver.

"Eline," he said, holding her closer. "I don't do any harm by it."

She couldn't speak. She choked, shivering and shaking her head.

"I've never killed a man in that shape or done injury to any human creature. All my sins have been committed as a man."

"This happens to you every time you go?" choked Eline. "Every time you leave me, you . . . you change?"

"Not every time. Only when I go hunting without Mirre."

Three times since she'd married him. Three times, the body she held, which had entered her own, had shifted and become the body of a beast. Eline sat up abruptly and swung her feet out of the bed. She bent over double, shaking with horror. Tiarnán knelt in the bed behind her. He put his hands on her shoulders; she flinched, and he took them away. She was afraid to look at him; she knew that if she did she'd see him turning into a beast, and then she'd scream. "How can we stop it?" she asked wildly. "How do we break the curse?"

"You don't understand!" he cried impatiently. "I don't want to stop it! I told you, I do no harm by it. It isn't wicked and there isn't any curse. It's the most marvelous gift!"

She gave an awful dragging moan and covered her ears. He reached out again to comfort her, and she flung herself out of the bed and away from him. He freely accepted the monstrous thing he had become; he delighted in it. She thought of her body being penetrated by a wolf, and knew suddenly that she was going to be sick. She scrabbled under the bed and got the chamber pot just in time.

"Eline!" whispered Tiarnán, appalled, as she stared bleakly down into her own vomit. "There's no harm in it."

"Just give me time," she whispered back.

"She'll get used to it; she'll get over it," she heard at the back of her mind. But she was already certain that she wouldn't. The thought of sleeping with Tiarnán ever again made her skin crawl; the fact that she'd slept with him already made her feel unclean. I can't, she thought privately. I can't, and I never will again. God help me.

For about a week after the revelation, Eline wandered about the manor house in a daze of horror. Every morning when she woke she would look at her husband's face, and for a moment think the whole midnight conversation had been a dream. It was the same face she had been so glad to gaze at on her wedding day, different only in the look of pain in the eyes. Then she would notice a previously unobserved wolfish quality to it and know that it was true. The hair on his body now reminded her inescapably of an animal's. At night she would lie rigid on the very edge of the bed, arms clutched against herself to keep from touching him, and if their hands happened to brush each other during the day she would rub hers anxiously against her gown. The manor servants began discussing her in concerned whispers, and when she went into the village there were curious or hostile looks.

She did not want to touch her husband, but she did want to talk to him. She was full of questions: How did he do it? Could he change himself any time, or did it just happen? Where did he go when he'd done it? What did he do? What did he eat? The details she raked from his unhappy replies she piled together and turned over obsessively in her mind. Like the sight of blood and mutilation, they both repelled and fascinated her. She told Tiarnán that she was trying to understand, and that without knowing such things she could never grasp what it meant to him.

At first she believed that. But gradually, almost without her notice, "trying to understand" became inwardly "trying to understand how to stop it" and then, fatally, "trying to understand how to be free of him." The word "werewolf," which he had never uttered, hung perpetually in the back of her mind, and seemed more fearsome with each day that passed. She did not dare repeat what he had told her to anyone, first because everyone around her was her husband's servant, and second, and even more tellingly, because she herself was enmeshed in his secret. If what he was became known, he would be burned at the stake, but she would become a spectacle, "the werewolf's wife"—a scarecrow thing for all the world to gape at. Besides, who would believe her? The people of Talensac would be prepared to swear that black was white if Tiarnán was threatened, and everyone knew he was a favorite of the duke's. Who'd take Eline's bare word against that? To betray him would only invite a terrible retribution.

Tiarnán answered her questions painfully but freely. The vehemence of her revulsion stunned and wounded him. He could not feel himself any different from what he had been before, and yet Eline shrank from him. He was deeply ashamed of his weakness in confiding in her: the village held that a man of character should never give in to a woman's pleading. Yet he had done it because he loved her, because he had wanted to trust her and to comfort her. He told himself that the extremity of her revulsion was only because she must have heard horrible stories about *what he was*. (Even in thought he avoided the ugly word that haunted her.) She must believe that he ate children or killed virgins. When she understood that he really did nothing but wander the forest, then she would be reconciled to him. But with every word of explanation he uttered, the thing itself seemed to grow more bizarre and harder to grasp, as though it altered and became monstrous as it moved from his experience to Eline's horrified regard.

"Does anyone else know?" asked Eline.

Tiarnán remembered bitterly the only other time he had told his secret: when he had confessed it to Judicaël. Judicaël had not wept or recoiled in horror. The confession had distressed him, sent him stalking out of his hermit's cell into his garden, where he had attacked a row of onions savagely with a hoe—but Judicaël had instantly understood why Tiarnán would love it. He did not know, he said, if it was sin: it had come unsought

for, and no crime had been committed through it. He had repeatedly urged Tiarnán to give it up, but he had set no penance
for it, saying that if Tiarnán had committed no sin, he could
not absolve him, but if there were sin, they must wait for God
to reveal to them how to atone. Perhaps Judicaël could make
Eline understand as well.

Eline's understanding had by then progressed so far that
when Tiarnán urged her to visit the hermit, she dismissed the
confessor from her list of possible allies in shocked disgust. No
real priest would tolerate such an abomination. The hermit's
reputation for holiness was so much wind. Probably he really
did bless bonfires and other forms of demon worship.

After a week of tormented questions and painful proximity,
Eline begged Tiarnán to allow her to leave Talensac for a little
while and visit her married sister at Iffendic. "I need time," she
said. "I'm trying to understand; I am. But . . . I . . . I need to get
away."

He was inwardly relieved. Her questions had left him feeling
mauled, and her white face and horrified eyes lacerated him
every time he saw them. Staying with her sister would give her
opportunity to calm down and come to terms with what he was.
He readily gave her permission, and sent her off with a train
of servants and the excuse of needing to learn housekeeping.
As soon as she was gone, he set off alone for the forest. In the
shadows of Broceliande, past and future could become remote,
and this present torment would fade into the scents on the wind.

VII

The ducal court left Rennes in the early part of July and rode south to Nantes. The move took several days, but as soon as everyone was installed in Nantes castle, the court resumed its continual chattering in three tongues as though it had never been interrupted.

Nantes was a bigger city than Rennes, a port where ships came down the Loire from Tours and Orléans, and up the Loire from all the harbors of the world. The castle, however, was smaller than that in Rennes, built for Hoel when he was merely Count of Nantes. The ducal court filled it to overflowing. The knights of the household spent much of their time in the town, or practicing their weapons on the field to the north of the castle.

"There's a letter for you," one of the pages told Alain de Fougères when he came in from such weapons' practice at noon one day about the middle of September. "A man brought it this morning. I put it there, on the table."

"A man?" asked Alain, picking up the letter from the table in the Great Hall and looking at it with apprehension. It was a single piece of folded vellum and the seal was blank. He wondered if it concerned some debt he'd forgotten. Letters were not common things, even for a knight like himself who could read a little. "What sort of man?"

"A farmer from somewhere. Iffendic, I think. He said," and the page grinned, "a lady gave it to him for you."

Alain suddenly remembered that Eline's sister had married the brother of the lord of Iffendic. He almost tore the letter open on the spot—then decided to take it somewhere more private. He had been recalled to the court when it first moved to Nantes, but he was still under something of a cloud. Alain's position as knight in the duke's household was supposed to demonstrate Lord Juhel's loyalty to his feudal overlord. Alain's dereliction of duty had reflected badly on his father, and Alain still winced at the memory of some of the things Lord Juhel had said. It would never do to be discovered with a letter from Eline.

In the castle garden a few minutes later he broke open the seal and unfolded the paper. Inside it was a single lock of white-blond hair, tied with a strand of forget-me-not blue silk, and on the parchment, in a round, clerical hand, the words, "St. Maugan's Chapel. Iffendic. Three days before the Feast of Saint Michael. Nones."

He picked up the lock of hair with hands that shook: it seemed to shine like water. He remembered Eline in her bedroom at Comper with her hair loose over her shoulders. He had known, he told himself joyfully, that she would send for him one day. Tiarnán must have gone off hunting once too often, and she'd realized that she'd really loved Alain himself all along. She needed to send a message, but she couldn't write and didn't dare send a messenger, so she'd used some pretext to get a clerk to write out a time and place, and for signature and seal enclosed her hair, knowing that her lover would understand. He touched the hair to his lips. Three days before the Feast of Saint Michael—the twenty-sixth of September. That gave him a week.

He told the court that he wanted to go to St. Malo to see about a ship that was said to have arrived there with some hawks from Norway. The duke and most of the others accepted this without comment: one knight's absence from the crowded court meant more space for everyone else. Tiher, though, became suspicious when Alain declined his offer to come along.

"You're not going to Talensac?" he asked while Alain was packing.

"No," Alain replied coolly.

"Good," said Tiher, still suspicious. "Because, cousin, Tiarnán could kill three of you before breakfast, and I think that if he found you visiting his wife, he would. It was plain to see at the wedding that he's besotted with her."

"I am not going to Talensac," said Alain. He picked up the gold crucifix he wore on a chain around his neck and held it up in his fist. "I swear to it on this." He dropped the crucifix and crossed himself piously.

Tiher raised his eyebrows. "Oh. Good. Well, if you see a bargain in hawks, get me one. No gyrfalcons, though; too costly."

The evening of the fourth day before the Feast of Saint Michael found Alain at the inn in Montfort, a place of unpleasant association that he tried now to banish with hope. The following morning he washed and shaved and dressed with great care in a slashed riding tunic, red velvet with the new wide sleeves, and a pair of striped hose. This time he had left his armor at Nantes. He hadn't needed it for his invented hawk-buying expedition, and it would never do to lose it again. He strapped his sword to his side, mounted his bay charger, and rode off with a dry mouth and wet palms.

It was about eight miles from Montfort to the chapel of St. Maugan, the other side of Iffendic. He hadn't been sure where the chapel was, and had to ask for it, but he still arrived closer to noon than the midafternoon office of Nones, almost three hours early. The chapel was in fact the parish church of a small hamlet, and when he arrived he found the yard in front of it full of peasant women fetching water from the well and gossiping. After a few embarrassed minutes waiting under their curious stares, he remounted his horse and rode back toward Iffendic. She was sure to come along the road; he'd find somewhere private to meet her.

About half an hour before St. Maugan's bell in the distance rang for Nones, she came. She was alone, riding a plump white pony, her head bent as though in grief. Alain, waiting in an apple orchard just off the road, found his heart pounding so hard that he couldn't speak, and almost let her ride by. But she lifted her head just as she was level with him, looking toward the church tower ahead, and at the sight of her pale face he found his tongue again and shouted, "Eline!"

Eline had intended to talk to him reasonably, to explain that her husband had tricked her into the marriage by his silence over a terrible secret, to say that she considered the vows she had made in ignorance to be invalid. But when she heard Alain shout her name, the speech went out of her head. Safe at Iffendic, away from her husband's disturbing presence, any remaining ambivalence in her feelings toward him had been swept away. She had slept with a beast, and she felt unutterably defiled. When she saw Alain standing under the apple trees, shaven and elegant, keen with hope and *human*, she turned her pony, galloped toward him, and jumped off the horse's back straight into his arms. After a moment's stunned disbelief, his arms folded around her, and he kissed her passionately. His touch seemed to sweep away the clinging filth of the wolf's fur, and she leaned against him sobbing with relief. She had been afraid that he would not come, and that she would be trapped in the nightmare forever.

"My darling!" said Alain, kissing her tears. "Whatever has happened? — Here, we mustn't be seen; let's go under the trees."

Under the trees there were shadows and long grass; the apple branches, recently stripped of their ripe fruit but patched gold with autumn, cut off the light. She stumbled over the windfalls underfoot, and from everywhere came the smell of rotting apples, the buzz of drunken wasps. They stopped in a clear space well away from the road and faced each other. Alain's hair was gold as the apple leaves, and his wide eyes were full of astonishment and concern. She put her arms about his neck and kissed him frantically. Golden strength, sweet safety! "You came," was all she could say. "Oh, thank God!"

"Of course I came! I would come to the end of the earth for you. What in the world has happened?"

She remembered how she had pushed him out the window the last time they met, and began to cry. She gabbled incoherent apologies, punctuated by kisses; then, terrified at what she was doing, flung herself out of his arms again and hugged her trembling hands against her throat. "Oh, Alain! I'm so sorry!" she gasped. "I can't say . . . Swear to me that you'll help me, that you won't betray me!"

He took the crucifix from around his neck and unfolded her cramped, terrified hands to set it between them. Then he knelt in the long grass under the trees and placed his hands between her own. It was the act of homage, the gesture a knight would make to his feudal overlord. "I swear by this cross, and by your white hands," he promised solemnly, "that I will shed the last drop of my blood sooner than betray you, Eline. I am your liege man forever."

"Oh, my love!" gasped Eline, dropping to her knees to face him. Her face was burning with shame: such generosity, after such treatment as she had given him! "I don't deserve it of you!" she cried impulsively. "You can call me not liege lady, but mistress. Everything you want of me is yours."

Still scarcely daring to believe it, he put his arms around her and kissed her again. She responded to him not with the sweet yielding warmth he'd sometimes daydreamed of but with desperation. Anger began to stir even in the rapture. What had Tiarnán done to her?

Whatever Tiarnán had done, it had left no mark on her body. When she had undressed and stood naked in the shadows under the trees she was whiter and softer and more lovely than any dream he'd had of her. She blushed to take her shift off, and he thought it looked like the dawn flooding the white winter sky—but to touch her was the very heart of spring. He had never conceived of such ecstasy, such an intense, overmastering bliss; at the fulfillment of it they both wept.

When it was over, they lay together on the heap of their discarded clothes, and she rested her head on his chest and whispered, "Oh, my darling!" He stroked her tangled hair, and knew that he had all he desired of the world. It only remained to keep it.

"Now," he said determinedly, "tell me what has happened."

Eline told her story in a stumbling rush: Tiarnán's hunting

expeditions without the dog; the ignorance of the servants about the nature of them; her own desperate questions; Tiarnán's final reluctant reply. Alain listened in increasing amazement and, against his will, disbelief. When Eline finished, his first question was "Are you sure he wasn't making . . . well, some kind of cruel joke? To punish you, perhaps, for fretting over his absences?"

"A joke?" repeated Eline. "No, it's true. I know it is." She remembered again Tiarnán's eyes in the moonlight, and shuddered. Suddenly she was afraid to be there, lying with her lover under the trees. She had betrayed Tiarnán now, and perhaps he could find out. Even the leaves might whisper to him what she had done. She sat up and looked about for her shift.

"Yes, but . . ." Alain began — and trailed off helplessly. He had been at the duke's court for over a year and had often shared a table with Tiarnán. He'd slept near him in the duke's Great Hall, used the same latrine, practiced weapons on the same tilting field. He'd never liked the other man, but a werewolf? It didn't seem possible.

Eline was on her feet, hurriedly doing up the laces on her shift; she didn't notice Alain's expression of doubt. "He told me . . . everything," she whispered, and glanced around again uneasily at the shadows. "He told me where he goes when he . . . he changes. Most often he goes to St. Mailon's chapel in the woods, and he leaves his clothes under a hollow stone. He told me that he has to go back to them and get — something — he leaves with them, before he can become a man again."

She remembered that admission, and Tiarnán's voice as he made it, low and perplexed, his troubled eyes watching her. "But what is this thing you leave?" she'd asked, and he had replied impatiently, "I don't know! I only feel it. It must be the part of my soul that makes me human." She had taken that answer fastidiously between the tips of her mind's fingers, dropped it into her heap of details, and gone on asking — how did he leave it? was it visible? how could he separate out a part of his soul? — until Tiarnán had shaken his head in angry confusion and left the room. It was only after that, turning it over again, that she had realized it was the way to be free. Her first thought had been to use the information herself—but that was impossible. It was difficult for a young noblewoman to get away from the house unattended—even to get out from Iffendic manor house to the neighboring hamlet of St. Maugan had required complicated planning—and to travel on the road through the forest to St. Mailon's was dangerous and would never be allowed. Besides, she was afraid. The longer she was way from her husband, the greater and more frightful was the shadow he cast over her. So she had turned to Alain, the only man who might, she thought, be willing to take the risk for her. "Listen to me," she said to him now, urgently. "If someone went to St. Mailon's and waited until he'd become a wolf, and then stole the clothes and the thing he leaves with them—then he couldn't come back. He'd be trapped in his beastliness. And I'd never have to endure him again."

"Yes, but . . ." Alain repeated—and again trailed off helplessly. Eline had not claimed that she'd actually *seen* any of this: it was no more than something Tiarnán had told her. It couldn't be anything but a cruel joke.

Eline stared at him, her eyes growing enormous. He was hesitating; he was afraid. Or perhaps, now that she'd given him what he wanted, he didn't love her anymore. Perhaps he now despised her as a whore. "Aren't you going to help me?" she cried in anguish.

Alain jumped to his feet, naked as he was, and pulled her close against him. "Yes, yes!" he protested. "Of course. But . . ."

But there were no "but"s. There were only her lips, and the feeling of her body against his. He forgot what he'd meant to say. What did it matter if she was wrong? She wasn't asking him to fight Tiarnán, but only to check out some nonsense about a hollow stone at a chapel. "What do you want me to do?" he asked her.

She sighed deeply and tilted her head back to gaze into his eyes. *Alain, Alain,* she thought, *why didn't I marry you?* "Tiarnán told me that he always wants to go into the forest when the moon is full," she whispered. "He always leaves the house at cockcrow, so he must reach St. Mailon's an hour or so after dawn. If you go to St. Mailon's the night before the moon is full, in the morning you could go up the bell tower and watch until Tiarnán comes."

"What if he doesn't come?"

"Then you try again at the next full moon. But I think he'll go. He said he usually goes there."

Alain was quiet a minute, considering. He still felt very doubtful about Eline's story. On the other hand, there was no great danger in spending the night at St. Mailon's. Even if Tiarnán showed up to consult his hermit, he could be pacified with some excuse. "Oh yes, I was on my way back from St. Malo and I remembered I once vowed to observe a vigil for the saint, and I missed my chance of doing it there, so I turned aside and came here. After all, it's the Breton name of the same saint, isn't it? No, I swear I haven't been to Talensac. It's your manor; you'd know if I had. Eline's at Iffendic? Well, I haven't stopped there, either." Yes, Tiarnán would have to accept that. And if Tiarnán didn't show up, Eline might be willing to admit that her husband, cold, dark devil that he was, had played an unpleasant joke on her, perhaps for no other purpose than to distress her and make her cry. And for that, Alain thought with satisfaction, Tiarnán had already been repaid, with cuckoldry. "Very well," he told Eline, kissing her hand. "I'll do exactly as you say, and go to St. Mailon's the night before the next full moon. I swear it to you now."

She threw her arms around him again. "Oh, thank you, Alain! Please, please, be careful!"

He felt as though his heart had burst into flower, like a tree. "We must arrange somewhere to meet afterward," he said, "whether Tiarnán comes or not." Then he smiled and added, "By then we'll need somewhere warmer than this."

He was delighted with the way she blushed.

It was not difficult to find an excuse to go to St. Mailon's chapel the night before the full moon. When he returned

from his "trip to St. Malo," Alain told the court that the ship
he'd heard of hadn't arrived. It seemed natural, then, when he
said he'd heard it had docked and that he meant to try again.
Tiher was again suspicious, but, again, was easily put off with
a misleading oath.

Finding the chapel itself was more difficult. It lay off the road
from Iffendic to Comper, two full days' ride from Nantes. The
road was a narrow country lane, and for most of its length it
ran through thick forest. He missed the turning at first, and
rode all the way to the edge of the cultivated lands near Comper
before realizing his mistake, and had to turn and ride back. It
was dusk when he finally found the place. Only the tip of the
bell tower showed above the trees, black and dangerously sharp
against the evening sky. He turned his horse into the narrow
path that led toward it, but had to dismount and lead the animal. The branches of the young oaks hung low over the path
and made riding impossible. He had put his armor on this time,
just in case he met Tiarnán and the other wasn't pacified with
explanations. The hauberk weighed on his shoulders, and his
sword, hung to be comfortable when riding, kept tangling in
his legs as he twisted under the trees on foot. He was irritable
and out of breath when at last he led the horse into the clearing
in front of the church.

St. Mailon's was small, scarcely bigger than a peasant's hut,
a squat gray building that lacked even glass for its windows
and made do with wickerwork screens, like a house. Crane flies
swooped up and down in the fading light of the clearing, but
the night was already deepening under the branches of the sur-
rounding trees. The moon was hidden behind the forest. A bat
fluttered past like a falling leaf, but nothing larger stirred. Alain
had a sensation that he was being watched, and looked about
with his hand on the hilt of his sword, but no one was there;
there wasn't even a rustle in the undergrowth. Everything was
still. Not peaceful, though. It was as though the whole forest
were coming awake and was aware of him, staring at him with
hatred. The story he'd disbelieved in the apple orchard didn't
seem quite so impossible now, and he swallowed and crossed

himself. He reminded himself that he stood on holy ground, and that, anyway, all he had to do was stay hidden in the church and watch. And if the story was true, then Eline was married to a monster, and it was his duty to rescue her. To rescue her from a werewolf! That was a deed for a hero.

His tired horse butted him with its nose, and he realized that he would have to find somewhere to leave it, or it would betray his presence to any chapel visitor. He led the animal around the church, and found that the path continued away from the chapel. He followed it through the woods along the ridge of the hill, then down to a small stream. There was grass by the stream, and he tethered his horse there, tended it, and left it to graze, praying that no thieving peasant would come that way and make off with it.

He remembered that the hermit Judicaël was supposed to have a hut nearby, and he looked for it as he walked back up the path to the chapel but saw no sign. It was dark now, though, and the forest was thick and black. A whole village could be yards away, and he'd see nothing of it. He anticipated no trouble from the hermit, though, even if they met. All he had to do was say that he was keeping a vigil in honor of the saint, and the priest would probably offer him breakfast. The thought reassured him. The moon was higher now, and cast a cold gray light on the center of the path before him, and the leaves of the forest rustled strangely. He did not like the thought of being entirely alone.

The church was unlocked and empty, and he went inside, sat down by the open door, and ate the bread he'd brought for his supper. An owl hooted repeatedly outside, and the sense of being watched did not fade. He went farther into the church and closed the door, but the sense did not ease. Sitting there in the black interior of the church, he grew steadily more and more afraid. He began to feel that if he opened the door he might see anything: devils dancing about the church, black and hideous with red tongues, waving the bones of men; or the fairy hunt riding by, magnificent and fair upon white horses, their bridles decked with bells, but death to anyone who saw them.

He became terrified that for some reason he would open the door; that his very fear would force him to open it, and then he would die. In the end, he drew his sword, went up to the altar, and knelt, gripping the crosspieces of the blade and repeating all the prayers he knew. He told himself that his fear was irrational, that he was kneeling in a small church not three miles from a manor he knew well, and that there was a hermit, a holy man, sleeping in a hut just down the hill. After a while, and after nothing had happened, the fear ebbed. He lay down on the rushes before the altar and went to sleep, his hand still clasping the hilt of his sword for comfort.

He woke before the dawn, cold and stiff; rolled over and tried to go back to sleep; failed; and got up. The fear he had felt the previous evening now seemed ridiculous. He went boldly to the door of the church and flung it open: the clearing lay before him, gray and still in the light of the setting moon. It was the middle of October now, and the grass sparkled here and there with an edge of frost. Judging by the moon it was already after cockcrow. Alain strode round the church a few times, stamping his feet and stretching his arms to take away the stiffness of sleeping in armor, then went back in and drowsed for another hour. The morning chorus of the forest birds awakened him once more.

Eline had said that Tiarnán, if he was coming, should arrive about an hour after dawn. Reluctantly—because he again believed that his presence at the chapel was pointless—Alain looked for the entrance to the bell tower. He found it to the right of the altar, and almost decided not to use it. The tower itself was solid enough—stone-built and squat, like the chapel—but inside there was nothing but a ladder leading up to the single bell, and a rope hanging down from it. No comfortable platform to sit on while he waited—not even a stair. Eventually, however, he climbed reluctantly up the ladder and propped himself against the wall at the top, looking out through the wicker surround of the bell. By changing position and turning his neck he could see the whole circuit of the clearing. He ate some more of his journey bread and had a drink of watered wine from his flask.

He'd only been watching for half an hour when there was a sudden flash of movement in the path that led to the road, and then Tiarnán walked quickly into the clearing. He was dressed in his plain green hunting clothes, hooded against the chill of the autumn morning, but his light, rapid step was instantly recognizable. Alain caught his breath at the unexpectedness of it. Tiarnán started to go around the side of the chapel, then paused and turned back toward the church door, disappearing from view in the shadow of the wall. There was a small bell hanging by the door as well as the larger one next to Alain's head, and it rang sweet and high for a moment, then stopped. Alain, waiting for his rival to appear again in the clearing, suddenly heard his footsteps in the church behind him. Tiarnán had come to consult the hermit, his confessor. Alain clutched his sword, not daring to move. He tried to remember where he'd left his helmet—was it behind the door, or right up by the altar in plain sight? He tried to think of ways to explain what he was doing up the bell tower of St. Mailon's. The worst thing was, if Tiarnán found him, he would probably think it was funny. "Are you as much afraid of me as that, Alain de Fougères?" he would say with that superior smile, and Alain would be ridiculous again, the man who hid up a ladder when he saw his rival. He set his teeth and prayed frantically to Saint Mailon that nobody would try to ring the big bell.

A minute later, a tall man in a plain brown robe came out of the trees along the same path; from his viewpoint, Alain could clearly see the neat clerical tonsure in the graying black hair. Judicaël the hermit—a younger man than Alain had expected. He went into the church, and a moment later Alain heard his voice, very close in the chapel below.

"I thought it would be you," said the hermit.

"God be with you, Father," replied Tiarnán's low voice. "Have you time for me?"

There was a sigh, and the sound of a man settling himself

on his knees. "You know I have. Well, *Dominus tecum,* my son."

"*Et cum spiritu tuo,* Father. Bless me, for I have sinned . . ."

Alain writhed and bit his knuckles. He had not the least desire to intrude on the privacy of the confessional, but he didn't dare come down. He pressed his hands against his ears and tried not to listen, but the voices were only a few feet away, and some base but irresistible curiosity ensured that he heard everything, despite himself.

Tiarnán solemnly confessed a number of venial sins: harshness to a servant; anger over some lawsuit; eating a pottage made with meat broth on a fish day. The priest listened patiently, assigned him a penance of prayers, and absolved him. There was a long silence, and then the hermit said, "Your wife has not come back to you, then?"

"No," said Tiarnán. The low, light voice was unexpectedly wretched.

"And will she be coming here to talk to me?"

"She said she might. But I don't think she will."

"You've seen her, then, the past week?"

"I went to Iffendic last Tuesday. She looked at me as though I were a monster. Even her sister has finally noticed that all is not well between us. When it was time to go to bed, Eline . . . she would not even sleep in the same room as me. I lay down to rest on the floor, but she still huddled awake in the bed, and every time I stirred, she gasped. I couldn't bear it; I went home in the middle of the night."

There was another silence.

"I should not have told her, I know!" Tiarnán exclaimed vehemently. "I certainly shouldn't have told her so soon. She did love me. If we'd had even a year together, she wouldn't be able to reject me like this. But she promised it would make no difference!"

"What you told her would make a difference to most people, I think," said the priest drily. "Tiarnán my son, God has given you an atonement for what you are. If you can bear it with humility and courage, it will lead you to his mercy."

"I have borne it humbly! I've given her what she wanted—

time, freedom to think among her own kin, money. Everything she's asked me for. I go to visit her at her sister's like a penitent with bowed head. In response she seems to loathe me even more than she did at first. I thought when she went to Iffendic that it would be for a week, a fortnight, but it's been over a month, and there's no sign of her coming home! What am I to *do*, Judicaël?"

There was a pause, and then the hermit said slowly, "Am I right in thinking that your mother was cousin to her grandfather?"

"You think," said Tiarnán in a harsh voice, "I should get the marriage annulled on the grounds of consanguinity?"

"You could get it so annulled, then?"

"She has not asked me to."

"Have you offered it?"

"She has not asked it! And I do not want it. I married her because she had the best part of my heart, and she has that still. She hasn't asked for that, Judicaël, and she must be aware of it."

"She is a woman and barred from the courts. It may not have entered her mind as something she *could* ask for."

There was a pause, and then Tiarnán said, "She keeps saying, 'Give me time; I'm trying to understand; give me time.' She must *want* to understand, and come home. And it's such a harmless thing!"

"No," the hermit answered sharply. "It isn't that. It's done harm now, to her and to you. It takes a rough man to say 'I told you so' to a bleeding victim, but, child, I wish you'd stopped years ago."

"I can't. I need it. I hate the smell of my own skin after a few weeks without it, and I make all the household miserable with my temper."

"That could have been dealt with — but the damage is done. Well, if neither you nor she wants the marriage annulled, perhaps you should bring her home. You say her sister realizes now that something's wrong; it would probably be easier for everyone if she went back to Talensac. If she's trying to understand, she'll understand more easily where she can see you, even if you sleep in another room. The imagination can shape devils more freely in darkness than when it has real forms to feed upon in daylight."

"Yes!" said Tiarnán, eagerly now. "Yes, I'll bring her home. She'll have to see then that I'm no monster."

"You'll go fetch her . . . tomorrow?" said the priest, and there was an edged significance to the word.

There was a silence.

"You never come here so early just to see me," the hermit said wearily. "I know that. I know what you've come for. You should have stopped years ago, but you should certainly stop now."

"I need it," replied Tiarnán defensively. "Now especially."

"You should look to God for support in your troubles, not to the forest of Broceliande! You come here in those clothes with that look in your eyes, and I know what you're thinking of, even when you're confessing your sins before our Lord and Savior Jesus Christ. I know it! I've been drunk on the beauty of creation myself, many times, though never so deep as you. But drunkenness of any sort is a sin, and more trap than escape in the end. Go home, Tiarnán. Bad luck will come of it if you go hunting today. I can sense it; you came into my prayers suddenly last night, and I was troubled for you. Please, pray here, and then go home."

Silence.

"Well, then!" said the priest, grunting as he got up. "I'll be off to my vegetable patch and my prayers, and stay well away from the whole business."

"God be with you, Father," said Tiarnán.

"Oh, child!" cried the hermit with anguish. "Of all men on earth, you are the one closest to my own heart—and because of that, I've advised you most badly. I know well enough what the world and the Church would say about it, and I should have been harsher on you years ago. God and his saints preserve you."

The priest came out of the chapel and walked out of the

clearing with long strides, not looking back. Alain chewed his knuckles, trying to grasp what he'd heard, and growing increasingly afraid as he did. It seemed a long time before Tiarnán, too, left the church.

Alain watched, scarcely daring to breathe, as the figure in the green hunting clothes walked slowly into the churchyard. It looked back at the path to the road—then turned and went the other way, toward the forest behind the church. At the edge of the trees, where the undergrowth was thick, it stopped. It knelt and heaved up one of the boundary stones, a large, rounded stone partially hidden by a bush. Carefully, it propped the stone up on one edge with a stick. Then it pulled off its tunic, folded it, and set it in the hollow under the stone.

Alain let out his breath in a hiss of shock. Almost as though he'd heard, Tiarnán lifted his head and looked around; Alain had to stop himself from ducking his head. He reminded himself that the wicker screen that protected the bell from the rain would look solid from a distance. Tiarnán stood still for a moment, his shirt showing white against the gold-splashed brown of the October trees. Then he edged deeper into the undergrowth and continued to undress. Alain's heart seemed to beat harder and harder, sounding hollow in his ears and making him dizzy. He felt that he was witnessing something which should never be seen, a violation of nature—and he stared so fixedly that his dry eyes burned.

Tiarnán sat down to remove his boots and his hose, then stood, his nakedness half-concealed by the bushes. He turned toward the church and bowed his head for a moment, his hands crossed on his chest. Alain wondered incredulously if he were praying—then noticed the movement of the hands, as though they were pulling something away from the heart. Tiarnán held the whatever-it-was out for a moment, then bent over and set it down on top of his clothes beneath the stone.

There was no slow transformation. One moment a man stood among the bushes; the next, there was a wolf. It was as though the eye, sweeping the clearing, had misinterpreted the shapes it saw and imagined a man where there was only an animal.

The wolf lifted its nose, scenting the air. It seemed uneasy. It took a few steps out into the clearing, its ears flat against its head—then shook itself, and turned back. With its forepaw, it knocked away the stick which propped up the hollow stone, and the stone fell back into place with a soft thud. The wolf sniffed it, then slid off among the trees and was gone.

Alain stayed at the top of the ladder for a long time. His legs were trembling, and he could not trust himself to come down. He began to cry, but he couldn't have said whether the tears sprang from horror, terror, or shocked amazement.

At last, he slid unsteadily down the ladder and stumbled back into the main body of the church. His helmet was on the floor, only partly concealed by the half-open door; he was lucky the others hadn't noticed it. He put it on and fastened the strap, then went to the door. The churchyard was peaceful and deserted, and it was still only the middle of the morning, though it seemed to Alain to have been days since he woke. He drew his sword, took a deep breath, and strode toward the boundary stone, his legs stiff with terror.

When he heaved the stone up, the clothes lay beneath it in a hollow lined with dry leaves. The other thing Tiarnán had left there, the thing he had drawn out of himself on crossed hands, was not to be seen. But Eline had said it was probably invisible, and something set the hair upright on Alain's forearms as he looked, so that he had no doubt that it was there. He knelt and propped the stone up with the same stick Tiarnán had used. He had to put his sword down to do so, and he glanced about fearfully, listening for any rustling warning that the wolf had come back. There were only the usual noises of the forest, the chirruping of birds and the shifting of the leaves. With fumbling hands, Alain rolled the clothes up into a bundle and took them out from beneath the stone. He tried to fit them into his food wallet, but they were bulky, thick weaves for the cold nights of early autumn and far too big. He didn't dare walk off with Tiarnán's clothes visible in his hands. Anyone who saw would be able to call him a murderer. Fumbling with haste, he cut the wallet open and wrapped the leather around the outside of the clothes, tying it in a roll with the cord. Then he jumped up, picked up his sword, and hurried along the path to the stream where he'd left his horse. Halfway there he realized he'd forgotten to let the stone down again—but he was afraid to go back.

His bay stallion was grazing peacefully beside the stream. He saddled and bridled it hurriedly, and shoved the leather package into the saddlebag. It was too big to fit properly, but he pulled at the buckles on the bag and got it in. He mounted, started along the path—and had to dismount again for the branches. Leading the horse, stumbling over his sword's scabbard, with the blade itself wavering in his free hand, he at last got back to the church, past the church, onto the path that would bring him to the road. He was almost there when he saw a flash of brown through the undergrowth and stopped, heart thundering, holding his sword before him.

Judicaël appeared from a side path which, in the dusk of the evening before, Alain had not noticed. Seen on a level, the hermit had a long, narrow face dominated by a pair of intense dark eyes; he looked to be in his mid-forties. He was carrying a bucket of water, which he dropped when he saw Alain.

"Lord have mercy!" he exclaimed, looking from Alain's face to the sword in his hand. "What have you come here for?"

Alain sheathed the sword. "I came to pray in the church," he said. "I'm sorry I startled you, Father. I had my sword out because I saw a wolf in the forest." He was amazed at his own coolness.

Judicaël bent slowly to retrieve his bucket. "I didn't hear you come. I am the priest in charge of this place. Did you wish to speak with me?"

"I only stopped to pay my respects to the saint," returned Alain. "I was just leaving."

"Something has frightened you," said Judicaël flatly. "Your face is still white. What was it?" His searching, sceptical eyes reminded Alain suddenly and uncomfortably of Tiher.

"The wolf startled me," Alain replied loftily, "but you're mistaken, Father: I wasn't frightened. I'm a son of the lord of

Fougères and not frightened of any animal, however savage. Good day to you." He clicked his tongue to his horse and started on along the path.

But Judicaël had stepped in front of him. "You're Alain de Fougères? I've heard of you. When did you come here? And why?"

"I came to pray at your church, Father," said Alain proudly. "Does that offend you? If so, I shall stay away in the future. Now, get out of my way: I'm expected back at the court, and I must hurry."

Judicaël didn't move. His own face had gone white. Alain realized that the priest had guessed *which* son of the lord of Fougères he was: he must have heard the name from Tiarnán, in connection with Eline. That had been enough to let him guess the whole plot, and know that Tiarnán had been betrayed.

Alain realized suddenly that it didn't matter. There was nothing Judicaël could do. He didn't dare even admit that he knew what Tiarnán was: the bishop of Rennes was already uneasy about the hermit, and if Judicaël confessed that he'd tolerated magical practices by a member of his flock, he'd certainly lose his priesthood, and perhaps his life as well. Judicaël had no way of knowing what Alain had in his saddlebags, and even if he had known, and understood its significance, he couldn't take Tiarnán's things by force from an armed knight. Tiarnán's only defender had already lost the contest.

Abruptly, all Alain's remaining fear was buried in a storm of joy and triumph. Tiarnán had indeed lost—lost the struggle, lost his wife, lost everything. And Alain had won. Fortune's wheel had completed its turn. Eline, and Talensac, and all that Tiarnán had owned would find another lord now, and that lord would be Alain. It had been stupid to be afraid of the wolf. What could a wolf do to an armed knight? What use were teeth against armor and a sword? Tiarnán didn't even have a voice to complain with: he would have to go howl his loss to the moon.

Alain laughed out loud at the thought. He tugged at his horse's bridle again and forced his way past the hermit. Judicaël staggered against a tree, then straightened and hurried after Alain as far as the road. Giddy with joy, Alain jumped up into the saddle and gathered up the reins.

"Wait," said Judicaël hoarsely. "Wait—what you're doing is wrong. It's the wrong way. Only grief will come of it."

"I don't know what you're talking about!" shouted Alain and laughed triumphantly. He set his heels to his stallion's sides and galloped away.

VIII

The wolf did not return to the chapel until the evening, three days later. He approached the building cautiously, as he always did, circling downwind of it and pausing frequently to sniff the air. There were no scents but the ones expected: leaf mold; earth; a rabbit; the recognized scents of Judicaël the hermit and the goat he kept for milk; wood smoke, hours old; other human scents, faint and unstable with age; the sweetness of the herbs in the hermit's garden. The human scent, even a known human scent, was dangerous and to be avoided whenever possible—but it came from the hut by the stream near the road and not from the chapel itself. Reassured, the wolf trotted through the thick undergrowth toward the boundary stone behind the church.

Even before he reached it, he realized that something was wrong. The usual sense of everything within him realigning itself as he approached, the tingling of each hair and the awakening—that was gone. He ran the last few paces toward the stone and stopped before it. It was still propped up on its edge, and the space beneath it was empty.

The wolf's mind was more animal than human. It took him some time to comprehend what had happened. He sniffed the empty space and pawed it, then knocked away the stick and let the stone fall. He circled back the way he had come and approached again. Only when the space remained empty, and his paw failed to drag out from under the stone the thing that was not there, did he begin to understand. He whined and began to cast about for a scent. It had rained during the time he'd been away, and there was not much trace of the intruder, but here and there—under the bush that half-concealed the stone;

on the stick; at the side of the stone itself—he caught a whiff of an unfamiliar human smell, rank with fear. He cast about more widely, trying to track it, and caught it here and there, but never enough to follow. He sat down; got up again; ran back and forth beneath the trees; and at last crouched, shaking, his ears flat against his head. From a deeper and more fundamental part of him came a desire to scream in horror, and it confused him: he had neither instincts nor ability for screaming. After a time, a single human word surfaced in his mind: "Help." He turned away from the stone and made his way slowly through the forest to the small round hut beside the stream.

It was a long time before he could bring himself to go near. It was contrary to all his instincts to approach men: the shape and smell of them were flagged with warnings of death. He crouched outside the small garden plot, trembling, listening to the priest's voice saying the office of Compline, distorted and unintelligible to his wolf's ears. But at last, when the voice stopped, the deeper part of himself forced him through the garden to scratch at the door.

Judicaël had been lying down to sleep when the scratch came. He was heavy with exhaustion: since meeting Alain he had been keeping a vigil every night from Lauds to Prime, preparing himself to face disgrace and possible death. He knew nothing about the thing that Alain had stolen: he'd never wanted to know any details of how Tiarnán transformed himself, and Tiarnán had never told him any. He had indeed guessed that Tiarnán's wife had sent her former suitor to the chapel, but suspected only that Alain had seen the transformation and had gone to inform the authorities. Soon, he thought, men from the bishop's court would arrive to question him about the werewolf and to set a trap for it. Then there would follow a long nightmare of courts and angry interrogations, public humiliations, and the anguished bewilderment of friends. For Tiarnán it would end inevitably in a slow and painful death, and for himself . . . who could say what the Church would decide? All he could do was commit himself, and Tiarnán, to the mercy of God. At the scratch on the door, his first thought was that the devil had come to tempt him with false promises of safety.

Judicaël sat up and crossed himself. His windowless hut was completely dark: he hadn't bothered to build up the fire during the evening, and there was only the faintest of glows from the embers in the hearth. The scratching came again. Judicaël whispered a prayer to Saint Mailon and felt for his breviary on the table beside his bed. Its leather binding, soft at the edges from use, comforted him. He clasped it firmly, went to the door, and flung it open.

The wolf in the moonlight outside leapt backward and ran to the edge of the garden—then stopped, trembling, tail between his legs. Judicaël stared for a moment, then lowered his breviary. The wolf whined and moved back toward him, then checked and stood with his head down, watching. The moonlight gleamed greenly in his eyes. Judicaël took a step forward. The wolf didn't move. The hermit moved closer again, and finally dropped to his knees on the path in front of the wolf. "Tiarnán?" he whispered.

The wolf whined. His ears could not hear the low notes of most consonants, and the name that had once belonged to him was only a confusing hiatus: Iarr'a? Judicaël held his breviary out, and the wolf sniffed at the book, then whined again and licked the priest's hand.

From the time that Tiarnán was orphaned, Judicaël had thought of him as a foster son, the child he would never have in the flesh. He had always believed that to see the one he loved best transformed into an animal would horrify him. Faced with this cowering beast, though, he felt only an overwhelming pity. Proud, self-possessed Tiarnán reduced to this!

He stroked the wolf's fur and spoke gently, and the animal whined in a distress that no animal could know. After a little while, the wolf tugged at his sleeve, led him up the hill, and showed him a hollow stone behind the chapel. Then Judicaël understood what Alain de Fougères had really done, and was appalled far more than he had been afraid.

On the evening of the twentieth of October, there was a knock on the door of Talensac manor house, and the clerk Kenmarcoc opened it to find Judicaël standing in the dusk outside. The clerk gaped for a moment. Hermits were not supposed to leave their hermitages. Some put the world behind them so completely that they enclosed themselves in their cells with the office for the dead. Judicaël had never gone so far — but equally he had not left St. Mailon's since he first went there, eleven years before.

"Christ and his saints have mercy!" exclaimed Kenmarcoc, crossing himself. "Father Judicaël! I pray God it's not bad news of the machtiern that brings you here?"

The old word "machtiern" leapt out at Judicaël and touched him painfully with pride. That was what the people of Talensac made of the boy he'd helped to raise for them. Not "lord" or "master," but guardian of the law. He answered the question with a misleading shake of his head. "I saw Tiarnán four days ago," he said. "He asked me to speak to his wife for him. He said she was at Iffendic, and I went there this morning, but it seems she's come home."

The explanation was natural enough — a hermit might leave his wilderness for the solemn purpose of reconciling an especially dear pupil and his wife. Even fully accounted for, however, Judicaël's presence flabbergasted Kenmarcoc. He believed firmly that a holy hermit was far superior to a flesh-loving failed priest like himself, and to have so admirable a creature on his doorstep disconcerted him more than if it had been the duke himself. He gabbled out an agreement — yes, Eline had returned to Talensac the day before — then remembered his manners, begged Judicaël to come in, and began shouting for his wife to fetch food and drink. "You will eat and drink with us, Father, and spend the night under our roof?" he asked anxiously, as a crowd of children and servants gathered to gawk at the holy man.

"That will depend on the lady of the house, won't it?" replied Judicaël. But he came in and sat down at the table near the fire. It was more than fifteen miles from St. Mailon's to Talensac by way of Iffendic, and he ached with weariness. His heart was aching, too. He had left the wolf in the forest near his hut. It had watched him go with human hope in its eyes, but he knew that there was no hope for it if this mission failed—and the signs were not encouraging.

"I'm sure the lady will be pleased to welcome you," said Kenmarcoc, while his wife, Lanthildis, hurried in with a jug of wine and a cup for the visitor. "As I said, she came back from her sister's yesterday. If Tiarnán asked you to speak to her, he must have told you that they quarreled. The silly girl took exception to his hunting trips. I don't know why she expected a husband to stay beside her every hour, adoring her, but when he didn't she felt herself ill-used and took herself off to her sister's, making up some excuse about needing to learn housekeeping. She did need that, but she could have learned better from my Lanthildis than from anyone at Iffendic, from all I've heard. My daughter Driken went with her, as serving maid, poor thing; she didn't like Iffendic at all, and cried from pure homesickness every night. She says it was a scandal, the way the lady treated the machtiern when he came to visit her. Acted as though she was too fine to say three words to him, and made him sleep on the floor. I'd have given her a beating and dragged her home by the hair, but he was quiet and patient, and it seems to have worked. At any rate, she's home, and says she's determined to make him welcome when he comes back. She's over at the dairy now. Shall I tell her you've come, Father?"

"Let me catch my breath," said Judicaël. He had refused the wine Lanthildis offered, but the woman was back with water now, and he let her fill his cup. The crowd of servants were whispering to one another that it must be because of Judicaël's prayers that the lady's heart had been softened. God would answer such a holy man. Judicaël drank his water slowly. The noisy admiration around him disturbed him, and he wished himself back in the forest, where the birds sang without regard to the spirituality of man.

"The machtiern is still off hunting," Kenmarcoc went on. " — I suppose you guessed that already."

"Yes," said Judicaël, and was silent.

Kenmarcoc felt rebuked. He was always ready to feel rebuked by Judicaël. "I've already said too much about the affairs of my masters," he said penitently.

Judicaël smiled. He had a peculiarly sweet and gentle smile, unexpected in such an intense, ascetic face. Kenmarcoc had almost forgotten it, and there was an element of surprise in his own answering smile. "You've talked honestly," said the hermit. "So, your daughter Driken is the lady's serving maid? I remember her as barely higher than my knee."

Driken herself pushed shyly through the crowd around the hermit and knelt to get his blessing. Judicaël made the sign of the cross above her head, then leaned forward to kiss the neat parting of her lank black hair.

The door opened again and Eline came in, pale in the dimness and shadow-eyed. She stopped in puzzlement — then recognized Judicaël, whom she'd seen before on a visit to St. Mailon's with her father. The puzzlement was instantly replaced by resentment and hostility.

Judicaël rose slowly to his aching feet. "May God keep you, Lady," he said. "Your husband asked me to speak to you on his behalf. May we speak privately?"

Eline hesitated. She had not the least wish to speak to Tiarnán's too-tolerant confessor and was tempted to say so — but that would scandalize his hallful of admirers. She had to pretend that she was reconciled to Tiarnán and awaiting his return to make peace with him: she and Alain had agreed on that. She forced herself to smile. "Of course, Father," she said. "I'm honored that you've come so far. Can I offer you some refreshment?"

"Let us talk first," said Judicaël. "The chapel would be the best place."

The manor house's chapel was a small wooden building, little more than a shed, on the other side of the hall from the kitchen.

Judicaël had occasionally conducted services in it himself when he was parish priest of Talensac, and its familiarity was disconcerting. When his hand reached instinctively for the candles in the bronze chest by the door—kept there to protect them from the mice—and found them ready waiting, it was like reaching backward in time. He remembered saying prayers before the same altar, with Tiarnán—a small, thin, big-eyed boy—watching him solemnly. The memory was peculiarly painful, and he had to stand still for a moment. Kenmarcoc had followed Eline and the hermit with a rushlight lantern from the hall. He lit two of the candles, set them in the holders on the altar, and left the two to talk.

Judicaël crossed himself and knelt before the altar with bowed head. Eline's smiling, deceitful answer had filled him with a rush of anger that verged on hatred, and he struggled to surrender it. The girl was young and inexperienced, he told himself. She had been deceived in her marriage and she was very much afraid. God had created her, and Tiarnán had loved her: two reasons that Judicaël should hold her in affection. He had not come to condemn her, but to help her. He was quite certain that this thing she had done would blight her life and her immortal soul unless she acted at once to undo it. He must speak from that awareness, and from love, and not out of anger. *O God, O my dear Lord Christ*, Judicaël prayed, with a sudden flare of passion, *soften her heart, and let her listen to me!*

Eline had also knelt before the altar, though well to one side. She watched the hermit impatiently through her eyelashes. Alain had told her how he'd met Judicaël just as he was leaving St. Mailon's. This was hypocrisy, she thought angrily. Pretending to pray when really they both knew he'd come to ask her to tolerate Tiarnán's abominable practices.

After what seemed ages, Judicaël crossed himself again and turned to Eline. "May I speak freely, Lady?" he asked.

"There's no point in speaking at all if we don't both speak freely, Father Judicaël," she replied tartly.

Judicaël nodded. "Yes. Lady, I know that you quarreled with your husband and why. I have not come here to argue with you the rights and wrongs of that, but to help you set fear aside and act justly. However the situation appears in the eyes of God, for you to conspire with a lover to betray your husband will only make it worse."

"However the situation appears to God?" repeated Eline sarcastically. "How do you think it appears, Father? Tiarnán told me that you were not sure whether he was committing a sin or not. But I would have thought," savagely now, "that there was no question how the situation would appear to our mother the Church. The most mercy Tiarnán should have expected was the chance to repent before being burned at the stake."

Judicaël flinched but he answered her evenly. "Which is why I repent that I didn't advise him better," he said. "You don't need to tell me that God will hold me to account for all my dealings with your husband. But you haven't sent him to the stake, Lady. That's why I've come."

Eline sniffed. "We were supposed to be speaking freely. Say what you want."

"Your de Fougères knight has taken something, something that belonged to Tiarnán. I've come to beg you to give it back, for your own soul's health as much as for your husband's sake."

"Has my husband been to see you, then?" asked Eline. "He came running to you, did he? Running on four legs, and scratching at your door like a dog, begging you to find the humanity he so carelessly left beneath a stone?"

Judicaël's face changed. It seemed to grow narrower in the candlelight, and paler, and his dark eyes became even more intense as he grew angry despite himself. He thought of the wolf cowering in the moonlight outside his door. Could this beautiful child really dismiss a man who had loved her to that forever, and in a tone of such satisfied disdain?

He forced himself to answer quietly. "Yes. If you give it back now, he can still come home without scandal. People will say his hunting trip this time was a little longer than usual, no more. But each day you wait will make it harder to explain where he's been, harder to restore him. Harder for you to repent."

"What do I have to repent of?" demanded Eline angrily. "I

was tricked into marriage with a monster. I've escaped in the only way I could."

Judicaël's patience snapped. "Don't you see what you are doing, Lady?" he asked furiously. "You didn't want the shame of a public trial, so you betrayed your husband secretly. You are pretending to be his loving wife—and soon, I think, his grieving widow—so that you can inherit all his lands and possessions. I think you mean to take a new husband with the old one still living. What good do you think will come of so many sins and lies? Everything you get by them will turn to bitterness, and the fear of what you have done will poison everything you touch. You said just now that you were tricked into marriage, and got out in the only way you could—but there are three other ways you could have chosen, all better than the one you took. The first was to bring the whole matter before the judgment of the Church. We neither of us want that judgment, but at least we would all have had to submit to it. The second was to take your dowry and a settlement from your husband and retire to a convent. I think that does not appeal to you. But the third is this. When your husband last came to me for counsel, I suggested that he offer you an annulment of your marriage. It would be possible, and I am ready to promise you that Tiarnán will now agree to it. Give back what your lover took from St. Mailon's, leave your husband honestly, and marry your lover truthfully. Otherwise, I am afraid for all of you."

Eline was silent for a minute, her head bowed. "You churchmen are always telling women that they must be loyal to their husbands," she said at last. "If he is harsh to you and neglects you, bear it patiently. If he beats you, be humble. If he goes with other women, try to be cheerful and uncomplaining. Your husband, say all the lords of the Church and all the lords of the land, your husband, woman, is your lord and master, and you should fawn upon him like a spaniel. But one thing I've never heard them say, and that is that a wife is obliged to accept damnation for the sake of a husband who is damned." She looked up and met the hermit's eyes. "I know about these annulments. Every husband who gets tired of his wife suddenly discovers that he's related to her, and calls in witnesses to prove it. There are always plenty of men to laugh at the wife, and say, 'I'd be tired of her, too.' And I know what they say about me already. 'Silly woman,' they say, 'making such a fuss about her husband going hunting!' If Tiarnán got this annulment, I'd be ridiculed. I probably couldn't get the whole of my dowry back. As for my maidenhead, no one can ever restore that. And if Alain is brave enough to stay faithful to me and marry me despite all that, the whole court will whisper that that's why Tiarnán suddenly discovered that we were related: because I was unfaithful to him. It's always the woman's fault, isn't it? Alain and I would be left impoverished, ridiculous, and disgraced, eking out a living on whatever Alain's father would spare us—and I know Juhel de Fougères; he's a hard man. Tiarnán, meanwhile, would have Talensac, and he'd be perfectly free to remarry, probably to an heiress—that pious Penthièvre woman, perhaps—and if he did, you may be sure he would keep his mouth shut about what he does when he goes hunting. And his new wife, like me, would be married to an animal, a filthy, savage *brute*," her voice rose hysterically, "but unlike me, she'd never find out. Not until it was too late. Then on the Day of Judgment, when she went before the throne of God, the recording angel would say to her, 'We gave you a lovely body to be a temple of the Holy Spirit; but you have given it to wolves, and slept with wild beasts. Depart from here, you wicked one, and be forever accursed.'" Eline drew in her breath sharply, and cried, in a much louder voice, "No! No, I won't agree to be the humble, submissive wife, and I won't let him drag anyone else to damnation! I was an innocent virgin when I married Tiarnán and he wronged me. I will not take an annulment and go quietly away to poverty and disgrace, leaving him in wealth and honor! I will keep Talensac. He owes it to me, after what I suffered from him!"

Judicaël stared at her, stunned. "But it isn't that way," he said. "You didn't marry an animal! No recording angel would ever say otherwise, or punish you for an abomination of which you were never guilty."

"You have no right to advise me!" Eline said vehemently. "You've admitted yourself that you advised him badly. You can't come here and preach me a sermon. The bishop of Rennes has already had complaints about you. Without Tiarnán's protection, you would probably have been called to account long ago. Well, don't expect any protection from the lords of Talensac now! If you're stripped of your priesthood it's less than you deserve. As for Tiarnán, he *chose* to be what he is now. Let him stay that way. I'm not giving anything back." Eline got proudly to her feet and snatched up one of the candlesticks. She blew the other out and marched to the door, then paused with her hand on the latch. "And if you say anything about this to anyone else, I will simply deny it. It won't hurt me, and it won't help Tiarnán. But it will certainly make trouble for you." She flung open the door and strode back toward the hall.

Judicaël stood for a moment in the door of the empty chapel. Failure, total and irredeemable, weighed on him so heavily that he could barely see. He had not comprehended the depth of the girl's bitterness, her hysterical sense of defilement. He had hurt her when he should have healed, and she would not hear him again. He would have to go back to his hermitage, and the wolf . . . the wolf would remain until its death a prison for the soul of the man he loved as a son. It seemed for an agonized moment too much to bear. He turned back toward the chapel's dark interior. The cross gleamed faintly on the lightless altar. That had once seemed too much to bear, too: *Father, if it be thy will, take this cup away from me.* Judicaël knelt painfully in silence and bowed his head.

Kenmarcoc and his wife hurried in a few minutes later, looking apprehensive. Eline had stormed into the manor house, slammed down her candlestick, and gone upstairs in tears: it was painfully obvious that Judicaël's counsel had not pleased her. Lanthildis smiled nervously. "Will you be staying to supper, Father Judicaël?" she asked.

"No," said Judicaël, and climbed heavily to his feet. "I'll go down to my old house in the village and stay with Father Corentin. It's been a long time since I've been in Talensac, and who knows if I will ever come here again?"

When Tiarnán had been missing for a week, Eline sent villagers from Talensac to all the neighboring manors to ask for news of him. When he'd been gone ten days, a message was sent to the duke, and a wider search was instituted, a search that grew less and less hopeful as the days went by. Everyone knew of Tiarnán's habit of disappearing into the forest for days at a time, and the forest was huge, full of dark peat bogs and dangerous animals. It was impossible to search thoroughly for a man who might be anywhere within its boundaries. The peasants of Talensac whispered in dismay that the machtiern, grieving over his quarrel with his wife, had ridden off into the hollow hills and would never come back. In Moncontour and in several other manors, they said that he'd been murdered by Éon, the werewolf. More prosaic communities shook their heads over the dangers of hunting alone. Duke Hoel waited for a month with gradually decreasing hope, and at last declared that his favorite was dead, and sent one of his own officials to take charge of Talensac and set the estate in order while its lord's widow went to court to do homage for her husband's lands.

The ducal court had by then moved to the castle of Ploërmel, which lay in the forest a day's ride southwest of Rennes, and only half a day's from Talensac. Ploërmel was only a village, and the old-fashioned wooden castle sprawled comfortably within it, more hunting lodge than fortress. The gardens were large and very fine. Marie was sitting in them when Eline arrived. It was a chill, damp day at the end of November and really too cold to sit outside, but she'd wanted to be alone. It was an empty gray afternoon; she had a book, but after reading three pages and realizing that she hadn't taken in a word, she put it down and simply sat, looking at the sparrows hopping among the branches of the rose arbor above her. After a while, she heard laughter and greeting from the Great Hall of the castle behind her, and she guessed who had just come in. But she didn't go inside. The thought of having to smile at the company and offer condolences appalled her.

A little later, a man began to sing. The sound carried out through the heavy air, clear and sweet.

> "The leaves are falling from the trees:
>   now all that's green has died.
>   All heat has slipped from everything
>   the sun has turned aside.
>
> "No river now that's not in flood,
>   no meadow flowers catch the light.
>   Our golden sun has taken flight,
>   and snowy day follows freezing night.
>
> "Now everything that is, is chilled —
>   but I alone am filled with heat.
>   My heart within me's set alight:
>   the fire? a girl, for whom it beats.
>
> "On kisses the fire is fed within
>   and on the girl's soft touch.
>   Light's light shines in her eye; this age
>   contains no other such.
>
> "Greek fire, sad thing, can be put out
>   if splashed with sour wine.
>   But my fire yields to no sour thing:
>   a richer drink I need for mine."

Marie remembered Tiarnán in his huntsman's green that spring, leading her confidently through the whispering darkness of the forest. She remembered him standing in the Great Hall at Rennes, looking into his bride's face with solemn joy.

> The leaves are falling from the trees
>   now all that's green has died.

Suddenly she found that she was crying. Leaves would return to the forest, but Tiarnán was gone, and earth's new season would not match or renew what she had lost. Marie leaned forward, cradling the pain, and whispered a prayer for the dead.

There was a crunch of feet on the gravel path, and she looked up to see Tiher standing over her. She wiped her eyes hurriedly.

Tiher tried to look at her critically. Shapelessly swathed in a plain gray cloak trimmed with rabbit fur, and huddled on the bench with her nose and cheeks red from cold and her eyes from crying, why should she stir a man's heart? It was no use: his heart picked out the odd detail—the way one arm in its tight sleeve braced gracefully against the bench; the clear, unashamed sweep of her beautiful eyes as they lifted to him—and it was stirred anyway. It stirred too much these days. He would have to do something about that. "You're crying for Tiarnán?" he asked, sitting down on the bench beside her.

There was no point in lying about it now. Marie nodded. "I have a right to grieve for him," she said defensively. "He saved me from Éon of Moncontour."

Tiher scuffed the gravel with his foot. He had been in the hall when Eline came in, but he'd walked out when Alain started singing love songs to her. He disliked his cousin's feverish excitement about the young widow, and wished Alain would be less blatant about his hopes. The way Eline encouraged her old suitor disgusted him. It was true that he, too, had been hoping that Alain might now be able to marry the woman he adored, but this was too soon, too crude, too *convenient*. Perhaps Alain was right, and Eline really had preferred him all along, and only taken Tiarnán for the sake of Talensac. But to listen so greedily to the man she wanted, when she'd just acquired the land she wanted through tragedy, seemed discourteous to the dead. Here was Marie, with less cause, paying Tiarnán the tribute of her tears. Tiher looked again at her reddened eyes and sighed. Alain's precious swan was a cheap creature compared with this one.

"If *I* saved you," he said to Marie, "would that make you change your mind and accept me? Should I hire a party of ruffians and give them instructions to carry you off and stand over you with threatening gestures until I arrived to rescue you?"

She had recovered her poise by now and gave him a wide-eyed look of mock alarm. "Not real ruffians, please. Why don't you hire some peasants from your uncle's estate and get them to dress down a little? Oh yes, and borrow a pacing palfrey for the carrying part. I might as well be carried off in comfort."

"I'm not sure that would be convincing. I can just see Paul from my uncle's estate being ruffianly: 'I'll throttle 'ee then, if it please your ladyship. Oo, mind the ho-orse; mind the ho-orse! Fifteen marks he cost my lord last Michaelmas!'"

Marie laughed the soft gurgling laugh that always made Tiher grin in answer. "It wouldn't work with real ruffians, either," she said.

"No, I don't think it would," he said, the grin fading. "What was Tiarnán's secret? I've felt all along that if he'd wanted to, he could have taken your castle by storm."

Marie stared for a moment, surprised. Tiher was usually too sensitive to spoil his wit by touching on real pain. But he was looking at her with an unusually serious expression on his ugly face.

"I don't know," she said, answering the seriousness. "But even if he had been free, and had asked me to marry him, and I'd said yes—even then it would have been a mistake. I'd have had to betray my father to accept him."

"Your father, from all I've heard, never gave a moment's thought to your happiness from the minute you were born. He couldn't be bothered to arrange a marriage for you before he went off on crusade. He dumped you in a convent but refused you permission to take vows, in case later on he needed to toss you into the bargain of some alliance. Your father's overlord, Robert, is a perjured, violent, profane man little better than a bandit—no, worse than one! What has either of them ever done to deserve your loyalty?"

Marie was stung. She glared at Tiher with the proud lift of the head that always made his disobligingly susceptible heart skip a beat. "All the world knows that my father is a brave and honorable knight!" she said angrily. "And anyway, people don't have to *deserve* loyalty to get it. If Duke Hoel fulfills his obligations to you, then you're bound to be his liege man, whether he worries about your happiness or not. I can't just break off a loyalty I was born into. And I'd be stupid to choose two contradictory loyalties at once."

"You're really not going to marry any of us, are you?" said Tiber thoughtfully.

She met his eyes and found that they were sad. "No," she replied levelly, her anger fading. "I really am not going to marry any servant of Duke Hoel. It's what I've said all along."

"They ought to carve your image over the doors of convents," Tiher said. "An allegory of the Triumph of Virtue and Honor over Love. They can put me in as one of the poor lost souls crushed under your chariot." The words were light but the tone was bitter.

"Oh, Tiher!" Marie exclaimed with great tenderness. "You know perfectly well that you and I and all the court have had a delicious game with love all summer! We've all enjoyed it. You can't seriously expect me to believe that you, of all people, are going to die of a broken heart now you realize I meant what I said. You told me once yourself that if you have good soil and cultivate it properly, you can grow what you like in it. Even poor soil will produce something if you work it well. As you said, we can make do with such scrapings of happiness as we can find."

Tiher caught her hand. She had small, soft hands like a child's: there was no hint in them of the strength inside her. He ran his thumb along the index finger she always bit when she was distracted. "I think I could have been very happy with you," he told her, "even if you didn't have Chalandrey." Then he folded her into his arms, all billowing cloak, awkward elbows, and surprise, and kissed her.

When he let go, Marie slid away sideways along the bench and stared at him, flushed and gasping. Kiss still tingling on his lips, Tiher grinned. "I've been longing to do that ever since we caught up with you on the road to Bonne Fontaine," he told her. "Don't worry; I won't do it again. But I had to do it once. My sweet white hind, you unattainable animal, I'm giving up the chase. My heart's come into it too much, and there's no pleasure in it anymore. Since I can't have you, I must give you up. But let me say that, since you've lost one champion, I'll be your surety against a forced marriage. Of course, the duke doesn't want to force you into anything, and the duchess wouldn't let him if he did — but some of the Marcher lords have been pressing him to secure Chalandrey to the duchy, and if you have a champion at court it's a convenient excuse to do nothing."

Marie went even redder. She stifled a sharp cry of protest and tried to do the same with the even sharper pang of regret. "Thank you, Tiher," she whispered, struggling to keep her voice steady.

"Mind you, I'm no Tiarnán when it comes to fighting," he said with all his old lightness. "The thought of facing him on the field put the rest of us in a cold sweat. The thought of facing me will only bring out ordinary hot ones, from practicing sword swipes. But I should do as an excuse for the duke." He grinned again. "Better than Tiarnán, in fact. It's my uncle Juhel who's been pressing Hoel hardest." He got up.

"Tiher . . ." she said.

He paused, looking down at her with immense affection.

"I think I could have been very happy with you, too," she said quietly. "If I'd really been free to marry any of the knights at this court, it would have been you. I made up my mind on that a long time ago."

It took him a moment to take it in. Then he leaned over her, beaming, one hand against the rose arbor. "Really? So I'm a fool to back off now?"

"No. I'm not marrying anyone. We've agreed on that. But you are the one I like best." She looked up into his familiarly ugly face, and suddenly she felt an immense welling up of happiness, simply because he was who he was and they liked each other. "And I liked the kiss, too," she admitted.

"I'll give you another," he said, beaming wider and leaning closer.

"No, no! In fact . . ." She leapt up directly into his arms, flung her arms around him, and kissed him soundly. "There! I've given you your kiss back. We're quits now. And let's leave it at that."

"I suppose," he said, smiling into her face, "it's happiness enough."

IX

The court in November was less crowded than it had been in June, but if there were now beds enough, there remained a shortage of blankets, and the duchess assumed that Marie and Eline would once again share. Marie noticed that Eline looked displeased at the prospect, and quietly told the duchess that she thought the widow would prefer to be alone. It was clear that Eline had suffered considerably in the past few months. She had been slim before; she was now thin. Her collarbone pressed through her skin like a yoke, and her jaw was whittled to a point. Her eyes were deeply shadowed and moved restlessly, never fixing for long on the person she spoke to. There was a broody irritability about her, too, quite unlike her former happy, open impulsiveness. She still looked extraordinarily beautiful, however. Black suited her fair complexion admirably.

"Of course!" cried Havoise apologetically. "I'm sure it brings back painful memories just to be here, my dear: I'm sure you'd prefer to be alone. Let me see—I think there are plenty of blankets in the stables. Horse blankets, but perfectly clean and usable. If we put you in—"

"Never mind," snapped Eline with an impatience that would have been improper toward a duchess from anyone except a grieving young widow. "I'll share with Marie."

"I'm very happy to share, Lady Eline," put in Marie. "But please do say if you'd prefer to be alone."

At this Eline gave a weak smile. "I'd prefer not to be alone, Lady Marie. But thank you."

When they were in bed that night, lying side by side in the chill darkness under the pile of blankets, Marie at last found the strength to whisper, "I am very sorry for your loss, Lady Eline."

Eline was silent for a long time. In the blackness at Marie's side, her breathing was shallow and quick. "Do you remember when I was last at court," she said at last, "you wished me joy of discovering over many years all the many things Tiarnán had never told me about himself?"

"Yes. I am very sorry you never had the chance to learn them."

Eline shook her head; Marie felt, rather than saw, the movement. "No. I learned one of them, and it wasn't joyful at all. I'm glad I never had the chance to learn any more."

Shocked beyond words, Marie lay still.

"I won't say any more about it," Eline continued abruptly. "He's gone now; I won't speak ill of the dead. But marrying him was the greatest mistake I ever made, and I'm glad I'm free of him."

"I . . . I can't believe . . ." stammered Marie. "Whatever you discovered, it can't have been . . ."

"You think well of him because he rescued you from Éon of Moncontour," said Eline impatiently. "You didn't know him. He was a worse monster than the robber. I won't say any more about it! But you don't need to be sorry for me, not now."

Marie bit her lip, struggling to keep quiet. Everything she could think of to say seemed impertinent. She had not known Tiarnán. Perhaps he really had been a monster in private, and addicted to some unnatural perversion.

She could not, did not believe it. Not because she knew anything to convince herself that it was false, but simply because her heart and mind refused to be convinced otherwise. Eline, they insisted, had taken offense at gossip and quarreled bitterly with her husband without real cause. But to think that ignorantly was grossly unfair to Eline.

"I will pray for you," Marie said at last, solemnly. "For you, and for your husband's soul."

"Thank you," Eline replied, quietly now. "I'd welcome your prayers, Marie."

In the end Marie prayed for most of that night, in a torment of denial. She had accepted Tiarnán's marriage and endured his death, but she could not accept the destruction of her faith in him: to do so would destroy a portion of herself.

In the small hours of the morning she at last fell into an exhausted sleep. Almost at once, she dreamed. She was walking again in the forest with Tiarnán, holding onto his belt to keep from stumbling. The trees towered blackly over them, their leaves whispering mysteriously; owls hooted, the bats fluttered overhead, and from somewhere nearby came the sound of wolves howling. "Are you afraid, Marie?" asked Tiarnán's low voice out of the darkness.

"No," she whispered. And she wasn't; once again she stepped in a perfect, dreamlike peace, body and soul moving as one.

"Good. There's no reason to be afraid. Wolves are gentler beasts than they're given credit for. Look, here we are!"

He stopped, and she saw that they had reached a mound in a clearing, faced with two standing stones like a door. It had somehow become day again, and she could see it clearly. Elder trees fringed it, and the grass was scattered with dark red wild poppies, tall white hemlock, and purple-flowering bittersweet.

"This isn't the pig keepers'!" she protested, and Tiarnán smiled the smile she remembered so vividly, one side of his mouth going up, the other staying serious, and the warm brown eyes laughing.

"Did you want it to be?" he asked. He caught her face very gently between his hands, and with a flush of delight she realized that he was going to kiss her.

Then suddenly there was a crash of thunder and a burst of rain, and he was gone. She was alone and in tears in a land gray and wet with winter.

She woke and found that she'd slept late and Eline was up already. She sat up slowly, crossed herself, said another prayer for the dead, and rose heavily to face the undesired day.

———

I t was a Sunday. After attending Mass in the castle chapel, Hoel held court in the Great Hall. The hall of Ploërmel was larger than that of Rennes, and being older and less sophisticated, it was in some ways brighter. The castle's wooden walls had been plastered inside and whitewashed, and the clay floor was strewn with rushes — pale yellow rushes now, in this bleak season. The smoke from the central fire rose blue to the high ceiling, and the white winter light fell steeply through the narrow windows, barring the oak tables with light, picking out armor, rich clothing of blue or scarlet, trimmings of fur and gold.

The duke took his place on his chair at the center of the dais, the table was moved aside, and Eline formally presented herself as the heiress to the manor of Talensac. She walked slowly through the tables toward the dais, looking tiny and fragile, her black mourning standing out starkly against the bright colors all around. She was leading the lymer Mirre on a leash of scarlet leather.

With Tiarnán declared dead, the fief of Talensac had returned to Hoel's control, and Eline, as the widow of the duke's liege man, had become the duke's ward. It was a sign of the exceptional favor Hoel had shown to her husband that she had been invited to do homage and take control of the estate. Eline was miserably aware that the gesture was meant to remove her from the number of marriageable heiresses under the duke's authority, and to leave her free to mourn Tiarnán for a long time. Hoel would not be pleased when she asked his permission to remarry at once. She knew that the whole court thought it was much too soon. Already the way she smiled whenever Alain looked at her had provoked disapproving frowns. She was desperate to be near Alain, however, and she couldn't bear the thought of continuing for months or years alone at Talensac. The "simple, honest, good-hearted peasants" had turned against her. She had quarreled with the machtiern. It was because of her that he had disappeared. They did not dare disobey the lady of the manor, but they avoided her: when she entered a

room, everyone else left. The only person at Talensac who
would speak to her comfortably was the duke's bailiff Grallon,
who'd come to set the estate in order. For Eline, who had
never known anything in her life before but love and admiration,
it was almost unendurable: she was torn between rage and helpless bewilderment. Alain's love, his adoring gazes and reassuring
words, were like warmth to her frozen spirit. She needed them,
and to get them she was willing to scandalize the court and dare
whatever the duke would say to her. But she dreaded it.

She stopped before the duke and curtsied gracefully to the
ground. Then she took one more step forward and offered Hoel
Mirre's crimson leash. "My lord," she said shyly, "when you
were so kind as to summon me to court, I thought to myself
that I must offer you a gift, and the best gift I could think of
was this fine lymer, whose quality is known to every man in
Brittany who hunts. She has been grieving for her first master:
I beg you to accept her, and make her joyful with hunting
again."

Hoel reddened with pleasure to the crown of his balding
head. He took the leash eagerly. "Lady Eline," he said, beaming,
"you judged it very well. I don't think you could give me a gift
that could please me more, except to see your husband in my
hall once again. Thank you. Here, Mirre! Good girl!" He
snapped his fingers to attract the dog's attention; then, when
she came politely to his hand, he roughed her long ears and
patted her.

Eline was glad. The duke's obvious delight would make it
harder for him to refuse consent to her second marriage — and
she hadn't wanted to keep the lymer anyway. Mirre had been
unambiguously Tiarnán's dog, and since his disappearance she
had moped about the house, always lifting her head in hope at
each new opening of the door. Eline had begun to hate her.
Better far to give her to Hoel.

Hoel put Mirre's leash over his arm and got to his feet. The
business to be conducted wasn't an exchange of gifts, but the
rendering of homage and its acceptance, in court and before

witnesses. "Do you wish to become wholly my vassal?" he asked solemnly, in a loud voice so that all the court could hear.

"I do," Eline replied, so timidly that the witnesses had to strain to hear her soft voice. She knelt down before the duke and raised her hands, palms together, and Hoel took them between his own. "I promise faithfully," she said earnestly, "that I will be loyal to Duke Hoel, and in all my dealings I will abide by the homage I give him, in good faith and without treachery."

Hoel pulled her to her feet and ceremoniously kissed her. Then he sat down in his chair again, and one of his attendants handed him a beechwood rod to symbolize the fief of Talensac. Hoel took it firmly in both hands and presented it to Eline. Eline took it, then knelt down to the ground and bowed her head. When she got up, the company applauded. The act of homage was completed: Talensac was hers.

At this point she was expected to disappear back into the crowd in the hall. Hoel turned his attention back to Mirre, the company began to talk, and the servants started moving the high table back onto the dais for lunch. When Eline knelt down again, a ripple of surprise spread around her: the servants stopped, the talk died down again, and Hoel turned back to her in surprised inquiry.

"My liege lord," said Eline, desperately gathering up her courage and speaking much more loudly than she had done when she swore fealty, "you've been generous in allowing a woman to pay homage to you, but I know that a manor is better governed by a knight. I don't have the wisdom or the strength to manage Talensac by myself. I am young, I am suffering great loss and confusion, and I need a strong arm to lean upon. I beg you, my lord—and you, lords and ladies of the court, all of you—not to think me fickle and inconstant because I wish to remarry at once. I was true to my husband while he lived, but he's gone, all my searching hasn't brought him back, and I cannot stand alone in his place. An old suitor, who's loved me for many years, has presented himself to me as a helper: I ask you, my lord, to permit me to marry him, and confer on him the lands you have just confirmed to me."

Hoel frowned in consternation. A mutter swept through the hall. Eline remained as she was, kneeling silently before the duke. Hoel glanced over at Alain, who was standing among the household knights at a discreet distance. His friends were all staring at him in scandalized admiration. Alain to acquire a manor, a lovely, profitable manor—and a hot young wife!

"Lady Eline," Hoel said warningly, "think carefully. You've lost a husband who was reckoned the finest knight in Brittany. To take another so soon would expose you to criticism and slander."

"I have thought carefully," Eline replied with a wobble in her voice. "But, my lord, I can't stay at Talensac all alone, and a manor is more use supporting a knight to fight for you than one weak woman who doesn't even know how to govern it. Alain is noble and your own liege man. And, my lord, as a widow and a lady, I have the right to choose."

The duke gave in. He had no legitimate grounds for refusing. He allowed Eline to summon Alain from among the knights, and the two were officially betrothed. But he pointedly did not offer them the use of the cathedral and court for the wedding, and treated them both with cold disapproval. Since Advent was just begun and marriage celebrations were inappropriate to the season of preparation and repentance, the date was set for Christmas.

"She'd have taken him even before that, if she could," Duke Hoel said sourly at lunch an hour or so later. "She should have waited six months at the least, out of respect for the dead. She didn't have to stay at Talensac alone: my man Grallon has things in hand there. She could have gone home to Comper, or retired to a convent for a while. And to take that idiot de Fougères after a man like Tiarnán! I'm amazed she can stomach him."

"He's very good-looking, and he obviously loves her," soothed the duchess. As Tiher had observed long before, she had a soft spot for young lovers. "He was her suitor before her marriage. And they do make a very pretty couple."

Everyone who was sitting at the high table looked at Eline and Alain, who sat together at the second table of the hall:

Alain, tall, wide-shouldered, and golden in a new yellow tunic trimmed with fox fur; Eline, slight and pale and liquid-eyed in black, smiling at him over the meat. Eline should have been at the high table, but had been moved into a less honorable place as a sign of her liege lord's displeasure. It didn't seem to bother her.

"He's a shallow, self-indulgent, vainglorious peacock!" snapped the duke. "Tiarnán was a reliable man." He glanced moodily around the high table. "I've told this tale before, but I'll tell it again, in his honor," he declared. "When Robert of Bellême came raiding five years ago, I was caught napping."

The high table fell silent, sat up, and paid attention. Most of the listeners had heard the story before, but they were happy to hear it again. Robert of Bellême, son of a notorious poisoner and disloyal vassal simultaneously of the king of France, the duke of Normandy, and the king of England, was one of the most savage and brutal men of a savage and brutal age. Forever eager to launch a private war, he was the terror of those unlucky enough to neighbor any of his thirty-four castles — and Domfront, one of the more important of those castles, stood in Normandy neighboring the Breton March. Robert of Bellême and his crimes were a familiar topic at the table of the duke of Brittany; the tale of his discomfiture was welcome.

"A Friday in Lent, it was, flat contrary to the Truce of God," continued Hoel, "but what does Robert care for God or man? He crossed the Couesnon at Pontorson and began to ravage like a starving wolf, killing and robbing on all sides. They brought me the news at Rennes, and I rode out to meet him in a hurry. I had with me only the knights of my household. I sent messengers off at a good round gallop to summon my vassals, but I didn't expect many of them to reach me in time to be any help. But when I came to the Rance River, there was Tiarnán with a dozen men from his household and three or four knights he'd met along his way and badgered into coming with him. He hadn't waited to be summoned: he'd come as soon as he heard the news. And he hadn't wasted his time by looking for me at Rennes. No, he'd decided that I would necessarily go by way of the Rance and had ridden directly there. All his men were well equipped and supplied, and all were contented with their leader's orders — which counts for a great deal, you know, if a man must fight in a holy season.

"We went on up the Rance, for we'd heard that Robert was attacking the land about Dinard — Géré of Dinard had some dispute with him. When we were approaching the city, we learned that Robert's brother, Geoffroy, had separated from the main party of raiders, and was with his own men somewhere to the east, keeping the road for the others and pillaging a bit on his own account. Geoffroy had a bloody reputation, as you all know: he once lopped off a peasant's legs because the poor devil walked too slowly. I didn't want to engage Robert and find Geoffroy attacking my rear, so I turned to Tiarnán and said, 'Make sure that fellow stays out of the way.' Tiarnán never boasted and made great protestations, like some: 'Yes, my lord,' he said, and he took his followers and went to find Geoffroy. The rest of us continued toward Dinard. We encountered Robert about two miles from the city, and we fought him as soon as we encountered him. I take Christ to witness, it was a fierce struggle! When we were all well blooded, Robert fell back and offered to parley. He suggested that we withdraw and that he and his followers go home. He didn't offer to return the plunder he'd taken, or even to refrain from plundering any more as he went. He would simply call the raid successfully completed then, instead of later.

"I didn't like the terms. But I wasn't sure I'd be wise to press for more, with only my household knights to support me. Géré of Dinard, by the way, who'd offended Robert to begin with, was nowhere to be seen. He'd locked himself into his city and stayed there. He said afterward that he didn't know I was there. So I stood there parleying with that wolf of Bellême, trying to judge if I dared to ask for justice.

"Then there was a stir, and we all looked up and saw Tiarnán, and his men, riding across the plain toward us, leading a war-horse by the bridle. Straight up to us he rode, and when he stopped he bowed his head to me and said, 'My lord, the fellow is out of the way.' Then he gestured to his men to give the led horse to Robert. It was Geoffroy's horse, and Geoffroy's body was tied across the saddle. 'I give you your brother's body for burial,' Tiarnán told Robert. 'He was a nobleman and distinguished in battle, and I ask no ransom for it.'

"Robert had gone gray as vomit: Geoffroy had the reputation of being the best knight in his service. 'How did he die?' he asked Tiarnán, and Tiarnán said, 'Bravely, in single combat. Five of his men are dead, and the rest are bearing the bodies home.' 'Who killed him?' asked Robert. He did not think, you see, that it could have been Tiarnán: Tiarnán was only twenty at the time, and he sat there looking as stiff as a nun at an alehouse. Geoffroy had been a big man, and in his prime, and we could all see that his head had been cleft open right through his helmet. God, what a blow! Then Tiarnán told Robert quietly, 'I killed him.'

"Robert looked at me, and I thanked God, and said, 'This is my liege man Tiarnán of Talensac, Lord Robert: he is one of the finest knights in Brittany, and I would rather have another like him than a whole troop of foot soldiers. But I thank God that I have many brave men in my service, and they are even now hurrying to my aid. Now I want you to return the plunder you've taken, and surrender your arms, and go home.' And Robert did what I asked."

Hoel again glared down the hall at Alain. "But even that wasn't the sum of the reasons I had for prizing Tiarnán. It never mattered to him which table he sat at and who sat above him, or which cut of meat the servants gave him. He wasn't offended, like some, if I gave honors to others. He never caused any grief to his neighbors, and he was courteous and easy in all dealings. When it came to hunting, he knew every beast of the forest as though it were his cousin: I have watched him entice a fox cub from its earth right to his hand. There never was a man so terrible on the field of battle who was so gentle off it. I can believe the lady Eline isn't happy at Talensac on her own. She'd quarreled with her lord and it will be a long time before his people forgive her for it. And they won't be any happier when

she sets that beribboned juggler up in his place. Damn!" Hoel
suddenly wiped his eyes with the back of his hand. "He adored
her. She should have waited six months."

There was a silence. The duchess was blinking rapidly as
well, and for once made no move to defend young love. Marie
thought about what Eline had said the night before, and was
ashamed at the way her heart had chimed its agreement with
Hoel.

"Don't judge her too harshly, my lord," she said aloud. "If
Tiarnán had listened to her, he would still be here. She did beg
him not to go hunting alone."

Hoel snorted. "There is that," he said. "Yes, I suppose there
is that. And he did adore her, and would want me to give her
his lands and make her happy. Well . . . If I ever catch that brute
Éon of Moncontour, I'll have him disemboweled and burned.
Hanging's too good for the creature." He shoved his trencher
of venison aside and rinsed his fingers in the silver bowl of
water, then dried his hands on the napkin his steward hurried
to offer. He looked round the table. It was flanked by the of-
ficers of his household—chancellor, chamberlain, constable—
and their wives, and on every face he saw reflected his own
angry resentment. Hoel at once regretted his harshness: one
woman's fickleness shouldn't cast a shadow over the whole state
of Brittany. He glanced about again, looking for a way to
lighten the air, and this time his eyes fixed on Marie. "You look
tired, Lady Marie," he said in a much more cheerful tone. "Were
you losing sleep over the suitor who's abandoned hope?"

Tiher had earlier announced to the hall his intention to "give
up the chase" and act as surety for Marie.

"It wouldn't be a wonder if I had," Marie replied. She had
understood instantly what the duke was about. "Of all my suitors, he's the one most worth losing sleep over."

Hoel glanced down the hall again, this time to the table of
the household knights (the fifth, in this less crowded court),
where Tiher sat talking animatedly with his friends. "Do you
think so?" he asked. "I'd always paired him in my mind with
his cousin. The one plays the peacock with his face and cloth-

ing, the other with his cutting tongue. But there's more to Tiher than that, is there?"

"Yes," Marie agreed warmly. "In fact, my lord, I think you waste opportunities in the use you make of him. He is as honest as he is clever, and his nature is considerably gentler than his tongue—which, I grant you, has an edge to it. He is loyal and faithful where he's committed, but he always looks before he leaps. Also, he can read very well and knows Latin. He was educated at Bonne Fontaine. He's a man who could serve you with distinction."

Hoel squinted thoughtfully at Tiher. It had been out of the question to promote a de Fougères nephew above a de Fougères son: to do so would have offended Lord Juhel. Hoel's claim to his dukedom was through his wife: he was aware that many of the powerful Marcher families disliked him, and he dared not offend them for fear of losing their allegiance. But if Alain became lord of a manor, he would leave the ducal household, and a court office for Tiher would become a compliment to the family instead of an affront.

Havoise was also looking thoughtfully down the hall toward Tiher, who joked on obliviously. "You know, my dear," said the duchess softly, "Marie's right. She has good judgment when it comes to lovers."

The duke grinned and turned the squint on Marie. "So Tiher was wrong to withdraw his suit?" he asked lightly again.

"No, my lord," Marie said firmly. "I would not marry him, or any man here, without my father's blessing."

"The old song!"

"I'm tired of singing it myself, my lord."

Hoel grunted. "So instead you sing the praises of your surety against forced marriage? Why did he swear to that, I wonder, if he's really given up the chase? He knows you're not threatened with any such thing. Havoise would throttle me in my sleep if I even suggested it."

"Tut!" said Havoise disapprovingly. "I'd never throttle a man in his sleep. I'd do it when you were awake, my dear." He grinned at her and kissed her little finger.

Marie leaned toward Hoel and lowered her voice to a whisper. "He said it would be a good excuse for you to do nothing when his uncle presses you about Chalandrey."

Hoel stared a moment, then burst out laughing. "Did he really?" he asked. "He is a witty fellow, isn't he? By God, he deserves promotion."

Éline stayed in Ploërmel for three more days, and, though the court disapproved of her second betrothal just as much as she'd feared, she started back to Talensac only very reluctantly. The court at least disapproved unobtrusively, and Alain was there; at Talensac the cold dislike of the servants cut into her like a freezing wind, and there was no one to shelter her from it. She had thought of going home to Comper until her second marriage but she was afraid to. There was too great a gulf between the happy girl she'd been before and the embittered woman she was now. Her father would pamper her in a way that now seemed childish and silly, and give her orders as though she were still under his authority, and she knew she'd lose her temper and snap at him. Then he'd be hurt and angry. He was annoyed with her already for her decision to marry Alain; he'd said so many dismissive things when Alain was Tiarnán's rival that he still felt bound to disapprove. She felt she couldn't bear it if her loving father quarreled with her, too. So it had to be Talensac, despite the coldness of the servants and the sullen resentment of the peasants. At least Duke Hoel's bailiff would be there, she told herself. And by the time the bailiff left, Alain would come to marry her.

It was only an afternoon's ride from Ploërmel to Talensac, but she didn't set out until noon, the winter days were short, and she arrived at the manor house after dark. She dismounted at the house door and sent the servants who'd escorted her back to the stables with the horses. The door was bolted, and she knocked on it impatiently. No one answered. She knocked again, shouted, and kicked it. After another cold minute's wait, the bolt was finally shifted, and Kenmarcoc opened the door and stood aside for her. Eline strode angrily in, but the words of reproach at the way she'd been kept waiting froze on her lips. The hall, lit by the red embers heaped in the fireplace and by a single candle on the central table, looked as though it were in the process of being torn down. Heaps of linen were piled in corners, and chests and boxes—stacked on top of one another, falling off one another, open and half-emptied—were strewn everywhere. The floor was bare of rushes, and the packed clay was scarred and gouged. There was a smell of dirt and spilled wine. The only things on the table besides the candle were a jug and an overturned cup, and when Eline turned furiously toward Kenmarcoc, she discovered that his breath reeked of drink. "What on earth has been happening here?" she demanded.

"I'm leaving," replied Kenmarcoc in a loud, drunken voice.

"Leaving? Leaving where?"

"Home," he declared. "Here. I know you'd send me off as soon as your new fellow arrives and finds someone prettier, and I'm not staying for that. But I wouldn't stay if you begged me to. I'm not going to see that Fougères fellow sitting in the machtiern's place—no, by Saint Main! We've been packing all day. We'll tidy the place in the morning, before we go."

"You're drunk," said Eline in disgust. "Where are you going to go?"

"Lots of places," replied Kenmarcoc. "I'm a good clerk. I have a letter from the machtiern that says so." He went over to one of the half-emptied chests, walking with the exaggerated steadiness of one who doesn't trust his balance, and fumbled at a pile of parchments. Several of them joined the mess on the floor, but Kenmarcoc ignored them and pounced on the sheet of vellum he was looking for. He flourished it above his head, then stalked back, set it down before the candle, and read it aloud in harsh triumph. " 'Kenmarcoc son of Alfret is a man I prize highly, for no lord ever had a more estimable and honest bailiff, and any man he seeks service with should count himself fortunate.' " Kenmarcoc thrust the letter under Eline's nose and shook it. "See?" he demanded. "It's his seal. That's what he said.

He gave it to me once when he went off to a war, in case he never came back. He thought of things like that. And he gave me the linen for all the family's beds, and a wooden chest full of cutlery and pans, and five bolts of good woolen cloth, and my horse and the brown mule. We've been sorting it out all day; we won't take anything that's not ours." He sat down at the table, set the cup upright with heavy concentration, then poured himself some more wine from the jug.

Eline glared at him wordlessly. She'd sent one of her attendant servants back to Talensac the day before to tell the manor when she was likely to arrive: this, clearly, was the result. She and Alain had indeed decided that they ought to find a new bailiff for the manor, but she hadn't planned to dismiss Kenmarcoc suddenly. She'd meant to find him a new job first. She didn't want to share her house with him, but she had hoped to part without too much rancor.

"I've bought a cart," Kenmarcoc told her, and gulped some wine. "We're going tomorrow." He took another gulp.

"There's no reason to go so suddenly," Eline said stiffly. "I'm happy to find you another place first."

"I'm not staying under the same roof as you," he declared. His eyes, red with drink, fixed her with a glare of absolute contempt. "It's because of you that the machtiern left. The finest knight in Brittany, and the best master. You quarreled with him and sent him off."

"You have no right to talk to me like this!" Eline cried. She was horrified to find her eyes brimming and a lump in her throat. She felt a wild desire to scream at Kenmarcoc, *The machtiern you thought so marvelous is a monster: go fetch him from the forest if you want him!* But to frame those words even in thought turned her throat to ice. "You're nothing but a servant!" she choked instead. "I was his wife! And I didn't send him off; I begged him not to go!"

"I know what you did!" Kenmarcoc answered in a strangled hiss, looking at her with such knowing malice that she fell back a step. "You begged him to tell you where he went when he went hunting, and he loved you so dearly that he did. You treated him afterward as though he were filth. I don't care what the secret was! I don't care if he did go hunting with the people of the hills, or visit some lady of a well. A soulless creature from the hills would make him a finer wife than you!"

"You can't say that to me!" shrieked Eline. There was the creak of a door opening up the stairs, and the duke's bailiff, Grallon, appeared on the landing in his shirt, looking down into the hall in bewilderment.

"I can say what I like!" Kenmarcoc roared back. "Twenty-four years I've lived and worked in Talensac! The best part of my life! But I'm not staying, not now." He began to cry. "I'm not staying here to see that swaggering minstrel take Tiarnán's place."

Eline stamped her foot helplessly. "Stop it!" she shrieked. "Stop talking to me like this, or I'll have you punished for it!"

Kenmarcoc glared, his face red with drink and wet with tears. "You whore!" he exclaimed bitterly. "You weren't fit to clean his boots."

Eline burst into tears and slapped him. He blinked at the blow and grunted, but didn't stir. There was a stamp of feet outside, and she realized with relief that her escort had finally finished stabling the horses. "Take Kenmarcoc and put him in the stocks!" she screamed as they came in.

The three servants who'd escorted her to court and back gaped at Kenmarcoc in consternation. The duke's bailiff hurried down the stairs. "Lady Eline!" he exclaimed. "I didn't realize you were back."

"Kenmarcoc's drunk," she sobbed, turning to him. "I told him to stop calling me names, but he wouldn't. He called me a whore. Put him in the stocks!"

Grallon opened his mouth and shut it again. He nodded at the servants. They remained motionless, staring at Kenmarcoc, who glared drunkenly back.

"He treated your lady with great disrespect," Grallon told them. "I heard it. Put him in the stocks."

"I'm not putting *Kenmarcoc* in the stocks!" one of the servants exclaimed. He turned and walked back out the door. The remaining two looked at each other uncertainly.

"Let her put me in the stocks!" exclaimed Kenmarcoc, staggering to his feet. "Let the whole village see me in the stocks! Warn them what to expect, now the machtiern's gone! I'm safe; I'm leaving tomorrow. It's the rest of you that need to worry now!"

One of the servants caught his arm to steady him, and he stumbled toward the door. The other glanced back nervously at the duke's bailiff, then carefully went to one of the chests and took out an armful of blankets. He collected Kenmarcoc's cup and jug of wine and followed.

Eline stood in the middle of the dim hall, crying in bewilderment. She had always considered herself kind and gentle — and here she had sent, not just any servant, but the bailiff, to the stocks, in the middle of the winter. Grallon looked at her in pity.

"You should rest, Lady," he told her. "Don't worry about what he said: he was drunk."

"Yes," said Eline, and, still crying, went upstairs past him to her bed.

The two servants, Donoal and Yann Ruz, put Kenmarcoc in the stocks very tenderly, wrapped a couple of blankets round him, and sat down beside him to help him finish the wine. Most of the village was asleep, but after a little while Justin Braz and Rinan came staggering up the road from their own drinking session at the alehouse on the Rennes road. They roared with pleasure when they saw that the stocks were occupied, relishing the prospect of pissing upon some local enemy, but when they came closer and saw who occupied them, they fell silent. Kenmarcoc had put Justin in the stocks on innumerable occasions, and Rinan on a good number, but the bailiff's downfall provoked shock rather than triumph. Justin took great pleasure in the position of worst man in the village, perpetual threat to good order and the virtue of decent women. But if good order could be pinned out by the hands and feet on a cold winter night, what would become of Justin? "What's happened here?" he asked anxiously.

It was Donoal who answered. "He called the mistress a whore."

Kenmarcoc's fury had had time to cool. He used the last of it to repeat that Eline was indeed a whore, but then he began to mourn his imminent departure from Talensac. "Twenty-four years," he repeated dolefully. "Twenty-four years, oh God! And my children all born in that house. And to leave it like this!"

Justin was horrified. He called Kenmarcoc "Uncle" and begged him not to go. "We've lost the machtiern," he said pitifully. "Don't you go away, too."

"I must; I must," replied Kenmarcoc, now once again weeping. "If I don't go, I'll be sent, soon enough. And I won't let the whore and her fancy man dismiss me."

At this Justin began to cry, too, and decent manor servants and the worst men in the village united round the stocks, weeping for the lost past, and the fearful expectation of the future.

Kenmarcoc was released from the stocks early the next morning, so as not to offend the villagers with the sight of him there any longer than strictly necessary. He returned to the manor house pale and subdued, and helped his wife and children to finish their packing in silence. It was afternoon by the time all their belongings were strapped onto the cart. Lanthildis and the older children were in tears as they walked away from the manor house; the younger children, riding on the cart, howled with grief. Eline heard them from her room, where she'd stayed all morning, but she didn't come out until the sound had faded into the distance.

When she came downstairs, the hall was swept clean and missing a quarter of its furniture, and Grallon was standing in the doorway looking out at the gray, overcast afternoon with a worried expression. She walked up behind the bailiff, and he started and looked round apprehensively.

"I would have found Kenmarcoc another place if he'd let me," Eline said bitterly.

The bailiff grunted noncommittally. "He'll find one himself without too much trouble," he said. "He's planning to go to court. He worked for the ducal chancellery originally, you know. And he has a letter of recommendation which would get him a place with most men. I'm sure the duke will find a place for him." He hesitated, then went on, "He said there was a wolf in the village last night."

Eline felt the old constriction of her stomach. "A wolf?" she whispered.

"Yes. He told me just before he went. He said that when the moon was setting, a wolf came onto the green. He thought at first it was just a dog, but it came close to him and he couldn't mistake it. He shouted for help and it ran off. The servants who put him in the stocks and some of the villagers had stayed with him. They woke up when he shouted, and they saw it, too." The bailiff looked at Marie questioningly.

"I've never heard of a wolf coming right into the village before," she said, so as to say something. She felt queasy and faint.

"No," said the bailiff. "Nor had Kenmarcoc. He took it for an omen." He crossed himself. "I pray it doesn't mean famine and a hard winter."

Eline thought of the wolf walking deliberately up the narrow street of the village. It was looking for her; she was sure of it. Could it get into the manor house? She shuddered. She thought of Alain, and how she'd said good-bye to him in Ploërmel. It was still a long time until Christmas.

"We should set wolf traps," she said.

Grallon nodded at once. "I'll give orders about it today," he said. The prospect of traps made the wolf less ominous and more ordinary. He'd heard of lone wolves causing trouble. It was said that when the king wolf of a pack was supplanted by a younger animal, he lost all his normal caution in his rage, and might take sheep from the byre or even snatch children from gardens. "We'll set the traps until we catch the beast," he told Eline. "It will cheer the villagers up, too, when they kill it." That, he thought, was very necessary: a more sullen and gloomy set of peasants he had never seen.

A sudden horrifying image leapt into Eline's mind: the body of a wolf, caught and killed by the villagers, being skinned to reveal Tiarnán's body inside. She pressed her hand against her mouth, trying to swallow down the sickness that choked her. He left what made him human under the stone, she told herself; he won't turn back into a man even if he's dead. He won't. And he can't get into the manor house. The palisade is tall and has good, deep, foundations, and the gate and the house door are both bolted at night.

"What's the matter, Lady?" asked Grallon.

"I'm afraid of wolves," Eline whispered.

"Never fear," he replied, his own anxiety over omens forgotten now. "We'll trap it. I'll have the villagers dig a pit trap as well, and bait it. They all hate wolves, and they'll enjoy that. It's really a piece of luck that the beast turned up, Lady Eline. They'll forget their worries in the excitement of killing a wolf."

"I'm . . . I'm glad," Eline whispered. "Tell them I'll pay a reward to the man who kills it. I . . . I don't feel well, and I'm going to lie down. Have Driken bring me something in my room."

"Driken's gone with her father, Lady."

Eline bit her lip, remembering that this was true. She didn't regret Driken, but she couldn't face trying to pick another serving girl from the village. The villagers' sullen stares seemed suddenly to be part of the same horror as the prowling wolf. She knew all at once that she wasn't going to stay in Talensac, not just now: she'd go home to Comper, whatever her father thought, and, at Christmastime, ride to Fougères and marry Alain there. She hated Talensac. She couldn't stay here at all, not without Alain.

Like a rock amid the tumbling water of her thoughts, she remembered Judicaël's voice: *Everything you get by your lies will turn to bitterness, and the fear of what you have done will poison every-thing you touch.*

But she told herself that all would be well again, once she was married to Alain.

X

The wolf left the forest cautiously and paused, nervously sniffing the air. He was still a couple of miles from the village of Talensac, but he didn't like the open, exposed stretch of farmland, even now, at night. The scent on the wind, of wood smoke and human dirt, was one which his instincts flagged with danger. His instincts were strong, and had always governed most of what he did. The self beneath them was struggling now to override them, but the struggle was made brutally hard by that self's own confusion. It knew that it was human, but it was drunken and dazed, swimming in a sea of alien perceptions and desires. Reasoning was difficult, and words came to it only slowly, dragged from within as though pulled up by a diver from deep water. Images and memories came more easily, but they, too, were confusing. It was hard to map the world recalled onto the world apparent. Sounds and scents were different; colored memories bewildered eyes that saw only shades of gray.

The wolf whined and glanced back at the shelter of the trees. Then he lowered his head and dashed quickly across the corner of a field to a boundary ditch. The ditch was better: it smelled of wet and rotting vegetation, with a trace of rabbit. The wolf's instincts forced a momentary pause, tracking the rabbit smell toward its burrow, and the self had to wrench him back again. Hunger wasn't as fierce as the gnawing sense of loss. The wolf ran quickly along the ditch, splashed through a stream, and found another ditch to take him onward.

About a mile from the village he came to the mill. He circled downwind of it, then crept slowly back toward it, shaking from the violent conflict between his decision to approach and his instinct to run away. The choking smell of flour struck him first, then the smells of pigs, cows, and smoke, of humans and dogs. Then came a sound: voices. They frightened him, but he crept closer still, then crouched, trembling, to listen. The effort of trying to drag up the drowned words inside and match them to the distorted din from the mill house was painful and exhausting. Then the wind shifted slightly, and a dog inside the house scented him and began barking loudly.

One of the distorted voices shrilled whiningly in response. The dog barked even more furiously. A door opened and the dog shot out, then stopped short, barking frenziedly. A man followed it, holding a stick of firewood for a torch. The man's presence made the dog bolder; it jumped two steps toward the wolf and leapt up and down, baying madly. The wolf snarled, and the man saw him. He shrieked and swung his torch back and forth through the air so that the fire blazed up. The hot crackle terrified the wolf, and he turned and ran. Neither man nor dog followed, but the wolf could hear other voices from the house joining in the wild gabble.

He ran into the stream below the millpond, cold though it was, and splashed along it for a short distance, then climbed out of it on the same bank, ran downstream, doubled back in his tracks, went back into the water and ran upstream a few paces, and climbed out on the opposite bank. He shook himself and crawled under a bush. There was still no sign of pursuit. He rested his head on his paws, and struggled again to match the words he'd heard to their drowned meanings. The shout "wolf" emerged from the depths easily. But the man had said "wolf" before, too, while he was in the house. "Is it the wolf?" he'd asked the dog. The people here knew he'd come before. They expected him. And they would attack him without hesitation. Danger! screamed his instincts. Run!

But the image of Eline's face in the blue silk wimple perplexed his mind; then the image of Eline in bed, smiling up at him. The desire to weep at the memory was a torment: tears were as alien to his shape as wings. Surely, if she could see him, realize what she'd done to him—surely then she'd relent and give back what she'd stolen? She had loved him. He was sure she'd loved him once. Even if she now wanted to be free of him, she couldn't mean to deprive him of everything forever? He slid out from under the bush on the far side of it, ran up the bank, and found another boundary ditch that led toward the village.

He was still afraid, though, and because of that he saw the first wolf trap before he was caught in it. It was lying in the narrow path that led up from the fields to the village's muddy main street, and it looked like nothing more than a wooden plank scattered with leaves and dung. He almost walked over it—but he was nervous, and stopped. He noticed the three small box shapes along the plank's surface, and the pattern connected suddenly with an image. A wooden box, part buried, its lid set with three small trapdoors that gave way if they were pressed. Inside the lips of the doors were angled spikes, ready to catch any foot that dropped past them, and hold and tear it when it tried to pull free again. There was a memory of Mailon the carpenter building one, and another man, himself, saying . . . his own words were drowned. He hadn't wanted one, but Mailon had made it anyway: wolves were bad; it was good to be able to catch them.

He backed away from the trap and tried another way into the village. Every pathway he tried had been prepared for him. At last he was forced to enter the village by the main street, with the wind on his side. A dog began to bark inside a house as he went by, and he broke into a run, bristling with fear— but still anxiously watching the ground. Then he caught another smell: fresh meat. His instincts again drew him toward it before he could stop himself. There was a pig's head hanging from the branch of a tree, freshly killed and dripping blood. He stopped, staring at it hungrily. But another memory stirred: a pit covered over with branches, and bait hung above. He looked at the ground beneath the dripping head, and, sure enough, saw there the branchy covering of the pit. Heart pounding, he hurried away and loped into the square before the church.

The stocks were empty tonight, which was a relief. The night before, it had taken him a few minutes to recognize Kenmarcoc, and then the slow understanding of where the man was had been painful, and his shout of terror more painful still. It had made him run off before reaching his goal. Now he ran on, through the stream and up the hill toward the manor house. Another dog had started barking. He had to hurry.

There was a bridge over the dry ditch defense outside the gate. His instincts disliked it, and when he reached it, he stopped short. He struggled with himself, forced himself to set foot on it, then dashed across—and nearly ran into the closed gate. He laid his ears back, cowering against the door. This was all wrong. He couldn't get in this way. He had been following his human memories of how to come back to Talensac, forcing them against his wolf's instincts, but they'd misled him. The gate that had always opened to welcome him as a man was barred to him as a wolf, and he couldn't get in. He wasn't even downwind of the house here.

Even as he realized that, he heard the dogs begin to bay. Hunting hounds that had once belonged to him shouted now for his blood. Answering sounds came from the lodge beside the gate. Voices creaked and shrilled distortedly. He crouched, whining as he tried to make sense of it. "Catch," he managed, "Lady," "sou reward." Catch the wolf, and the lady will pay you a sou as a reward.

Mercy, he thought, the word shaping itself slowly. *Mercy, Lady. Oh God.*

But he realized that there would be no mercy. It wasn't enough to take away his house, his lands, his humanity: she wanted his life as well. For a moment he was so wrenched by agony that he couldn't move.

But the speakers inside would come out soon. They would loose that baying mob from the kennels. He had memories of dogs. Their colored images poured across his mind: running after a quarry, pulling it down, tearing it to bloody scraps with their heavy jaws. He turned and tore back across the bridge, raced with the wind down the hillside, and ran desperately for the shelter of the forest.

The baying of the hounds in the night woke Eline, and she lay awake for a long time after the dogs were quiet. She imagined the wolf prowling about outside the enclosure of the manor house. It was waiting for her, she was certain. In her mind it loomed big as a horse, black, fiery-eyed, and savage with hatred. It was waiting to kill her. She cried quietly from misery and terror.

She ached for the wolf to be dead, but she was afraid of what might happen if it were. The image of the wolf skin peeling off Tiarnán's body refused to be banished. What would the villagers do if they discovered what she'd done? She imagined the sullen contempt on their faces turning to bestial rage.

She told herself that if they knew what Tiarnán was, they would have to admit that she'd been right to reject him — but her heart remained unconvinced. *I don't care what the secret was!* Kenmarcoc had shouted. *You weren't fit to clean his boots.*

In the morning when she learned that the traps had caught nothing, she didn't know whether to be disappointed or relieved.

She set off for Comper that same day, taking along an escort of four servants, armed with bows for fear of the wolf. She stayed there until the last Sunday in Advent. The quarrel with her father happened exactly as she'd foreseen, and hurt just as much as she'd expected — but at least there were no wolves.

The week before Christmas, though, it seemed that the long night of misery would finally end. She rode with her escort to Fougères, and her father patched up the quarrel enough to come with her. Lord Juhel de Fougères received them both very graciously. He was perfectly willing to forget that he'd once called Eline a "fancy white-haired child slut" now that she was bringing his younger son land — "a very pretty manor, too, with some of the best hunting in Brittany." This warmth from the grand Lord Juhel thawed the rest of Lord Hervé's resentment. As for Alain, he greeted Eline with such tender joy that it brought tears to her eyes.

Fougères was a very grand place, much larger and finer than either Comper or Talensac. It was a stone-built castle, not just a fortified manor house, and its estates covered forty square miles of the Breton March. At Fougères they celebrated both Christmas and the wedding with a splendor that was not inferior to that of the ducal court. In fact, Eline thought happily, it was better than the court. There her marriage celebration had been only a minor occasion, while here at Fougères it was a major feast. And here she was marrying her true love—marrying him at long last, and bringing as her dowry not just the few acres she'd brought Tiarnán, but the whole of Talensac. She looked across the table, spread with the Christmas feast of boar's head and marrow-fat pie, and there he was, looking lovingly back. He seemed impossibly handsome: golden-haired, blue-eyed, his wide shoulders set off to perfection by a new tunic of crimson velvet trimmed with lynx fur. She felt a tingling in her groin, and touched his foot with her own under the table. He smiled back at her eagerly and kissed her hand.

Lord Juhel noticed the hand-kissing and laughed. "Christmas is a better time to marry than midsummer, isn't it, Lady Eline?" he joked. "The last thing newlyweds want is a short night."

Eline glanced at him unhappily. The last thing *she* wanted was to be reminded of her first wedding. But Alain only kissed her hand again. "Any night would seem short," he whispered, "with you."

When that long night was still beginning, though, she remembered the midsummer night, and Tiarnán's tenderness. The girl she had been then seemed so remote that it was as though the memory belonged to another person, and for a moment she forgot what Tiarnán was, remembering only the sweet delight in which she had lost her virginity. For a moment it even seemed to be part of this present sweetness. It was all love.

Then she remembered, and the memory was contaminated with sick disgust. She froze in her new husband's arms. It was a long time before Alain could coax her into warmth again.

———

lain was eager to leave for Talensac after Christmas; Eline was reluctant. They discussed it on the morning of the Feast of the Innocents while they were getting up. "I've never even visited the place!" he told her. "And it's mine now. I want to look it over and set it in order at once."

"It's in perfect order now!" protested Eline. "And the duke's man Grallon is still there, collecting the relief."

Alain grimaced. The "relief" was the large sum which the new lord of a fief paid to his feudal overlord on his succession. It usually amounted to about a year's income from the estate. An overlord with an urgent need for money might ask for more, and a bad overlord might refuse to accept the homage of his vassal indefinitely, and strip the estate while it was under his control. Hoel was a good overlord, and Grallon was carefully collecting no more than what was customarily due. Tiarnán had kept a reasonable surplus in his coffers, and even though the wedding and the flurry of repairs on the estate had dented this, there'd been enough left to pay off most of the relief at once. Grallon only needed to collect the rents for the Christmas quarter to get the rest. But even that seemed a lot to Alain. He had never had money of his own before, just an allowance from his father, and his father had always disapproved of the way he spent it.

"Do you suppose," he said to Eline, "that the duke might agree to reduce the relief if—"

"Alain!" she exclaimed in alarm. "Duke Hoel only let me keep Talensac because he was so fond of Tiarnán. He's angry with us for marrying so soon: we *can't* ask him to reduce the relief."

Alain grimaced again. "Very well. So, no money from the estate until after Easter. Oh well, I still have fifteen marks of what I borrowed: that will last us till then."

"Borrowed?" repeated Eline in surprise. Then she bit her tongue: of course, she and Alain would need some money in hand to set up house together. Silly of her not to have seen that. Fifteen marks, though, sounded like a lot.

"I borrowed fifty marks from a Jew in Nantes," Alain told her casually. "He was happy to lend it to me on the strength of Talensac. But he does charge a ruinous usury, and I was hoping to be able to pay him back this year. But never mind, next year will do."

Eline gaped at him stupidly. She could not read and she was not good at sums, but she knew that fifty marks was more money than Talensac brought in in a year. Fifty marks was . . . two years' rents from Talensac? More than that? And there was *interest* to pay on that enormous sum? "But . . ." she stammered helplessly, "but—why did you need to borrow so *much*?"

Alain grinned at her. He went to his clothes chest and dug into the bottom of it to bring out a small box of polished rosewood. He brought it over to her, sat down on the bed beside her, and put it in her lap. "Open it!" he ordered.

Breathlessly, she obeyed. The box was lined with white silk, and on the silk lay a necklace, a large sapphire set on a chain of silver and pearls.

"Oh, Alain!" she breathed, lifting it from the box. "Oh, how beautiful! It's the most beautiful thing I've ever seen!"

Alain took it gently from her hands and fastened it about her neck. The sapphire gleamed against her sky-blue gown, less vivid and less brilliant than her eyes. "You're the most beautiful thing *I*'ve ever seen," he whispered. He straightened the stone, then let his hand slip from it to her breast. "I wanted to get you a present worthy of you."

"Oh, dearest!" She had always loved getting presents, and this one transported her to the innocence of her girlhood again. She flung her arms around him and kissed him. "Oh, I adore you!"

No more was said about the debt of fifty marks, not even later, after it emerged that the necklace had cost only six marks, and that Alain had disposed of the other twenty-nine on a new warhorse, a pacing palfrey for Eline, a gyrfalcon, his new red velvet tunic, and an assortment of wines to stock his new cellars. How could she complain at anything he did, when he loved her so much?

She agreed to go back to Talensac for the new year, as well. Alain found a clerk to replace Kenmarcoc as bailiff, and the party set out for their estate on the thirtieth of December, arriving in Talensac on the first of January.

Talensac's new bailiff was the son of one of Lord Juhel's bailiffs, a small, morose, clever man by the name of Gilbert. He was glad to leave Fougères, where he had no prospects, but he was impatient with Talensac people even before he arrived at the manor. He spoke no Breton, and only two of the four servants Eline had brought in her escort spoke French.

They arrived in the middle of the afternoon on a day of clammy fog. They saw no one as they rode into the village, but that was natural enough given the weather. In the manor hall the fire was burning brightly and everything was in order. The servants bowed correctly, and the duke's bailiff greeted them warmly and congratulated them on their marriage. He welcomed Gilbert as well—then had to welcome him again, in French. Eline left the bailiffs to talk, and showed Talensac manor to its new lord: the horses in the stable, the hounds in the kennels, Tiarnán's goshawk and merlin in the small mews; the house and the kitchens and storerooms and the servants who looked after it all. Alain was as thrilled and delighted with it as she had been when Tiarnán first showed it to her. It was possible for a few hours to believe that they could be happy in the manor.

Dinner dampened the enthusiasm. "The wolf seems to have left us," Grallon told Eline as they all sat down.

"Wolf?" asked Alain sharply. Eline had not told him about the wolf while she was at Fougères. She'd been too busy being happy.

"Didn't your lady tell you?" asked Grallon, smiling. "You must have kept her occupied! We had a big wolf coming into the village when she was here last. He scorned all our traps and put all our dogs off his trail. We couldn't catch the beast, but it seems we frightened him off."

"Where did he go?" asked Alain.

"Thinking of having a try for him yourself, Lord Alain? The

stable lad Donoal tracked him into the forest west of here, toward Tremelin."

"That's my land, isn't it?" said Alain. "And Tiarnán had a
good pack of hounds, didn't he?" Once again, he was astonished at his own coolness. "Yes, I think I will have a try for
him."

"Don't," said Eline. She was sitting very white and still, and
she felt as though something inside of her had fainted at the
very mention of the wolf. She wanted nothing to do with the
creature.

Alain looked across at her angrily. "Why not?"

She looked down. "I'm afraid of the beast. He might hurt
you."

Alain smiled. For a moment he'd thought she might be afraid
for the beast. "Don't be afraid," he said gently. "It's only an
animal."

Later that night, when they were lying together in the bed
she had once shared with Tiarnán, she whispered, "You mustn't
go near the wolf, Alain! You know what he really is. He's dangerous!"

"It's an animal," Alain repeated firmly. "And you're right; it
is a dangerous one. Too dangerous to be left alive." He understood now why she'd been so reluctant to return to Talensac.
What woman wouldn't be afraid with that eerie creature roaming about? He should have killed the wolf before: he should
have run after it into the woods at St. Mailon's and ended it
then. Only when the monster was dead would she be wholly
safe and entirely his.

Eline lay still, staring up into the blackness. The air of the
bedroom was damp and chill, heavy with the fog outside. No
light came through the wicker shutters tonight, and sound and
feeling alike seemed curiously deadened. "Alain," she whispered, "I had the most horrible thought. What if they kill him
and skin him—and find Tiarnán inside?"

Alain was silent for a long time. The memory of Tiarnán's
transformation appeared in his mind with a strange, remote vividness, like something glimpsed in a dream. It had been com-

plete in an instant: there was no man inside that wolf skin. "It isn't like that," he said at last. "He left that part of himself under the stone at St. Mailon's. And anyway, if I catch him with the hounds, he won't be skinned: there won't be enough hide left intact to make it worthwhile." That thought cheered him.

Eline shuddered: the horrible image simply transformed itself to Tiarnán's dogs howling in terror as they found that the body they were tearing was their master's. She felt no pity for the wolf — she was far too frightened of it for that — but she was afraid of discovery, of the peasants turning on her: *I don't care what the secret was! You weren't fit* . . .

"Maybe we should burn his things," she whispered.

When they were at Fougères, Alain had secretly showed her the bundle of Tiarnán's hunting clothes, wrapped in the slashed leather wallet. He had not unwrapped them since he first fumbled up the knot at St. Mailon's, but he'd shrouded the leather bundle in an old altar cloth bought from a church and sprinkled it with holy water as a safeguard. The whole package was now buried in his clothes chest, under a false bottom to keep it from the servants' eyes. They'd discussed burning it before. When they first snatched a meeting after St. Mailon's, Alain had been eager to burn the clothes, afraid of being accused of murder if they were found in his possession. Eline had dissuaded him. If the clothes were burned, who could say what would happen to the other, invisible thing that had been left with them? It might fly back to its owner. Fire was unlikely to destroy something without weight or form.

"You said before that we shouldn't," Alain told her now impatiently. "After all, we know that it works, that he can't turn back with them as they are. We don't know what would happen if we changed things."

"Yes," she whispered unhappily. "I suppose that's right."

"I'll kill him," Alain promised. "I'll hunt him down, wherever he goes. Don't be afraid. He's no match for me now."

She turned and suddenly clung to him passionately. "Be careful, then, dearest. Oh, please, please be careful!"

Talensac, watching warily to see what its new lord was like, was reassured at first to find that he was interested in nothing but wolf hunting. The bleak expectations of the night Kenmarcoc was put in the stocks showed no sign of being fulfilled: Alain didn't even learn the villagers' names, let alone care what they did. The new foreign bailiff, though, soon proved himself to be a foul person. He insisted on being spoken to in French, and gave anyone who addressed him in Breton a box on the ears or a cut from the little riding whip he always carried. He was greedy, too. He would wait until a villager had a cousin's wedding to attend, or a trip to a fair planned, and then he would demand one of the day's labor owed on the domain lands, and smirk as he was bribed to be excused. Even Justin Braz trod carefully with Gilbert, because it was clear that if a man put a foot wrong, the bailiff would fix on the most brutal punishment he could find, and then take money for lessening it: a foul person. Still, it could have been worse. Talensac approved of wolf hunting.

"Though Lord Alain's no huntsman, mind," Donoal told Justin over a mug of ale. The night of unity at the stocks had carried over into a prickly friendship, and the responsible stable lad had taken to recounting events at the manor house to the village terror and his friends. "He can barely tell a wolf's tracks from a hound's when they're printed side by side in mud. And he loses his temper if anything goes wrong." Patience was a cardinal virtue among huntsmen. Things invariably go wrong on hunts. Donoal loved hunting himself, and had no respect for lapses of temper—which was why he had previously looked down on Justin.

"Lord Goldilocks doesn't know how to shit in the woods" was Justin's reply. Donoal thought it very witty, and laughed into his ale.

Alain killed several wolves over the next couple of months. First he tried the usual wolf hunter's tactic. An animal carcass was left in a small wood which stood separate from the main body of the forest. Once wolves had found and eaten it, it was replaced with fresh, for three nights in succession. Then, on the fourth night, the carcass was hung up in a tree, with only a few bones scattered about on the ground beneath. The wolves were tempted to wait in the wood during the hours of darkness, hungrily crunching the bones and hoping for the meal they could smell above them. Shortly before morning, Donoal, whom Alain took to employing as his huntsman, went into the wood and cut down the carcass: the wolves gathered to feed on it, then stayed in the copse, afraid to return across the open fields to the main forest in daylight. Each time this was done, Alain found a number of animals to hunt when he came with the dogs in the morning. But he was certain they were no more than animals.

"It's not the king wolf," Donoal told him, examining a body after a chase. "Not the one that came into Talensac. He came the nights we left the meat, though. I've seen his tracks — a big dog-wolf that comes in from a different direction from the others. He snatches meat from the rest and runs off with it. He doesn't stay and feed with the pack, and when he sees the bones, he goes off at once, and leaves the others to be caught. He's a crafty creature."

Alain looked at the servant critically. "You're good at tracking, aren't you?" he asked.

Donoal shrugged. *Taken you a while to notice, hasn't it?* he thought. *You don't know how to shit in a wood.* "I like it," he said noncommittally.

He'd always liked it. Tiarnán had given him permission to hunt rabbits anywhere on the manor lands, and had assigned any forestry work on the estate to Donoal, or to Sulmin the swineherd, because he knew they enjoyed it. Donoal's most prized possession was a lymer, one of Mirre's pups, which the machtiern had given him. He'd gone after the noblemen's game of deer or boar with Tiarnán, too, and sat about the manor house fire afterward, talking over the chase. Tiarnán had been born a nobleman, Donoal a peasant, but that difference was less important than being the same age in the same village and sharing the same interests. They had grown up together. They shared memories of swimming in the fish ponds in hot summers before they were eight years old, of wrestling matches, daring raids on orchards, illicit bonfires by standing stones.

Donoal knew that to the new lord of Talensac, he himself would never be anything more than an obedient pair of hands. Well, that was the world: the good died, and change was always for the worse. He looked at Alain expressionlessly.

"I want you to find that wolf for me," said Alain. "You can have leave from your work to track him, and I'll give you three sous if you can find him."

Donoal was impressed and suspicious. Three sous was nearly two months' wages, a great deal of money to offer for one wolf, however crafty. The new master was a careless, impatient man, too, liable to make promises and then forget about them — not like the machtiern. There was greedy Gilbert, too: if the master promised three sous, you could be sure that the bailiff would keep one of them for himself when he took them from the strongbox. And the master wouldn't want to know about that, but the bailiff would make a man's life wretched if he mentioned it. Still, hunting in the forest was better than mucking out the stables, and even two sous was a lot of money — if it came.

"I'll do my best to find him for you, my lord," Donoal told Alain.

He searched for the king wolf through the freezing end of January and the wet February snow. He found the trail several times — the wolf seemed to inhabit the forest to the west of Talensac, sometimes near Montfort, sometimes near Comper and St. Mailon's, but never too far away — and his master came and hunted it with the hounds. Each time the crafty animal slipped away, and the dogs were left chilled and discouraged, usually on someone else's land. The third time, it was the lord of Montfort's land. Lord Raoul de Montfort, when he found out, was furious, and accused Alain of poaching. He was the most powerful baron in the district, and it was not good to offend him. Alain was forced to make a humiliating apology.

When Donoal next found the trail, it lay on the edge of the

ducal forest of Treffendel. Alain did not dare follow the wolf onto the duke's land. He was not eager to be accused of poaching again, and by Hoel. But he remembered that there was another thing he could try.

At Christmas Tiher had been appointed the duke's Master of the Hunt. Alain had felt aggrieved when he learned this: the position was a salaried office in the ducal household, an administrative post of some influence in the hunt-loving court. It was a much better place than he himself had ever been offered. Still, it might now prove itself useful. What could be more natural than for him to write Tiher a letter inviting the duke to come and hunt the wolf? And that, thought Alain with satisfaction, would finish the beast. The monster would not find it so easy to slip away from a court hunting party. The duke had hundreds of hounds at his disposal and he had the finest huntsmen in Brittany. He had the lymer Mirre, too. Whenever Alain's hounds had lost the wolf's trail, Donoal's response had been, "Mirre might have found it." Alain had had to check himself from cursing Eline for giving the dog away.

By this time, the ducal court had moved back to Rennes. So it was in the Great Hall at Rennes, on a Sunday after lunch, that Tiher read Hoel a letter he had received from his cousin.

"'My dear cousin,'" he read, "'do you think our lord the duke would care to hunt the wolf? There is a most marvelously crafty animal near here, which has crossed onto his land. I hunted it myself while it was on my land, and once followed it into my lord de Montfort's forest—and I was not after boar, despite what he says—but it's always given me the slip. The people here call it the king wolf. It's a big animal, in its prime, and would give our lord good sport if he came to chase it.'"

Hoel took the letter and frowned at it with interest. "In which forest is this animal to be found?" he asked.

"From what he says, I imagine it's Treffendel," Tiher replied. "That's the only forest of yours that borders on Talensac."

Hoel nodded thoughtfully. He had a large hunting lodge in the forest of Treffendel. He had not used it for some years, but the resident forester and his family would have kept the place in order. It would not hold the entire court, but it was big enough to take a hunting party and had kennels for all the dogs.

"You really want to go wolf hunting?" asked the duchess resignedly. She could never see the point of hunting an animal one couldn't eat. If a wolf or a fox or an otter was making a nuisance of itself, it was much easier to set traps for it than to go after it with a hundred or so dogs and a couple score of riders.

Duke Hoel grinned. "But it's great sport, my dear! There's no beast of the chase as full of tricks as a crafty old wolf! It's been a gray, grim month, and next month is Lent and we'll all be repenting of our sins, *miserere nobis Domine*! Why don't we go to Treffendel for a week of pleasure first?"

"I don't see the pleasure in galloping after wolves through a soaking-wet forest at the tail end of winter, thank you!" Havoise exclaimed. "But it's true it's been a gray, grim month, and I'm heartily sick of this gray, grim castle. Yes, let's go to Treffendel! I'll sit by the fire and toast my toes, and see that you have hot wine to drink when you come back frozen and empty-handed after a day spent chasing this marvelously crafty wolf. Why is Alain de Fougères being so generous with his quarry, do you suppose?"

"Self-righteousness," replied the duke at once. "Lord de Montfort accused him of poaching boar: if I catch his wolf, he's vindicated."

Havoise chuckled.

The high table soon hummed with arrangements for the hunting party: who was coming and who wasn't; who among the noblemen of the region would like to be invited and who would be glad not to be. Alain had to be asked, since he had provided the quarry, but he would not be invited to stay at the lodge. "He can ride over from Talensac on the morning," said Hoel. "Treffendel isn't big enough to hold every knight in the region." Which was true, though no one doubted that Tiarnán would have been invited, had he still been lord of Talensac.

Marie now took it for granted that she would come in atten-
dance on the duchess, and she was not disappointed.

"But you don't need to sit by the fire at Treffendel; you must
come hunt the wolf," said Tiher, grinning at her. "You'll bring
me luck."

Tiher was responsible for organizing the hunt, and he knew
he needed luck. Since being given his office at Christmas, he'd
arranged a few boar hunts in the forest of Rennes, but this wolf
hunt was clearly going to be a much bigger affair. What with
the duke and duchess and a large group from the court moving
to the hunting lodge for a week and most of the nobility of the
region joining the hunt itself, a new Master of the Hunt who
made a mess of things was likely to find himself a mere household knight again. Wolves were difficult creatures, shy and hard
to find, and when found full of cunning ruses that could baffle
all but the best hounds. Hunts for them had to be organized as
carefully as battles, with relays of dogs stationed at strategic
locations and every attention paid to the terrain and the direction of the wind. Tiher felt that he could do the organizing as
well as any man at the court, but it would all count for nothing
if bad luck intervened—if, for example, the quarry had moved
somewhere else by the time the hunting party arrived to chase
it. Tiher crossed himself at the thought.

And then, too, it would be impolite to take on too much of
the organizing. It was, after all, the duke's wolf hunt. "I hope
my lord the duke will have mercy on a poor novice like myself,"
Tiher said carefully, "and take as much of the business as he
can into his own skilled hands."

Hoel laughed. "Prettily said! You knew perfectly well I'd
never be kept from the business, and you make a virtue of
necessity. But the first part of this battle I'll leave to you. Take
some of the servants and go to Treffendel today: have them get
the lodge ready, while you consult with my forester there and
with Lord Alain about where this marvelously crafty wolf is to
be found.—Oh, and take Mirre with you. She'll sniff the beast
out for you. The rest of us will come to join you tomorrow."

he wolf knew nothing about the arrangements for the duke's hunting party. He had been living in Treffendel forest for about two weeks by then, hunting by night and curling up in the dry leaves beneath a bramble bush to sleep during the day. He had decided to stay near Treffendel for a time: he remembered the forest, and knew that the man who had been hunting him could not come there. And he was tired, very tired, of being hunted.

For months, it seemed, he had been running, living from day to day with no company but Hunger, Fear, and Cold. Loneliness was worse than any of them. Wolves, like humans, are social creatures, happiest with others of their kind. Instinct and drowned memory agreed in longing for others, but humans and wolves alike treated him with fear and loathing. He met other wolves in the forest from time to time, and they always understood that he wasn't one of them. They would fall back at first, snarling and yelping. If he refused to go away, they attacked.

He went to St. Mailon's sometimes, but only when he couldn't bear the loneliness, when the vastness of the forest seemed to crush him, and the ache of longing for what he'd lost swelled to become unendurable. It was an immense relief to scratch at the door of Judicaël's hut and be welcomed. He would lie on the floor beside the fire, and the hermit would talk to him and stroke his head, and then say the offices and pray beside him. Judicaël gave him food, too: bread soaked in goat's milk. He ate it, though it made his stomach hurt. Warmth and food and company: paradise. But he never dared remain beyond a single night. He understood why he was being hunted, and it was easy to guess that if he went to St. Mailon's often, the way would be filled with traps. Besides, there was always a danger of meeting a stranger there. Judicaël was much admired, and the people of the region often came to him for advice. The wolf's instincts were afraid of any unknown human, and his struggling reason feared for the safety of his only friend. On top of that, Judicaël had only the food that people gave him, and always sternly refused to accept more than he needed: if he fed the wolf, it usually meant that he himself went hungry. So he went to St. Mailon's only infrequently, always coming after nightfall and leaving before the dawn. He tried to stay away from the hermit's goat, afraid that his hungry instincts would lead him to kill it.

Hunger, then, was his closest companion. It followed him devotedly, stepping in his shadow. A whole wolf pack will have difficulty bringing down a healthy hind, let alone a stag: one wolf on its own must live on smaller game, and small game is scarce in winter. The wolf caught rabbits, mice, and voles; he snatched roosting birds from bushes in the darkness; he ate rats on the edges of farms, and frogs and beetles dug from the frozen earth. Sometimes sheep were left overnight in the fields, but he rarely dared approach them, and they were more usually enclosed. The carcasses left as lures he'd welcomed as a feast. Other wolves were always there first, but he took advantage of their fear to snatch a part of the carcass and run away with it. And he knew all the wolf hunter's tricks, and never stayed near the baited woods until morning.

Fear was only a visitor, but a frequent one. He would catch the scent of men and dogs on the morning air, or hear the horns in the distance, and he would run from them. Chilled and worn from a night's hunting, he would strain every limb to escape, and wrestle with his buried memory for the craft to outwit the hounds. Even after escaping, he could feel no elation. The chases exhausted him, slowing him the next night, making it harder to catch food.

He knew who was hunting him. Judicaël had told him. He couldn't understand half of what the hermit said to him, but he'd understood that. Eline had married his one-time rival, and the two of them meant to kill him. When he thought of it, the anguish and helpless rage were so terrible that he tried to bury them. There was no point in remembering that he had ever been human: it would be far better to forget, to drown the struggling self and become entirely a wolf. But the self refused to drown. It struggled on, sometimes completely submerged, at other times horribly aware, freshly appalled at how it was trapped. He hated it for the pain it gave him, but he could not get rid of it.

He'd been reluctant to leave Talensac land. It had been comforting, in his intense loneliness, to at least be in country he knew, which he'd loved as a human and filled with pleasant memories. In the end, though, it was a relief to be away from it. Treffendel forest lay a little farther from farmland and it was guarded against poaching peasants by the duke's resident forester, so the small animals he lived on were more plentiful. Hunger dropped another step behind. It was the beginning of March now, too, and his other loving companion, Cold, was also retreating. Best of all, no one had come to hunt him during the whole of the time he'd been at Treffendel. He was beginning to relax, to feel that Fear had given up visiting him for a while. It was a numbing shock when he woke suddenly in early daylight to a scent of dogs and the sound of feet crackling in the brambles.

He leapt up and ran from them, twisting his way through the thickest snarls of bramble and dog rose. As he ran, he heard the horns begin to blow close behind him, the quick, stammering call of the view, for the unharboring of the quarry from its bed. Fast on the horn call came the baying of the hounds as they caught his scent. He did not think anything, not in that moment: all his being was taken up in running.

He had chosen his bed carefully, picking a place with thick cover and near water, a stream that flowed into the Chèze River to the south. He splashed into it with relief and ran along it, upstream because that direction took him with the wind, keeping his scent from the dogs. Where the stream turned he left it and continued to run with the wind. The sound of the baying changed from the full excited cry of hounds on the scent to the irregular and angry one of those that had lost it. He stretched out and ran at his full speed. It was a simple puzzle and would not hold them long; meanwhile, he must win some distance.

The hounds were in full cry again within minutes, but the minutes had been enough. He had enough space now to mislead them. He ran through a thicket, doubled back on his tracks, then leapt as far as he could sideways. He ran on, came to a tree that had broken in half during a gale and lay with its top branches sloping upward from the ground to the break in its trunk. He scrambled through the branches, up the slope to the top, doubled halfway back, and jumped off. He doubled his tracks again, and ran on, still going with the wind, but more slowly now. That would delay them a little. Now he must circle round and find a good place to lose them entirely.

The self had time to surface inside him now. It was furious that they had been able to get so close. He had been careless. And what did *he*, the enemy, think he was doing, hunting in a ducal forest?

The horns sounded again: *Da-∂a ta ta ta ta, Da-∂a ta ta ta ta* — the call for the quest, when the hounds have come to some check. The baying had again fragmented. Too many hounds, he realized suddenly; too many horns. This was not one man and his servants hunting with the remembered pack. This was a large hunting party. He did not try to puzzle out how or why. He had no energy to spare for the difficult and laborious business of reasoning. But he knew he was in even greater danger than he'd at first supposed. There would be more hounds, fresh ones, waiting elsewhere in the forest: there would be trackers and beaters. *Mercy!* he thought, the word surfacing and filling his whole mind as he ran. Oh God, have mercy!

No mercy, no more than he had found when last that plea had risen in his mind. The puzzle he'd set didn't keep them as long as he'd hoped. It was only minutes later that the strong, clear baying rose again, and the horn, joyful and merciless, sounded the *rechace*. He put his head down and ran.

He tried every puzzle, every ruse, that he had ever heard of. He doubled and redoubled his tracks; crossed and recrossed streams; fled through sheets of icy water, left in low patches in the forest by the melting snows, and through nearly impenetrable tangles of thorns. He nested one trick within another. Several times he thought he'd lost his pursuers, only to hear them taking up the call once more, faint in the distance at first, but always coming nearer, always too close. He could not circle back, as he longed to, to find the stretch of marsh or the lake where he was sure he could lose them. Instead he was forced downwind, northeast. As he'd feared, there were relays of fresh dogs in that direction: he heard the new cries, eager and excited, joining the old. Noon came and went, and the cries came steadily nearer. He could not shake them. His legs were trembling now, and his lungs hurt. The human part of him curled up inside, weeping in exhaustion and despair, and the wolf ran on blindly.

The hunt had forced him north and north again, and he burst suddenly from the trees onto the open space of a road. He recognized it as the road from Montfort to Plelan, the boundary between the forest of Tremelin, which had been his own, and the forest of Treffendel. He stopped, sides heaving. It was late in the afternoon now, and he knew he would not live to see the night. The human self suddenly awoke to full consciousness. Death was following him from the woods, the hunter whom no one can flee forever. Since in the end it must be faced, he would face it bravely. No one would praise the courage of a wolf, his body would be given to the hounds to tear—but he would die bravely still, for his own sake.

He began walking slowly along the road, not fleeing now, but only moving to keep himself from collapse. The forest to either side stretched wet and gray; the grass of the verges was deep. Early snowdrops were flowering in the shadows, and the sun rode brilliant in a wrack of windswept cloud. He heard the baying crowd of hounds burst from the forest behind him, and close on their heels came horses and riders. The horns were silent, the huntsmen too tired to spare breath on blowing idly. The wolf turned in the middle of the road to face them all, and the horns suddenly sprang to life again: *Ta ∂a-∂a ta ∂a-∂a ta ∂a-∂a ta ∂a-∂a taaa,* the beast is brought to bay.

There weren't as many of them as he'd expected, only a score of dogs and a handful of riders. The rest must be straggling through the forest, left behind by the furious chase over the rough ground. He saw with a surge of fierce joy that he had a chance to accomplish something before he was killed.

He waited until the hounds were almost on him, then lowered his head, gathered all his remaining strength, and raced
toward them. He rushed into their midst, snapping and tearing
on either side, and they fell back, snarling, yelping, and howling. But he wasted no time on them; he lengthened his stride
and raced on, through the dogs, and in among the astonished
horsemen.

Wild and distorted shouts rang on every side; horses reared;
white faces glared down at him. None of them was the face he
was looking for, the face of his enemy. Confusion began to
drown him, leaving only a wolf's instincts bewildered with terror. Then he glanced up at one of the white faces and recognized it. *My lord*, he thought, with a spasm of senseless hope.
On the thought, he leapt up onto his hind feet, slid a forefoot
into the rider's stirrup, and bent his head to lick the rider's foot.

Duke Hoel gave a shout of fear when the wolf leapt up
against his horse, and his companions cried out in horror.
No one had his sword out. Wolves never turned at bay, and
they'd expected their cunning quarry to be killed at last by the
dogs. Hoel's horse pranced in terror, and for endless seconds
he struggled to pull his weapon out of its scabbard, while his
attendants shoved and got in one another's way as they tried
to draw their own and come to help him. The seconds were
long enough that he noticed them, and noticed, when the sword
was at last in his hand, that the wolf had not sunk its teeth into
his leg and dragged him from his horse; that it was, instead,
licking his boot. He sat with his sword in his hand, staring in
perplexity. His horse stopped prancing and stood trembling
with its ears back. The other huntsmen had their own weapons
out now and drove their horses close to help; beyond them, the
dogs were boiling back up the road after their quarry.

"Stop!" Hoel shouted at them all.

"My lord!" cried Tiher, who'd been at his right hand all day.
His face was white with fear. "Are you hurt?"

"No," said the duke. "Look."

They all looked: there was the wolf they'd chased all day, balanced on its hind legs, licking the duke's foot. It raised its head, stared up at Hoel, whined, then licked the foot again.

"He's asking me for mercy," said Hoel slowly. "By God, I believe he really is begging for mercy." He began to laugh. "The crafty creature!"

"My lord, kill it quickly," said Tiher. "They're evil, dangerous animals. This is only another ruse."

"No!" said Hoel again. "He's begging me to spare his life — and I will. Beat off the dogs, there! Tiher, get a collar for the creature, and a muzzle. We'll take him home alive."

XI

Tiher was appalled at his lord's decision. He would have argued, but at that moment the dogs burst among the riders, and he and all the others had their hands full beating them off. When he next looked at the wolf, it was crouching in the road by the duke's horse. Shivering with terror and exhaustion, it did not look particularly dangerous. He did not trust it any better for that.

More dogs and riders came out of the forest onto the road, demanding to know if the wolf had been taken. Tiher was pleased to find that one of them was the duke's Master of Hounds. He at once told the man to get the dogs under control, and borrowed a stout collar, a thick leash, and a muzzle from him. He dismounted and, unhappily, approached the wolf. Lord Raoul de Montfort, who'd been one of only four hunters to stay beside the duke to the end, jumped from his own horse and came over beside him, his sword drawn. He looked at the collar in Tiher's hands, at the cowering wolf, and finally at the duke, still sitting high on his sweating horse.

"You expect your man to collar and muzzle that beast?" he asked Hoel bluntly.

"No," said the duke, smiling down at him. He slid off his horse beside the wolf. "Give me the collar, Tiher, and I'll put it on him myself."

"No, my lord," said Tiher firmly. "That is something I will not permit."

"You have no business 'permitting' me to do anything!" Hoel replied indignantly.

"And you, my lord, have no business taking stupid risks." Tiher knelt in the road beside the wolf and put the collar around its neck, trying not to think of the stupid risk he was now taking himself. But the animal didn't stir. He buckled the collar snugly and clipped on the leash, then stood up and put the end in the duke's hand. "Your wolf, my lord."

Hoel smiled. "Stupid risks?"

"Yes, my lord. There's no glory for the lord of Brittany in being killed by a wild animal."

The wolf whined and glanced up. He licked Hoel's boot again. Hoel laughed. "He heard you, Tiher. Look at that! He's trying to tell me he won't hurt me."

Tiher sighed in exasperation. He knelt down and, with even more trepidation, fitted the muzzle over the wolf's nose.

The wolf flinched as the man's hands forced the stinking leather over his mouth and nose, but he did not try to fight. The presence of so many men and dogs all around, stinking of fear and hatred, hemming him in on every side, had left his instincts numb with terror. His exhausted human self found it difficult to comprehend what had happened: he had recognized his liege lord, but no one had recognized him in turn, so why hadn't they killed him? He was aware of one of the men stand-ing over him with a drawn sword. Duke Hoel, though, held death in check—a godlike figure towering above on horseback, a man recognized, familiar, who had responded to him. He clung to that awareness like a sick child to his mother.

The muzzle had been designed for an alaunt, a hunting dog with much heavier jaws than a wolf. It did not fit. There was an endless interval of pinching straps and fumbled buckles.

Tiher had fully expected the wolf to leap suddenly at his throat, and was hoping that Raoul de Montfort, who was still standing there with his sword drawn, could strike quickly. When the muzzle was at last secure, Tiher leaned back on his heels and looked at the wolf. The wolf looked back, then low-ered its head, nervously pawed the muzzle, and whined.

"My God!" exclaimed Tiher. "It's tame as a dog."

"When I was a boy at Quimper," said Duke Hoel, "I once tried to tame a wolf cub. I've heard of other men who've tried it, too. Lord Alain said that his wolf came into the middle of

Talensac, but he never said it did any harm there. I think this beast must have been tamed as a cub, and went looking for human company because it was lonely."

"They're evil creatures!" exclaimed Raoul de Montfort angrily. "Yes, I've heard of men trying to tame the cubs. But I've never heard of anyone owning a full-grown tame wolf. The beast's natural savagery always comes to the surface before it's grown. It harms its master as much as it can, and is either destroyed or runs off to do more damage."

"That's what my father said when my wolf cub got into the chicken run," said Hoel with a grin. "And it was destroyed, poor beast. You're right; I've never heard of anyone having a full-grown wolf as a pet. All the more glory for me if I do, eh?" He bent over and patted the wolf's shoulder defiantly. The wolf flinched and cowered.

Still more dogs and hunters straggled from the forest. The duke's forester trotted up with the lymer on her lead. The brown and white bitch had been the first to solve every ruse the wolf set, but she was now limping with exhaustion. Hoel called to the forester to bring her over.

When the lymer came near enough to smell the wolf, she stopped suddenly. Her hackles rose and she stood motionless for a moment, nostrils wide and black. Then she gave a single short sharp bark.

Silence was imposed on all good lymers by breeding and training both. The forester immediately turned on her, gave her a slap, and told her she was a bad dog. Mirre looked embarrassed.

"Oh, be gentle with her!" exclaimed the duke. "She's had hard work today." He gave Tiher the wolf's leash and went over to pat the lymer and pull her long ears.

The other hunters straggled in in knots of two and three. The dogs were rewarded for their efforts with a mixture of chopped mutton and bread brought for the purpose — food that they should have eaten from the stomach of the gutted wolf, as several astonished hunters pointed out. Tiher had the horns blow the *appel de gens* to guide in anyone who had lost the trail, and the *retraite,* to advise them that the party would return to the hunting lodge.

"Have them blow the *prise,* too," ordered Hoel.

"But we haven't killed the quarry!" protested Tiher.

"No—but we have *taken* it." The duke had hold of his wolf's leash again by this time, and he once more bent over and patted the animal delightedly.

The call was added to the other two, and the whole assembly began to move off. Raoul de Montfort and his men departed for their own manor, still shaking their heads over the folly of trying to keep a wolf as a pet, and the other lords who'd joined the duke for the hunt did much the same. The duke's party turned back into the forest for the long ride back to Treffendel, occasionally blowing their horns to summon their companions and let the world know what success they'd had.

Alain de Fougères was still in the forest, walking his horse northward, when he heard the horns in the distance. The horse had gone lame shortly before noon; he'd whipped it and ridden on for a while, but it was no use: the beast could not carry him any more that day, and he'd fallen far behind the hunt. He stopped now under the bare gray branches listening intently. The *appel de gens,* the *retraite,* and the *prise.* His heart seemed to stop for a moment, and he remained motionless, listening, hoping the calls would be repeated. Quick and clear it came once more: the *prise.*

He crossed himself, then knelt down in last autumn's leaves and thanked God. The monster was finally dead. And it was the right wolf this time: he was sure of it. He had sensed it somehow from the moment the beast was unharbored, and every twist of the trail, every more than naturally cunning ruse, had made him more certain. The shadow that had haunted the fringes of the manor, that made his wife wake weeping in the night, was no more. It was a shame, a great shame, that he hadn't been there at the death himself, but he could go back to Talensac now and tell Eline that she was free at last. And nothing was discovered. They'd hardly blow the *prise* so cheerfully if they knew what it was they'd killed.

He wanted to turn toward Treffendel and see for himself that everything was indeed as good as it sounded—but it was miles to the hunting lodge, he hadn't been invited to stay there overnight, and the household knights would be disdainful if he invited himself. It was a long way back to Talensac, going on foot, and he wouldn't reach it until after dark as it was. Better to go straight there. Eline would be waiting anxiously for his news. He stood, brushed off his knees, and walked on toward his home, smiling.

Marie had almost reached the road when the ducal party turned back into the forest. She was mounted on her own mare, which was why she'd fallen behind. The vile-tempered Dahut had decided about noon that she'd done enough galloping in bad country for one day, and since then Marie had had to struggle hard to make her move at all. One of the household knights had stayed beside her to protect her, but he was, inevitably, not one of her favorites. Brient of Poher, his name was: a thin, awkward, silent young man whose notion of how to pay court to a lady was to suggest that they sit down and have a rest together, and then grope. She'd had two struggles to undertake at once: one with the horse, and the other with Brient's offers of assistance. It was a relief when the others appeared at the forest edge, riding toward her.

"Honor to the war leader!" she called to Tiher, who was at the duke's side in front of all the others. She spoke in the Breton which the whole hunt had been using all day: it now seemed so natural to her to slip between it and French that it was a shock to remember that only a year before she hadn't spoken any of the language. "I gather from the horns that your plan of battle worked!"

"Duke Hoel's plan of battle," returned Tiher sourly. "But, yes, we got the victory and are leading the enemy captive home." He gestured, and for the first time Marie noticed the muzzled wolf, towed on its leash behind the duke's horse.

She was shocked. She didn't know what to say, so she said

nothing. When the party came abreast of her, she turned her mare in beside Tiher's mount and let Dahut walk at the other's pace. Brient, looking disgruntled, fell in behind.

Hoel laughed. "Lady Marie, that look said more than all the scoldings the others have given me. 'Christ and Saint Michael!' it said. 'What is he doing with a wicked, stinking beast like that?'"

"My lord," she replied, "you are hunting in your own forest: you have the right to do whatever you like with a beast you've taken."

"Well said! Do you hear that, Tiher? Lady Marie doesn't like wolves any more than you do, but there's none of this 'I won't permit that' from her, none of Lord Raoul's 'It's an evil beast,' none of that carping about the poor, tired hounds needing their reward. 'I have the right to do what I like with a beast I've taken.' That's good!"

Tiher looked exasperated but restrained himself. "When the beast turned at bay, it ran through the dogs and jumped up to lick Duke Hoel's foot," he explained instead to Marie. "He thinks that it must have been tamed as a cub. It does seem tame, but I'd feel happier if I knew what had become of the man who tamed it."

"If a man had been killed by a wolf he'd reared, we'd have heard about it," said the duke confidently.

"Wouldn't we have heard about it if a man had lost his tame wolf cub?" Tiher asked.

"Indeed we wouldn't," replied Hoel. "If a man's tame wolf ran off into the forest, the next time any neighbor of his lost a beast to any wolf at all, or even to a stray hunting dog or fox, you can be sure his wolf would be blamed for it. No, a man who'd lost a wolf would be sure to keep quiet about it. But *I* won't lose you, eh, Wolf?" Hoel glanced affectionately at the wolf, which walked dejectedly at his horse's heels. "You're a fine beast. I believe he's the craftiest creature I ever hunted, Tiher. If we hadn't had the luck to surprise him this morning, and that wonderful lymer bitch to help us, he'd have got clear away from the lot of us. That was a chase to remember! And a fitting end to it, too! But what did you mean, saying you wouldn't 'permit' me, eh? — Marie, I told him to give me the collar to put on the beast, and he refused and said he would not permit me to take stupid risks!"

Tiher set his teeth. "My lord, how could any liege man of yours permit you to risk your life in such a trivial cause?"

"Huh!" said the duke, and beamed down at his wolf again.

It was perfectly plain to Marie that Hoel was very pleased with Tiher. It was odd that Tiher didn't realize that. She smiled to herself.

Hoel caught the smile. "What are you grinning at, Mistress Cat?"

"I was remembering a compliment the duchess paid my judgment," returned Marie. She glanced significantly toward Tiher.

The duke's mouth twitched. "You're lucky I like clever women. Tell me, what shall I call my wolf?"

"What does one call a wolf?" asked Marie. "Isengrim?"

"As in the fable?" said Tiher. "Reynard the Fox and Lord Isengrim the Wolf! A very wicked lord, as I recall, much like a Norman baron."

"This wolf is a good Breton wolf," the duke said reprovingly. "But the name . . . ye-es, I like it. I called the wolf cub I kept Wolf, but Isengrim is altogether grander. You hear that, Wolf? Your name is Isengrim! Good boy, Isengrim, good wolf!"

The wolf trailed after him looking more dejected than ever.

It was dark when they reached the hunting lodge, and the wind, which had gusted all day, had risen so that the bare branches of the trees rocked and hissed across the sky. It was beginning to rain, the cold, driving rain of early March, and the hunting party was very ready to go in by the fire. Instead it was forced to stand around discussing what to do with Isengrim. The Master of Hounds refused to have the animal in the kennels: "It would disturb the dogs." Duchess Havoise, who appeared to greet her husband and was brought into the consultation, adamantly refused to have the beast in the house: "I'm sure it's not housebroken." It was eventually decided to chain the wolf in the boiling shed by the kitchen. This was only used to prepare boar carcasses in the season, and was empty. When a chain had been found, fastened to the collar, and secured to a cauldron bracket, the Master of Hounds reluctantly fetched a dish of the bread and offal mix fed to the dogs, together with a bowl of water. The forester fetched a long forked pole and pinned the wolf's head to the ground with it so that the muzzle could be removed without any danger. Isengrim did not fight when this was done, and did not pay any attention to the food afterward. They left him crouching on the boiling room floor. The last thing Marie noticed was the red glare of the torchlight in his eyes.

She had not protested at the duke's decision to keep the animal, but she was still horrified. Wolves for her were inextricably bound up with what had happened to her in the forest near Bonne Fontaine. The thought of the creature crouching in the boiling shed, eyes gleaming, hung heavy on her mind. She fell asleep easily that night, healthily tired from the exertions of the hunt, but before morning she was tossing uneasily in a nightmare.

She was in the forest again, and a wolf was hunting her. She ran, her face whipped by the low branches of the trees, her clothes torn by the clinging fingers of the thorns. The mud of peat bogs dragged at her feet, and the icy rain stung her. She tripped at last and fell. At once the beast was upon her, snarling horribly, and its teeth locked in her shoulder. She struggled to her feet and tried to pull away from it, and she heard a rip, and saw the animal's red eyes glaring as it tore a long bloody seam of flesh from her back. She woke sweating and struggling.

She lay still for a minute, her heart pounding. She was alone tonight: the other ladies Havoise had brought to attend her were all married, and Marie had been given a bed and a partition all to herself. She'd rolled against the side of the bed and knocked her shoulder against the post.

She sat up, pressed her hands against her face, and said some prayers to steady herself. Her partitioned-off room was a corner of the hall, and she could tell from the soft breathing all around her that the rest of the hunting party was asleep. But she did not want to return to sleep, in case the wolf was waiting there to meet her again.

The cure for nightmares, she told herself, was to confront them. In sleep the wolf had hunted her, but in reality, she had hunted it. It was a poor, frightened animal and securely chained, and when she saw it she wouldn't need to feel afraid. She pulled her gown on, picked up her cloak, shoved her bare feet into her shoes, and picked her way carefully around the side of the partition and across the hall of the lodge to the door. As she opened it, Mirre padded over to her from some corner — the lymer was a favorite of the duke's and allowed the run of any of his houses. Marie patted her and allowed the animal to follow her out.

The sky was clear, and the rain-wet ground was dark with patches of ice. The sun was not yet up, but the stars were fading, and there was a smear of pink in the east. The servants were beginning to stir; she could hear sleepy voices from the kitchens, and the splash of water in a pail. Marie pulled her cloak over her shoulders and walked slowly toward the boiling shed.

The wolf was curled up in the middle of the boiling shed floor. He had drunk all the water left for him but had not eaten. The animal part of him was stunned with terror, and the human self bewildered with shame. He should never have begged for mercy. Twice he'd begged for it in thought and received none: he should not have degraded himself a third time. His life was not worth living, and he had been prepared to die bravely. It was only confusion, a moment's forgetting of what he was, that had made him turn to his lord in hope. Against all likelihood, he'd now been granted mercy — and what did that mercy consist of? Muzzles and chains, and the condescending goodwill or loathing of those who'd respected him as a man. *Good wolf, good boy!* Even in his voiceless daze, the condition seared his heart, and he wished he were dead.

He lifted his head from his tail when Marie came to the door, but did not otherwise move. He recognized her at once: she was one of the few humans of the court whom he'd seen in his present form. She had waved a stick at him in the forest once, and yelled "Scat!"

That had been just after his betrothal to Eline: he had gone out into the forest as a man, walking at random because the joy had been so great he had wanted to treasure it to himself for a time. And in the middle of the forest he had been over-come by the desire to lose himself completely in the sweet drunkenness of Broceliande in Spring. He had occasionally left the human part of himself somewhere other than St. Mailon's — casually, it now seemed to him, with a carelessness verging on the criminal. He'd left it then, and it was as a wolf that he'd seen the girl, and scented the robbers nearby, and reluctantly realized that he'd have to intervene. The human memory of how he'd found her imposed itself on the wolf's memory of the first meeting: the one robber crouching on her feet while the other two peeled her clothes off. He had rescued her and brought her to safety, and she had honored him and been grateful.

And what had become of that honor and gratitude now? He was nothing more than a beast from which the woman recoiled. He had smelled the fear on her the previous evening, and he could smell it again now.

There was a dog with her, too, a bitch, a house dog, with the scent of humans and smoke clinging to her fur. She stood beside the woman with her head down and her hackles raised, making a low singsong noise in her throat, part whine and part growl. He did not growl back, only stared at them both impas-sively.

The dog stopped growling, shook herself, and gave a soft, bewildered "Wuff!" She took a step nearer, her nostrils flaring. He could smell her distress and confusion, and began to be puzzled by them. All the other dogs hated him. They would hate any wolf, but they particularly hated him, because they could sense something unnatural about him. This dog was dif-ferent. It was the same one that had barked at him the day before, barked in greeting rather than defiance. It was a . . . he dragged the word up, a *lymer*. He had once had one that he had particularly treasured. *Mirre*, he thought, *it's Mirre*. And as he thought it, he understood suddenly that she had recognized him; that somehow, under all the other scents, she had smelled out the self, and was bewildered at where she found it. He climbed to his feet, pierced with joy. Someone, even if only a dog, had recognized him.

He whined, and Mirre gave up trying to understand what he'd done to himself, and bounded over. She licked his face and paws, her tail wagging so hard that her hindquarters slipped with a scratch of toenails back and forth across the floor. Here was the master. He had covered himself in wolf, for some reason, but it was him. *Good girl, Mirre!*

arie hadn't expected the duke's prize dog to bound up to the wolf: lymers were not expected to attack prey, just to track it. She gave an exclamation of dismay, then stared in disbelief as the lymer fawned happily upon the wolf. "Mirre!" she called urgently. "Here, Mirre!"

Mirre whined and looked at the wolf. He licked her ears gently, and she lay down in front of him, ignoring Marie. Isengrim lay down as well, and rested his chin on the dog's back, looking at Marie challengingly.

She suddenly remembered Tiarnán at his wedding, saying he was not afraid of werewolves because wolves are "gentler beasts than they're given credit for." The memory, which had been buried, leapt perfectly clear. She knelt down, facing the wolf, looking into the light brown, black-rimmed eyes. They were unreachably alien, yet they held neither malice nor hatred. The eyes of Éon's wolf skin had been hollow, she remembered: all the savagery she'd dreaded had been in the human eyes beneath. Was that always the case? Wolves were dangerous: they killed sheep, and occasionally, so the stories said, children; they followed armies and fed on human flesh. But in the end they were far less deadly than men.

Without pausing to reflect, she extended her hand toward the wolf; even as the gesture was completed, she realized it was lunacy to try to touch an unmuzzled killer from the forest. But

Isengrim only sniffed at her hand politely. Marie held her breath and touched him. The fur of his neck was unexpectedly soft and warm. Slowly she pulled her hand away and sat back on her heels, staring. The wolf stared back unblinking. He was, she thought, really a rather beautiful animal. "I won't have nightmares about you again," she said aloud.

She got to her feet. Mirre rose as well, then turned back and once more lay down beside the wolf. Marie left her there and walked back to the lodge, feeling unreasonably happy.

Isengrim, watching her go, felt much the same. The dog had recognized him, and the woman had not recoiled. It might be possible to go on living, after all.

Alain de Fougères arrived at the hunting lodge shortly after noon and found Duke Hoel settling accounts with the forester. He bounced up when he saw Alain, however, and shook his hand. "There you are!" he exclaimed happily. "I'm pleased you came; I wanted to thank you for your invitation. That was a chase, eh? Craftiest beast I ever hunted."

"Indeed, my lord," said Alain contentedly. "I was sorry I missed the death. My horse went lame."

"Ah, that was a pity! You missed a very fine sight, a very fine sight indeed." Hoel chuckled. "But you didn't actually miss the death."

Alain stared in incomprehension. "My lord?"

"Your wolf was tame," said Hoel. "When he was brought to bay, he ran through the hounds and jumped up to lick my foot. I couldn't kill him after that. We have him chained up in the boiling shed. He's a very fine beast."

The disaster was so overwhelming that Alain could not immediately comprehend it. He gaped at the duke stupidly. He thought he would be sick. The wolf was still alive. It was alive, and it was under Hoel's protection. Eline had been so delighted when he'd told her the good news. She'd sent him off that morning with kisses and smiles. Now — God! God in Heaven! Oh God, what was he to do now?

"Are you all right?" asked Hoel, suddenly concerned. "You look ill." He helped Alain to a chair.

"I . . . wasn't well this morning," muttered Alain vaguely. "Drank some bad water yesterday, I think."

"You shouldn't have ridden over today, then," said Hoel.

"I thought it would pass. And . . . and I was shocked at what you said. The creature ran through the hounds and leapt up at you? My lord, you can't really mean to keep a *wolf* as a pet? An evil animal like that would—"

"I can do what I like with a beast I've taken in my own forest," said Hoel complacently. "He's a fine animal and very well behaved. My lymer bitch seems to have adopted him, and he's settling down nicely. I'm calling him Isengrim."

Desperately, Alain tried again. "My lord, you can't—"

"Enough of that! I meant to thank you for your invitation to hunt the creature. I'm very pleased to have him."

Alain didn't hear him. His heart was pounding, and his mind reeled in distraction. Hoel said something more, and Alain came to himself and asked, "My lord?"

"You look very ill," repeated Hoel. "Shall I send for some hippocras for you, or some barley broth?"

"No, my lord," said Alain, struggling to master himself. "No, it's passing. I'll be fine in a minute."

Hoel left him sitting by the fire and went to have another look at his wolf. Isengrim got to his feet when the duke appeared and wagged his tail politely. Hoel was delighted. Like most serious hunters, he had a great affection and admiration for the beasts he pursued, and wolves, crafty and elusive, had always been particular favorites of his. It was for that reason that he'd once tried to tame his ill-fated cub. He had Isengrim muzzled, and then sat beside him and talked to him for a little while, patting him occasionally, letting him become accustomed to his master. Isengrim watched him attentively, flinched less and less at being touched, and seemed already far less afraid than he had been the day before. Hoel wondered if the muzzle was even necessary. When the duke went back to the lodge, he felt grateful to Alain for providing him with such a magnificent animal.

Alain was still sitting by the fire, but he'd regained his color, and when Hoel came in he jumped up and answered the necessary inquiry with the news that he was quite better now.

"Good," said Hoel heartily, then hesitated. He had something more he meant to say to this knight of Fougères, and it was hard to phrase it so as not to give offense. His bailiff Grallon had been concerned about the state of affairs at Talensac. He had given Hoel a complete account of the manor, and Hoel had been concerned in turn.

"My man Grallon," Hoel began, "told me that you wanted to raise the rents on your estate. He thought there was some question of repaying a debt to a Jew in Nantes."

Alain straightened his shoulders uncomfortably. He had asked Grallon's advice on the rents before the bailiff returned to the court. He had asked about reducing the relief, too, despite what Eline had said at Fougères: it had seemed worth at least trying. The longer he stayed at Talensac, the more he wanted money. He was sick of sleeping in Tiarnán's bed between Tiarnán's sheets, sitting in Tiarnán's chair, eating off Tiarnán's plates, and looking at Tiarnán's hunting tapestries on the walls. Eline was having nightmares in that house she'd shared with the werewolf. Alain wanted to clear out all the old haunted things and buy new. He saw nothing shameful in that. But it was humiliating to be in debt with a manor where the previous lord had always had a surplus, and Alain knew that Hoel did not think well of him to begin with.

"Well . . ." he said unhappily — and then, as there was no help for it, "that's true, my lord."

"You mean you are in debt to this Jew?"

"Yes," Alain admitted. "But it's not . . . that is, Talensac *is* mine, isn't it?"

"No," returned Hoel, more coldly. "It's mine. Tiarnán held it from me, in fee of service, and I permitted his widow to do homage for it: she married you. That makes you lord of it, but the land still belongs to me." He paused, then gestured for Alain to be seated on one of the benches and took his own chair. "Never fear," he went on in a gentler tone. "I recognize your rights in the place. So, you are in debt. Well, God knows, your father's a hard man and a strict one. You weren't brought up to manage an estate: I can understand if it went to your head. But, listen, this business of increasing the rents must be dropped."

That was what Grallon had said, but Alain had not been completely convinced. "My bailiff says they're low. He says my father charges twice as much."

"The rents have always been higher in the March than in the rest of Brittany," replied the duke. "Your father's peasants are accustomed to it; yours aren't. Listen and I'll give you some good advice. You've moved into the manor of a man who was more than ordinarily well liked by the people he governed. To make things worse, you're a foreigner to them, speaking a foreign tongue. I know, I know, you're a Marcher lord and you don't like hearing this from a Breton speaker from the wilds of Cornouaille, but the fact is, everyone born east of Rennes is a foreigner to Talensac. Your predecessor was the son of the family that had held the place for generations. If Saint Paul the Apostle became lord of Talensac, the villagers would still condemn him in comparison to a Talensac man. If you want to do well in the place, you will have to tread very gently."

"Do you think I care about having the good opinion of peasants?" demanded Alain angrily.

"You're a fool if you don't," said the duke. "Everything depends on them, and they can make an estate profitable or ruin it. Do you hope to earn any extra money by selling wood from your forest, or apples and beer from your orchards and fields? Do you expect to make money on charcoal or surplus pork? If the peasants hate you, you won't make a penny over the rents, believe me. 'Lord,' they'll say, 'the timber was all broken in a gale this year; the pigs didn't breed as we'd hoped; the apples spoiled, the barley wouldn't brew properly, and we have nothing left over our entitlement.' They'll spoil the things themselves sooner than let you profit from them. And even the rents can go. If a farmer comes to you and says, 'I can't pay the whole sum this year'—what are you going to do? Beat him and put him in the stocks? It won't produce the money, his friends will look after him, and you'll have to let him out to work. Turn him out of his cottage? Who's going to take his place? Nobody's going to move to a village where the lord has a bad name. You won't find anyone to till his fields, and next year you'll get nothing from that land at all. And beyond all that, a manor where you're hated is not a pleasant place to settle in with a young wife and raise a family. I've seen men who made it work, but they were very much stronger and crueler than you are, and even they weren't happy. That's no insult, Lord Alain. Think of it as a piece of advice from one who's seen many estates made and ruined, and wants yours to do well. If your creditor is pressing you, sell some of your horses and hounds. I'll even help myself, if you really can't find the money. But don't push the people into misery, or they'll drag you after them. If you tread gently for a few years, the peasants will get used to you and slowly forget their previous lord. It would help if you could get rid of that Marcher bailiff of yours. Grallon told me he's already made himself very unpopular. I could provide you with a reliable Breton speaker, if you like."

Alain gave him a look of loathing. He remembered all his father's acid comments on how they did things in Breton Brittany: the lack of discipline and refinement, the poverty of the nobles, and the insolence of the peasantry. "I'd rather keep Gilbert," he muttered resentfully.

Nobody, not even a man's overlord, could take away his authority over his own servants. "As you please," said Hoel. "He's your bailiff, and it's your estate. But I hope you'll give him a good talking to." He leaned toward Alain, gripping the arm of the chair. "You can ruin yourself, you know," he said seriously. "It's not just something that happens to other people. And I don't want to see it happen, for your sake, for your wife's, and for the sake of the estate itself." He looked at Alain evenly for another minute, then slapped the arm of the chair and stood up. "Enough of scoldings, then! I meant most of all to thank you for a fine hunt. Do you want to see your wolf?"

Alain wanted and did not want to see the wolf. Its presence had formed an ulcer of horrified fascination on his mind since Hoel first told him it was in the hunting lodge. He allowed the duke to show him out to the boiling shed.

The wolf shook himself and stood up politely as they approached, but when they had stopped in front of him, his black ears went flat against his skull and he began to growl—a terrible sound, low but tense, like noise of a distant war. Alain took a step back just as Isengrim leapt at him—not snarling and barking like a dog, but silently, with all the speed and ferocity of an animal that kills to live. The chain snapped taut against his collar in midleap, and he stood suspended on his hind legs a moment, man-high, leaning against the chain, his fangs gleaming white and his eyes glaring. Alain made a noise of inarticulate terror and drew his sword.

Instantly the wolf was crouching on all fours again, his hackles raised and lips curled in a snarl. He edged rapidly to his right, away from Alain's sword hand, eyes fixed in lethal desire on Alain's throat. Alain turned to follow him, and Hoel caught his arm.

"Put that back!" he snapped. "He's chained up; he can't hurt you. Isengrim! Bad wolf! No!"

Isengrim rose from his crouch. He looked at the duke, and his ears shifted forward. Then he looked back at Alain, and they lay flat again. His eyes met Alain's directly.

For a chilling moment Alain was aware of who he was facing, not just with a secret knowledge, but with a sense as clear as sight. The animal eyes were full of human rage. Tiarnán was alive, and would kill him at the first chance he got. The sense of the wolf's identity was so strong that Alain looked at Hoel with dread, certain that it *must* have touched him, too, that the duke *must* suspect. But Hoel simply looked puzzled. "My lord," said Alain thickly, "it's an evil, savage creature. I beg you, have it killed."

The wolf snarled again.

"He was tame enough this morning," said the duke in

bewilderment. "Well, I suppose it's too much to expect for a wild animal to become used to men all in one day. I hope he'll settle again. And it seems to me it's you he doesn't like. You hunted him before: perhaps he recognizes you. Come away from him now. You're disturbing him."

On the way home Alain burst into tears. The duke's lecture stung, his terrifying enemy was still alive, and he did not know what he was going to say to Eline.

XII

The duke's party left Treffendel the following morning. Isengrim, muzzled again, trotted on his leash behind the duke, and Mirre trotted happily at his side. The courtiers laughed at them: the lean, dark, dangerous wolf and the flop-eared lymer with her mournful face and wagging tail, following the duke's horse together. The duchess laughed harder than anyone.

"Lord!" she exclaimed. "He doesn't like being laughed at, does he? He's gone stiff as a bishop at a bastard's christening. Never mind, Isengrim; it's the dog we're laughing at, not you!" Isengrim glanced up at her with an even more dignified look, and she laughed again.

Marie smiled but didn't laugh. She had learned that St. Mailon's chapel lay not too far from Treffendel, and she was nerving herself to visit it. For some weeks she'd been considering whether to approach Tiarnán's confessor. Eline's bitter declaration that her husband had been worse than a robber was a continued torment, and Marie ached to learn that it was false from the one person who would know. Several times she had dismissed the idea: it was inexcusable for a woman who had been no relation to a man to question his confessor about him. But the idea kept coming back. It would not hurt, surely, to go to St. Mailon's and ask? The worst outcome would be that the hermit sent her off indignantly; the best, that her doubts were laid to rest. "My lady," she now said hesitantly, "do you want me at Rennes immediately?"

"Why do you ask?" Havoise said in surprise.

"I'd like to meet this holy hermit of St. Mailon's that everyone from the region was praising. It's near Lent, and I thought perhaps he could suggest some spiritual disciplines for me."

The duchess gave her a shrewd look. "By 'everyone from the region' you mean Tiarnán."

"Others praised him, too," Marie answered with a smile, "but, yes, I suppose that's the opinion I most respected."

"Well, certainly you may go and see him!" said Havoise. "Hoel, my dear! Marie wants to go see the hermit of St. Mailon's. Give her an escort, my love!"

"Tiher!" said the duke. "Escort Lady Marie to St. Mailon's, and bring her back to Rennes this evening."

"With pleasure!" said Tiher, grinning. He set his heels to his horse and made it prance to Marie's side. He bowed low in the saddle.

"And remember, you've given up the chase," Marie told him hastily.

"Sweet lady," he protested, kissing her hand, "what a Lenten and spoilsport thing to say!"

Judicaël was kneeling before the altar in his chapel when he heard the sound of horses outside. He rose to his feet and turned just as two people came in. The man wore the sword and spurs of a knight, and was well dressed in a red tunic and fur-lined cloak; the woman wore plain blue-gray, but of good quality cloth, and her cloak too was richly made and lined with fur. Both noble, reckoned Judicaël; the woman wants to consult me before Lent, and the man's escorting her. He sighed inwardly: he felt singularly unfit to counsel anyone, and pious young gentle-women were a trial at the best of times. "God be with you," he said reluctantly. "I am the priest in this place: may I serve you?"

"Christ be with you, Father," said the woman, crossing herself. "I'm sorry to interrupt your prayers. I've heard of your holy way of life here, and I wanted to seek your advice before the season of penitence. Do you have time to see me?"

"My time is not valuable," he said. "But my advice will be of no more use to you than that of your parish priest."

"I'd welcome it, though, if you would give it," said the woman.

Judicaël sighed again, out loud this time, and gestured toward the rushes in front of the altar rail. The man gave a nod of satisfaction and brushed the woman's shoulder with his fingertips. "I'll see to the horses and wait outside," he told her. "Shout if you want me." He nodded politely to the priest and went out.

The woman came up to the altar and knelt down, sitting back on her heels. She looked at Judicaël a moment in silence, and his irritation with her faded. She had a pretty, intelligent face, with a high forehead and level gray eyes, and her air was one of self-possession and quiet resolution. There would be no hysterical pieties from her. He knelt on the other side of the rail, facing her. "Christ be with you, daughter," he said again. "How can I be of help?"

Marie had wanted to speak to Judicaël because he had known Tiarnán. Now that she found herself face-to-face with the hermit, she realized that what she was trying to do was to pry into the secrets of the confessional. What Tiarnán might have told Judicaël was between him and God alone. She had no tie to Tiarnán that could excuse her interest: she was neither sister nor lover. Judicaël's severe, ascetic face and intense dark gaze invited no confidences. Wouldn't he merely rebuke her for meddling curiosity and send her off? Yet she still longed to hear that Eline was wrong. It was love for Tiarnán that had laid her mother's ghost to rest and set her free: if Tiarnán deserved no love, where was her own freedom?

She knelt silently for a long minute, trying to find a way to explain why she needed to know, and to ask for an answer that breached no confidences. "I heard of you from Lord Tiarnán of Talensac," she said at last, "a man to whom I was much indebted. My name is Marie, Marie Penthièvre of Chalandrey. Tiarnán saved me from a robber—I expect you heard the story."

Judicaël's heart jumped senselessly at Tiarnán's name. The wolf had not come to his hut for some weeks now, and he was fully aware of how bitterly Alain had pursued him. He had been praying for his foster son with steadily increasing fear.

"He told me of it himself," Judicaël said, keeping his voice even with an effort. "I was his confessor."

"I'd heard that. What I wanted . . . I don't know how to say this."

"You do not need to fear indiscretions, daughter," Judicaël told her. "I've heard many of them, in my time, and never repeat them, whether they're under the seal of the confessional or not."

"Thank you," said Marie, smiling at him nervously. "Very well. I . . . felt something for Tiarnán." She could feel the blush spreading across her skin at the admission, and she looked down hurriedly. The rushes before the altar were old and thinly scattered: between them she could see a patch of the gray packed clay of the floor. She stared at it as she went on. It was as difficult to open her heart to this man, knowing that he might condemn her, as it would have been to strip herself naked in front of him. But there was no other choice, if she was to have any chance of learning what she wanted to know. "Nothing dishonorable passed between us, and I don't think he was even aware of what I felt. But he mattered a great deal to me."

Judicaël looked at her in surprise. She knelt very still now, her voluminous gray cloak falling in folds from her straight shoulders, her head in its plain white wimple bowed. Her cheeks were stained with embarrassment. Clearly her admission had not been easy for her. Even on first acquaintance, she did not seem to be the sort of woman who fell in love casually. *Had* Tiarnán ever realized that she was in love with him? He had never mentioned it, and had barely mentioned her. Judicaël remembered more about her now: she had been abducted from a convent and was trying to escape back to it when Tiarnán had rescued her; she had since adamantly refused to marry at the duke's orders, out of loyalty to her father's Norman allegiance. Plainly she was a woman of some character. "Go on," he urged, his interest quickening.

"When Tiarnán disappeared," said Marie, her eyes still fixed on the patch of floor, "his widow came to Ploërmel, where I was attending Duchess Havoise. We shared a bed, and when I tried to condole with her on her loss, she told me — alone and in that privacy — that I shouldn't be sorry, that her husband had had a terrible secret, and she was glad that she was free of him. She said," Marie dragged the painful words out with angry force, "that he was a worse monster than the robber he'd saved me from. I would not repeat her words now, except that they have tormented me ever since. I know, Father, that I never had any claim on Tiarnán. I do not pretend otherwise. But . . . what I felt for him I have felt for no other man, and that I *could* feel it set me free from terrors that had long haunted me. If he was a monster and all that I felt was based on ignorant daydreams, then I am still in prison. What Tiarnán may have confessed to you under the seal of the sacrament is sacred. I do not ask to know it. But it would comfort me greatly if you could tell me simply this: Did his wife have real cause to hate him, or not? I swear now, by God and my immortal soul, that if you tell me I will repeat it to no one. I want to know it merely for my own comfort."

To Judicaël the question cut like a sword. He could not trust his own answer to it. He remembered the hysterical girl at Talensac. Could he really state that her distress was causeless? The church he served would champion her. All he had to set against it was the plea that Tiarnán had not become what he was intentionally, and that he had never deliberately injured anyone by it: that he knew the man to be innocent. It would never carry in an ecclesiastical court, so why should it carry his own judgment so completely?

"Child, what do you want me to say?" he asked harshly. "I was Tiarnán's confessor, but I was more than that. I was parish priest at Talensac when he was a boy, and the nearest thing he had to a father. Half of what he was is what I made him. So how can I judge between him and his wife? If he is condemned, so am I. Perhaps he was a monster. She certainly thinks so. I cannot believe it; no, never, not of a man I loved so dearly. But I am not to be relied upon. I failed Tiarnán, and I may fail you as well."

Marie raised her eyes at last and looked at him in amazement. She had expected reassurance or condemnation, but not this. "Why do you say you failed him?"

"Because I could never tell him whether the secret for which his wife condemned him was sin or not. If I had condemned it and burdened him with penances, he might be lord of Talensac still."

Marie gazed at him in silence for a long moment. "You're saying, then," she said with an effort, "that you cannot tell me the answer, because you do not know it."

"Yes," said Judicaël with relief. "Child, you said that your love for my foster son set you free of old terrors. If the door to your prison is open, does it matter whether the key that unlocked it was real or counterfeit?"

Marie bit her finger. A door had indeed been opened, and she had stepped through it. But if the key was counterfeit then what was outside the door might really be as terrible as she had always feared. Fleshly love had killed her mother, and at Nimuë's Well it had nearly killed her. She might never know fleshly love — her probable end was the convent — but if she never knew it, it was all the more important to understand the value of what she was missing, for she'd have no chance to experience it for herself.

"I was at Treffendel this week, on a hunting party with the duke," she said, after a long silence. The events there seemed somehow to have some bearing on her question. "He caught a wolf—"

"A wolf?" asked Judicaël sharply.

She looked at him, surprised by the fear in his voice. "Yes," she said.

Judicaël bowed his head. His hands clutched the altar rail before him until his knuckles were white, but he said nothing. There were many wolves in the forest. He had no reason for his heart's instant certainty that this wolf was the one that mattered to him. There could be no funeral, no burial — only private prayers for the dead, and private mourning.

Staring in puzzlement, Marie went on, "Duke Hoel caught this beast alive."

Judicaël's head snapped up again, and his eyes widened in astonishment.

"It ran up to him when it turned at bay," explained Marie, increasingly perplexed, "and it licked his foot, so he spared it and had it brought back to the hunting lodge. He thinks it must have been tamed as a cub. . . . What is the matter?"

The priest's dark eyes were blazing with excitement. "Nothing. Go on."

Marie shook her head in bewilderment. "I was afraid of wolves. I had a nightmare about this beast. When I woke I went to look at it, to convince myself that what I'd dreamed wasn't true."

She stopped for a minute. She saw now why she'd thought of the wolf. The nightmare of the wolf and its reality fitted into her torment like the tossed ball into the cup of a child's game. The thing she'd feared, the thing that lived in the cave where her mother died, was also a nightmare that lost all terror when it was confronted face-to-face. And she'd confronted it twice: once at Nimuë's Well, and once on the day Tiarnán was married. It didn't matter what Tiarnán had been: nothing could make her afraid of earthly love again.

"The wolf I'd been afraid of was nothing but a frightened animal," she said slowly, "a beautiful one. And it's the same with what I learned from Tiarnán. You are right, Father. I don't need to know what his secret was. Even if he was as guilty as his wife believes, what I learned from him is still true."

But Judicaël was not paying attention. "What is the duke going to do with this wolf?" he asked eagerly instead.

She was disconcerted and hurt to find the revelation that was so important to her brushed aside. She looked at the hermit closely; then understanding dawned and she exclaimed, "It's *your* wolf!"

But he shook his head. "No. No. But . . . but I know whose it is."

Marie began to be amused, despite her slighted revelation. "Does he want it back? The duke is very pleased with it. He wants to own the only tame wolf living."

"He has more right to it than anyone else," Judicaël said deliberately. He glanced over his shoulder toward the small crucifix set against the wall. "It seems . . . providential that it should have come to him, and that he should show it mercy." And his face broke suddenly into its peculiar sweet smile. For the first time since his failure at Talensac, he had hope. Tiarnán was safe, and had been accepted by his old liege lord. Accepted as an animal, perhaps, but at least he was among men again and secure from the merciless pursuit of his enemies. The thing was so miraculous that it was almost possible for Judicaël to believe he would one day hear his foster son's voice again. His whole being made one passionate bound of gratitude toward heaven.

"It's a good wolf, is it?" asked Marie, beginning to smile as well. "How did it get loose from its owner?"

"Theft," said Judicaël. "A sorry tale of theft and treachery. I'm very glad to hear that the creature is safe. I was concerned for its owner."

"But he doesn't want his pet back?"

"The duke has a right to keep it. Thank you, daughter." Judicaël gave her another smile of intense joy. "You've brought me news of an answered prayer."

"And you will repeat no indiscretions," said Marie, smiling back. "I see."

He noticed the luminous warmth of her eyes as they met his own, and felt a sweep of affection for her. He had seen her struggling to reach her revelation, and he had not meant to slight it; he was glad to see that she had forgiven him for doing so. He wondered suddenly what Marie would have done if she had learned the secret whose shadow had broken Eline. Recoiled in horror, like Eline? Condemned coldly? Or—was it possible that this woman who could out-face nightmares would have understood?

Judicaël reached over the rail and caught Marie's hand. He

wanted very much to give some answer, however inadequate, to the question she had brought to him. He was not so simple as to believe that her acceptance of ignorance meant she didn't still long to know the truth. She was in love with Tiarnán — deeply in love, for Eline's words to disturb her so much. And for his part, he felt suddenly that her judgment was one he could trust. "Daughter," he said, "I wish you to judge the secret I told you of."

She frowned at him. "I cannot judge a secret I don't share."

"Judge your own terrors, then, and Lady Eline's, as far as you know them. It will be close enough. Let me know when your judgment is complete, for I would accept your decision where I cannot trust my own. And in the meantime, I will pray for our Lord Jesus Christ to guide you."

What was the holy hermit like, then?" asked Tiher, when they were riding back along the road toward Rennes.

Marie was quiet for a minute, then shook her head. "Very odd."

"Well, they have to be, don't they? Holy men, I mean. If they were sturdy, respectable types, no one would take them seriously."

She laughed. "You should become a holy man."

"Perhaps I should. I'll grow out my hair and let my beard trail to my knees, dress in rags, and live in a hut in the forest, abusing everyone who comes near me as sinners, but particularly women, because they're so charming."

"Unfair! Father Judicaël was clean-shaven and very polite. He said, too, that he would trust my judgment on a particular matter above his own."

"Did he really? Sensible man. By Saint Anne, he's shot up in my estimation. I'll bring alms to St. Mailon's this Lent."

"Father Judicaël said he knew who'd tamed the duke's wolf, too," Marie told him.

"Really? So there's an anxious owner awaiting dear little Isengrim's return?"

"There was some story behind it which he wouldn't tell me. Isengrim was stolen from his owner by treachery. But the hermit thought that the duke should keep him now."

"So the court is stuck with the brute?"

"I think it's quite a nice wolf."

"I think it would be even nicer dead. When it jumped up on the duke at the hunt, I was so frightened I ... excuse the thought. The first serious hunt I organize for my lord, I thought, and he goes and spoils it by getting killed!"

"But he didn't."

"No. But he's offended with me over this 'permit' business. He keeps telling people about it. I wish I'd never used the word."

Marie smiled.

"What's that smirk for?"

She burst out laughing. "Tiher, don't you realize that he's delighted with you over that?"

"Is he?" asked Tiher in surprise. He gave it a moment's thought, then broke into a grin. "By God, I believe you're right."

It was late when they reached Rennes, and it had started to rain again. They left their horses in the stables and hurried up the steps of the keep, through the guardroom, and into the hall. The great room was dark, lit only by the central fire, and it was littered with the bodies of sleeping knights. The duke's party had been back for hours. Marie was saying good night to Tiher when a servant appeared from the inner door of the hall and told her that the duke wanted to speak to her and was waiting in his chamber.

Puzzled, she climbed the stairs past the solar to the private apartments of the duke and duchess, and knocked upon the door.

Hoel opened it himself and gestured for her to come in. The room, his dressing room and study, was one he shared with the duchess, and Marie had been in it before. Havoise was there now, sitting at the table by the window. A rack of three candles beside her provided light, and there was a fire burning low and red in the fireplace. Marie noticed, with amusement, that Isengrim, muzzled for safety's sake, had been chained in the far corner next to a large tray of sand. Mirre was curled up beside him. Hoel and Havoise had compromised on how to keep the duke's new pet.

"Marie, my dear," said Havoise, getting to her feet with a wheeze of effort. "I'm afraid that when we got back this afternoon we found a letter with some bad news which affects you."

Marie's amusement vanished. She stood frozen for a moment, staring at the duchess. Then she crossed herself and bowed her head. She felt sick. "What . . . what's happened?" she asked. But she had a horrible feeling that she already knew, that she'd stood before under the lip of this very disaster — only then it had passed over her; it had been her brother.

"Sit down first," ordered Hoel, pushing her over to the other chair at the table. "There. Now, I'm afraid I have to tell you that your father is dead."

She turned toward the blank wicker window screen. Dead. No, this time the avalanche had fallen, as she'd feared: he was dead. He would never be proud of her now, never be glad that she lived. They would never love each other. From the moment she was born, there'd been emptiness between them. Now the emptiness remained, with herself upon the edge, and he was gone, gone, gone forever. He would never return from the Holy Land, and his body would lie in a faraway country, which she could not visit to say good-bye; there would not even be a grave that she could deck with flowers. She wished, painfully, that she had loved him. She'd always wanted to. She'd always wanted so much to please him, and he had always looked impatiently over her head toward his son. What a dishonorable thing the heart is, she thought remotely. I was pleased when Robert was dead, because Father would have to pay attention to me at last. And now I'm repaid for it.

She felt the tears begin and covered her face behind her hands. Havoise came up behind her and put an arm around her shoulders, and she turned, jumped to her feet in a blind lunge that knocked the chair clattering against the wall, and buried her face against the duchess's shoulder.

"Hush, my dear, hush," said Havoise gently, patting her on the back. "I know; I know. He was your one true lord, the one man you would satisfy if you must disappoint all the others, and now you never can. But, my dear, if you cry for that, be glad for him. It's a good end to die crusading, and he's in paradise now."

They let her cry for a few minutes, and then Havoise sat her down again, and Hoel poured her a cup of wine. Marie swallowed a mouthful of it, gulping it with a painfully tight throat. "How did he die?" she asked.

Not, it seemed, valiantly in battle, as he would have wished. Hoel had received the news from his son Alain Fergant, who'd been writing regularly throughout the crusade. The duke gave it to Marie and let her read it for herself. It said that many brave knights had died of fever on the way from Antioch, the most distinguished of them being Guillaume Penthièvre de Chalandrey, a man universally respected for his courage and skill at arms. Marie guessed suddenly that the same writer must have reported Robert Penthièvre's death at the siege of Nicaea, nearly a year before, giving Hoel the news before Marie herself had heard it and allowing him to arrange the quiet abduction from St. Michael's. And that reminded her of her own position.

She usually forgot now that she was a captive, held for the land to which she was heiress. When she remembered, she always pushed the awareness away again with a stab of dread. One day, she knew, everyone would finally believe that she was not going to betray her family's honor—and then this delicious life at court would be over, and she would have to go back to the convent. Worse: she'd have to stay there. The contradictory loyalties she'd feared had forced themselves upon her, despite all her efforts to avoid them. How could she marry a Norman now, when he might make war upon Brittany and kill gallant young men who'd been her suitors? On the other hand, how could she marry a Breton, betraying her father and swallowing all her proud words? No, she could marry no one. She would have to swear to Hoel that she would marry no one and go back to the convent. And the hour for that oath and that departure was rushing down upon her.

She put the letter down and looked bleakly at duke and duchess. "So," she said. "The lord of Chalandrey is dead. That changes things, doesn't it?"

"My dear, we didn't mean to discuss this with you tonight," said the duchess. "No one is going to push you to make decisions in a state of shock."

"But it does change things, doesn't it?" she insisted. "The manor is now legally in the wardship of its overlord. As heiress, I need to do homage to him to obtain it. Only it's not clear who he is."

Havoise sighed, but Hoel squared his shoulders combatively. "I am the rightful overlord," he said firmly. "Marie, my girl, the decision as to the fate of Chalandrey isn't yours to make. I have documents to prove my title to any impartial court. They ought to carry even the partial court I have to take them to."

Marie stared stupidly, unable to understand him. What did courts have to do with it?

"We won't discuss this tonight!" said Havoise forcefully. "Marie, drink up your wine and go to bed."

"No! What do you mean, talking about a court?" Marie demanded, looking from duke to duchess and back again. "I thought you were relying on me to give you Chalandrey. I thought . . ."

"My dear," said the duchess, "I saw some time ago that you were not going to marry any of our men, not even poor Tiher, and I told Hoel so. Tiarnán might have changed her mind, I said, but he's married — and then, of course, he was gone. As for the other household knights, poor fellows, they had more chance of capturing Mont St. Michel, that impregnable fortress, than of shifting your resolution. They're giving up. The heart went out of them when Tiher pulled out. They keep on for the game's sake, but no one really expects you to give in now. No, Hoel and I haven't expected anything from you for some time.

What we plan to do instead is to take the case to court."

"What court could try a dispute between Brittany and Normandy?" asked Marie incredulously.

"There is such a person as the king of France," said Hoel. "I grant you, he's a fat old man who doesn't count for much, and he's mortally afraid of Robert of Normandy—but he is legally Robert's overlord as well as my own, and entitled to judge between us. And Robert, in case you hadn't noticed, is in the Holy Land, and I'm not. I have a good chance of winning. So you see, my girl, you don't need to fret over who's entitled to your homage, or break your heart with divided loyalties. You're not judge of the matter."

She gave him a stunned stare, then went bright red. So all her resolve, and all her determination and honor, had become irrelevant, and Chalandrey's fate was something to be decided drily at a law court in faraway Paris?

"Hoel, that's enough!" said the duchess. "How can you stand there lecturing her like that when she's just had the news of her father's death? Marie, come to bed." Havoise caught Marie's arm and helped her to her feet.

"I'm sorry," said Hoel, taking her other arm. "But you did ask."

They did not need her as a captive, they expected nothing from her—and yet, still, they were kind. Where her own father had given her only emptiness, these two gave her love. Marie began to cry again. "If it were really decided in court that you had legal title to Chalandrey," she blurted brokenly, "nobody would be happier about it than me."

Havoise kissed her on the cheek. "My dear," she advised, "don't say anything now that you might regret later. Rest first, my dear; rest."

When Marie had been escorted off to her bed, and the duke and duchess had gone to theirs, the wolf lay awake in his corner, struggling with words. They had used a name that had belonged to him, Marie and the duke and duchess. He recognized that name when he heard it now, despite its distortions: Judicaël had used it to him. He had been watching the scene, trying to understand why the woman was so distressed, and then he had heard his name. Now he lay still, laboriously trying to concentrate his sunken powers of reason and piece together what they had said. The badly fitted muzzle hurt his ears, and the human scents all around him kept his instincts tense with fear, while the shame of being chained up and voiceless in the house of a man who had once treated him with honor was a pain that would not let him sleep. He might as well exhaust himself trying to understand what was happening around him: it would at least distract him from the rest. He thought about it, wordlessly for the most part, shifting clumsy blocks of concepts about like an amputee maneuvering a tool awkwardly with his stump.

There was bad news for Marie in the letter: yes, he had that.

Marie had expected something else bad to happen, and Hoel had said something that surprised her. He turned it back and forth, dredging for words to fit it. Court. That was it. Marie was to leave court, stay with the court, what?

Then the duchess had said the words that had included his name. "Marry"? He had once gone surety for Marie that no one would marry her by force. Ah, that other often-repeated noise had been "Chalandrey."

The bad news in the letter was that her father was dead: that was why she had wept. And then she'd realized that her father's manor was now hers, and she had been afraid. Afraid that she'd be forced to marry? Then the puzzle about the court, and then the duchess had reassured Marie that they wouldn't force her to marry . . . no, that was not what had been said. The duchess had told Marie that they knew she would not marry. And then his name: *Tiarnán. Might have. Changed her . . . mind.*

Why might he have changed her mind? *Marry.*

It was only after a long weary session wrestling with the whole scene that he began to understand that Marie had been in love with him. He did not wholly believe his own labored interpretation, but even the possibility that he was right sank into him a shaft of bloody anguish. He again remembered her at Nimuë's Well, pinned naked on the grass by the robbers. She

was a lovely woman, and she was brave and loyal. He valued
loyalty much more now that he had known betrayal. What was
any lovely woman to him now?

Nothing, never, ever again. His body now would respond
with a rush of desire to the scent of any bitch in heat, though
his human self recoiled from the arousal with disgust. The
thought that he might have been loved once by Marie showed
him his degradation now more plainly than the muzzle and the
chains. He began to whimper quietly in the darkness. He
clawed at the humiliating muzzle and twisted it back and forth
against the floor. Mirre woke up and licked his ear, and he
forced himself to stop. It must be endured.

He remembered Alain looking at him in the boiling shed at
Treffendel. Alain, human and elegant as ever, but with the same
rank, frightened scent that had clung to the rock at St. Mailon's.
Alain, who knew who he was and had urged Hoel to kill him.
He had been able to do nothing, nothing, nothing but endure
it as helplessly as he had endured everything else Alain and
Eline between them had done to him. He had lost all hope of
returning to human form. But perhaps one day, if he endured
long enough, he would find it in his power to return to them
some of the destruction they had practiced on him. If he were
mild and patient, the muzzle would be taken off—and Alain
would have to visit court again one day. Judicaël would not
approve. But Judicaël had never approved of him killing, and
it had never stopped him before. What other reason did he have
now to stay alive?

The court stayed at Rennes for Lent. Few people traveled in
the penitential season, and the duke received a bare handful
of visitors. He couldn't even go hunting: between the ban on
meat and the need to let the deer produce their young in peace,
the forest was closed to the hounds. Hoel amused himself with
his wolf instead. After a week or so, the muzzle was quietly left
aside, and well before Easter, the chain joined it. Even Tiher
grudgingly admitted that Isengrim was perfectly well behaved.

He never even threatened to bite, didn't bark, never stole food from the table, and, as Hoel gleefully pointed out to his wife, was house-trained from the first. If the dogs barked at him, his only response was to walk away with an air of such disdain that the duchess laughed at his dignity. Hoel taught him to come, heel, sit, stay, and fetch, all in the same morning. "Marvelously intelligent animal!" he said, rubbing Isengrim's ears. "But I knew that from hunting you, didn't I?"

Isengrim understood him. The number of distorted words which he could recognize increased with each day that passed, and the continual effort of reaching for their drowned counterparts brought the words in his mind up into shallow water, where sometimes he glimpsed their meaning even before he touched them. Sometimes he could even follow a conversation — though always it took an effort of concentration, as though he were trying to understand a foreign language, once familiar but now half-forgotten. Constantly surrounded by human talk, human feelings and desires, the human part of him staggered out of the depths into the air, as though it had reached a beach where it lay gasping, still washed by the sea of animal instincts but no longer perpetually sinking beneath it.

He was content to wait on Hoel. The duke had always been the overlord he wanted, and there was no dishonor in serving him in any shape. The casual childishness of so much that was said to him — *Good boy! Here's a treat for you!* — shamed him at first, but moved him less and less as he grew accustomed to it. How else was the duke supposed to speak to an animal? He was very glad to see the muzzle and chain go, and he was careful to do nothing that would bring them back. It was tempting to snap back at a dog that barked at him; tempting to bite one of the pages who occasionally teased him for a dare — but the temptation was one he could resist. And if he stayed near Hoel, the duke protected him.

The castle got used to the sight of the wolf walking quietly behind its lord, or sitting by his knee at table. When visitors began arriving again for Holy Week, the courtiers pointed the wolf out to them with pride and reassurances. "That's the duke's

wolf Isengrim," they said. "A fine beast, isn't he? You don't need
to be afraid of him: he's tame, and you can see how he loves
his master."

Apart from his master, the wolf could be seen to love the
duchess and Marie. If they came into the room he would go
over to greet them, pressing his nose into their hands, and he
would follow them about the castle or lie at their feet. To others
he was merely polite. Time and a few dropped comments had
confirmed Isengrim's first horrified conjecture that Marie had
loved him — or rather, had loved the man he had been once. It
made him watch her with a bittersweet regret. He began to be
able to pick out her scent quickly from a roomful of others, and
increasingly he found himself searching for it. He liked the way
her body moved within her gowns, the shape of her above him,
the controlled poise with which she held herself. Her voice was
never shrill, but always low and pleasant, and she laughed easily, tossing her head back at her suitor's jokes and replying to
them lightly. If he licked her hand, her skin had a sweet taste
all its own.

He could not remember clearly what she looked like to human eyes. Her body on the grass at Nimuë's Well, yes, and the
way she had stood afterward, with her rich brown hair in tangles over her shoulders. But he could not remember the color
of her eyes. He had never paid attention to her eyes when he
was a man, and now there were no colors in the world.

He knew, bitterly, that the reason he had never noticed her
was because he had been in love with Eline — sweet, beautiful
Eline, who had betrayed him so easily and so entirely. He did
not like to remember Eline at all. He did not dream of killing
her, as he dreamed of killing Alain: to see her again at all would
cause him too much pain. He would be glad if she died, and
were buried and placed forever beyond his eyes. It was much
better to think about Marie. Those thoughts, too, were full of
pain, but at least the pain was sweet. If that scene at Nimuë's
Well had been played out one year earlier, he might have married Marie, and Eline would never have been more to him than

the daughter of a neighboring lord. Marie, he was quite certain, would never have wept and badgered him to tell his secret. Even if he had told it, she would not have betrayed him. She might have left him for a convent, but treachery was one thing that would never stain her. If he had married Marie, he would be human still, happy and at peace with his wife in his own manor. Sweet pain to imagine it!

The clerk Kenmarcoc, who'd been given a place in the duke's chancellery, took a particular interest in Isengrim. He exclaimed when he first saw the wolf, and Isengrim, who was still chained and muzzled at the time, got to his feet eagerly and stood looking at the clerk with his bright feral eyes. It was in the hall after Mass on a Sunday: the duke was conducting business with his officials, and Kenmarcoc was bringing in some accounts. Marie was nearby with the duchess.

Kenmarcoc edged cautiously up to the wolf, then, even more cautiously, held out his hand for the beast to sniff. Isengrim touched it with his muzzle and sat down again, still watching the clerk.

"That's the wolf I saw my last night in Talensac, when I was in the stocks!" Kenmarcoc exclaimed. "Seems I didn't need to be so afraid of him."

"How can you tell?" asked Tiher sceptically. As Master of the Hunt, he was among the officials beside the duke.

"He looks just the same," said Kenmarcoc. "And I won't forget in a hurry how I saw him. He walked right toward me: at first I thought he was a stray dog, but when he was only a few yards away, I saw he was a wolf. His eyes were all green in the moonlight. I was pinned in the stocks and couldn't move, and I thought he'd kill me."

"What were you doing in the stocks?" demanded Hoel, shocked and curious. A cleric should have been exempt from such punishments.

Kenmarcoc snorted. "Said something to the lady of the manor which I shouldn't have, my lord. I won't repeat it. I was upset over leaving Talensac, and I'd had a few drinks to comfort myself. Well, I went too far: I can admit that now. But I was upset. She'd quarreled with the machtiern — Lord Tiarnán, that was — and I still think she was to blame. He was so grieved over the quarrel that when he went into the forest for the last time I don't think he really wanted to come back. And even when she'd come home and said she meant to make the quarrel up, when we were still expecting him back, she still wouldn't admit she was to blame. Father Judicaël came from St. Mailon's to reconcile her to her husband, but she quarreled with him, too. And Father Judicaël, you must know, my lord, is a man of such holiness that the people of the region thank God for giving us one of his saints. Tiarnán — well, I was his man. I was angry for him, particularly when his lady was in such a hurry to marry that de Fougères fellow."

"My cousin, you mean," said Tiher dryly.

"Forgive me, my lord," said Kenmarcoc. "I talk too much."

Marie could not say why she felt unsettled by what the clerk had said. She went over it several times in her mind afterward, always with the feeling that she wasn't remembering it right, that something more must have been said, or she wouldn't have this sense of disquiet when she thought of it. But the missing element remained obstinately missing, and at last she put the problem from her mind and concentrated instead on the disciplines of Lent.

On the evening of Palm Sunday the castle was full. From every corner of Brittany, Hoel's vassals came to pay their respects to their liege lord and to join in the celebrations at Rennes cathedral. Marie was surprised when the duchess took time from her busy schedule to summon her to her chamber. When she went there, she was even more surprised to find Havoise in consultation with Sybille and with her dressmaker, Emma.

"So here you are, my dear," said Havoise, breaking off her discussion. "I want you to try this gown on." She picked it up, a beautiful sweep of dark green. Marie looked at it in bewilderment. It had been embroidered in gold across the bodice and along the long sleeves from elbow to midhand, and was held together at the sides with gold buckles.

"This is far too grand for me," she said. "And I'm in mourning." She was, in fact, back in the old black gown which she'd worn from St. Michael's. Even the duchess couldn't ban it when it was worn in mourning for her father.

"Marie," said the duchess sternly, "you are *not* going to Paris in that horrible old black thing. I forbid it. You are the heiress to an estate about which Hoel and I are making a great deal of trouble, and you are going to look worth every bit of it, or you are not coming at all."

"Coming to Paris?" asked Marie in amazement.

"Coming to Paris to see the king," agreed the duchess. "King Philippe has agreed to hear the case. We'll meet in Paris at the Feast of Pentecost. But you will *not* come in that old black gown. You can wear this at court, and for the journey I've ordered some other clothes for you. Emma here can make any adjustments that are needed."

Sybille giggled. "Look at her trying to say no," she said.

"Yes," said Marie, blushing and laughing. Her heart fluttered helplessly with excitement. To go to Paris, to see the king of France! She'd never left Brittany and the March in her life, and the King in Paris seemed like something from a fairy tale. "Oh my lady, thank you!"

"Just like a normal girl sometimes, isn't she?" said Sybille.

"Just occasionally," agreed the duchess.

XIII

Judicaël was praying in St. Mailon's chapel on the evening of Easter Sunday when the bell tinkled sweetly.

He had had a difficult Lent. Officials had come from the bishop of Rennes to talk to him, and they had questioned him at length about his conduct over bonfires and other manifestations of demon worship. It was true that he'd never viewed these with the same dismay as the ecclesiastical authorities, regarding them rather as courtesies paid to the land's original inhabitants than as works of the devil. He was able to swear that he had never blessed a bonfire in honor of any fairy being, but he doubted that was enough to satisfy the bishop. Since Tiarnán had been lost he'd had no confidence in his own opinions about anything. He found the dry, impatient questions of the bishop's men almost impossible to answer. It might well be, he thought, that this Easter at St. Mailon's would be his last; that he would be forced from the chapel and given some minor place in a monastery or at the ecclesiastical court, or even stripped of his priesthood. And perhaps that was indeed what he deserved.

Despite this, Easter itself had been particularly rich. He had kept the vigil for Easter Eve, and at midnight, alone in the chapel, he had lit the paschal candle and sung the Exultet, the anthem of joy for the moment when all the dark inevitability of age, death, and the ruin of innocence was overturned, and the forces of evil worked backward to their own destruction. When the sun rose in the morning, he had gone out and stood in the clearing: the primroses were in flower, with the wood anemone, celandine, and sweet violet; the trees were just breaking into leaf, and the birds sang to one another. Then he had peace.

Whatever happened to him, however wrong he had been, still he could trust in God.

A number of the people who had come to him during the year turned up for the service of Easter morning, as they always did, and he celebrated Mass with them happily. Many of the worshipers had brought food, and when the service was over they all sat together on the grass outside the church and ate and drank and talked, laughing because Lent was over and they had eggs and meat to eat once more. Judicaël provided goat's milk and cheese and the last jar of last summer's honey. It was sweet.

On Easter evening he was happily tired from the vigil and the day and looking forward to his bed. When the bell tinkled, he assumed it was simply another worshiper, come to pay his respects, and he turned from the altar with a smile of greeting. But if it was a worshiper, it was not one who'd come before: a tired and anxious-looking peasant woman, carrying a young baby wrapped in a blanket.

"God be with you, daughter," said Judicaël. "What do you wish?"

She knelt down in front of him and touched her face to the floor. "You are Judicaël the hermit?" she asked. When he nodded, she said, "There is a man dying in the forest not far from here, Father. I beg you, for the sake of Christ's mercy, come and do what you can for him."

Judicaël fetched a lantern from his hut, and a bag for the bread, wine, and consecrated oil; when it emerged that the woman had not eaten that day, he gave her the remains of the worshipers' picnic, and they set out together into the forest.

"Is this man known to you, daughter?" asked Judicaël. "Or did you find him by chance?"

"I was looking for him," she replied. "He is . . . a friend. I once meant to marry him."

"But you didn't." He glanced at the baby she carried. Only a part of its face was showing, but from its size it was not much above three months old.

"No," she said. "I . . . was prevented. I married someone

else." The baby gave a snuffling cry, and she rocked it against her shoulder and crooned to it. It seemed to Judicaël that she was relieved not to have to answer any more questions about her dying friend. That probably meant that he was some kind of runaway serf or criminal.

The man was in the deep forest about two miles southwest of St. Mailon's. He was lying in a lean-to built of brush and sticks upon a flea-infested deerskin rug, with another tattered skin for a blanket. He was filthy, hairy, and dressed only in a patched hemp shirt. There was a fire in front of the shelter and fresh water in a cup beside him; some hemp hose, still damp from washing, were hanging from a bush. Judicaël guessed that all this care had been bestowed on him only recently, by the woman. Before that the man must have been lying ill alone for some time. His face was gaunt and wasted, with sores around the mouth from sickness and malnutrition, and his stomach was bloated with starvation. He was asleep when they arrived, but when the light of the lantern fell on his eyes, he opened them. They burned darkly in the tangle of his hair. "What's this?" he asked the woman.

She set the baby down carefully in the warmth of the fire and went over to kneel by the man. "This is a priest," she told him. "I fetched him from St. Mailon's. Please talk to him."

The man turned his hot eyes on Judicaël. "Go away," he ordered.

Judicaël knelt down opposite the woman and touched the man's forehead. It was, as he'd expected, burning with fever. "Are you hungry?" he asked quietly.

"No," said the man. "I'm too far gone for that. I don't want you: go away."

"I think your name is Éon," said Judicaël. "How long have you been ill?"

"Too long," replied Éon triumphantly. "Even if you go running to the lords' manors and say you've caught the robber at long last, I'll still be gone by the time they come to fetch me. I'm dying and I'm going to hell, but I'll go in my own time, not the duke's."

"I'm not running anywhere," said Judicaël. "That I've seen you here is between you, me, and God. But you have a friend here, who has gone to some trouble to fetch me; out of courtesy to her, you ought at least to talk to me before you send me off."

Éon hesitated and looked toward the woman. She nodded earnestly, and he sighed. "It won't make any difference," he told her. "But to please you . . ."

She smiled and kissed his forehead, then went back to the fire and picked up the baby, which was snuffling unhappily again and beginning to cry. She sat down a short distance away and put it to her breast. Éon followed her with his eyes.

"The child isn't mine," he said abruptly. "She hasn't let me touch her since she was married to that fellow in Plèmy. She told him she was going on a pilgrimage this Easter, and came to look for me because she was worried about me—but she hasn't deceived him otherwise. That's true, as God hears me."

"I believe you," said Judicaël. "I pray God rewards her for her fidelity, to him and to you."

"Yes," said Éon, with a hint of a smile.

"As for yourself . . ." Judicaël paused, praying silently for guidance, then went on. "I believe you have consigned yourself to hell far more readily than God would."

Éon glared. "Now comes the sermon," he said bitterly. "Wicked man, repent! Robber, murderer, rebel against your lord, runaway serf, werewolf—crawl on your belly like a worm and cry for mercy, and maybe you'll be let off with beatings and Purgatory. I'd rather die like a man."

"You're no werewolf," said Judicaël.

"I'll tell you who is, though!" snapped Éon. "That lord of Talensac I've been accused of murdering. But because he's a lord, he's held in high honor. I was born a serf, and any filth flung at me sticks."

"How do you know he's a werewolf?" asked Judicaël, curious.

"Saw him," replied Éon. "Near Carhaix, autumn before last. I saw him riding along the road and thought he'd be worth robbing. I didn't know who he was, but he had a fine horse, and I had three men with me, in those days. I could think of robbing armed men, then. We followed him, looking for a good place to take him. He left his horse on a farm and went into the forest on foot, as though he were going hunting. Better and better, we thought. He stopped. We went ahead to fix an ambush for him, and waited. But he never came into it. After a while we went back and followed his tracks. A man's tracks led up to a hollow tree in a dell, but only a wolf's tracks led away. The clothes were inside the tree. We didn't touch them. We were afraid to. The next time I saw him, he killed two of my men — poor men who'd been wronged by their lords and forced from their lands, like me. But the story the world heard was that a noble knight of Talensac had met a wicked robber and got the better of him. The nobles can do anything they like, anything, but if a poor man raises his hand to defend himself, he's condemned."

"God has exacted his own penance of Tiarnán of Talensac," said Judicaël evenly. "And your responsibility is for your own soul, not for his. Do you think God is ignorant of what you've suffered? I've heard the story of how you came to be a robber. It was a great injustice, and in the final judgment of it, there will be no rich or poor, no noble or serf, and all things will be made plain and equal. Answer to God for yourself, Éon, and he will listen to you. Christ is your friend and defender, and he will plead for you. But you must repent and accept his help. When your two fellows were killed, you and they were not sitting innocently in the forest: you were assaulting a young woman."

"And I wish we'd all finished with her!" returned Éon savagely. "She was a fine lady, a kinswoman of my lord of Moncontour. I wish I'd known that at the time, and I wish I'd had a chance to enjoy the bitch!"

"As Ritgen mab Encar enjoyed your friend there?" asked Judicaël.

It was a low blow, and Éon was shocked into silence.

"There's no noble or ignoble with God," said Judicaël, following the thrust quickly. "If it's good to rape a young noble-

woman you happen to meet in the forest, it's good for a lord's
bailiff to rape a serf in her sweetheart's hut. There are no dis-
tinctions: the women both suffer. Oh, as I said, it is my belief
that God will even the balance, that he will say to the lord's
bailiff, 'You were entrusted with power, and you abused it,' and
to the runaway serf, 'You were brutalized by others.' But you
know, Éon, that most of the people you have terrorized were
as poor as yourself: peasants working in the forest; poor tenants
on pilgrimage; parish priests with a handful of tithes from their
flocks. Peasant women, perhaps, who had the misfortune to
cross your path."

"No," said Éon sullenly. "Just whores, or willing ones. A man
needs women. I thought the Penthièvre girl was a whore."

"Did you? When she struggled with you?"

"No, but she had no business being there alone if she wasn't!
She deserved it."

"Did she? And the man you and your friends robbed and
beat outside Paimpont two years ago, who was going to offer
his life's savings to Saint Main for the recovery of his sick son,
whom you left blind, penniless, and broken-ribbed—did he deserve it?"

"We didn't know what the money was! We got angry when
he tried to stop us from taking it! We had to rob: there wasn't
any other way for us to live."

"Did you ever try any other way of living? You could have
slipped into a town, somewhere you weren't known, and ap-
prenticed yourself to a trade. You were a strong man: you could
have found work. You could have found a place on a ship, gone
to another country. There are always other ways to live than
off the flesh of others."

"That's right! I'm condemned, whatever I do. Push a man
out into the wilds like an animal, and then despise him as one.
Leave me alone, and let me go to hell!"

"Éon, why would I have walked all this way tonight if all I
wanted was to condemn you? I could do that sitting at home
in my cell. I came to offer you absolution. That is my function
and God's urgent wish. All you need to do to receive it is hold

out your hand. We are all sinners: I have certainly done things that I regret most bitterly, and all I can do is beg God to have mercy on me. Do you regret crippling the man at Paimpont?"

Éon was silent for a long minute, then put one weak hand against his burning eyes. "Yes," he mumbled into it, and began to cry. "I was sick with myself when I heard the story."

"Then, God forgive you, my son. As by his death and resurrection, which we celebrated today, he is able to. Are there others you regret?"

He regretted all of them, in the end, even Ritgen mab Encar, strangled as he slept beside his wife. He threw off the whole blanket of degradation and violence which had covered him, and Judicaël gave him absolution and extreme unction. Then he consecrated the bread and wine, and gave both the man and the woman their Easter Communion. When that was finished, Éon went to sleep, smiling as contentedly as the baby.

"What will you do now?" Judicaël asked the woman as he packed the oil and wine back into his bag.

"I will stay here until he is gone," she replied simply. "Then I'll go home."

"Come to me if you need food," he told her. "With the little one, you need to keep your strength up. And when the man has gone, tell me, and I'll help you bury him."

"I think it won't be long now," she said, looking at Éon. "He is very weak. He was here by himself for a long time. And he's stopped fighting it now. He was afraid of hell, but now he will have a good end." She looked back at Judicaël, her eyes bright with tears, then took his hand and bowed her head to it. "Thank you, Father," she said quietly. "May God reward you!"

"What I have been allowed to do for your friend is reward enough," replied Judicaël quietly. "But, daughter, may I ask one favor of you? He has told you, I think, about the knight of Talensac?" She nodded in surprise, and Judicaël went on, "I beg you, then, not to repeat what he told you. I was that knight's confessor."

She believed instantly, as he'd meant her to, that he feared that the story about Tiarnán would harm his own reputation.

She would have repeated the story otherwise: if a rumor of viciousness clung to the reputation of a nobleman who had harmed her friend, so much the better! But to protect Judicaël she would let the story lie buried with Éon under the forest floor. It was a small deception, and Judicaël almost regretted it—and yet, what good would it do anyone if Tiarnán's memory were spat upon?

"Of course, Father," said the woman. "And again, thank you. Some priests wouldn't have come at all, and most would have turned around again when they discovered who they'd come for. All his life he's been treated like a beast, but you accepted him as a man. You saved him."

"No," he replied, "you did."

On the way back home he walked quietly, feeling the forest breathe around him in the darkness. What had just happened appeared to him as a gift from God, justification enough for any hermit's existence, and he was deeply happy. But he had time to wonder what he would do if he were stripped of his priesthood. Bereft of that, and the chapel, and the forest with all its infinite variety, shut up copying manuscripts in a monastery or episcopal office, disgraced, suspected—what would he do?

There is always something one can do, he told himself. I said it to Éon, and it's true. And God's ways are wonderful and mysterious beyond my imagining. My trust, O Lord of my life, is in you.

He went back to his cell, blew out the lantern, and went to sleep in peace.

Duke Hoel left Rennes on the twenty-sixth of April, and arrived in Paris on the tenth of May. It was a leisurely journey, not pressing the horses, stopping in monastery guest houses or the castles of his friends, seeing the sights and joining in any offered entertainments. To Marie, it was all new and all delight. The world was in the last spring of an old century, and it was sparkling with life, and beautiful. Everywhere they passed, the fields were being tended, or were shooting green with new grain. Horses strained at the plough, sheep grazed the fields, pigs foraged in the greening woods, and men and women stopped their work and children ran out into the road to watch the Duke of Brittany riding by. Everywhere they stopped, the masons were busy: new castles were going up; monasteries were building new chapels, new guest houses, or new refectories; new churches sprouted in what seemed to be every town. The whole world was bursting with life like the leaves.

Hoel was determined to make a good impression at the court, and was bringing all his household knights, together with another twenty who owed him service, as well as trumpeters, musicians, his herald, his priest, his doctor, and his clerk. Rather to Marie's disappointment, the other court officials, including Tiher, had been left behind. Havoise brought a dozen ladies besides Marie, and the ducal retinue was followed by some sixty servants, together with baggage mules, horses, hunting dogs, and hawks. Mirre and most of the serious hunting dogs were left behind: it wasn't the season for hunting with hounds. But Isengrim came along, in a new silver-studded collar, together with a few favored alaunts and greyhounds, for the sake of the show they made. It took a large monastery to accommodate them all.

Isengrim was intensely relieved that they had left the hunting dogs behind. Mirre had been coming into heat, and he had found the rank, erotic smell of her almost unendurable. The thought of coupling with a dog, and perhaps begetting puppies gifted with some part of a human soul, was unspeakably monstrous. The smell was so arousing, though, that he was afraid to have Mirre near him. She was used to following him, and the way he suddenly turned on her snarling and drove her off hurt and confused her. It made it worse that Hoel and the duchess simply found it funny to see a wolf chasing off an amorous bitch. It was much, much better to be on the road to Paris.

Paris itself, when they finally reached it on the afternoon of the tenth, was not very much bigger than Nantes. They passed the great abbey of St.-Germain-des-Prés, and rode down through its green vineyards to the left bank of the Seine. Beyond the wide brown stream lay the Ile de la Cité, the clear spring air above its ancient walls stained with the smoke of its many cooking fires. They clattered over the Pont St. Michel and through the city gates, into a stink of sewage and rotting vegetables. Most of the people of Paris lived on the island, though some had moved across to the less crowded river port on the right bank. Here, in the heart of the old city, the houses were jammed one on top of the other, and their noise and filth far surpassed that of Rennes. The street was the city's main market. Street vendors were crying their wares, shoppers bargained with them, and everyone cursed when the duke's knights rode up to clear their lord's way. The duke's dogs barked at the cats slinking about the narrow alleys, and the town dogs barked at the duke's wolf. They hurried through it all, turning left through the marketplace, and arrived at last at the palace of King Philippe of France, where they were expected and made welcome.

The Bretons had worked hard to make the most splendid impression possible. The dogs and the wolf had been washed and brushed that morning until their fur stood out in soft ruffs about their necks. The horses had been groomed until every hair gleamed, and their hooves had been blackened with a mixture of oil and charcoal—most of which came off in the filthy streets. All of Hoel's fifty knights had polished and oiled their armor until, as their lord said, they glistened like fresh sardines. The duke himself wore a new tunic of scarlet trimmed with ermine and fastened with a belt embroidered with gold; the duchess was even more magnificent in dark burgundy silk glittering with jewels. Marie's green and gold looked plain by comparison. They rode through the gates of the palace into the cobbled courtyard to a flourish of trumpets, and the fifty knights fanned out across the yard with a ringing of hooves on cobbles, then dismounted all at once with a clash of armor and knelt down as the duke descended from his white charger. Marie thought it the most magnificent sight she had ever seen.

Hoel's magnificence, however, made no impression at all on the king's court. Philippe might be just a fat old man who didn't count for much, but all the great nobles of France nonetheless occasionally found it expedient to visit him. What was Hoel compared with the fabulously wealthy count of Flanders, or the mighty dukes of Anjou and Normandy, or the cultured Duke William of Aquitaine? Brittany was one of the poorer and more isolated parts of the kingdom, and of no great interest to the Parisians. The king's seneschal, Lord Guy de Rochefort, who had come into the courtyard to greet the visitors, merely smiled politely at the display and waved to the servants to stable the Bretons' horses.

What did make an impression, however, was Isengrim: a tame wolf was a much rarer animal than a mere duke. When Hoel strode into the king's Great Hall with the wolf on a leash of crimson silk, the courtiers along the benches nudged one another and whispered. Even King Philippe, a crafty and indolent man not often stirred by anything, sat up at his place at the high table, twitched his ermine robe straight, and belched.

Hoel knelt and did homage to his overlord. The king drew him to his feet, kissed him on both cheeks in a rather perfunctory fashion, and asked, "Is that really a wolf?"

"Yes, my lord," said Hoel with great satisfaction and patted Isengrim on the shoulder. Isengrim licked his hand.

"Eh!" said Philippe doubtfully. "It seems very tame."

"He's a very well behaved beast, my lord, and much more intelligent than a dog. Isengrim! Bow to your king!"

Isengrim had been taught this trick on the journey. He stepped forward and dropped his head and forequarters to the ground, tail held out straight behind him, and touched his nose to the king's shoe. Philippe pulled the shoe back hastily, then smiled. The courtiers applauded. Isengrim stood up again and went back to his place at Hoel's side.

"A most respectful animal," said the king. "I'd always believed that wolves were incapable of honoring anyone. Well, well. Be welcome, my lord of Brittany, to Paris."

The women and higher-ranking men of the Breton party had

been given a suite of rooms in the north wing of the palace. The knights had to share the hall with King Philippe's own men, and with their counterparts among the Norman delegation, which had already arrived. The hall was large enough to hold them all. It was comparatively new, and had been rebuilt, like the rest of the palace, by King Philippe's grandfather Robert the Pious. There was a banquet in it that evening to welcome both the Normans and the Bretons to the court.

Even before she entered the huge room that evening, Marie was struck by the sweet overpowering scent of flowering may, and when she followed the duchess through the low door, it was to see the hall spread with dazzling white. Fresh-cut may had been scattered in thick drifts over the rushes of the floor, and the tables were covered with cloths of bleached linen, and set with silver salt cellars and dishes. Candles blazed in racks along every wall, casting a pure soft glow over the scene. The magnificent clothing of courtiers and visitors alike blazed against the whiteness in a rainbow of rich colors, as though they had walked from the fabulous tapestries which decorated the palace walls. Once again, Marie had the sense that this journey was part of some fairy tale, or a dream from which she would awaken to the drabness of St. Michael's convent.

The king's seneschal had been involved in some anxious reckoning of dignities before the places were assigned at the banquet tables. The king's son, Prince Louis, was absent, chastising a rebellious baron—a piece of luck Lord de Rochefort thanked God for, because the king's wife was unfortunately present, and she and the prince loathed each other. (Queen Bertrada was the king's second wife. The king's first wife, Bertha of Frisia, Prince Louis's mother, was still living. So was Bertrada's first husband. Her elopement with the king was the scandal of the age, and had provoked a papal excommunication for Philippe which everyone quietly ignored.) Also fortunate from the seneschal's point of view was the fact that Duke Robert of Normandy was not present, which meant that there was no one to contest Hoel's position on the king's right, while Duke Robert's steward, Count Ranulf of Bayeux, who headed the

Norman delegation, could take the place on the queen's left unquestioned. But farther down the tables there were hot disputes.

Marie was escorted to the high table — partly because she was a kinswoman of the duchess, but largely, she suspected, because the few women at the feast provided convenient blanks to shuffle about the contested seats. She found herself wedged between the king's constable and a Norman she knew, Hoel's old adversary Robert of Bellême, who'd once visited her father at Chalandrey. Robert was a tall, powerfully built man with a cruel face, sleekly gray and magnificently dressed. He tapped his fingers impatiently against the table as the company stood waiting for the king. There was a fanfare of trumpets, and Philippe and his queen entered the hall in a blaze of cloth of gold and jewels. They took their places at the center of the table, and the rest of the company could finally sit down. Then there was another blare of trumpets, and the first course of roast lamb and gravy-soaked pasties was borne into the hall upon a dish of silver so heavy it took two men to carry it.

Robert snorted and began to tap his fingers again. Before the company could be served, the royal seneschal had to ceremoniously carve for the king, taste the meat himself, and at last hand it over with more bows and flourishes of trumpets. Then the same ceremony had to be repeated with the wine. But at last the ritual was completed, and the servants began to carry the food about to the guests. The meal was superb: Philippe was a connoisseur of the pleasures of the table, and had come by his bulk honestly.

Robert of Bellême turned to Marie with a leer. "God prosper you, Lady," he said. "I must've done something right, to be seated next to a beautiful woman. You're with the Breton party, aren't you? But you're too pretty to be a daughter of Hoel's. What's your name?"

"You know me, Lord Robert," she said. "Marie, Guillaume Penthièvre's daughter."

He blinked. "By God and Saint James!" he exclaimed. "So it is. I never would have believed it. Fat, bookish little Marie, turned into a vision like this! Captivity must agree with you."

Marie was very grateful to the duchess's dressmaker, and grateful, too, for the jewels loaned by the duchess herself. "Not exactly captivity, Lord Robert," she said without thinking.

"But I'd heard that Hoel had you abducted from a convent and kept at his court by force, imprisoned until you agreed to marry one of his men."

"I haven't been imprisoned," she said, smiling. "As you can see. I swore an oath to Duchess Havoise that I wouldn't try to escape unless I were forced into a marriage, and she made me one of her attendants. She and Duke Hoel have treated me with nothing but kindness."

Robert was frowning. "Kindness? To abduct you and keep you by force?"

"I've refused to do what they wanted, but they still treat me as their friend and cousin. Yes, kindness."

Robert continued to frown, and she suddenly remembered comments from her first days at the ducal court: *What you expect from us, shows what the Normans are.* She could see now that it was true. Robert would not have allowed her liberty and freedom if she'd resisted his plans. Robert would have had one of his men rape her. He found it difficult to understand why Hoel hadn't.

"But you've refused their choices of a husband for you?" he asked.

She nodded, no longer trusting herself to speak to him, and Robert gave a grunt of satisfaction. "I'd heard of your loyalty," he said. "I hope it counts for something with the king when the manor's fate is decided."

Marie bit her lip, not knowing how to admit that she hoped it wouldn't.

She was saved replying by an extraordinary noise from the center of the table, where Hoel was sitting beside the king. She looked up to see the duke bending over his wolf and imitating a howl. Isengrim looked embarrassed.

"What on earth is he doing?" said Robert to the king's constable.

The constable had just asked his own neighbor the same question, and he turned back and said, "It seems the king wants to hear the wolf howl."

The king's chancellor and several peers of the realm began howling as well, pausing, like the duke, to encourage Isengrim to do the same. Isengrim flicked his ears back and forth and looked the other way, pretending he didn't understand. Marie caught Duchess Havoise's eyes and had to cover her mouth to stop herself from giggling. The king tapped his heel impatiently against the ground and his courtiers bayed harder. Finally Isengrim, with a put-upon air, lifted his head and howled.

The sound rose from its half-sob beginning to its high, trailing finish, lonely, chilling, achingly sad, and completely unlike the noise made by its imitators. The rest of the banqueters turned from their food and stared, and for a moment the whole hall was absolutely still. Then every dog there—and there were many of them, from the king's white greyhounds to the ladies' lapdogs—began to bark. Isengrim lowered his head and flopped down on the bed of may behind the duke's chair.

"Wherever did Duke Hoel get that wolf?" Robert asked Marie admiringly. "I'd pay a pound of gold for a beast like that."

It emerged, after the banquet, that the king had offered three pounds of gold for Isengrim, and, when Hoel refused, increased the offer to five pounds. Hoel was exultant.

"I said I wouldn't sell him for a hundred pounds in gold!" he said, roughing the fur of the wolf's neck with both hands. "Nor would I. Nobody in this place has ever given a damn about anything I owned before. You've brought honor to your master, eh, Isengrim? I'm the envy of the court. There's a good wolf!"

The wolf grinned at him and gave his face a lick.

"You know he only howled to stop you from doing it," said Havoise. "Really, Hoël, I thought I would burst trying not to laugh at you."

"The king's men howled, too," responded Hoel, and imitated them, howling in a Parisian accent. Havoise doubled up with laughter.

"But what are you going to do about the other thing the king wants to see?" she asked her husband when she'd collected herself and wiped her face.

This, it seemed, was a fight between the wolf and some hounds. The Norman leader Ranulf of Bayeux had offered to set his two best hounds against the wolf, and the king was very taken with the notion.

Hoel shrugged. "If we can possibly avoid that, we will. As I said to the king, Ranulf can get more hounds easily, but where would I get another wolf? Though I'd wager anything you'd beat those Norman dogs, wouldn't you, Isengrim?"

Marie didn't like the sound of that. It made a wolf fight seem rather probable, and she'd grown fond of Isengrim. Havoise obviously shared her apprehensions. "Hoel," the duchess said, "you don't even know that he *can* fight. He's such a gentle creature. He won't even snap back at a dog."

"I'm certain he can fight if he wants to," replied Hoel. "The only time I ever saw him try to attack someone, he was properly terrifying. It was the day after I caught him, and I brought that de Fougères fellow out to look at him. If he hadn't been chained, I believe he would have killed the man. Lord Alain went white in the face and told me I ought to have him killed."

"Really?" said Havoise. "I've never seen him misbehave at all."

"Nor have I since. But he's an intelligent beast. I think he recognized Lord Alain as the one who'd been hunting him. I'm sure he could fight like a devil if he had cause."

This, too, was not reassuring.

The king was in no hurry to try the dispute over Chalandrey. Royal dignity demanded that he entertain his tenants-in-chief when they visited his court, so over the next few days the two parties, Breton and Norman, were taken hawking in the royal forest of Rouvre, separately, and amused with dances and music in Paris, separately. The duchess went shopping and purchased, with great satisfaction, items ranging from cloth of Flanders to spices and dye stuffs for the castle stores. Marie continued to attend her, though she was uncomfortably aware that the

Norman party regarded this as improper, and had complained to the king. On the morning of the second day of entertainments, King Philippe had her called over to him and asked her whether she'd prefer to stay with the Normans, the Bretons, or his own servants. She stammered that she preferred to stay with her kinswoman the duchess of Brittany. The king raised one eyebrow quizzically and sent her back to Havoise. She was glad to get away, but she could feel Robert of Bellême glaring at her as she went.

That evening there was another formal banquet, and she was once again seated beside him. He launched into a complaint at once. "What do you mean, saying you'd prefer to stay with the duchess?" he demanded. "We all heard back in Normandy that you refused to go along with Hoel, and we all admired your loyalty. But ever since you arrived here in Paris, you've acted like a member of the Breton party."

"I am," she replied quietly. "I came here with them, as their guest. Duchess Havoise is my kinswoman. My lord of Bellême, apart from any other considerations, neither you nor Lord Ranulf have brought your wives along. It wouldn't be fitting for me, as an unmarried woman, to be alone in your company."

Robert snorted impatiently. "We can find you a chaperone. We were hoping to take you back with us as soon as the king's heard the case and find you a husband. You're old to be still unmarried."

All these months of postponing the inevitable, and it had finally arrived — not in Brittany, but here; not with Hoel or Havoise, but with this brutal ally of her father's. Marie looked down at her trencher of bread, then looked up again resolutely. At least it was not Hoel she disappointed first. "My lord Robert," she said calmly and clearly, "I do not intend to marry."

His black brows pulled down over his cold eyes. "What?" he brayed incredulously.

"I will not marry. I've been loyal to my father and his overlord, and refused to marry one of Hoel's knights. But I owe the duke and duchess a debt for all their kindness to me. The least I can do to repay it is to refuse to marry any of Robert of

Normandy's men. My firm intention is to take vows as a nun, and give all my father's lands to St. Michael. The best owner for Chalandrey is God."

Robert stared at her for a long minute, his expression slowly changing from stupefaction to rage. Absolute master in his own territory, he wasn't used to controlling his temper when he was crossed, and he lost it now. "You little bitch!" he exclaimed. "Hoel's given you far too much liberty, and it's given you the idea that you can please yourself! You will marry who you're told, when you're told!"

"Your opinion is contrary to canon law, Lord Robert," Marie said coldly. "I am allowed to refuse marriage."

"Then canon law's flat against the laws of nature!" Robert's voice was rising to a strangled roar, and the other diners began to look at him. "A woman does what her lord tells her, and if she doesn't, she should be beaten like the rebellious donkey she is. You little traitress!"

It was the one word Marie had done most to avoid. She felt her cheeks going hot. She lifted her chin and looked Robert proudly in the eye. "I have betrayed no one!" she cried in a clear, ringing voice that could be heard down to the far end of the table. "Never in my life! Nor will I, not for Normandy or Brittany or the whole world! I would sooner be dead than guilty of such dishonor!"

Robert struck her violently across the face with the back of his hand. The blow sent her flying from her seat to land heavily on her side in the rushes, cracking her head against the floor. There was a shout of protest from someone up the table, and then Marie heard a snarl just above her, and dragged a blurred gaze into focus to find Isengrim crouching protectively over her, his teeth bared at Robert of Bellême. Robert was on his feet, glaring down. At the wolf's snarl he drew his sword with a hiss of oiled metal. Marie felt the wolf shift his weight above her, and saw the animal's eyes flicker to the man's left with a lethal concentration that was not animal, and that was somehow familiar.

"My lord Robert!" exclaimed King Philippe, heaving his bulk

up from the table and hurrying over. "Stop!" Behind him came
Hoel, red with anger, and Robert of Normandy's steward,
scowling with annoyance, and behind them Havoise and half
the king's courtiers. Panting, the king faced Robert over the
wolf, and Robert's raised sword sank down again. Marie could
feel the wolf relaxing, too, though he remained crouched above
her head.

King Philippe belched painfully and rubbed his stomach.
"What does this mean, eh?" he demanded.

"The little bitch says she won't marry a Norman, no matter
what you decide in the case, my lord!" said Robert hotly.

"You had no right to strike her, whatever she said!" shouted
Hoel. "Marie, my dear, are you all right?" He held out his hand,
and Marie took it. Isengrim moved reluctantly aside, and Marie
pulled herself slowly to her feet. Havoise pushed past the king's
steward and came over to put an arm around her. Marie's head
ached savagely where she'd hit it against the floor, her mouth
was full of blood, and her cheek stung outside where Robert
had struck her, and inside where she'd bitten it. She swallowed
several times. Isengrim licked her hand, then looked at Robert
and made a low singing growl in the depths of his throat.

"You had no right to strike her," agreed Count Ranulf, glaring at Robert of Bellême. "Apologize. And put that damned
sword away."

"The sword was for the wolf!" protested Robert, shoving it
back in its sheath.

"The wolf ran to protect what's mine!" yelled Hoel.

"Yours!" Robert shouted back. "She's not yours! She belongs
to Duke Robert!"

"She's my wife's cousin and a member of my household!"
replied Hoel furiously. "And if she really has said she won't
marry a Norman, it's because she's finally realized what sort of
people you are!"

"I did say I wouldn't marry a Norman," said Marie, wiping
blood off her chin. She pushed Havoise's supporting arm away
and stood straight. "But it wasn't because of that." Inside her
like a pillar of bronze rose the conviction that she didn't belong

to anyone but herself and God; that all these people who clustered about her, protectively or aggressively, were building nets to catch the wind. She turned to King Philippe. "My lord, you know yourself that there are strong claims to Chalandrey on both sides. If the matter were straightforward, why would we all be here awaiting your judgment? Duke Hoel says he can prove legal title; Duke Robert has been the recognized overlord for forty years. I am bound to respect my father's loyalties, and I have done so. But I am also bound to respect Duke Hoel's claims, and I am, besides, indebted to him and to Duchess Havoise for the favor they've shown me. I said to Lord Robert here, and I repeat to you now, that whatever you decide about the manor, I myself will betray neither loyalty. If I am not permitted to choose a husband, still, canon law and custom allow me to refuse one. I say now that I refuse to give Chalandrey to anyone but God and the abbey convent of St. Michael's. Anyone else who takes it will have to disinherit me first."

There was a stunned silence. Then King Philippe smiled.

"So, my two barons are now contesting this manor with an archangel?" he asked. "A fearsome adversary! But, my lady Marie, the case has not been heard yet; it would be better to leave such declarations until it has."

She curtsied. "Forgive me, my lord."

The king greatly admired handsome, high-spirited women: it was the reason he'd run off with Bertrada. He gave Marie a warm smile. "My lady," he said, "I think I'd be prepared to forgive a woman such as yourself almost anything. As for my lord of Bellême" he turned to Robert, "sir, you have struck one of my guests at my own table and drawn your sword in my hall. You will surrender your sword and go down on your knees and apologize, to me and to this lady, or you will leave this court tonight and never return."

Robert glared. Ranulf of Bayeux glared back at him. "Apologize!" he ordered. "Or I'll give the same order in Duke Robert's name."

Not even a vassal as insubordinate as Robert of Bellême could afford to have two out of three overlords angry with him at the same time. Stiffly and reluctantly, Robert knelt down and grated out an apology, first to the king, then, even more reluctantly, to Marie. He unbuckled his sword and handed it to Philippe. Hoel laughed.

"That makes twice I've seen you hand over your sword, my lord of Bellême," he said. "Once to me, and once to the king. I remember I made you pay ten marks to get it back; I hope he charges more."

Robert gave him a bloody look. "Next time we meet, I pray God permits me to put my sword somewhere better than your hands."

"You think you can manage against me better than your brother Geoffroy did?"

The look became even more savage. "The knight of yours that killed my brother isn't here," he said. "I heard he met with an accident in the forest. I hope he died slowly, and I pray that God rewards all your knights with such an end!"

"It's true that I've been deprived of the services of Tiarnán of Talensac," Hoel replied proudly. "But God has given me many other brave men to fight for me. And even if he took one of my finest, still, he gave me another servant from the same forest where the man was lost." He rested his hand on Isengrim's head. "Even this animal rushed to defend what was mine."

"Though you're afraid to let him fight," Ranulf put in quickly.

"By God, I am not!" exclaimed Hoel. "I wasn't afraid when Lord Robert here invaded my lands, and I'm not afraid to set a good Breton wolf against a pair of Norman dogs. Bring them on, my lord Ranulf; bring them on by all means. Isengrim will see them out, won't you, boy? Just as I'll see out any Normans who treat my lands and people with contempt. Bring on your dogs tomorrow morning, my lord, and Isengrim will kill them both."

XIV

Isengrim lay in the corner of the duke's chamber, watching as Havoise washed Marie's bruises. Hoel sat beside him, in the chair just above, one dangling hand toying with the fur of his neck.

"Oh, Hoel," sighed the duchess, "I wish you hadn't said that."

The wolf understood her easily. He could follow most conversations now, Breton or French, though still only with an effort of concentration. If he relaxed, the human noises flowed over his head in an unmeaning blur. He was concentrating now.

"Isengrim can kill Ranulf's dogs—can't you, Isengrim? Did you see the way he snarled at Robert? Scared the man witless."

"Not that," said Havoise impatiently. "God knows, I'd be sorry enough to see the beast killed or maimed—but I'll be sorrier still to see Robert of Bellême invading again. And you practically invited him to try."

Hoel's hand in Isengrim's fur went still, gripping painfully hard for a moment. "Havoise," he said, "I am a duke. I have a place to keep up for the honor of Brittany."

"You were angry, and you let your pride run away with your tongue," said Havoise. "Marie, you'd better lie down, and I'll make you a compress of borage leaves to take up that bruising."

"Well, I was angry," said Hoel defensively. "It was a vile, loutish blow."

"Yes, but he'd been reproved for it by his overlord's steward and the King of France! He was a bull being led off by the nose already. You know the bull will charge for any provoking rag, so why provoke him?"

"If he invades again, he'll get the same response he did last time," said Hoel. "Only with luck, we'll be able to kill the brute and have done with him. You can't expect to have peace with a neighbor like that, and Robert of Normandy has never done anything to check him."

"Hoel, my dear," said the duchess in exasperation, "you and I both know that the Normans are stronger than we are. Don't provoke them!"

"Oh, I know," said Hoel wearily. "I know we're not even going to get Chalandrey outright. I saw that the evening we arrived, when there were more Normans and Parisians at the high table than Bretons." He began roughing the wolf's fur again. "All the more reason to give them a bit of a fight, eh, Isengrim?"

"I'm sorry," said Marie, suddenly sitting up with the compress of borage leaves pressed against her face. "I wish I had given you Chalandrey. Robert will use it as a base to invade you, won't he?"

"My dear, I don't think he'll be able to," said Havoise. "King Philippe is unlikely to give it to Duke Robert outright, either. Don't worry: the person who's behaved best throughout this whole dispute is you. I was so proud of you this evening. Did you see the way old Ranulf's jaw dropped? He looked like a carp. I couldn't have been more delighted with you if you were my own daughter."

Hoel snorted. "She's sunk whatever chance we had left of getting the manor. King Philippe's never going to miss an opportunity like that. If two dukes and an archangel can claim a manor, and either duke will be offended at losing it to the other, it's not hard to guess that piety will triumph and the archangel carry the day."

Havoise smiled. "And do you mind that so very much?"

Hoel looked at her a moment, then got up, crossed the room, and kissed her. "Well, it was never a question of rents anyway, was it? If Saint Michael has it, he'll at least keep the border secure."

Marie all at once bitterly regretted her own proud devotion to honor. She should have given them Chalandrey. She should have married Tiher and given Chalandrey to Brittany. But it was too late now. The king would award it to Saint Michael, and she would be left to the convent, with her cold honor uselessly secure. She began to cry silently into the duchess's compress of borage leaves.

The tears were invisible behind the compress, but Isengrim could smell them. He came over and pressed his nose into Marie's hand, then licked her chin. Her skin kept its sweet taste, even under the sharpness of the borage and the salt of tears. For one aching moment he had an image of himself as a man, stroking back her hair, lifting the compress of leaves away, and telling her not to cry. He could almost imagine her eyes meeting his own, and the way her lips would part as he leaned down to kiss her — but he could not remember the color of her eyes. He was not a man. He was only an animal, and what comfort he could bring her was limited. He had leapt furiously to protect her that evening, but he knew with infinite grief that his protection, like his love, was the inadequate offering of an inferior.

His touch was still enough to make Marie fling her arms around his neck and cry into his fur. The pressure of her body meant nothing to his now, but the closeness was comforting to them both. "Oh, Isengrim!" she said after a moment, sitting up straight again and stroking his head. "I wish you weren't fighting tomorrow!"

Isengrim merely licked her hand. He was perfectly happy to be fighting tomorrow. He'd never been reluctant to fight for Hoel as a man, and he was no less willing as a wolf. It was just a pity that his opponents would be dogs, not men. He would have been glad to fight Robert of Bellême. It would have been easy to kill the man in the hall that evening — cut round to his left, brace against the bench, and leap on his sword arm from behind. Robert wouldn't have expected the move from an animal. He would have dropped his sword, and it would have been a matter of seconds to tear his throat out. Isengrim would have died himself afterward, of course: an animal that killed a baron would undoubtedly have been destroyed. But Hoel's bitter enemy would be dead, and the insult to Marie avenged. Alain de

Fougères, unfortunately, would have been left secure — but still, it would have been a notable deed for a wolf, and a glorious end. Killing a couple of dogs would be a lot less satisfying.

He ate a good meal that night and settled down to sleep quickly and easily. In the morning, when he was offered only water, he overrode his protesting instincts without difficulty: it was better to fight fasting. He stood still to have the leash clipped to his collar, and followed the duke out into the king's hall.

The court was excited about the fight, and bets were being placed eagerly, most of them favoring the wolf. Isengrim stood motionless in a crowd of admirers while Hoel ascertained where the fight would take place. There was a bear-baiting pit in the palace garden, and it emerged that the king had already gone there with Count Ranulf to decide its suitability for a wolf fight. Hoel and the rest of the court threaded their way through the maze of the palace into the garden to join the king.

The royal garden lay on the very point of the Ile de la Cité, which jutted out into the river like the prow of a ship pointing downstream to the distant sea. They crunched down gravel paths among the beds of herbs, under an arbor of newly leaved roses, and found the bear pit. It was sunk into the ground more deeply than a man was tall, and its sides and floor were lined with stone rubble set in cheap mortar. The pit itself was ringed with banks of seats for the spectators. King Philippe was standing at the entrance to these, talking to Ranulf. Both men turned and greeted Hoel cordially when he appeared. "What about this, eh?" said Philippe, waving a hand at the bear pit. "Do you think it would suit?"

"It's a bit small," said Hoel, glancing into the pit. "A confined space will favor the dogs, my lord. But my lord Ranulf's dogs probably need favoring. Yes, it will do."

Ranulf smirked. "You sound very sure of your wolf, my lord Hoel."

"He's a good wolf," replied Hoel, patting Isengrim. "I'll back him for twenty marks against your dogs."

"Taken," said Ranulf at once, and shook hands on it. King

Philippe looked uneasy. "And you, my lord," Ranulf said, turning to him, "will you be placing any bets?"

Philippe hesitated uncomfortably. "I think I will bet on your dogs, my lord," he said slowly. "But I think Duke Hoel should see them before he accepts the bet."

Ranulf gestured to one of his attendants, and a moment later, the two dogs were led up.

Isengrim had expected a pair of alaunts, the usual hound for wolf or boar—tall, handsome dogs about his own size. Ranulf's hounds were a good four inches taller than he was at the shoulder—hairy, heavy-chested beasts with the massive, crushing jaws of a mastiff. Their ears flattened when they scented him, and their hackles rose. They lowered their powerful heads and began to growl. He could smell their hatred. One of them might be a fair match for him. Two of them—two of them could kill any wolf.

Isengrim's mind went dim, numbed with shock. He was aware of the duke protesting, and of Ranulf taunting him smugly—"You didn't specify the breed of dog, my lord of Brittany. These are wolfhounds, a gift from my cousin in England. Are you afraid for your good Breton wolf?" The duke's leg, pressed against the wolf, began to shake with anger and indignation. But the wolf realized that Hoel would not, could not back out after all his boasts. Rather than give up, he would allow his wolf to be torn apart before his eyes. Isengrim glanced back at the rest of the Breton party. Havoise's scent was sharp with anger, and Marie's, still bruised and smelling faintly of borage, was salty with distress. Isengrim looked back at the wolfhounds. The human self struggled up inside him and said, *If I am a man, I am more than equal to these dogs. If I'm not, I should have died before now. And if I die now, fighting for my liege lord, it's a good end.*

He licked Hoel's hand, and the duke looked down at him angrily. He trotted forward to the end of the leash and snarled deliberately at the two wolfhounds. At once they both flung themselves toward him, nearly dragging their handlers off their feet. They hung against their collars, choking, growling, and barking with rage. He coolly sat down just beyond their reach and glanced back at Hoel. I'll fight them, he tried to tell the duke with his eyes. You will not be made ashamed.

Everyone, even Ranulf, exclaimed at him. Hoel, with an oath, accepted the king's wager as well as that of the Count of Bayeux. But there were tears in his eyes when he led Isengrim down to the barred door of the underground passage that was the bear's entrance to the bear pit. The king's man opened the door, and Hoel bent and unclipped the leash — then knelt and put an arm around him, rubbing his ears. "You're a brave beast," said the duke, not in court French but in plain Breton. "The best I ever owned. By God, I've been glad of you." He kissed the wolf's head. Then he stood up. "Kill them both for me, Isengrim!" he shouted in French for the courtiers to hear. "Kill them both!"

Isengrim whined and trotted into the round pit, and the door swung shut behind him.

The dogs were still behind their door, in the other kennel entrance to the bear pit. Isengrim sat down in the pit's center, gathering himself for the combat. He had to be prepared for death, but he hoped to live. The dogs were bigger and heavier than he was. They were stronger and had a longer reach. Their jaws were terrible. One bite in the wrong place, and he'd be crippled and torn to pieces. And from the look of the wolf-hounds, they'd fight like mastiffs: once they got a grip, they'd hang on. On his side, he was probably faster than they were, and more agile, though these were not qualities an animal could use to full advantage in the cramped, sheer-walled pit. Even if he did somehow manage to kill or maim the dogs enough to end the fight, if he were crippled himself, he'd die. Hoel might prize a pet wolf, but he'd certainly destroy it if it were maimed. Yes, the wagerers above, now busily readjusting the odds in the dogs' favor, were right. A wolf's chances here were bad.

But he had another advantage, one that none of the wagerers above was aware of. He shaped it in his mind, forcing himself to use words: *I am not a wolf.* He glanced upward at the wild, white faces pouring along the benches all around to watch, smelling the excitement and the lust for blood. *I am one of them,* he told himself. Crippled though his reason was, he still had more than an animal's cunning, subtlety, and the power to deceive. He had once been reckoned one of the best fighters in Brittany. If he could strike first, fast, and hard, he could win.

The door opposite was being unlocked now, and he got to his feet and reached into himself for that familiar rage that had always accompanied him into battle. *You black-dog-shit bastards,* he thought, the Breton words coming for once without effort. *Come get me then. You'll regret it.*

The door opened, and he could hear the wolfhounds beyond it begin to bay. He howled.

Howling, for dogs as for wolves, was a call for the gathering of the pack and for the shared communion after a kill. It was not a reply to a bloodthirsty bay. The two dogs that rushed into the pit were momentarily bewildered, and in that instant's bewilderment, Isengrim leapt on them. He must cripple at least one of them at once or he had no chance of surviving the fight. He sprang past the belatedly flashing teeth of the nearest and sank his own fangs deep into the middle joint of its hind leg. He tasted blood and felt the bone crack. The wolfhound yelped in pain. It lunged at him, but he was already away from it. He sprang against the wall and used the force of his rebound to turn, bringing him down at the second animal's side. He landed running and slashed at its muzzle as he passed, tearing it open from nose to ear, blinding it. Then he danced away, licking the blood from his lips. *Good, good, good!* screamed the fury inside him.

He could hear shouting above him, but he paid no attention, all his concentration focused on the dogs. His wolf's body remembered the man's instruction in weapons: strike quickly, strike hard, and strike while they're off balance. He must not strike directly, though, like a true wolf: he must confuse them. Both dogs were running to attack him, but the one he'd lamed was slower, giving him the opportunity to take them one at a time. He turned as though he were trying to flee, then leapt against the wall of the pit again and used it to change direction, bringing him down, this time directly on top of the half-blind dog. He twisted while they fell together to the ground, looking for a place to strike. The hound's head was stretched up in its effort to bite him, and he tore at its throat, but his teeth caught harmlessly in the heavy collar. And now the second wolfhound had caught up. It flung itself snarling and yelping onto his back and sank its jaws into the base of his tail. He pulled his nose away from the first hound's throat and twisted to get at the second. His instincts screamed at him to slash stingingly and pull away, but he ruthlessly overrode them, remembering the mastiff grip. Instead he closed his own jaws on the hound's nose.

Suffocated by its own blood, it let go, and he sprang away. His tail hurt horribly, might be broken — but a tail wasn't something he needed for fighting. *Strike while they're off balance.* He darted in toward the half-blind hound again, on its blind side, and ripped savagely at its forepaw. Then he circled behind both of them and ran to the far side of the pit, where he crouched panting to catch his breath. He had reached the state he had found sometimes in battle, when the noise and the hate and hitting gave way to a great, exhilarating clarity, and for all the pain in his tail he felt invulnerable.

Both limping now, the wolfhounds edged toward him. They still barked and bayed, but more hesitantly. They were beginning to be afraid of him. He howled again, tauntingly, and dropped to his side on the ground, as though he were in no danger and had decided to rest. Again they were bewildered, and again he took advantage of that instant of confusion to strike. He leapt up and shot diagonally in front of them to catch the half-blind one on its blind side yet again. The hind leg, this time; again the sweet salt taste of blood. He ran on to the other end of the pit, leapt to turn, and tore back eagerly to attack again; the less severely injured dog had turned to face him, though the blinded one cowered. He crouched snarling, muzzle to muzzle with it for a moment, then feinted at its injured nose.

It flinched, and he twisted and tore at its foreleg, then danced off again.

The two dogs, both doubly lame, their muzzles rippled open and bleeding, crouched in their places, their hackles up and their tails down. The onlookers were shouting and screaming; Isengrim could make out the yell of the Count of Bayeux, urging them to attack. But the wolfhounds were afraid. This creature smelled like a wolf, but it didn't behave like a wolf. And now that they were afraid they noticed the strangeness of their opponent: even the scent was wrong. They had been bred and trained to kill wolves, but this was an unnatural thing, and a deadly one. They wanted to run away.

Isengrim walked slowly along the wall of the pit toward them, and they backed away. He stopped and stared at them insolently, then turned his back on them and walked the other way. One of the wolfhounds picked up its courage at this appearance of retreat and made a staggering lunge; at once the wolf leapt up against the wall, turned himself against it, and crashed down upon the lame and half-blind dog. It managed to keep its head up, and its fangs tore his face as he landed, ripping open his jaw, but then he had pinned it to the ground with his weight and caught its heavy collar in his mouth. He drew his head upward, drawing the collar tight, and then twisted. The dog yelped and struggled, but with its cracked leg bone it couldn't push him off, and he flung his weight repeatedly against its shoulders, banging it down again and again, and twisting the collar tighter all the time. The other dog ran forward, yelping and barking as it tried to work up the nerve to attack. Its fellow's struggles were feeble now. Isengrim stopped banging it and met the other animal's eyes. He held those eyes with his own as he strangled its fellow, and it stood, whimpering, until the other wolfhound was still. Then he let go of the collar and got up.

The remaining hound fell back. It put its tail between its legs, ran back to the kennel entrance, and cowered there, whimpering in terror. Isengrim stood in the center of the pit, bleeding from face and tail. His fury, no longer needed, ebbed away. *Poor beast*, he thought. The onlookers screamed and bellowed all around. Kill them both, the duke had said. But what honor was there in killing a terrified animal? He glanced about, looking for Hoel.

The duke was beside the king, in the front tier of onlookers, hanging beaming over the railings and banging the wall of the pit with his fists. "Good wolf, Isengrim!" he shouted, catching the wolf's eyes. "Good boy! That's it, you brave beast: he's surrendered; spare him!" In his excitement he was shouting in Breton, but Isengrim understood that better than French. He grinned at the duke, and, turning his back on the cowering hound, went over to the space beneath the royal bench and sat down. Hoel swore, vaulted over the railings, and dropped into the pit beside him. He embraced the wolf, blood and all, then grinned up at the king and count of Bayeux. "Well, my lord Ranulf?" he said. "My wolf wants to spare your miserable cur. Do you want to have it taken out, or shall I tell Isengrim to finish it off?"

The half-blind dog would have been killed anyway, but the remaining beast might recover. The Count of Bayeux had his hound taken out, and the Duke of Brittany clipped the leash back onto the his wolf's collar and led it victorious from the ring. The courtiers who'd placed bets on the wolf, and who hadn't been able to retract them after seeing the dogs, rushed over with congratulations. The Normans came scowling and more slowly.

"You owe me twenty marks!" Hoel crowed triumphantly to Ranulf.

"The beast is a witch!" snapped the count. "It didn't fight like any natural creature."

"So? I've told everyone that he's an intelligent animal, far cleverer than any dog. You trust too much to strength, you Normans. Skill counts, too. Twenty marks, my lord — or do you want to default on your bet, eh?"

The king appeared beside the count. "I owe you twenty marks as well, my lord Hoel," he said. "And I'll pay the sum gladly, and five times more as well, if you will let me keep the wolf."

"Not for a hundred marks, and not for a thousand!" exclaimed Hoel. "Truthfully, my lord, if you were in my place, would you sell him?"

"If I were in your place, I would thank God and keep him," replied Philippe with a smile. "Very well. You had better take him off and have his injuries seen to."

For the Breton party, nothing was too good for the duke's wolf. Most of them had bet on him to beat the dogs, and had the pleasure of collecting money from Parisians and, even better, from Normans. They went out and spent most of their winnings in the taverns of Paris, staggering home drunk and shouting out to all the world that Count Ranulf had had two wolfhounds, and the one was dead and the other turned coward because of one good Breton wolf. Isengrim had his lacerated tail bandaged in silk and was fed on steak, minced to spare the stitches in his jaw. For his own part, the wolf was glad to have shamed the Normans and delighted his liege. But the sweetest thing was to have fought beasts like a man, and won.

The following day, the king finally heard the case of the rival claimants to the manor of Chalandrey. Law was a man's affair, and Marie and the duchess waited in their allotted quarters in the palace to learn the decision. Marie had profited from Havoise's shopping expeditions to buy a couple of books, and she read to the duchess and her ladies from one of them. Inwardly, she was queasy with tension. She regretted declaring her intentions to the king. He might otherwise have decided on the evidence that Chalandrey was Hoel's.

The court recessed at noon, and Hoel returned for a quick meal. No, he told them: there was no decision yet. He'd presented his evidence to the king and argued his case; now the Normans were presenting theirs. Afterward, both sides would sum up, and the king would give his verdict. Hoel kissed Havoise and went back to the court.

Marie sat down in the rushes beside Isengrim and scratched the wolf's ears. He rested his head in her lap, on one side to take the weight off the slash on his jaw. It was a deep cut, and ran from the middle of his lower lip halfway down his throat, and it was sore and inflamed. Marie noticed the inflammation and fetched a basin of salty water and a sponge to bathe it. "Good wolf," she whispered as she stroked the cut gently. He looked up at her affectionately.

She was sitting there, bathing the wolf's injury and thinking about anything but the court case, when Kenmarcoc's story about his night in the stocks leapt suddenly to her mind, and she finally realized why she had found it so disquieting. According to what the clerk had said, Eline had returned to Talensac after her husband had gone away for the last time, but before anyone realized he was missing. And yet she hadn't wanted to be reconciled with her husband: she'd quarreled with Judicaël when he came to help her do just that, and Judicaël had not seemed to Marie a man given to quarreling. Marie remembered exactly that voice in the darkness: "Marrying him was the greatest mistake I ever made, and I'm glad I'm free of him." If Eline hadn't wanted to be reconciled, why had she returned to Talensac?

Because she knew that her husband was already dead, and wanted to appear innocent of his murder.

Marie's hand froze in midstroke, and she reasoned with herself. It was tragic that Eline should have decided to try for reconciliation too late. Tragic, not suspicious.

But Alain, who had loved Eline all along, had left Nantes shortly before Tiarnán disappeared. Marie could remember it now: the two journeys to buy hawks in St. Malo; the two returns hawkless, and Tiher's caustic comments about it. Had that really coincided with Tiarnán's disappearance, or was she misremembering? The first time Alain went to St. Malo, it had been about the time of the Feast of Saint Michael: that was a festival she'd always observed with special devotion, and she could remember he'd been absent for it. And the second time? A couple of weeks later. He'd even armed then: Tiher had commented on that, too, laughing at the absurdity of wearing all that fine mail just to buy a hawk. If there was no certainty that the fit was exact, still, it was close. Frighteningly close. He could have gone once to see Eline and hear her plea for freedom, and once to murder his rival, who was hunting alone and lightly armed.

Isengrim whined. She'd been pressing the sponge against his wound. She stroked his head apologetically, squeezed the sponge out, dipped it back in the brine, and began stroking the cut with it again. The possibility that had just occurred to her was monstrous, and it would be utterly wrong to breathe a word of her suspicions to anyone — yet. She would have to check some of the details first. She could talk to Kenmarcoc, find out exactly when Tiarnán had disappeared, and see if he had more to say about his former master and his hunting expeditions. That should be easy: Kenmarcoc was a talkative man, and particularly fond of telling anyone who'd listen about the excellence of Talensac in general and "the machtiern" in particular. The other thing that could be checked was more difficult: she needed to know if anyone had sent Alain a message before he went to St. Malo. But with thought . . . she could ask Tiher about ships, how one knew what ships were docking, how Alain had heard about that ship with the hawks . . .

Judicaël probably knew more. The hermit would reveal no secrets, though; she was certain of that. She remembered now, however, his baffling comment about how she should tell him when her judgment was complete. There was something he hoped she could determine — something he considered himself too partial to decide. Eline's guilt.

Was it really her place to decide that? Was it good, even for Tiarnán's sake, to question the matter any further? He had had a secret: Eline had made that clear, and Judicaël had only confirmed it. If she dragged the facts of his disappearance out into the light of day, the secret might come with them. Whether Eline were innocent or guilty, to pursue her might destroy the only thing her husband had left on earth: his reputation.

If Tiarnán really had been betrayed by his wife and murdered by her lover, then justice was due. All her beliefs cried out that it was false to think a crime could lie buried and poison no one as it decayed. If there really was a case, she would present it to Duke Hoel, and he would see to it that justice was done.

The door was flung open, and Hoel stalked in, his face crimson from his throat to the bald patch on the top of his head. He flung himself into his seat and glared at Marie. "Well!" he said. "The archangel won!"

"Well, at least the Normans didn't," soothed Havoise, jumping up and coming over to him. "My dear, have something to drink: it's far too hot a day to talk law with a dry throat." She nodded to Sybille, who hurried over with a jug of watered wine and a cup.

Hoel gulped the wine thirstily, then flung the cup into the fireplace, where it shattered. At this Isengrim got up and pressed his nose into the duke's hand. Hoel softened at the touch and began roughing the wolf's fur. "The archangel won," he repeated, wearily this time. "King Philippe listened to all our summing up, and then said sweetly that the matter was too complicated to decide easily, but that since the rightful heiress to the manor had announced her intention of giving all her lands to Saint Michael, and since this was a pious and godly intention, and the prayers of the holy monks would support peace, the land should go to God. If Marie wants, we are to let her join St. Michael's convent and take vows; if she doesn't want, the land is still to go to the saint, but she may keep whatever goods the manor house contains and use them as her dowry. If she declines to give the manor to Saint Michael, the whole estate is forfeited to the crown. To the crown! What right does the *king* have to Chalandrey, I'd like to know?"

"My dear," said Havoise after a moment's thought, "I believe that if the archangel hadn't entered the contest, the crown would have claimed the whole."

Hoel snorted. "He could never have made that stick."

"Which is probably why he decided on the archangel."

Hoel laughed ruefully and ran his hand over his bald patch. Marie was staring at him in confusion. Her heart was beating fast, as if with hope—but she could not believe she had any hope. "The king suggested that I give away the manor of Chalandrey but keep its contents?" she asked.

The contents of Chalandrey, as she knew very well, included an enormous amount of silver, plate, and jewels—spoils of England, which her grandfather had helped to conquer under Duke William. She had never before thought of the money as divisible from the house or lands. Like the serfs who farmed the estate, her grandfather's wealth had been part of Chalandrey, a resource which its lord could draw on at need. Now she saw that it was indeed something that could be taken away, and that it would, indeed, form a perfectly respectable dowry.

Hoel grinned at her question. "That was a good thought of the king's, wasn't it?" he said. "He doesn't want you to follow your lands to a convent any more than I do."

Marie stared even more stupidly, like a young child who cannot understand her elders' meaning. "Do you mean," she said slowly, "that you don't want me to go back to St. Michael's when we return to Brittany?"

"Of course," said Hoel, his eyebrows bobbing up in surprise. "Why would I?"

Havoise looked at Marie's face and laughed. "My dear," she said, "is it really so surprising that we like you? You know what the court's like. It's full to bursting with *men*, and noisy young men at that. There's no pleasure in living in an armed camp all the time. Even the men don't like it. A pretty, clever young woman like you adds more joy to the place than I can say. You've certainly been a delight to me ever since you arrived. Stay with us for a little while longer, at least, and don't hurry to make up your mind to be a nun. You've got a dowry now, and I can think of at least one court official who might have been willing to take you without a penny."

"Tiher wants land," Marie stammered, blushing with embarrassed astonishment.

"Tiher will have land," replied Hoel. "Just as soon as one of my vassals dies without heirs—and there are two or three that might pop off at any time. I'm not going to let a man like Tiher go wanting when idiots like his cousin hold manors. Let me give Tiher an estate, and then see if he doesn't decide to take up the chase again, eh? But whatever you do, stay with us awhile longer."

Marie looked from him to Havoise in confusion, and the duchess chuckled.

"There's nothing I'd like better!" exclaimed Marie, running to kiss her.

And I'll stay, she thought privately, at least until I can settle whether Eline has a case to answer or not.

XV

Duke Hoel returned to Brittany in the first week of June. His manor of Talensac, which had paid little attention to its overlord's departure, paid even less to his return. For Talensac, that June would be remembered bitterly as the month Lord Alain doubled the charges at the mill.

Since Easter, Alain had been growing more and more desperate for money. When he'd returned home after the disastrous wolf hunt at Treffendel, he'd decided that the best way to stop his wife's tears was to strip Talensac manor house of every trace of its former owner. He'd got rid of all the old furniture, burning what he couldn't sell, and ordered new, of the best quality that could be made. He'd torn down Tiarnán's hunting tapestries from the walls, bundled them up with all Tiarnán's clothes, his armor, bow, spears, and the sword which had once sunk through Geoffroy of Bellême's helmet a hand's breadth into his skull, and he'd taken them to Nantes, together with the chestnut warhorse, and offered them to the Jew as partial payment of his debt.

The Jew did not really want them. All members of his faith were banned by law from riding horses or bearing arms, and he was a banker, not a merchant. However, he did not want to offend his debtor, and he knew the fabulous cost of warhorses and armor, so he accepted the things and placed them with a Gentile associate until they could be sold. Alain then went shopping with the fifteen marks left from what he'd borrowed, and spent it all. Vast amounts of new linen for the new beds, new blankets, a new cupboard, one new tapestry hanging . . . he ran out of money before he could buy the rest. He'd hoped that the quarterly rents, due on Easter Monday, would provide him with more. But the amount that came in was disappointing, and the household expenses had by then begun to grow alarmingly.

His clearing-out had utterly appalled the manor house servants. The house was *their* home, too. The oak tables in the hall had been there since the days of Tiarnán's grandfather. They were too big for any common house, and could not be sold, so they were burned. Some of the women servants, watching the flames lick the dark wood which four generations of their kind had polished, wept—and the bailiff Gilbert cursed them, and slapped one or two with his little riding whip. Some of the men servants, like Donoal, had vivid memories of the duke's wars, and they watched the weapons and the chestnut warhorse depart for Nantes with bitter faces. When Alain returned from Nantes with his purchases, it was to find that a dozen of his servants had left. Those who remained were all serfs, and not free to go. Some of the free-men and -women who'd gone had simply moved in with friends or relations in the village; others had left Talensac altogether. "They'll come crawling back with their tails between their legs," said Gilbert contemptuously. "They won't find work or wages as good as here in the towns." Perhaps—but in the meantime, the house was short staffed, and there was all the new furniture to arrange.

Alain went to some of the servants who'd moved down the hill and told them that he would overlook their defection if they came back. Not one would come. It astonished him: not one of them had a house or field of his own. They'd all lived by working on the domain lands and in the manor house, and now they were rootless hirelings—but they obstinately refused to return to the only place they had. Alain was particularly infuriated with the stable lad Donoal. Since the time of the wolf he'd thought of Donoal as the servant he knew best, and had favored him. But Donoal, too, had gone, down the hill and over the brook to the house of Glevian the blacksmith, where he helped his friend Justin in the fields. Alain went to Glevian's house and offered Donoal higher wages if he returned. Donoal, like the others, refused.

"What is the matter with you?" Alain asked him furiously. "You're upset that I sold some furniture?"

Donoal looked at him impassively. "Lord," he said, "the lis is your house now. You may do what you want with it."

"Then why did you leave it?" demanded Alain.

"Lord," replied Donoal in a tone of deep stupidity, "I lived at the lis when the machtiern was there. Now it is your house."

Alain raged at him but received no better answer than that. When the lord of Talensac had stamped off, Justin slipped in from the garden, where he'd been listening. "But why did you leave?" he asked Donoal in mincing March-accented Breton.

Donoal grinned savagely. "Lord," he said, "I don't care to work for a whore's darling, a whore and a thieving bailiff. You're not half the man your predecessor was, Lord Goldilocks, and if you think you'll make everyone forget that by trying to scrub out every trace of him, you're wrong!"

"May they all rot in hell!" agreed Justin. "And may they go there soon!"

The only place Alain went soon was to Fougères, where he recruited new servants from among his father's tenants. He had to offer them high wages, though, to get them to leave their homes and come to live among the wild folk of the forest, and when they arrived and saw how the people of Talensac detested them, Alain had to offer them more again to make them stay. Therefore, he needed more money.

He still wanted to increase the rents, but after what the duke had said to him at Treffendel, he did not quite dare. So he looked to his other sources of revenue. The most obvious one was the mill. It was his, and the villagers were obliged to use it to grind all their grain. He doubled the charges.

To the villagers the coarse buckwheat bread baked from the mill's flour was the footing of life itself. Alain could have chosen no more devastating blow. Was the village to pay double for its life because the lord wanted new furniture? The day the charges were raised, there was an impassioned meeting in the parish churchyard. Talensac assembled, united in outrage, and swore as one that it would not pay the cruel and iniquitous charge. And so that June, and the summer after it, became something that marked its people for the rest of their lives.

arie spent the early part of June painstakingly checking whether her suspicions of Alain and Eline were justified. She questioned Kenmarcoc first. He was, as ever, very willing to talk, and found nothing odd in her questions: events at Talensac were so inherently interesting that it was only surprising more people hadn't asked him about them. Yes, the Lady Eline had decided to be reconciled to her husband shortly after he went away for the last time. She'd returned from Iffendic two days after he left on his final hunting expedition. When was that? Oh, about the middle of October. Yes, the middle of October: Kenmarcoc remembered that they'd finished the threshing by the full harvest moon the night Lord Tiarnán left. What had the lord and lady quarreled about? Well, the lord had a habit of going hunting on his own, without even the dog, and the lady had got it into her head that he was visiting another woman. That was nonsense: he'd adored her. But she'd been offended with him, and had taken herself off to her sister's. Why *did* the machtiern go hunting without the dog? At this Kenmarcoc grew suddenly awkward and reserved . . . well, there were foolish stories—but really, the best guess was that the machtiern had simply liked time alone in the forest, and didn't want the trouble of caring for a dog.

Marie recognized, with resignation, that she had again come up against the blind wall of Tiarnán's secret. She doubted that Kenmarcoc knew what it was. But it seemed likely that it had been divulged to Eline, and she had gone to Iffendic to escape from it. She had only returned in October, just after the full moon—the time when Alain had, indeed, been absent from the ducal court on his second unsuccessful trip to buy a hawk.

The second part of her investigation was, as she'd anticipated, more difficult. In fact, it proved impossible to carry out unobtrusively. Tiher was far too quick-witted to be deceived by her casual air when she asked him how Alain had known that a ship carrying hawks had arrived in St. Malo.

"Uncle Juhel has a shipping agent in the city," he said. "Why are you interested, sweet lady? If you want to take up hawking, you don't need to wait for a ship. I'll buy you a merlin tomorrow."

Marie smiled. "You don't need to buy me a hawk. I'll have lots of money when Chalandrey's been consigned to the priory. Did your uncle's agent send Alain a letter, then?"

But Tiher's eyebrows were beginning to slide up to their angle of mockery. "Your father must have hawks at Chalandrey," he said. "He wouldn't have taken them to the Holy Land. You don't need to buy hawks." He paused and looked at her with candid curiosity. "Why this interest in my uncle's agent in St. Malo?"

"I was just wondering how Alain knew when to go there."

Tiher stared at her for a long minute, and then his amusement vanished. "You aren't really interested in ships at all, are you?" he asked. "You're interested in Alain, and whether he really went to St. Malo that time."

Tiher had been suspicious of the expeditions at the time. Alain was quite capable of suddenly deciding that he *must* have a gyrfalcon and chasing a ship rumored to be carrying one right round the coast of Brittany—but it had been very unlike Alain to refuse company on his shopping trip. When he set out he had had the self-satisfied air that in Tiher's experience usually preceded a disaster. There had not been much doubt about what sort of disaster Alain would have been courting at the time: Alain was a fool for Eline. "But he swore to me," Tiher said out loud, "on the holy cross he swore it, that he wasn't going to Talensac."

Marie hesitated, then replied quietly. "I believe that Lady Eline was in Iffendic with her sister at the time."

"Christ and Saint Michael!" The self-satisfied air, the smile after the oath. Tiher looked at Marie a moment longer, now with a strained expression. She could see him checking the dates of his cousin's two trips in his mind, matching them against another event, and recoiling. "Have you said anything about this to the duke?" he asked sharply.

"No," said Marie. "I don't want to say anything about it to anyone. Not unless there's more reason to believe it's true."

"I'll find out," promised Tiher grimly.

There was absolutely no doubt that Alain would have gone at once to meet Eline if she had summoned him; there was no doubt that he had hated Tiarnán, and for Eline's sake would have been willing to kill his rival. And yet . . . how could Alain ever have got the better of a knight like Tiarnán — even given that Tiarnán would have been carrying only a bow and a hunting knife, while Alain wore full armor? Tiarnán had been a superb huntsman, and Alain in full armor would never have got anywhere near him, not unless he pretended to be carrying a message for him, or Tiarnán was asleep. And Alain couldn't have killed him then. He simply couldn't have killed a rival without making a long speech to him first. He was not the stab-a-man-in-the-back sort: he'd thirst for some glorious single combat, and he'd stand there under the trees waving his sword and declaiming, while Tiarnán disappeared into the bushes to shoot him dead.

The ridiculous image comforted Tiher. It was plain, though, that Marie had started a bird of suspicion from cover, and somebody was going to have to bring it down. Tiher was going to have to discover the truth, for Alain's sake.

So Tiher made his own cautious inquiries about the court. One of the pages remembered that Alain had received a letter the previous September — but that had been nearly a year before, and a year is a long time for a ten-year-old boy whose mind and body are fully occupied learning to be a knight. The details had all been forgotten. Tiher tried another tack: he wrote to Lord Juhel's agent in St. Malo, asking about the ship carrying hawks that was said to have docked there the previous autumn. Early in July came the puzzling response that no such ship had ever existed.

When this letter arrived, Tiher kept it to himself. Marie was away from court, and wasn't expected back until the Feast of

Saint James, on the twenty-fifth of the month. She was going
to Chalandrey with Duke Hoel's bailiff Grallon to take an inventory of the contents of the manor, then continuing to Mont
St. Michel to make a formal gift of her lands to St. Michael's
priory. There was no one else at court to whom he was willing
to entrust such damaging information. Alain had lied about
where he was going and been absent when Tiarnán disappeared. Alain had gained a wife and a manor from Tiarnán's
death. Tiher still couldn't believe that his cousin would have
gone up to a man with a friendly greeting, then stabbed him
through the heart — but he could not shake off the doubts that,
to gain Eline, Alain might have been willing to do even that.
The image of handsome, impulsive Alain, the young fool of a
cousin whose enthusiasms Tiher had always tried to curb, secretly burying his victim's body in the forest sickened him.
Tiher didn't want even to think about it — not until Marie returned to the court, when he knew he would have to. So he
threw himself into work. The stag-hunting season had begun,
and there was much to keep him busy.

The court had by then moved back to Ploërmel, and the duke
was much occupied with hunting in the nearby forest. Tiher
had to find suitable quarries for him, arrange hunting lodges
and servants for him, and see that any guests invited were ac-
commodated. There was besides a particularly splendid hunt to
organize for the last week of July, when Bishop Quiriac of
Nantes was expected to visit the court. The bishop was Hoel's
brother, and he shared the family enthusiasm for the chase. As
the best quarry for him, Tiher eventually settled on a sixteen-
tined stag reported to be in the forest at Treffendel.

Hoel was pleased with the suggestion. "I had good luck at
Treffendel in March," he said, glancing affectionately at Isengrim, who was, as usual, at his heels. "Yes, send a messenger
there to tell them we'll arrive the evening after Saint James's
Day. And make arrangements for the ladies to come as well.
Quiriac is fond of the ladies, and he sees little enough of them
in his palace, poor fellow."

If the duke planned to arrive in Treffendel the evening after

Saint James's Day, then Tiher and the court servants should arrive on the feast day itself, to prepare the hunting lodge and seek out the quarry. Tiher decided, though, that the servants deserved their holy day rest, and decreed that his party set out a day early, to give them Saint James's Day free. It was only after making this decision that he realized that the extra day would give him time to visit his cousin Alain at Talensac. He took the opportunity with a mixture of eagerness and dread. He had never had a high opinion of Alain's good sense, but they'd grown up together from infancy, and the suspicion that his cousin was a murderer had become like a blister in his heart.

He had never been to Talensac before, but he'd always heard it described as a pretty place. Certainly it had a pretty setting: he rode from the green forest out into wide fields, gold with the harvest, green with neat rows of vines, or silver-green patched with grazing cattle and sheep. A tall wooden church tower poked from a dell ahead, and his road became the main street of a village of good-sized houses sitting in well-tended gardens. The place was not welcoming, however. The peasants working in the fields stared at him sullenly as he rode by, and when he entered the village, the street was empty, though suspicious faces peered at him from doorways. No one called out the ordinary greetings of the country. No one spoke at all. The stocks in front of the church were occupied to overflowing. One wretch who'd evidently been flogged sagged bloody-backed in the stocks themselves, while beside him sat shackled two other peasants in leg irons and yokes. They glowered at Tiher, and he noticed that one of them had been branded on the forehead. Next to them stood a pillar of raw new wood with a pair of hand shackles dangling from it. It was stained with blood, some fresh, some darkly brown. Talensac had plainly seen more than one flogging recently.

The gate of the manor house was shut and bolted. When Tiher knocked on it, an eye peered at him through a slitted window in the lodge, and then a voice called down, "What do you want?"

"My name is Tiher de Fougères!" Tiher called back. "I've come to visit my cousin Alain."

There was a moment's silence, and then the bolt was shot back and the gate cracked open. "You'd best come in, my lord," said a nervous peasant. The peasant's face was vaguely familiar, and he spoke in the French of the March. When Tiher had ridden through, the gate slammed shut behind him. Tiher began to wish he hadn't come.

"I'll tell the master you're here, my lord," said the gatekeeper. "Can you stable your horse yourself? Sorry to ask it of you, but we're a bit shorthanded."

Tiher raised his eyebrows, but took his horse off to the stables without comment. He was still seeing to the animal when Alain appeared and greeted him very warmly.

There were apologies for arriving unexpectedly, and effusive welcomes in reply, and at last Alain showed him to the house. Eline was waiting in the doorway. She, too, welcomed him very warmly, but her beautiful face was pale, thin, and lined with strain, and her eyes were red. And if the air in the village had been tense and sullen, the air of the Breton manor servants was frightened and subdued, while the large group of servants from Fougères was bullying and shrill.

The house had an air of guilty debauchery. The rushes on the floor had not been changed for some time, and everything was slightly dirty round the edges, as though it had been wiped now and then but not washed properly. The furniture was all new and fine, but there wasn't enough of it: the servants' bedding lay in unraveling heaps in the corners instead of being folded away in chests. One wall of the hall was partly covered by an insipid embroidery of the life of Saint Martin, but the rest were bare.

The evening meal was late. They waited for it, talking of the court, the hunting party for Bishop Quiriac, and similar irrelevancies. When the food finally appeared, the meat was burned and the rosee of rabbits underdone: the short-staffing evidently extended to the kitchen. The servants were anxious, and hurried in and out whispering. Alain ignored them and drank heavily. There was no shortage of wine.

"Are you having some kind of trouble here?" Tiher asked when he had been decently silent long enough for the question not to be offensive. "You've got three men in the stocks, and there's a flogging pillar that's seen some use recently."

"I had a man flogged this morning for taking his grain to the mill at Montfort," said Alain at once, flushing with anger at the memory. "The other two in the stocks are guilty of the same offense, but only for the first time—the first time I've *caught* them doing it, that is. Most likely they've done it several times before without my knowing."

"Taking their grain to Montfort? What's wrong with your own mill?"

"Nothing! Nothing at all! It's been sitting idle for weeks, though, and the stubborn, greedy fools have been going to Montfort, or grinding their grain at home, or even living on pottages of unground barley. I increased the charges at the mill, and they're refusing to pay."

Tiher looked at his cousin for a long moment. Alain had a frantic, feverish look, not entirely due to the wine he'd been drinking. Alain's foolishness, Tiher thought grimly, had involved him in another disaster—a worse one than ever. "Well, what do you expect, if the mill at Montfort is cheaper?" he asked harshly.

"They're *my* tenants; they're *obliged* to use my mill! It's my *right*. And I'm *entitled* to increase the charges if I want to. And I do want to."

"Why?"

Alain's flush of anger faded, and he looked down. "I borrowed some money in Nantes last November," he mumbled. "The usury on it is ruinous, and I'd like to pay it off as quickly as I can. Duke Hoel told me flatly that I shouldn't increase the rents, and I don't like to disregard him. I thought it wouldn't hurt to increase the mill charges instead."

He felt uncomfortable as he said it. He had, in fact, paid off half the debt already, with Tiarnán's things, and the Jew in

Nantes had never been pressing him for repayment to begin with. He had been content to collect his interest and wait patiently. Any Jew took a risk in lending to a Christian nobleman, a class always likely to default without the slightest sense of shame, and the rates of interest on such loans were correspondingly high—but the rate on his fifty marks had been standard for such a transaction. The problem was that Alain now wanted *more* money. He needed more furniture and tapestries. He had to pay the servants from Fougères, and the four men-at-arms he'd hired to protect the house when the trouble about the mill began, whose salaries were even higher. Things kept getting lost or broken now, too, which meant replacing them, and some of the serfs had tried to run away, which meant that men had to be sent after them and rewards offered. He would have borrowed again, only nobody was willing to lend him any more money at the same rate until he'd paid off his first debt.

Tiher sat for a minute in a cold silence that would have made Alain angry if it had been anyone else. "I see," said Tiher at last. "But it sounds as though increasing the charges has hurt, and you're not even getting any extra money from it."

"No," Alain said angrily again, "because of the pure perversity of the people here. They could afford to pay—the rents here are half what they were in Fougères—but they think they have a right to have their grain ground at the old price. They'd rather do without flour than pay a farthing more a week for their bread."

Tiher slapped the table. He had never run a manor himself, but he knew that villages consisted principally of people, who might be expected to behave with all the unreasonable conservatism and perversity of human nature. "For God's sake, Alain, what else did you expect?" he demanded in exasperation. "Would *you* tamely agree to pay more for the same old thing, when you could get the old price by going a mile up the road? If you raise the price of bread, of course the peasants hate you! You never did have any sense. I could have told you this would get you nothing but ill-will."

"I can't back down now!" protested Alain. "The people here

all hate me as it is. If they think they can disobey me and get away with it, God knows where it will end."

Eline, who'd said virtually nothing since Tiher arrived, suddenly jumped up from the table and ran from the room. Alain looked at his cousin accusingly. "You've upset her," he said.

"I? I didn't say anything."

"It was that bit about ill-will. She's been very worried about that. The servants keep running off, and people call her names behind her back. I try to have them punished, but it's hard to catch them. And she's . . . she shouldn't be upset just now. She's going to have a child, Tiher."

"Oh!" exclaimed Tiher, with a stab of pity for the white, sick, frightened seventeen-year-old who'd just fled the room. He delivered the conventional congratulations without conviction. "I pray God send you both joy of it."

Alain shook his head, then sank it in his hands. "I pray God does send joy, because there hasn't been any joy of it yet! Tiher, we ought to be so happy, but right now it's just one more thing to worry about. She's been so wretched the past few months that I'm afraid for her. I want to take her away from here. She needs peace—but I don't have anyone I could trust to run the place in my absence. That bailiff of mine, Gilbert, is a thief, and the people here hate him even more than they hate me. Anyway, I can't afford to buy her a house, not with this debt hanging over me." He looked up at Tiher with the old, familiar pleading blue-eyed gaze. "I'm so glad you came," he said. "I don't know what to do, Tiher! The people here hated me even before I arrived, and everything I do only seems to make it worse. They always compare me to their machtiern. If they knew what their precious machtiern really was, they wouldn't want him back!"

"What do you mean?" Tiher asked impatiently.

Alain grimaced and shook his head. "He wasn't the noble knight everyone took him for. Eline found that out."

He did not explain, and Tiher wondered if Eline had "found out" anything more than that her husband lost his temper when nagged about his hunting expeditions, or if Tiarnán had produced a bastard by some village woman. He doubted it was more than that. Alain had been a fool as a landless knight, and becoming lord of a manor seemed only to have made him a worse fool. Why, by all the saints, had he borrowed money?

"I hated the fellow before," Alain went on abruptly, "but not nearly as much as I hate him now. I'm sharing the house with his ghost — and it's a wicked, dark, deadly ghost. I don't know how much more of it I can stand. Tiher, you're clever, and you have the duke's favor. Help me, please!"

Tiher set his teeth and wondered miserably if this "dark, deadly ghost" was the shadow of Alain's own guilt. He wished desperately that he knew where his cousin had gone when he told that story about buying hawks in St. Malo.

But that was a question he did not dare to ask — not then, with Alain waiting anxiously for hope, for the help that he was sure his prickly older cousin could supply.

"Listen, then," Tiher said after a long silence. "Duke Hoel owns houses all over Brittany. He might lease one to you at a nominal rent, for Eline's sake, considering the condition she's in and the way things are here. If you like, I can suggest it to him. But you're going to have to admit to him that you haven't been able to manage Talensac and do something to get your lands in order. If you know your clerk is a thief, sack him and find someone else."

"I can't!" moaned Alain. "I told you, the people here all hate me! I don't dare trust anyone in Talensac as bailiff."

"Then ask the duke to find you someone trustworthy."

"I can't. He offered to do that last March when he was at Treffendel. He told me to get a native Breton speaker. I said I'd rather have Gilbert."

Tiher stared at Alain incredulously. The thought that Hoel had offered Alain help and advice, and that Alain had turned it down, made him wish he could wash his hands of the matter: Alain was so pigheaded in his folly that there was no saving him. But of course he couldn't leave his cousin in the pit, staring up desperately and begging Tiher to toss him a lifeline. Tiher contented himself with making his opinion clear. "Jesus, Mary, and Joseph!" he exclaimed. "You brought this on yourself. *And* on your wife. You went into a perfectly respectable manor, your overlord gave you advice on how to run it, and you blithely ignored him and pulled the whole thing down on top of yourself! Alain, what do you want to do? Stay here and be hated, or put in a reliable bailiff and go live in a comfortable house in Nantes or Vannes until things here have calmed down a bit?"

Alain had stared guiltily down at the table during Tiher's scolding; at this he looked up again. For once he made no attempt to justify himself. "I want to get away," he said instead, very simply. "For Eline's sake, and the child's, I've got to."

"In that case, you're going to have to go to the duke and ask for help. Look, he's not going to do anything worse than say 'I told you so,' and if I make a few excuses for you first, he won't say even that very loudly. What you must do is come to Treffendel and join in the stag hunt. Then you can pick your moment to talk to him. I'm inviting you now in the duke's name. Eline can come, too. The duchess and her ladies are going to be there, so it will be perfectly natural for her to come along, and when they see her, they'll want to help her. Hoel hasn't forgotten how much Tiarnán adored her. He'll be willing to help her for his favorite's sake, even if you have offended him by ignoring his advice."

He noticed how Alain flinched at his rival's name, and all at once ached for the morning so that he could leave. Talensac might not be haunted, but Alain certainly was, and the blister in Tiher's heart reminded him that a ghost will seek out his murderer.

When the ducal party arrived at Treffendel, two evenings later, Marie was with them. The sight of her riding in on her bad-tempered roan mare was like rain on thirsty ground to Tiher. The blister in his heart ached now, and he wanted it to burst soon, one way or another.

He waited until he saw Marie going out to the yard, then managed to catch her privately before she came back in. In silence he handed her the letter from his uncle's shipping agent in St. Malo. She took it, read it quickly, stood staring at it for a long time. Then she sighed, crossed herself, and handed it back to him.

"Alain was lying when he said he was going to St. Malo," Tiher said flatly. "Do we go to the duke?"

"You don't need to ask me that," Marie replied quietly. "You know the answer already. We go to the duke. But let's do it privately."

Tiher nodded heavily. It was the duke's responsibility to administer justice for his vassals. If he were presented with the problem privately, he could check whether there was an innocent explanation for the lies before the whole matter emerged into the public disgrace of a court hearing. Tiher still hoped that Alain could explain, but the circumstances gave him little grounds.

"I'm sorry, Tiher," Marie said gently. "I shouldn't have involved you: he's your cousin."

"You didn't involve me," Tiher pointed out. "I guessed what you were doing and involved myself. But a member of Alain's family should be involved. Just to help him with his case."

This was true, but Marie still grieved for it. Tiher's distress for his cousin was only too apparent. Moreover, as far as Tiher knew, the murder, if there was one, had been committed purely from lust and greed. She knew already that it had involved more than that: at its heart lay a secret so alarming that it had turned Eline against her husband, and perhaps driven Eline's lover to violence on her behalf. Moved partly by an impulse to comfort Tiher, and partly from a solemn sense that the whole truth should be served, she decided to tell him everything she knew.

Tiher was bewildered by it. "Are you sure this isn't just chasing chaff?" he asked. "The man was mad about hunting; it doesn't need a terrible secret to explain that."

"There was a secret," she said wearily. She would have given half her dowry to be able to say that there weren't. "His confessor as good as admitted it. And if we press Alain and his

wife too hard, it will probably come out. Which is another reason to make sure that the duke talks to Alain privately. I don't
want to blacken the reputations of the living or the dead. It
would be good if we could think up some excuse for Hoel to
use when he summons Alain, so that no one else is aware that
anything is happening at all."

"He won't need to summon him; Alain and his wife will be
coming here tomorrow," said Tiher. He found himself telling
Marie all about Talensac and his visit there. It was a relief to
confide in her. The memory of the men glaring from the stocks,
and of Eline's sick, white face and Alain's feverish one, had
clung stickily to his mind since he left, whatever else he tried
to do.

"Poor Eline," she said when he'd finished. "And poor Alain,
and poor Talensac. Dear God, it's easy for people to be miserable."

He stood for a moment looking at her. She was dressed in
one of the gowns Havoise had given her for the trip to Paris,
a fine tawny thing, and she was wearing a necklace of rubies
he hadn't seen before. The richness suited her, reinforcing the
air of calm self-possession that she had had even in monastic
black. Her face, though, was vulnerable and troubled. Tiher
wanted suddenly to kiss her, but held back: what he'd told her
of Talensac was something she'd taken into herself, and it would
be wrong to disturb her so soon. "Do we go to Duke Hoel
tonight, then?" he asked instead. "Or tomorrow?"

"Tomorrow," Marie decided firmly. "After the hunt. Let Hoel
enjoy his day with his brother first."

"As you say." Tiher paused, still watching her. "I almost forgot," he said, forcing a smile. "How was Chalandrey? And your
convent?"

She smiled back, also with some effort. Their eyes held for
a moment in a wordless salutation. People could easily be made
miserable, so they would work at their scrapings of happiness.
"Confusing," she answered. "They were the same, and I wasn't."

He offered her his arm, and they began walking back to the
lodge. "Chalandrey was stunned by you?" he asked.

She smiled more naturally. "They were stunned anyway. They didn't know what to make of an archangel as an overlord."

"They wouldn't have gained much experience in the ways of angels from Duke Robert of Normandy."

"No," agreed Marie solemnly. "Still, they were prepared to attend to him. In fact, they were relieved that he was all they had to worry about."

She had seen, as soon as she got to Chalandrey, that she had been right to cling to her honor. So many other people had depended on it. The officials and servants in the manor house had been afraid that Hoel would get the manor and they'd all lose their positions. The peasants on the estate had been afraid that a Norman would come in and raise the rents. They were all pleased to think that everything would go on as it had been, expect for the rent money going to Saint Michael. She could not have lived in that house if she'd had to throw out all the old faces from her childhood. It had been desperately strange, though, to be back in a place still so familiar and to find herself so different. Her father's bailiff had tried at first to lecture her, the old chaplain who'd taught her her letters had tried to give her advice, and the manor officials and servants had tried to condescend the way they'd done in the past. After a little while both she and they had realized that they were talking to someone who didn't exist anymore, and they had stopped, and looked at her with baffled eyes, and started to call her "my lady." Yet it had been only four years since she was last at Chalandrey, and all the rooms had been exactly as she remembered them; the faces of the people had hardly changed. She had known that she had changed, but so much? It was disconcerting and unpleasant to be a foreigner in her own home. She had taken the inventory with Grallon, collected some of the movable property, and gone on to Mont St. Michel, already suspecting that she would never go back to Chalandrey again.

At St. Michael's it had been just the same as at Chalandrey. When Lady Constance met her at the convent gate, she'd called Marie "my dear child" and praised her pious intention of bestowing such a fine manor upon the priory. She, too, had eventually faltered to a stop and looked at Marie in confusion. Then Marie had found herself treating the prioress in a way she hadn't expected—not with the earnest respect she'd had when they first met, and not with the mixture of dutiful obedience and secret contempt that had replaced it by the time she left. Instead, she'd noticed how much Constance resembled her half-sister Havoise, and plied her with sly jokes, like Sybille's, until the prioress began laughing and talking with a pleasant worldly frankness. Of course, Constance lacked Havoise's honesty—but she was a kind woman, too, and this time, Marie had liked her. When the ceremony of bestowing the lands was over, and the bailiff of Chalandrey had been confirmed in his post, Constance had suddenly embraced Marie and said, "You will come back, won't you, my dear? I know you wanted to stay here once, and really, I'd be delighted if you did."

Perhaps, Marie thought now, perhaps. There are worse fates. I could be in charge of the convent library and ride out on expeditions to buy books; I could work in the hospital or the school. I could pray and find peace. It wasn't St. Michael's fault that I was miserable before, but my own. Perhaps you need to be at peace with the flesh to be a nun as much as to be a wife. Yes, I could be happy there, after all. As I could be happy with Tiher, if the duke does give him an estate big enough to support us, and if he still wants to marry me when he has it. But I'm wrong to count on him: I don't dare take his love for granted. He only needs to meet a pretty girl, livelier than me, who falls in love with him because she loves laughter, and he'll take her and thank God. I haven't given him any reason to be faithful. But I don't know my own mind yet, let alone his. Leave it a little longer. There's no hurry to decide.

"So: you stunned them," said Tiher, grinning at her, and she looked at him sideways and smiled back. "And you've duly disinherited yourself?"

"I have duly rendered myself as landless as you are."

He stopped, just outside the door of the lodge, and caught her hands. "Why don't we run away and get married tonight?"

"No doubt you've decided what we'd live on if we did?"

"Take no thought for tomorrow, for tomorrow will take thought for itself. Sufficient unto the day the evil thereof."

"Ah, so you still plan to be a holy man, taking no thought for the things of the body! I applaud you. Perhaps I'll become a holy woman and join you. We will live in a hut in a forest glade, eating nuts and berries and drinking fresh springwater. But holy saints don't marry. We will live together as brother and sister."

"Your brother has a wicked, incestuous heart," said Tiher, grinning, but he let go of her hands to open the door for her. "But I don't fancy a diet of nuts and berries. There's marrow-bone pie and pigeons in red wine on the menu tonight. Maybe we shouldn't run away until tomorrow."

The following morning dawned cloudless and bright, with a white sun rising tremulously from a shimmer of pink summer haze. The air was warm and nearly windless, and around Treffendel the great forest seemed to be drawing a deep green breath, as though it were about to sing. Alain arrived at the hunting lodge early, with Eline sitting behind him on their gray palfrey and holding onto his waist, and two servants following behind them with some hounds. A little color had come back into Eline's face, and she was smiling. The prospect of getting away from Talensac and spending a day with the court had stopped her tears—and the further prospect of getting away from Talensac altogether and settling in a house in Nantes had given her hope for the first time in months.

The yard of the lodge was full of noise and motion. Horses were being saddled for the hunt; hounds in couples barked at each other and ran back and forth whining with excitement; men and women sounded their horns and admired each other's clothes. Alain spotted Tiher, locked in a discussion of stag's droppings with the duke's forester and Bishop Quiriac of Nantes. He drew in his horse beside his cousin, jumped down, and helped Eline off. As Alain had expected, Tiher broke off his discussion to greet them.

"God prosper you, cousin!" he called cheerfully. "Greetings, my lady! Duke Hoel is still in the lodge with the duchess. She has indigestion and doesn't want to come hunting today. It might be best if you stayed with her, Lady Eline: I understand you shouldn't tire yourself."

Eline smiled; she hadn't been sure that a daylong hunt would be good for her, either, and she had no objection to staying comfortably in the lodge with the duchess. Alain thanked Tiher for the suggestion and escorted Eline toward the lodge, leaving his servants to hold his horse.

Hoel was in the main hall of the lodge, standing by the unlit fire and talking to Havoise, who was cossetting her indigestion on a chair in the shade. Marie, who was attending the duchess, saw the newcomers enter the room, glance about, and then start toward the duke, smiling.

In the next instant, everything changed. Eline stopped short, halfway across the room, and went white. Alain stopped beside her with an oath. Havoise stared in surprise, and Hoel began to turn to see what she was staring at. Isengrim, dark and deadly, had slipped from the duke's side and was walking purposefully toward the pair, head low and hackles raised, his eyes gleaming with triumph.

Eline screamed, a horrendous long wail of terror that turned every head in the room and forced silence even on the crowd outside. Alain reached for his sword. The wolf dashed the last few paces across the floor and leapt upon him.

The next moment, Alain was rolling screaming on the rushes, with Isengrim's teeth locked in his sword hand, and Eline shrieking, "Someone kill it, kill it, kill it!" helplessly over him. None of the onlookers stirred: everyone was paralyzed with shock. The wolf released Alain's mangled hand and made another lunge, this time toward his throat. Screaming, Alain caught the wolf's head with his left hand, and stopped the reddened jaws inches from his neck. Isengrim snarled horribly and drove himself on, his paws flailing at Alain's body as he forced all his weight down onto that trembling left hand—and the hand bent, and the jaws drew nearer, the fangs dripping blood and saliva onto Alain's face. Eline, still shrieking, seized the wolf's collar with both hands and tried to haul him off. The great dark head whipped round, and for a moment the eyes, passionate with human hatred, stared directly into her own. She let go of the collar and struck the animal's face with her hand, shouting now in wordless loathing and rejection. Isengrim turned from Alain toward her, and her shout shrilled into anguish. The wolf's jaws closed on her face.

"Isengrim!" bellowed Hoel in horror, and at last charged across to his pet, grabbed the wolf's collar, and dragged him off. Eline collapsed half-sitting beside Alain, her face a mask of blood. Her hands waved helplessly to fend off empty air, and she gave short high panting shrieks of pure horror.

Alain was on his knees, drawing his sword left-handed. "Monster!" he shouted. "I'll kill you this time!" Isengrim snarled and lunged toward him again, almost tearing free of the duke's grasp.

"Put that down!" yelled Hoel. "De Fougères, see to your wife! Somebody fetch the doctor for the lady! Isengrim! Bad, bad, bad!" He dragged the wolf toward the fireplace, picked up his silver-handled riding whip from his chair, and began to beat the wolf savagely. Isengrim crouched unresisting under the blows, but his eyes were still fixed on Alain with a desperate and lethal desire.

To Marie, still standing stunned beside the fireplace, the scene suddenly seemed to freeze: Eline lying on the floor; Alain standing over her but looking in hatred toward the wolf; and the wolf, under the blows of Hoel's riding crop, staring back. And in that frozen instant everything fell into place, and she could see it plainly. She made a choked sound of protest and steadied herself with one hand against the wall.

"My lord!" shouted Alain. "Look what the creature's done to my wife! Let me kill it!"

"It's my wolf," said Hoel. "And he's never hurt anyone before. Isengrim! What got into you? Have you gone mad?"

People were running in from outside: Tiher appeared, and Bishop Quiriac. Havoise was kneeling beside Eline now,

pressing a cloth against her face to stop the bleeding and looking wildly around for someone to help her.

"Mother of God!" exclaimed the bishop. "Did your wolf do
that, Hoel? I thought you said he was tame!"

"He is!" said Hoel, throwing the riding crop down in disgust.
"He's never done it before."

"It's an evil creature!" yelled Alain. "A stinking, evil, savage
monster! Look what it's done to my wife! And to me!" He held
up his torn and dripping sword hand for everyone to see. "My
wife is with child: this may kill the baby before it's even born.
My lord, I beg you, kill the creature! Kill it now, before it harms
anyone else!"

Hoel looked down at the wolf—his good Breton wolf, the
only tame wolf in the world, the bravest beast he'd ever owned.
No sane animal would attack humans with such frenzy. Alain
was right: such an animal was not safe to keep, and would have
to be destroyed.

"My lord," said Marie faintly, "I think I understand why Isengrim attacked these two."

Hoel looked up again, sharp with hope. "What's that, Marie?" he asked eagerly.

"My lord," she said, her voice unsteady, "the most important
thing now is to see to Lady Eline. She needs a doctor, and she
needs to be taken out of this crowd to somewhere quieter. Her
husband should stay with her to calm her. We can discuss what
to do with the wolf afterward."

"Very good, Marie!" Duchess Havoise exclaimed approvingly. "The lady needs help. Lord Alain, will you please put that
sword away and come see to your wife?"

Alain looked at Eline, then shoved the sword back in its
sheath and knelt to put his arms around her, clumsily and one-
handed. She gave another gasp, flung hers around him, and
began to cry. More helpers rushed up, the duke's doctor appeared, and Eline was carried out of the hall, clinging to her
husband, into a quiet room where she could rest and be tended.

The bright hunting crowd stood about murmuring, shaking
their heads over the wolf, who still crouched bloody-muzzled

at Hoel's feet. The duke's forester pushed his way through them. "Are you going hunting now, my lord?" he asked respectfully. "Or do you want to cancel the hunt, after what's happened?"

Hoel looked at his brother. "You go, if you like, Quiriac," he said. "It's a shame to waste all the preparations."

"You're not coming?" asked the bishop.

"I haven't the heart. I've never prized any beast the way I've prized Isengrim. I wish you could have seen him fight the Count of Bayeux's wolfhounds: it would have done you good."

"More good than seeing this sight, I'm sure," said Quiriac, kicking at a spot of blood on the rushes. "You're going to have to have the beast destroyed, Hoel. And, to tell the truth, though I'm sorry that you'll lose your pet, I'm sorrier for that lovely lady. Well, if you haven't the heart to hunt the hart, I do. Come follow the horns if you change your mind."

The bishop left with the forester to find the stag of sixteen tines. Most of the crowd, murmuring to one another, left with him. Tiher started to go, then looked at Marie and turned back.

Havoise returned from seeing to Eline. "She's quiet now," she reported. "The doctor says she'll be scarred for life, but there's no reason to suppose she'll lose the baby, thank God."

"Thank God indeed," said Hoel gravely. "What Isengrim did is dreadful enough without that. Well, Marie? Why did he attack Lady Eline?"

"My lord," she said—and swallowed, for her voice was still unsteady with shock. "I think we'd better discuss this in private. Can we use your own chamber?"

XVI

Like all the ducal residences, Treffendel was crowded, but the duke's own chamber was the largest and finest room available, and the most private. It was above the Great Hall, and, like his chambers in Rennes, consisted of a small bedroom and a larger dressing room. They went up to the dressing room now: Hoel, Havoise, Marie, and, at Marie's request, Tiher. Hoel clipped the leash on Isengrim's collar and pulled the wolf along as well. When they reached the room, he tied the animal to an iron candle stand in a corner. Isengrim lay down with his head on his forelegs, watching silently as the four humans settled themselves, Hoel and Havoise in the two chairs, Tiher on top of the clothes chest, and Marie, standing, in front of the empty iron fireplace.

Isengrim's muzzle was still wet with blood. Its taste filled his mouth, and the sweet, thick smell drowned every other scent in the room. It was Eline's blood, mostly. He had not meant to attack Eline. He had meant to kill Alain. His failure was double, and he knew that the next thing to expect was death. Hoel would lead him out into the forest, pat him on the head, and then draw his sword and position it carefully to catch the heart and kill instantly. He had already decided to pretend he didn't understand what the duke was doing. He had begged for mercy before, but he would not do so again. The life he had was not worth preserving—though he still wished he could have killed Alain. It was bitter to die like an animal, without having exacted any payment from those who had made him one. But no—he hadn't meant to exact anything from Eline.

He looked at Marie with tender regret. She stood with her back to the fireplace, as straight and tense as though she were braced to enter an icy river. He did not see what she could possibly urge on his behalf, but he was grateful to her for trying. It was something to have won her affection, even though he'd missed the prize of her love.

Marie stood so straight because she was afraid that otherwise they would all see her trembling. He mouth was dry, though she was sweating, and she swallowed repeatedly, trying to loosen the tightness in her throat.

"Well, Marie?" said Hoel. "You know why Isengrim acted so wickedly?"

"My lord and lady," Marie began formally, "I hope you won't be offended if I talk first about something else. It is connected, though it may not seem so. Tiher and I had meant to talk to you today about the very people Isengrim attacked."

Hoel glanced quickly at Tiher, who gave a small, tight nod of agreement. "Have they been having trouble at Talensac?" asked the duke.

"They have," said Tiher. "But that's not what we wanted to talk about."

Slowly and heavily he spelled out the case against his cousin. Hoel listened, impatiently at first, still worrying about his wolf, but gradually, as he understood the implications, with close, unhappy, frowning attention.

"This is a very bad business," he said when Tiher had almost finished. "I should have thought of it before."

"Everyone knew Tiarnán liked to go hunting alone," said Havoise quietly. "Everyone knows that's a dangerous thing to do. And everyone knew that fellow Éon had sworn to kill him. We were all quite worried about the robber at the time, though I haven't heard a word of him for months."

"I heard a rumor recently that he died last April," said the duke. "Certainly the last time he was reported to have robbed anyone was in March. But you're right; any suspicion of murder fell on him, and not on those nearer who had more motive."

Tiher squared his shoulders. The problem of whether his cousin was a murderer might have tormented him, but here, before the duke, he was free to play the part he had always played and defend Alain once more. "My lord, I believe that Alain is innocent," he declared firmly. "Or, at least, innocent of murder. Certainly, he loved Eline, and he may have been to see her when he told us he was going to St. Malo — but that doesn't mean that Lord Tiarnán's death wasn't an accident. My lord, you know my cousin: he's always been more lover than fighter. Most likely he simply visited the lady and told her of his undying devotion, and she fluttered and wept and committed herself to nothing. I agree that you must question him to clear the matter up, but I firmly believe he never murdered Lord Tiarnán."

"And you, Marie?" asked Havoise. "Tiher defends his cousin. Are you taking the part of the accuser?"

"I don't believe that Alain murdered Tiarnán," Marie replied, and was surprised at her own voice's steadiness in the face of what she must say next. "But I've just come to believe that Tiarnán is still alive."

She glanced round at the three surprised faces, and let her eyes slip momentarily to the fourth face, that of the wolf, who watched her with dark intensity from the corner. She looked away from him quickly, afraid now of what she might find in those black-rimmed eyes. She locked her hands together behind her back to keep them still.

"Tiarnán had a secret," she went on quietly. "I ask you to remember that, and to consider what it could have been, because it's the heart of the whole matter. Kenmarcoc, who was his bailiff, says that his master used to disappear alone into the forest for three or four days at a time, never admitting any company, and leaving behind even his dog. What he did there was so frightening that when his wife learned of it, she fled to her sister at Iffendic and treated him afterward with horror. She told me that he was a worse monster than the robber he saved me from, and that she was glad she was free of him. But his confessor, who knew his secret, was never sure whether or not it was sin, and reproached himself before me for his own refusal to condemn it. He said that he was partial and could not judge."

She took a deep breath. Already she had broken confidences on every side, and dragged things out into the light which were meant for shadowed privacy. She was bound to go on. Everything would have to be laid bare to judgment. How the duke would judge she could not be sure; she could only hope that his heart's sympathies would match her own. "My lord and lady," she said, lifting her head higher, "another thing the hermit told me was that he knew the first owner of your wolf Isengrim. He said the wolf had been lost through theft and treachery, that it was providential that he had come to you and you had shown him mercy. I could not understand why the fact that you hadn't killed a wolf should bring the hermit so much joy, until now.

"I think I have told you how, when I was being brought to Rennes for the first time, I met a wolf in the forest, and then met Éon. I dreamed that Éon was a werewolf, and afterward when I heard the story about him I was afraid that my dream was true. But when Éon first saw Tiarnán, he recognized him and shouted 'Bisclavret!'—speaking in Breton, which at the time I didn't understand. When I remembered it afterward, I thought he must have been threatening Tiarnán, saying, 'I am a werewolf, and if you attack me, I will make you suffer!' But I could see at the time, and can see now, that he was calling *Tiarnán* a werewolf. I had heard, as we all have, that wolves are evil, savage creatures, and I transferred the name of werewolf from the man who'd come to help me to the man who attacked. I was wrong. Éon was no werewolf, and Tiarnán is."

The three human faces were incredulous, only their respect for her and the sweeping force of her exposition keeping them silent. She did not dare look at the wolf. She had betrayed his secret now. She could only pray that her listeners, knowing the wolf as well as the man, would not hate him even when they believed.

"Think!" she urged instead. "A man disappears, hunting in the forest, and a wolf appears in the main street of Talensac. A marvelously crafty wolf, as you've said many times, my lord, far more intelligent than any dog. More intelligent, in fact, than an animal has any right to be. How would a hunted wolf have known how to beg you for mercy? What did Count Ranulf say after Isengrim beat his wolfhounds? 'It's a witch!' he said. 'It doesn't fight like any natural creature.' And we all know it was true. Isengrim fought like a man, with a man's courage, a man's cunning, and a man's willingness to spare the vanquished. My lord, you saw just now in your own hall how well Isengrim understands that he must disable a man's sword before he can kill him. How would a wolf know that? There's more, my lord! The lymer Mirre, Tiarnán's dog, barked in greeting when she saw Isengrim and fawned on him. He welcomed her, except when she came into heat, when he drove her off: What animal would behave like that? And Isengrim has shown himself perfectly gentle with all people, except two. When he saw Alain after he was first captured, he lunged at him. When he saw the same man again just now, coming into your hall with Lady Eline, he attacked them both. And the enmity between those two and the wolf was on both sides. When we came here in March, we all heard how bitterly Alain had pursued his quarry, and how many rewards he and his wife had offered, and traps they'd had set for it. And what did Alain say in the hall just now? 'Monster!' he said. 'I'll kill you this time!' "

Tiher suddenly stirred. "He said at Talensac the other night that if the people there knew what their machtiern really was, they wouldn't want him back."

"When I told him last March that we'd taken his wolf alive," said Hoel slowly, "he went gray and I thought he would be sick. He said that he'd drunk bad water. But he begged me to kill my wolf, begged me again when he saw the wolf — and begged me again just now."

Hoel turned and looked at the wolf, which lay motionless, head on paws. The bright animal eyes now seemed so full of humanity that it shocked him that he had been blind before, that he had not guessed that this was not a natural creature. "Tiarnán!" he called, and they all saw how the animal's head lifted and ears flicked forward in response. Then the ears flattened and the head dropped to the forepaws, and the wolf looked back at them blankly—afraid, Marie realized now, afraid, and quite horribly ashamed.

"My God," whispered Hoel. "Marie, you're right."

"All I've said is guesses," she replied. "But there are two people in this house who know."

"And they will tell us," said Hoel grimly. He went to the door and roared for the servants to bring in Lord Alain and Lady Eline.

"Hoel, not the woman!" protested Havoise. "She's injured and pregnant."

"She will have to answer anyway," Hoel said firmly. "If this is true—and, by God, I believe it is!—then she betrayed her husband and handed over his lands and servants to her tyrannical lover while setting a price on her lord's head. But we'll show some consideration for the unborn child: she can be carried up here in a chair."

Alain and Eline were not alarmed when the duke's servants came to fetch them. They expected apologies from the duke and a promise that the wolf would at last be destroyed. They entered the room confidently, Alain with his sword hand in a sling, and Eline carried in a chair by four serving men, her face bandaged from eyes to lips. The doctor had given her a drug to dull the pain, and it seemed to her that she was floating in the chair as though on gray waves. But she saw the wolf lying tied up in the corner, and she looked away from him quickly, shuddering. Alain caught her hand and kissed her forehead, and she huddled against him, hiding her bandaged face. He glared at the wolf, then looked challengingly at Hoel. Hoel nodded to the servants to leave, and they went, closing the door behind them. Alain's challenging look faltered at the duke's bleakness.

"Why did my wolf attack you?" demanded Hoel as soon as the servants were gone.

"Because it's an evil animal," replied Alain fiercely. "All wolves are."

"No," said Hoel. "Not this one. He has some reason to hate you: What is it?"

"My lord," Alain said, taken aback but still confident, "there is no such thing as a tame wolf." He began to feel angry. "The creature attacked me and injured my wife: Why should you question me about what *I've* done? A savage brute attacked a beautiful lady, and you seem to think *she* is at fault for it! It's grotesque!"

"Isn't she at fault for it?" asked Hoel levelly. "Lady Eline, what happened to my servant Tiarnán, your first husband?"

Eline's head jerked away from her husband's side, and her beautiful eyes locked on the duke, so enormous and impenetrably blue that it seemed that his question had struck her blind. Alain was cooler. "Nobody knows that, my lord," he said impatiently. "Why do you ask me?"

"Because at the time he disappeared, you had gone off in armor, saying you were going to look at a ship carrying hawks that had docked in St. Malo, and no such ship existed. And the lady there, whom you had loved for some time, had quarreled with her husband and fled him. Where did you really go, Lord Alain, when you said you were at St. Malo? And what did you do when you were there?"

Alain went white with shock. He looked at Tiher in bewildered appeal.

"Alain," said Tiher, "we know that you were lying. Tell us the truth, please. It can't be any worse than what you're suspected of."

Alain opened his mouth and closed it again. He shook his head. "Tiher!" he said pleadingly, and licked his lips.

"My God, Alain, you think I don't want to help?" Tiher shouted, his voice suddenly raw with pain. "But I think this time you've dug such a pit for yourself that nobody can pull you out again. What did you do? Just tell us!"

"Alain is a hero!" Eline cried suddenly, her drugged mind numb to everything but the danger that her husband would be charged with murder. Tiarnán's clothes, hidden under the false bottom of her husband's chest, blazed into her mind: evidence enough to kill Alain, if they were found. The truth, however disgraceful, was not something Alain could die for. "He was brave, and kind, and came to help me!" she protested. "You have no right to talk to him like that! You don't know what he faced for my sake!" She rose from the chair and tottered to her feet, swaying in the gray waves. She gazed with fixed revulsion at the shadowy wolf in the corner and screamed, "There he is! There's your Tiarnán! Look at him! A foul, stinking, savage *animal*! I was tricked into marrying it, a monster, a werewolf, a devil creature! Was I supposed to take it into my bed and cherish it, knowing what it was? God forbid! Alain rescued me from it, and you ought to love him and prize him for his courage, not accuse him!" She collapsed into the chair again, convulsed with sobs.

Alain encircled her protectively with his arm and looked at the duke. His wide-eyed good looks were suddenly quite gone: his face was brutal and self-satisfied. "What she said is true," he said in a voice so cool and unperturbed that it was far more disturbing than a scream would have been. "Your favorite Tiarnán, my lord, is a werewolf. I didn't murder him, but if I had, it would have been an easier death than the one the law would give him. Spare him, and you're guilty of heresy."

Tiher looked away from that suddenly unfamiliar face. For a long minute he stared instead at the wolf, and wished in anguish that Alain had been guilty of simple murder. It was much, much worse to have reduced a brave man to that cowering animal, and then urged the liege lord who'd grieved for the man's supposed death to cause that death in fact. *My dear cousin, do you think our lord the duke would care to hunt the wolf? There is a most marvelously crafty animal near here, and it would give our lord good sport if he came to chase it.* Alain clearly felt no remorse, no awareness even that he had acted amiss. He had written that inhuman letter and felt merely pleasure at his own cleverness. Tiher looked back at his cousin's face, and knew that he had lost everything that there had been between them, and that the trust of his childhood had just been destroyed forever. He pulled himself farther back onto the clothes chest, dropped his hands between his knees, and was still. He had no more part in this, except to wish that it were over.

Alain did not even glance at his cousin and made no more appeals. Tiher could not help him anymore.

"What did you do to Tiarnán?" demanded Hoel furiously. "How did you trap him in that shape?"

"Who cares!" Alain replied triumphantly. "You can't defend him: he can be either killed as a wolf or burned as a witch!"

"And you can be either beheaded as a traitor or flogged as an adulterer!" roared Hoel. "You foul, arrogant man! Tiarnán was the best of my knights, and had done no harm to any of his neighbors; he'd treated you, in particular, with more generosity than you ever deserved. In recompense, you got the better of him by some treachery, stole his wife, stole his lands, tyrannized his servants, got his manor into debt, and hunted him, hunted him without mercy, with his own dogs! Worse, you tricked *me* into hunting him, too! You know perfectly well you don't dare whisper a word of what you've done: you would be condemned on all sides—both of you! You treacherous little bitch, he adored you!"

"He's a monster!" shrieked Eline, her tears soaking the bandages. "Look at him!"

The wolf had slid farther back against the wall, where he cowered with his tail down. Hoel merely glanced at him, then turned a furious glare back on the couple facing him. "You're the monsters!" he shouted. "He's a wolf, no more—and a good wolf that's served me faithfully and fought for me bravely, just as he did as a man. Everyone at court can testify to that. What did you do to him?"

"He's a thing from hell!"

"He isn't," said Marie quietly. "Lady Eline, he isn't. Whatever made him what he is, it was nothing to do with the devil. Tiarnán was not an evil man, and the wolf is not an evil animal. The monster you're afraid of is a shadow in your own mind. Take your own advice: look at him. Can't you see? Had you even seen him in this shape before?"

"I saw him this morning, and he attacked me!" sobbed Eline. "He's evil." She did not look at the wolf as she said it.

"And weren't you screaming for us to kill him, kill him, kill him?" asked Hoel harshly. "No — not even that! Kill *it*, you said, knowing that *it* was a man who'd loved you, and whose house and lands you'd stolen. You cold-blooded, unnatural whore!"

"I hate his house!" Eline declared passionately. "Judicaël was right; it's all bitterness! I wish now I'd taken what I was offered, got the marriage to the monster annulled, and married Alain honestly instead."

"He offered you that?" asked Havoise, speaking for the first time.

Eline shot her a look of panic and began to sob more loudly.

"What did you do to him?" Hoel asked for the third time. "Why can't he turn back into a man?"

"We won't tell you!" declared Alain feverishly now. "You can't force us to. You don't dare tell anyone about this!"

"I would dare as much as you do!" replied Hoel vehemently. "If this comes to trial, you have almost as much to lose as Tiarnán. You two would lose every penny you stole from him, declare yourselves guilty of bigamy and adultery, and make your unborn child a bastard. And I think that even the Church would insist that the werewolf be allowed to speak for himself: they always demand a full confession before an execution. You will tell me what you did, or by God I *will* take it to trial, and have both of you questioned under torture!"

Havoise stirred, and was about to protest, but the threat had already broken Alain. Torture was routinely used in judicial investigations, and he knew what it involved. "No!" he cried desperately. "I'll tell you! Don't touch her: she's with child; she's suffered too much already! She mustn't be hurt anymore!"

Hoel's eyes glittered in triumph. "Then tell me now," he commanded.

Alain looked lovingly down at Eline's bowed, bandaged head. "Don't worry, my dearest," he told her tenderly. "I won't let them touch you. It will be all right."

Eline sniveled against his chest, and he rested his bandaged hand upon her hair.

"Tell me," repeated Hoel, his voice heavy with disgust.

"Tiarnán left a part of himself with his clothes when he

turned into the thing he is now," Alain said, yielding at last in a tone of sullen spite. "Without that part of himself he can't turn back. Eline told me where he went to transform himself, and I went there and hid and waited for him. When he'd gone into the forest, I stole the clothes and the thing with them, and took them away."

The duke let out his breath in a long sigh. He leaned back in his chair and regarded the two narrowly. "And where is it now?" he asked.

"In the bottom of my clothes chest at Talensac," admitted Alain. "Under a false bottom. I sprinkled the things with holy water and wrapped them in an altar cloth, because I was afraid of the creature. That's the truth."

Hoel sat still for another moment, fixing Alain with his eyes. Eline sobbed on, quietly now. "Tiher," said the duke. "Go to Talensac at once and fetch the things. Don't spare your horse going or coming: get a fresh mount at the manor, and hurry."

Tiher bowed silently and went out. Hoel leaned forward again, the stern gaze now fixed on both Alain and Eline.

"You're right," he said quietly. "I don't want this business to come out. I loved Tiarnán, I prized Isengrim, and I found no evil in either: man or wolf, I want to keep him in my service. You say, Lady, that you were offered an annulment of your first marriage. Well, we can get that. If you have it, then the second marriage sacrament should be considered valid, you will not be guilty of bigamy, and your child will not be a bastard. I know, Lord Alain, that you're in debt. I can see to that, too. In fact, I will offer you money to go away. The crusade is, they say, doing well, and may carve out a kingdom in the Holy Land; if that's true, there will be places for landless knights, perhaps even manors. I'm sorry to wish creatures like you upon the people of the east, but I'll pay for you both to go there, if you go quietly. What you do there is your own affair, but you'll have the opportunity to make yourselves a new life. Your alternative is to bring the matter to trial, tell everyone the truth about Tiarnán—and take the consequences for yourselves as well. You've both had much to say about what a monster he is, but I think you know how your own conduct would be regarded: the eagerness with which you've kept the matter secret shows as much. I hope you'll think hard about your position. You may go downstairs now, both of you, and rest. I want you to stay in this lodge until I give you leave to go, but you are otherwise free to please yourselves. I'll speak to you again when I have spoken to Tiarnán."

Alain picked Eline up gently in his arms and carried her to the door. Marie ran to open it for him. Alain shot one more self-righteous glare at the duke, then silently carried his wife out and down the stairs.

"They won't tell anyone the truth," said Havoise.

"No," said Hoel, leaning back in his seat again. "If they were afraid to before, they certainly won't now. It's a filthy, ugly thing they've done. They can't admit even to themselves what they did; they certainly won't tell the world. They'd only tell the truth out of spite, if they saw no way out for themselves — and I've just given them a way that will appeal to them. It's a kinder fate than they deserve."

"You're too harsh," said Marie. "They were afraid. Eline, in particular, was sick with terror. I understand her; I understand her very well. Tiarnán was very much to blame for marrying her, and for not understanding how terrible she would find the thing he was. You are far too harsh."

"I can forgive her for being afraid," said Hoel. "If I'd learned what I did today and hadn't known the wolf as well as the man, I would have been horrified myself. But I do not forgive her for rejecting the man but keeping the manor."

There was a moment's silence, and then, drawn by the same bewildered pity and fascination, they all looked at the wolf, who still crouched motionless in the corner. Marie went over and knelt beside him, and the light brown eyes looked up at her with the same blank, wary expression she remembered on Tiarnán's face. "We will bring you back," she told him. "Do you understand me? We will bring you back."

The wolf did not respond. She was suddenly afraid that perhaps he could not come back, that the human part of him had withered away in its long isolation, and that only this unnatural animal remained. She did not dare mention her fear, in case putting words to it would somehow make it come about, but her hands by her sides twisted in pain.

"Where will we tell everyone he's been?" asked Havoise.

Hoel shrugged. "He was distressed over the quarrel with his wife, and decided, on the spur of the moment, to make a pilgrimage. If we can bring him back, we can find excuses for him. His own people will probably be so pleased to have him back that they won't dare question their good fortune."

There was another long minute of silence, and then the duke slapped the arm of his chair. "There's no point sitting here until Tiher gets back. It's a good eight miles from here to Talensac, and even in a hurry, he won't be back until after lunch. Havoise, my love, I can't sit still, I don't want to be with the court, and I don't want to be alone, either. Come for a walk with me in the forest."

The duchess rose slowly to her feet. "Why not? It should settle my stomach."

Duke and duchess left the room together. Marie fetched a basin of water for the wolf and stood for a moment looking down at him. He stared back, his eyes once again alien and unfathomable. That morning she would have knelt and stroked his head, but now that she knew what he was she could not. She remembered him standing under the rushlight with Eline on his wedding night, and her eyes stung with tears. Then she thought of Tiher's anguished silence when he understood what his cousin had done, and wished that she had not involved him. It had seemed right that a member of his family should be there to defend Alain, but now she saw that it had hurt Tiher badly. She had also complicated a situation already fantastic and unpredictable, and burdened another soul with a dangerous secret. And for what? For Tiarnán, because she had loved him? Or from an abstract hatred of the treachery that had been committed, and a longing to establish a truth that would only be suppressed again?

Both, both. She crossed herself, and went to the lodge chapel to pray for them all.

Isengrim lay in the corner, numb with shock and bewildered with shame. He swam dazedly among the words that had been used that morning, unable to hold onto any one argument for long. Only two things stood clear in his mind: the taste of Eline's blood in his mouth that morning, and the memory of her body against his on their wedding night. She had been so near to him then, so happy, so much beloved. He was the one who had turned her into the wounded thing that had sat weeping in the chair that morning. He had not understood how much he terrified her until he scented her horror, raw and reeking even over the smell of blood and drugs. The bite to her face had only been the last injury he'd inflicted on her. He saw that now. The fact that he was what he was had cut her far deeper than his teeth. He had been wrong to attack her: he had already hurt her more than she deserved. When she had looked into his face and struck him with such loathing, though, rage had overcome him. Marie had said he was very much to blame. Marie was right.

And yet, Marie was trying to help him. He shaped her words silently in his mind: *We will bring you back.* Did *she* want him back? Her hands had curled with pain as she looked at him. It hurt her, too, to know what he was. He had not been able to interpret the expression on her face when she stood looking down at him, but she had smelled of grief. What had she, and the others, felt when they looked at him? Disgust? Contempt? The very most he could hope for was pity.

Monster, Eline had called him, again and again. *Foul, stinking, savage* animal*! Devil creature! Werewolf.* He saw himself in her terrified eyes and her white-faced recoil. That was the normal human reaction to what he was. His own sense of himself as still human and natural had been, he saw now, something he had kept only by keeping his secret. He had told it to Eline, and she had nearly destroyed him. Now Marie had guessed it, and told it to the duke, the duchess, and the man who loved her. What would become of him now? The longing to be human again was almost unbearable, but what would he do in a human world to which he was a monster?

His whole being ached with the effort to think, but the words blurred endlessly around the taste of blood, and it was impossible.

About noon, Isengrim suddenly sat up straight. Everything inside himself had turned like a weather vane in a gust of wind, pointing in a different direction, realigning itself. He knew the feeling: he had felt it before when he came back to the part of himself he left behind when he changed. He had never expected to feel it again. The door of the room was flung open, and Hoel and Havoise came in, followed by Marie, looking as composed as ever, and Tiher, dusty from the road and carrying a linen bundle under one arm.

Tiher hefted the bundle and set it down on the dressing table. "It was where Alain said it was," he told the others. He unwrapped the patterned linen altar cloth, slid a leather thong off a leather wrapping, and there was a set of woolen hunting clothes, folded, with a few dry leaves from the space under the stone still clinging to them.

Isengrim turned his head away. The others gathered over the clothes, and he could sense their shock as the sight of the things brought home to them again just what he was. He did not listen to what they said; he felt as though his skin would split from the swelling of shame and fear, and he longed to be far away, out in the forest, with only the smell of the trees for company.

Hoel came over and unclipped the leash from his collar, and Havoise set the things down on the floor, where he could look at them. He turned his head away again, though he could feel a trembling in every muscle from the longing to touch them. He had never changed in front of anyone—not knowingly. It had been a pleasure as intimate as making love, and how could he do it in front of these four watchers, and make himself still more monstrous in their eyes?

"Something's wrong," said Hoel anxiously. He smelled sharp with apprehension. "Something's been lost."

Isengrim looked pleadingly up at Marie, begging her to understand. And, miraculously, she did.

"He's ashamed," she said. "He doesn't want to transform himself in front of us."

There was a silence — and then, incredibly, Havoise laughed.

"Of course!" she exclaimed. "He'll be stark naked. Man or beast, he's always taken great care of his dignity. Very well, very well, we can spare his blushes." She picked the clothes up again, went to the small bedroom she shared with Hoel, and laid them out on the bed. "There you are!" she said, turning back and speaking to Isengrim directly. "Privacy."

Silent, shaking inwardly, he went through the door, and she closed it behind him.

He could smell the thing he had left with the clothes now, the insubstantial yet pervasive, alien and familiar scent of his own humanity. Hope and terror held him motionless before it for a long moment. Then, eyes shut, working by scent alone, he made his way to the bed and took up what he had set down so long before.

Instantly, as though his nose had been struck blind, that scent and all the scents vanished; the sounds of the lodge went dead, as though the whole world were a harp string muffled suddenly with a block of wood. But inside, the world of words, so long drowned, rose all at once shining from the ocean of sense. What had been heavy and laborious, done with an immense effort of will and concentration, became effortless, easy as opening an eye or lifting a hand, so simple that that the doer was unaware of doing it at all. He could think again; he could reason. It was like recovering suddenly from paralysis. He opened his eyes, and there were colors. He was crouching naked on all fours in the duke's bedroom, his chin resting on his old green hunting clothes.

He began to cry, shaking with tears and making no sound. He sat back on his heels and rubbed his face with his hands, then held the hands out before himself and watched them open and close. He jumped to his feet and looked down at his own body, hard and bare and thin and as he remembered it. Humanity, more precious than ermine and cloth of gold. Humanity.

The duke was waiting for him. Fumbling and clumsy, he picked up his clothes and began to put them on.

He was still crying when he'd finished dressing, and he sat down on the bed, trying to stop himself. He couldn't. All the tears he'd been unable to shed as an animal poured from his eyes, and he bent double, holding himself, remembering returning to St. Mailon's and finding the space beneath the stone empty; remembering Kenmarcoc screaming at him from the stocks; remembering the night of the wolf traps, the cold, the baying of the hunting dogs, the muzzle, the chains. He lay down, rolled over onto his back, and struggled to ram the tears back inside himself. At last successful, he lay still looking up at the light on the ceiling and breathing in quiet gasps. And all at once he was both profoundly grateful, and immensely, irresistibly tired. He closed his eyes and slept.

The others sat in the next room and talked quietly, about how Tiarnán could best be returned to the human world, then about what Alain and Eline might do, about the state of affairs at Talensac, and finally, about whether Bishop Quiriac was likely to have caught the sixteen-point stag. At last they ran out of things to say and sat silently looking at one another. Then Hoel got to his feet. "He's been there long enough to grow parsley, let alone get dressed," he declared. "Let's learn the worst." He went to his bedroom door and opened it.

For one horrible moment, Marie, following on his heels, thought that the room was empty. Then she saw the body lying on its back on the bed, a long, limp dark-haired shape in green. Hoel was staring at it rigidly, not sure whether it was alive or dead. She slipped past him to its side. There was the face which for a long time she'd seen only in dreams—the same arched eyebrows and narrow jaw under the close-clipped beard, changed only by a jagged line of whitened skin and white hair which ran from the lower lip down across the chin to the middle of the throat, in the place where a wolf had been injured in a fight with dogs. She touched his chest, and felt his heart beating under her fingers: he was asleep. And at the touch, his eyes opened, and met hers, and he sat up, staring at her.

"Your eyes are gray," he said in a hoarse, uncertain whisper.

"Yes," said Marie, "but you knew that."

He shook his head. "No. I couldn't remember, and couldn't tell." He touched the side of her face, very lightly, then took his hand away again. His eyes had moved beyond her to Hoel, still standing motionless in the doorway. He jumped up, then knelt down before the duke and bowed his head. "My lord," he whispered, "thank you."

Hoel drew in a breath that was almost a sob. "Tiarnán," he said. "Oh, damnation!" He leaned over, pulled the knight to his feet, and embraced him, thumping him on the back. "Damnation!" he repeated. "Oh, thank God!" He held Tiarnán at arm's length for a moment, looking at him, then shook him and embraced him again.

"Tiarnán, my dear!" exclaimed Havoise, drawing him away from her husband and into the dressing room, then embracing him herself and kissing him on both cheeks, "Oh my dear, it is so good to have you back!"

Tiarnán stood motionless, bewildered. When the ducal couple had let him go, he looked around the room, first toward Marie, who was in the doorway to the bedroom, and then at Tiher, who stood opposite, in front of the closed door that led to the rest of the lodge. Tiher looked back levelly for a moment, then said, "You'd better take off what's round your neck."

Tiarnán put his hand to his neck and touched Isengrim's silver-studded collar. His face went blank. He unbuckled the collar in silence and set it down on the dressing table, and he looked so like Isengrim, turning his head away from the clothes, that Marie wondered why she hadn't seen at once that the two were the same, just from their mannerisms. "Thank you," he said quietly.

Tiher raised his eyebrows and shrugged. "Glad to be of service. In case you're wondering: no, I am not going to tell anyone where you've been the past year or repeat anything of what was said and done in this room today. As far as I'm concerned,

I wasn't here, and know nothing about it. And it's best if you say the same."

Tiarnán nodded, then glanced around the room again. "Within this room, though, it must be different," he said in the same hoarse voice. "You all know what I am. I'm sorry."

"Why?" asked Hoel.

Tiarnán looked at him steadily. "It might be reckoned a disgraceful thing to be the liege lord of a werewolf."

"You brought me honor as a man and as a wolf. I'm the one who should be sorry."

Tiarnán shook his head. "My lord, you have done nothing for which you should be sorry from the time I first became your man."

Hoel reached out and touched the white mark on his chin. "I wouldn't have risked a man in that wolf fight," he said quietly. "It was a vainglorious exercise, undertaken from nothing more than pride. I was lucky you weren't killed. And there was worse—the muzzle, and the chains, and the 'good boy' 'bad wolf' business. It wasn't surprising you tried so hard to keep your dignity; I allowed you little enough space for it."

"You are a good master to man or beast," replied Tiarnán. "There's no blame due to you for treating a wolf as an animal. My lord, you gave me mercy when most men would have killed me—gave it twice: once on the road north of here, and again today. My life is doubly forfeit, and I owe you more than I can ever repay."

"You owe something to Marie, too," said Havoise drily.

Tiarnán looked at Marie, and she felt short of breath. "I owe everything to Marie," he agreed, and smiled hesitantly. It was the lopsided smile she had never expected to see again, one side of the mouth curving up, the other staying serious, and the brown eyes that were and were not Isengrim's brightening. She felt weak and silly, and bit her finger like a girl.

Tiarnán turned back to Hoel. "My lord, you told Lord Alain and Lady Eline this morning that you would speak to them again when you had spoken to me. I am here, and, by the grace of God, you, and Lady Marie, able to speak. What should I say?"

XVII

The duke and duchess didn't ask many questions. They wanted to know how Tiarnán had become what he was, for reassurance against suspicions of demon worship, and they wanted to be sure he could get an annulment of his marriage. When these points had been cleared up, he was told, gently but firmly, that it would be best if he left the lodge at once by the back door, before the hunting party returned. Hoel would tell the court that he had killed Isengrim and buried him in the forest. It was what everyone expected, and would cause no surprise. Tiarnán's return from the dead, however, would cause a great deal of surprise, and if he were to live unsuspected it was essential that no one connect him with Isengrim. He must turn up at his own manor first, and with luck no one would even realize that he had come back on the same day that the duke's pet wolf died.

"Come see me at court when you've got your lands in order," commanded Hoel, and hurried his liege man out the door.

So in the middle of a hot July afternoon Tiarnán found himself standing in the forest behind the lodge of Treffendel, still giddy and disoriented from his sudden transfiguration. No one had seen him leave the hunting lodge, and no one had suggested that he see his wife, for which he was grateful. The leaves hung limp on the trees, and the air was full of midges and mosquitoes. He was hot in the heavy tunic and hose he'd chosen the previous October, and he took the tunic off and slung it over his shoulder. The simple human action disoriented him again, and he had to stand still, breathing hard, while a prickle of nausea ran over his skin. His humanity was still so new and his experiences as a wolf so near that he felt fragile, as though his mind were a broken glass that someone had glued together and which needed time to set again. When his heart had stopped thundering he glanced around, getting his bearings. He had not forgotten the forest of Broceliande, not in any form. He turned to the northeast and began walking quickly homeward.

He arrived in Talensac at the time when the peasants had stopped their work in the fields and were tending the animals on their farms. He had been eager to reach the manor, but as he left Treffendel's forest and came into his own, his quick steps slowed. The walk had given him some time to collect himself, but he still felt shaken and exposed, vulnerable to the opinions of others as he hadn't been since he was a child. He had heard none of the discussions of what had been happening in Talensac, and felt none of the duke's certainty that he would be welcomed there. What could he say to people? What would they think of his sudden reappearance? He'd been aware that his manor worked smoothly and that his people approved of him, but he'd taken this very much for granted: that was what Talensac was like. It needed little governing from him because the way they did things at Talensac was right. He'd been dutiful in administering justice and managing disputes with neighbors because Judicaël had taught him that this was his responsibility, but it hadn't taken much of his time. Talensac, he thought now, as he walked through the fringes of his trees toward the empty fields, Talensac was a paradise, and he'd never understood his own unmerited good fortune in having it, until he was cast out.

He stopped on the edge of the fields and saw it there in the dell before him: the whole sweep of field, wood, and thatch, church and village and manor house, wrapped in the silvery haze of a summer afternoon. There lay a part of himself which he had left behind with the same careless confidence with which he had set that other piece of his soul beneath the stone, and as disastrously lost. Could he take it back? He remembered now what Tiher had reported Alain as saying—that the people here wouldn't want him back if they knew what he really was. *Monster, devil creature, werewolf.*

He drew up his shoulders with a small jerk, as though he

were pulling on a cloak, and began walking again. This was home. He could go nowhere else.

When he came up to the blacksmith's house at the edge of the village, old habit reminded him that he was hot and thirsty from the walk, and he stopped to get a drink. He was just setting the bucket down when the mistress of the house came out with a yoke of buckets to fetch some water for herself. She stopped dead when she saw him and her face went white. Then she dropped the buckets and screamed. She backed rapidly away from him, crossing herself and still screaming.

Tiarnán got up. The screams shivered inside him, making the new joins of his self ache. He was not sure what to do: it seemed that she must have heard some rumor of what he was, after all. He was determined that as a man he would not to be driven off as easily as he had been as a wolf. "Judith, Conwal's daughter," he said sharply, "what are you screaming for?"

She stopped screaming just as her husband and brother came rushing round the corner of the house to see what had happened, and also stopped dead. Donoal ran up behind Justin and crashed into him, and Tiarnán wondered what he was doing at the blacksmith's house.

"Oh, Machtiern!" cried Judith. "Is it you?"

"What do you mean by that?"

"Machtiern!" said Justin Braz, running forward and then stopping with a timid expression on his big-boned face that Tiarnán had never seen there before. "Is it really you?"

"Why are you all asking that? Who else would I be?"

Judith's husband Glevian gaped. "You're not . . . dead?"

"Would I be drinking water from your well if I were dead?" demanded Tiarnán impatiently.

Four faces broke into grins of utter delight. More people were hurrying from the neighboring houses, stopping, then running toward them. "It's the *machtiern*!" they shouted to one another in incredulous joy.

"Oh, my lord!" exclaimed Judith, laughing and crying and wringing her hands with happiness. "I thought you were a ghost!"

"Are you coming back?" asked Justin with the same unfamiliar timidity.

"Isn't this Talensac, and my home?"

Justin gave a howl of joy. "Thank God!" he said, and ran over, dropped on his knees in front of Tiarnán, and kissed his hands.

Justin had always regarded hand kissing as fit only for serfs, women, and foreigners, and Tiarnán jerked his hands back in astonishment. Justin beamed at him and slammed a massive fist repeatedly against the ground in inarticulate delight. He had been flogged for taking grain to Montfort, the first man in the village to suffer so. He had been shackled to the new post on the green, and one of Alain's Fougères hirelings had given him twenty lashes with the whip, counting them out in French. Trapped and helpless, unable, with his face against the wood, even to see the blows coming, he had screamed at *neuf*, wept at *seize*, and begged for mercy at *dix-huit*. He would not forget it till the end of his life. And now the machtiern was back, and the nightmare was over, and he could wake up into a world which was as it should be.

Donoal was hovering behind Justin, beaming so that his face hurt. "Machtiern," he said, "thank God! Lord Tiarnán, we all thought you were dead. It's been almost a year. . . ." And he wondered even as he said it whether Tiarnán realized it had been almost a year. The machtiern stood there in the same green hunting clothes he had worn when he left Talensac the previous autumn, and the expression on his normally reserved face was of utter bewilderment. It was always said that time was different in the hollow hills, that a man could go there for a single day and find that seven years or a century had passed when he came home. Donoal had long felt that if any mortal went riding with the fairy hunt, it would be Tiarnán, whose knowledge of the forest had always seemed more than human. His eyes fell on the white mark across his lord's chin, and at once his suspicions were confirmed. That was not a scar, but the kind of discoloration called an elf mark and attributed to some supernatural weapon of the Fair Ones. Tiarnán had been to the hollow hills, and the people there had tried to stop him coming out again.

To say as much out loud, however, might remind the people of the hills to come back and snatch their runaway. Donoal reached out and clasped Tiarnán's hand, as though he had to touch him to hold him to the human world. "My dear lord, welcome!" he said. "Welcome home!"

More people were arriving every second, and all of them were beaming, shouting excitedly, clapping their hands. The noise and the emotion were hard for Tiarnán in his battered state to comprehend. He shook his head in confusion, and, for want of anything better to do, began walking on into the village. Everyone followed him, shouting out to newcomers that it was the machtiern, alive! and at the same time explaining to him that his wife had remarried, she'd done homage to the duke for the manor and then married a foreigner from Fougères who had cruel, foreign ways and a foul, greedy, foreign bailiff.

"For God's sake, don't ask him where he's been!" Donoal whispered to Justin as they hurried after the others.

"Do you think I'm a fool?" Justin snarled back. "Did you see the mark on his chin? *They* didn't want him to go, did they?"

Even before Tiarnán reached the brook, someone had run into the church tower and begun ringing the bell, and the whole population of the village boiled onto the green. Tiarnán was horrified to see two of his serfs shuffling after the others in leg irons; horrified again to see one of them branded, and another with his ears cut off. Then he saw the stocks, overflowing with new victims, and the stained flogging pillar, and he stopped short. The sight of the new instrument of punishment shocked him as deeply as it would any other villager.

"What is that?" he demanded, pointing to the pillar.

"The foreign lord had it made," said Glevian. "I didn't want to forge the shackles for it, Machtiern, and Mailon didn't want to cut the wood, but we had to. He ordered us to, so we had to. We didn't think you were ever coming back, you see."

"And it's been used?"

"Oh yes, Machtiern. Ever since the foreign lord doubled the

charges at the mill, it's been used. Justin was the first man flogged at it, and then Rinan, and Guerech, and Géré, and Gourmaelon . . ."

Tiarnán glanced at Justin, finally understanding the look of timidity and the rapture of the villagers' welcome. The jolt of white-hot rage that went through him burned his soul into one piece again. He remembered the taste of Alain's blood in his mouth that morning, and he wished passionately that his fangs had succeeded in reaching that tantalizing throat. How dare he — God in Heaven! — brutalize *Talensac*?

"Take it down," said Tiarnán between his teeth, "and burn it. Take the iron off first if you like, Glevian, and turn it into something useful. Who has the key to the stocks?"

Alain's clerk Gilbert came down to the village a few minutes later to see what they were ringing the bells for. He brought the four men-at-arms Alain had fetched from Fougères, armed with knives and cudgels. He found a bonfire being lit on the green, the flogging pillar heaved on top of it, and the whole assembled village fanning the flames. For a moment he considered retreating to the manor house at once, but then he remembered that the duke was only a couple of hours away at Treffendel, and could be called on for help if needed, and he pressed on. The villagers fell silent as he approached, grinning and nudging one another. In the middle of the crowd, talking to the parish priest and the blacksmith, was a man he didn't know, a lean, dark-haired man in a sweat-stained white shirt and green hose. The stranger turned to look at him as he approached, and the priest and the blacksmith whispered something to him. Before Gilbert had a chance to say anything, the stranger rapped out a question in Breton.

"You will speak to me in French!" said Gilbert angrily. "Are you responsible for this disorder?"

The crowd laughed and stamped its feet as though he'd said something funny, which disconcerted him.

The stranger gave him a look which made him take a step

backward, a look blank except for a concentrated fury in the eyes. "I asked for the key to the stocks," said the stranger, in French this time. "They tell me you have it."

"I do," said Gilbert, plucking up his courage again, "and it seems I'll need it, to put you in. How dare you come into my lord's village and make trouble?" The villagers roared delightedly. "What's your name, where are you from, and what are you doing here?" shouted Gilbert, going red.

The stranger looked at him with contempt. "My name is Tiarnán, son of Maencomin," he said evenly. "I am lord of Talensac, and I am coming home. Now you know. You will release my people from the stocks this instant, or I will send you to your lord with your tongue slit to teach it courtesy and your hand cut off to keep it from other men's money."

When Tiher arrived the next morning he found the peasants singing as they worked the fields, the village green littered with the remains of a bonfire and a feast, and the clerk Gilbert sitting in the stocks, disconsolately guarded by the four men-at-arms. The guards must have been posted to keep the bailiff from being stoned or mutilated. Gilbert did not seem to have been damaged by the people he'd abused, and from the village's mood the first time Tiher visited, he would have expected them to go a fair ways toward killing the man. On the other hand, the villagers had been permitted to express their opinion of Gilbert: Tiher had never seen a man so covered with filth. He whistled and rode on across the brook to the manor lodge. This time the gate stood wide open. The gatekeeper from Fougères had disappeared, and piles of luggage sat before the lodge door: a Talensac man and his family were moving back in.

When Tiher had galloped up to Talensac the day before, he'd told the servants that Alain and Eline had been attacked by the duke's pet wolf, and that he'd come to fetch some things for them, as their injuries meant they'd be staying the night at Treffendel. He'd returned now to collect the horse he'd exhausted on the furious ride over. He made a methodical display of ignorance to the new gatekeeper, asking what had happened since the previous noon, and expressing astonishment at the answer. The gatekeeper was openly gleeful, and advised Tiher to go tell his cousin and his cousin's whore not to come back to Talensac. Tiher could make no reply to that. He was bitterly certain that the gatekeeper's hatred was justified.

The gatekeeper did not want him to see the lord of the manor, but Tiher eventually prevailed in Duke Hoel's name, and rode on to the manor house. One of the tables had been pulled out into the sun before the door, and Tiarnán and the parish priest were sitting at it, going over the manor's account books. A number of servants hung about watching them, and more men and women were carrying things into and out of the house. The Fougères servants were packing to go, while Talensac happily reclaimed its own.

"God prosper you, Lord Tiarnán of Talensac!" Tiher exclaimed, getting down from his horse. "Duke Hoel will be overjoyed to hear that you're alive. I wish you all happiness of your return."

Tiarnán had not expected to see Tiher again so soon. The appearance of someone who knew what he was sent another wave of disorientation through him. He half-expected to catch Tiher's scent and to find the other towering over him. He hauled his senses back to the human present with a shudder and got to his feet politely: Tiher had freely promised his silence about Tiarnán's secret, and was owed courtesy. "God prosper you, Lord Tiher de Fougères," he replied. "Be welcome to the manor. What brings you here?"

"I've come to fetch my horse," replied Tiher blandly. "I left it here yesterday when I came to fetch some things for my cousin Alain. I expect they've told you he's at Treffendel with the duke, recovering from an injury."

Tiarnán looked down. This smooth hypocrisy was something he did not feel equal to. He would have to speak to Tiher honestly and in private; he was anxious to know what Alain and Eline had decided. "You will excuse us for a time," he said to the priest. "I need to speak to Lord Tiher about how things stand with my lord the duke." A perfectly respectable reason to ask for privacy, and true, too. The priest bowed and beamed, and Tiarnán showed his visitor into the house.

Tiher found that the upheaval that gripped the rest of the manor was trebled in the Great Hall. Alain's tapestry of Saint Martin had been stretched facedown over the new tables, and Alain's new bed linen was stacked in mounds on top of it. Everywhere people were packing and unpacking. The group from Fougères formed silent knots in a noisy, glad, laughing crowd from Talensac.

The servants who'd been hovering about outside followed them in, and Tiarnán sent one of them to fetch wine for his guest, then impatiently told the rest that, unless they were particularly concerned with the duke's business, they could get on with their own. They reluctantly watched their lord and his guest climb the stairs to the privacy of the bedroom.

Alain's new great bed had been heaved up on its side and leaned against the wall, and the clothes chest that Tiher had ransacked the day before was gone. The light slanted through the open window onto the bare floorboards and scattered rushes of an empty room. Tiarnán hesitated, then went back onto the landing and shouted for the servants to bring a couple of stools with the wine.

Tiher laughed, and Tiarnán shot him an unfathomable look. When the servants came up with the wine and the stools, they showed a tendency to hover once more, and had to be shooed off.

"They're afraid to let you out of their sight, aren't they?" said Tiher, sitting down. "Perhaps you could give me some lessons in managing a manor some time. I'd love to be adored like that."

"They were grossly abused by your cousin," said Tiarnán. "They're still afraid he'll come back. I'll be pleased when they realize he can't, and stop hanging over me." He poured the wine, a cup for Tiher and one for himself, and set the jug down carefully on the uneven floor.

Tiher took the cup and sipped. The wine was not the fine Bordeaux that Alain had given him, but the local Talensac vintage, thin and sour. Tiarnán was obviously determined to touch nothing of Alain's, not the tapestry nor the linen nor the bed nor the wine. Which was just as well, as Alain had asked Tiher that morning to make sure that all his own property was removed from the manor. "I bought those things with my own money," he'd said, "and the monster has no right to them." No shame, no remorse, though his "own money" had been borrowed in Nantes on the strength of the manor of Talensac, to which he had never had the least right. It was left to Tiher to feel remorse — and he did. He was bitterly ashamed of his cousin. He supposed that he could try to see the situation through Alain's eyes, tell himself repeatedly that the man whose wine he was drinking was an unnatural monster, and that Alain had been justified in . . . but he did not believe that Alain had been justified in what he had done to Tiarnán, still less in what he'd done to Talensac. It was as Marie had said. The man sitting opposite was not evil, and the wolf had not been evil, either. That was not a matter of faith, but of simple experience.

Tiher looked thoughtfully at his rival for a moment. Tiarnán sat straight and self-possessed, his cup of wine on his knee, his face set in its old expression of guarded courtesy. The thought that that human body could change and become the body of an animal was disturbing and unpleasant, but full of strange questions which Tiher found himself itching to ask: What is it like, being a wolf? Can you sense things that humans cannot? *Have* you ever met the people of the hills? Are you forced to transform yourself, every so often, or do you only do it because you enjoy it? Are you going to do it again?

The questions were better left unasked. Tiarnán was human, had been so at heart even as a wolf, and probing too deeply into his private mysteries would only create monsters where there were none.

"My cousin won't be coming back here," Tiher promised out loud. "He's decided to accept the duke's offer of free passage for himself and his wife to the Holy Land."

Tiarnán let out his breath slowly in what was not quite a sigh of relief. "Tell him," he said, in an even voice, "to stay out of my way until he goes. I wish to respect your cousin's life, so as not to waste our lord the duke's care over me, but if he crosses my path I will kill him. There has never been a man I have had so much cause to hate." His face was studiously blank, but the pupils of his eyes had contracted to a deadly point like the tip of a spear. Tiher, looking at him, remembered the wolf lunging toward Alain's throat and shivered.

"He has no plans to meet you," said Tiher.

"Good," said Tiarnán, and sipped his wine.

Tiher cleared his throat. "Duke Hoel will start your appeal to have your marriage annulled as soon as he's officially informed that you're back and want it — which I imagine will be as soon as I get back to Treffendel today. I talked to Alain privately this morning. He was very eager to give me instructions for his servants here, telling them to make sure that everything he bought while he was lord here was returned to him. I told him I can't give them any such orders until he's officially heard that you've returned, but I thought I would warn you that he's likely to send you a long list. The duke is going to let him and Eline use a house in Rennes until the formalities are completed, and he wants everything sent there — armor, clothes, furniture, linen, horses, hawks, the wine, everything. Oh, and a cash sum in replacement of Eline's dowry."

Tiarnán's face stayed blankly furious. "He shall have his own things back, but he's spent every penny in the manor, and there's no money to give him — as indeed he must know. I hope to recover something from that thieving bailiff of his, but there are others who have a prior claim on his plunder. And, since your cousin sold my armor, weapons, and warhorse, as well as all my clothes and hawks and the furniture from my house and hall, there's nothing for me to sell to raise it. Indeed, I'm going to have to borrow money to get back my horse and arms, which I must have to serve the duke."

"Your clothes, too?" asked Tiher, looking at his clothes, a plain blue tunic and brown hose, and noticing for the first time that the sleeves were too short.

"My clothes, too. I've borrowed what I'm wearing from one

of my own servants." The blue tunic was Donoal's Sunday best.

Tiher suffered another stab of the shame that Alain had not felt. "Alain was thorough, wasn't he?" he said, trying to ward off the pain with cynical lightness. "I'm very sorry. You should be able to recover your horse and weapons and the rest from the man in Nantes when the duke pays off Alain's debt, and if you ask Duke Hoel I'm sure he'd be glad to help pay back the dowry as well."

Tiarnán shook his head impatiently. He felt that he had cost Hoel too much as it was. He was reluctant to ask even for the return of the relief, though he was entitled to take it back, since there had not, after all, been a new succession to the manor. And now a demand for Eline's dowry! That money had never existed in silver at all: it had all been settled between himself and Lord Hervé in forestry rights. It was true, though: when a marriage was annulled, the woman was legally entitled to take back her dowry. Tiarnán was determined not to leave either Eline or Alain with any legal claim upon him. "What Eline has a right to," he told Tiher, "she shall have somehow. Tell your cousin that I will deal with him honorably, and take nothing that isn't mine."

Tiher remembered how Tiarnán had returned Alain's sword and armor, lost at Comper. Then as now, the magnanimity would be squandered in vain. He shook his head. "That won't make him feel the least shame over what he did to you, you know," he confessed bitterly. "He thinks he was entitled to everything he stole, and is full of outrage at the way he's being treated now."

Tiarnán's blank fury was replaced by unambiguous contempt. "I'll deal with him honorably nonetheless."

Tiher sighed. "Well, at least you'll have the satisfaction of feeling thoroughly superior!"

Tiarnán's eyes glinted. "Why not? It's the only satisfaction I'll get from him."

Tiher had forgotten the man's straight-faced subtlety, and stared for a moment in surprise. Their eyes met, and all at once the grimness that had hung over the meeting was gone. What was between Alain and Tiarnán was excluded: Tiher had been no part of it. The shame was not his after all.

Tiher leaned back in his chair, feeling much happier, and swallowed some of the wine. "Your servants would love to treat Alain the way they've treated Gilbert," he said brightly.

Again the glint. "You may take Gilbert back to his master when you go."

"In the highly scented condition he's in? No, thank you! He can walk by himself."

Tiarnán smiled. He had expected this meeting to be very much more difficult. The awareness that Tiher knew his secret had at first made him feel as though he were facing the other without a layer of his skin. Tiher, however, was behaving as though that secret were irrelevant, and Tiarnán was grateful. Tiher, he thought now, had always been an honorable man — unlike his cousin. He would probably make Marie very happy.

Tiarnán's wolf memories always seemed vivid but strangely oblique to him when he was a man, half-wordless, like the memories of early childhood. His human mind had only just begun to digest Isengrim's experiences, interpreting them in its own terms. He already knew, however, that what he had begun to feel for Marie as a wolf translated into passionate human love. When he had lain down to rest the previous night, he'd thought of her and been swept by another wave of disorienting sickness, one that brought tears of anguish to his eyes. She had been in love with him once, but now she knew what he was, and the sight of him caused her pain. He longed to see her again, but he was afraid to. He had scented what he was to Eline: he did not want to recognize that same revulsion on Marie's face. She had said that she understood Eline very well. Marie, it was true, had saved him from certain death and restored to him a life worth living, but her motives for doing so he could only guess at. Truthfulness, principally, he thought, and concern for an abstract justice. He dared not tempt himself into another disaster by hoping she still loved him a little. All his confidence had been crushed by the enormous weight of his humiliations, and he dreaded meeting her again. The particular bitterness of being regarded as a monster by a woman he loved was one he had already tasted; he did not think he could bear to sample it again. Let Tiher marry Marie and make her happy. When she was happily married, the tempest of feelings that tormented him now would calm.

"When you inherit your manor," he said to Tiher deliberately, "you'll manage better than your cousin did, Tiher de Fougères."

"I should hope so, or I wouldn't keep it long!" replied Tiher with a grin. "But I don't have any prospect of one, more's the pity."

Tiarnán looked at him levelly, then said in a low voice, "Duke Hoel told Lady Marie that you would have land the next time one of his vassals dies without heirs. He said that he would not let a man like you go wanting. He urged the lady to marry you."

Tiher was stunned. He put his cup down, staring at Tiarnán in disbelief. Tiarnán stared back, his eyes once again as unreadable as Isengrim's. "When did the duke say that?" asked Tiher.

"It was while we were in Paris."

Tiher caught his breath. Of course, the wolf had gone to Paris, would have overheard, but . . . "You were listening then?" he asked. "You could understand?"

Tiarnán looked away, down at the bottom of his wine cup. "If I concentrated, I could understand. It was not easy, but I was listening then. And I remember it now more clearly than if I hadn't had to concentrate. If the duke has said nothing about this to you, it is probably because he wishes to surprise you. You're a favorite of his."

"Me?"

"Ever since you would not 'permit' him to risk his life." Tiarnán's voice was dry. Tiher had a sudden vivid memory of how he had not permitted the duke to risk his life: the exhausted wolf crouched trembling by the duke's horse, and himself fastening on the collar and the muzzle.

"My God!" whispered Tiher. After a moment's reflection, he demanded harshly, "Why are you telling me this?"

Tiarnán was gazing into the bottom of his cup as though he were looking for his fortune in the wine sediment. "You have an interest in a certain lady. I thought you should know that you could support her if you married her."

"Do you mean you have no interest in the lady?" asked Tiher incredulously. What Marie felt for Tiarnán had been perfectly clear to him the day before, and it had seemed far too much to hope that Tiarnán would be indifferent again.

Tiarnán's head jerked up again. "For Christ's sake!" he exclaimed in a suddenly passionate whisper. "Stop pretending you don't know what I am! How can I go to a lady like that, when she knows I . . . You saw what it did to Eline!"

"But . . ." began Tiher, then paused, struggling with himself. It was clear from Tiarnán's face that he was as about as indifferent to Marie as tinder is to fire, but thought he had no hope with her. For an instant Tiher balanced on a raft of considerations. He loved Marie, and if Tiarnán became her suitor, his own chances of winning her were slight. On the other hand, Marie had known, that evening at Treffendel when Tiher had issued his half-serious, half-mocking proposal of marriage, that he had expectations of land — and she'd said nothing, and turned the whole thing into a joke. If she was so reluctant to entertain his suit when she thought Tiarnán was dead, what chance did he have with her now that she knew his rival was alive? Besides, Tiarnán had just magnanimously shown Tiher fresh grounds for hope: How could Tiher respond by cheating his rival with despair? That was the sort of trick Alain would have played.

"It's true Marie knows what you are," Tiher said in an easy, unemotional tone that betrayed none of the pang he felt at heart, "but it doesn't seem to matter to her much."

Tiarnán stared just as Tiher had a few minutes ago. "But I could smell . . ." he began — and stopped and looked away abruptly. What he'd sensed as a wolf should not be spoken of; it would only make him more monstrous.

Tiher looked at him curiously. "Be that as it may, I certainly regard you as the most dangerous rival I have."

Tiarnán looked back at Tiher with wonder. His eyes began to brighten with an incredulous hope. "You're a more honorable rival than your cousin," he said, after a silence, and smiled.

"Stupid of me, isn't it?" said Tiher, and grinned back. I don't know why I like the fellow, he thought to himself. If he decides to press his case with Marie, my chances fly out the window: I could tell that from the way she looked at him yesterday. And he's a *werewolf*, of all impossible things! I ought to abominate him. Instead we sit here grinning at each other. Ah, well, Marie loves him, and he'll adore her like the Mother of God. As for myself, I'll try my luck with Marie while I can, and then scrape up what happiness I can find. With a manor of my own, that ought to be quite a lot.

He picked his cup up, emptied it, and set it back on the floor. "Well, thank you for the wine," he said. "Now I must collect my horse and get back to Treffendel."

"Of course," said Tiarnán. "I'll walk you to the stables."

When Tiher was mounting his horse, Tiarnán asked suddenly, "Was Eline badly hurt?"

Tiher settled himself in the saddle and looked down at the other. "The right side of her nose was ripped off and there are lacerations on both cheeks," he replied evenly. "They say that the wounds are clean and should heal. But she'll be scarred for life."

"Oh," said Tiarnán, dropping his eyes. He remembered again the taste of her blood; remembered her face smiling up at him. "Tell her I'm sorry."

Three days later, when the duke left Treffendel, Marie again asked for an escort to St. Mailon's. Tiher offered to come with her, but she declined: she wanted space to think and to consider her position, and he was no longer making any pretense of having given up the chase. She found instead one of the duke's servants who was going to conduct some business on an estate in the region, and who agreed to ride with her to the hermitage and collect her a couple of hours later on his way back. She pretended to pay attention to his discussion of his business all the way to the chapel, and took polite leave of him with relief. It was with a sense of arriving at a peaceful harbor that she rang the small, sweet bell above the church door and went in.

The chapel was shadowy and empty. A handful of wildflowers lay upon the altar, and the sunlight came crisscross through the window screens and patterned the blossoms with light. All at once, Marie was happy. From the moment she'd understood Tiarnán's secret, she'd felt a restless anxiety that had only grown when none of the disasters she'd feared came about, but here at last there was peace. She knelt down before the altar and began to pray.

When Judicaël came in a few minutes later, the pattern of light had spilled from the altar onto the floor before her and lay like a heap of jewels upon the rushes. Marie knelt in her tawny gown, as straight and simple as a young tree, her bowed head veiled in dark gold. He stood for a time in the doorway watching her. Tiarnán had sent him a letter from Talensac, and he knew what Marie had done. His joy and his gratitude were immense, but he was in no hurry to unload them in words. Time might yet deform many things, but in this moment was distilled a fullness of God's grace.

"God be with you, daughter," he said at last, and she turned, lifted her luminous eyes to his, and smiled.

"God be with you, Father. You asked me to come back when I'd completed my judgment."

He walked slowly up the nave, bowed to the altar, and knelt facing her behind the rail. "I had a letter from my foster son two days ago," he told her quietly. "He said he owed you much. I am grateful, more than I can say."

She looked down, blushing. "I made some guesses."

"Which you could not have made if you were content to see the world with the world's eyes. So, your judgment is complete?"

She shrugged. "Complete? I don't know. How can anyone but God make a final judgment? And you know Tiarnán far better than I do. But, in all I can see or know or feel, I believe, with you, that he is not a monster. The world God created is not monstrous. And for what we are by nature, however we came to it, we cannot be blamed—our guilt lies only in the thoughts of our hearts and the actions that spring from them. So I think Tiarnán's wife was afraid of shadows, and you were right in the eyes of God to set no penance on Tiarnán for being what he is. Though from the world's view he would have been safer if you had, still, someone has to see the world with God's eyes, with love and not fear."

Judicaël let out a long sigh and bowed his head. "You've given me more than I expected," he said after a long silence.

"It's only my opinion," said Marie with a smile. "I am not to be relied upon."

They were talking quietly a few minutes later when the chapel bell sounded again, and they both looked round to see Tiarnán himself walk in. He stopped abruptly, looking shocked. Marie, equally shocked, went red.

Judicaël leapt to his feet, sprang over the altar rail, ran to Tiarnán, and embraced him fervently. "Thank God we have you in your right shape again!" he said fiercely, holding him by the shoulders and shaking him. "Thank God!" Then he stood back and glared. "What are you in those clothes for?" he demanded. Tiarnán was wearing green hunting things again.

"My other ones have all been sold," Tiarnán replied with a lopsided smile. "You need not worry: I'm not even alone today. I have two men outside, and I was lucky to escape with so few. All Talensac has been hovering over me like a nursemaid over a new baby."

"Good!" said Judicaël sternly. "Perhaps they'll keep you in order."

"I came here to see you, Father," Tiarnán said hesitantly. "I did not expect to find Lady Marie. God shield you, Lady, you didn't ride here on your own?"

"I have an escort who will come back for me in a couple of hours," said Marie, then bit her lip at the prim stiffness of her own voice. The sting had gone back into her heart at Treffendel when he had touched her face and said, "Your eyes are gray." She had not expected that particular disquiet. On the night of his wedding she had surrendered all hope of marrying him, and the possibility that his marriage could be annulled had not occurred to her. Now she was afraid of that ache, and afraid of his gratitude. She had not intended to see him until he came to Nantes to see all the court.

"Could I take his place?" Tiarnán offered quickly.

"All the way to Nantes, Lord Tiarnán? I'd heard that your estate needs a great deal of attention, and I'm sure you'd prefer not to leave it for the court yet."

"My clerk Kenmarcoc came back last night; I'm freer than I was. I could go to the court briefly. I'm bound to go to Nantes in a couple of days anyway, to see if I can get my horse and armor back. Lady Marie, if I can do any service for you at all, I would be more than glad of it. I know how much I owe you."

Marie felt short of breath again. "Lord Tiarnán, I owe you a great deal, too, for a service you once did for me. Let's say that we're even now."

Judicaël had been looking quickly from Marie to Tiarnán and back again, and now his intense face altered with its sweet smile. "Perhaps, my son," he said pleasantly, "if you're in no great hurry to confess your sins, we could all go to my hut and share a meal together? It's about lunchtime."

When they came out of the chapel, Tiarnán's two men hurried over exactly like anxious nursemaids. Tiarnán looked at them with immense displeasure, and Marie bit her finger to stop a giggle.

The two came along to Judicaël's hut as well, taking some food they'd brought with them, and the five of them sat in the garden among the sweet scent of the herbs and ate bread and cheese and cherries, washed down with goat's milk and ale. Then Tiarnán glared at his two servants and told them to go see to the horses. "Lady Marie's as well," he told them. "That's the roan mare tethered in the shade. Take them all down to the brook and let them drink, and give them a good grooming."

"You'll stay with Father Judicaël and the foreign lady?" asked one of the servants suspiciously.

" 'The foreign lady' is called Lady Marie Penthièvre: she's kin to the duchess, the duke himself honors her for her wisdom, and you, Donoal, should not speak of her so disrespectfully. What on earth do you *think* I'm going to do? Go see to the horses. I didn't ask you to come, so you can't complain if you find it dull."

The two went off, with several anxious backward glances, and Marie bit her finger again.

Tiarnán flicked a cherry stone irritably in the direction of their departing backs. "I don't know what they think will happen if they let me out their sight," he said in disgust.

"You disappeared from this place suddenly once before," said Judicaël sharply. "And they were left at the mercy of people who treated them with contempt. Naturally they're afraid to leave you here alone again. What happens to you does affect them: you should remember that, Tiarnán."

Tiarnán looked at once more sober. "I can hardly forget that now. Justin Braz, Conwal's son, was flogged, did you know that? They told me he wept and begged for mercy. Justin, who was never afraid of any man living! Shackled to a pillar and whipped by one of de Fougères's men for carting his grain to Montfort. And he was only the first."

"I know what's been happening at Talensac," replied Judicaël quietly. "I've had a stream of people from there all summer, asking help and advice. What I want to know is, will you abandon them again?"

There was a silence. "I do not know," Tiarnán replied at last, in a strained voice. "I don't want to."

He felt at that moment that he never wanted to leave his humanity again. What he'd done in the forest before now seemed to him to have been nothing but playing at being a wild animal: after a few days as a wolf, he had gone home to his comfortable manor and rested and eaten his fill. The reality had been cold and hunger without hope of escape, desperate loneliness and constant danger. He could never forget it, and had no desire to taste it again. But he had several times before tried to give up his transformations, at Judicaël's urging, and always the desire had become so powerful that it overcame all his scruples.

"I would be glad if I could escape from it," he told Judicaël in a low voice.

"Other men have strong urges and master them," said Judicaël sternly. "For your people's sake, and your own, so should you. It was dangerous before—but now you've vanished for nearly a year and returned after being presumed dead: you won't be able simply to slip away anymore. Your comings and goings will be followed much more closely, and the risk you take will be much greater. If you do it again, I warn you now, I'll give you a penance for it—not for the thing itself, but for taking a stupid and unnecessary risk with your life and with the safety of those around you."

Tiarnán bowed his head. "I would deserve it."

Marie imagined Isengrim fasting on bread and water and humbly saying Paternosters, and bit her finger again. I'm being silly, she warned herself. It's not funny at all.

Tiarnán had caught the gesture, and he looked over and met her eyes; his own brightened, and the laughter went out of her. She wanted suddenly and desperately to touch his face, stroke the white line on his chin, kiss him. She made herself look away.

Tiarnán looked at her demurely bent head, and thought of her body as he'd seen it, white against the grass at Nimuë's Well. He'd thought of her frequently since Tiher's visit, uncertain whether to trust what Tiher had said or not. He had been watching her surreptitiously since his arrival, anxiously searching for signs of revulsion—and there had been none, only an ease that when he thought of it seemed nothing short of miraculous. He had caught the laughter in her eyes when Judicaël threatened him with penances; to see it fade at his own perplexed him. He did not know how to proceed, or whether to proceed at all. He wanted to proceed, to coax the laughter back into those dark-lashed eyes, and see her smile for him. He did not want to part quickly, leaving nothing settled, nothing said. "My lady," he said, "when is your escort coming?"

"He said he'd be back no later than Nones," she replied promptly, looking up again. "We were to catch up with the duke at Redon, and if he's later than that we won't arrive until after dark."

Tiarnán nodded. The court usually stayed at the great monastery of Redon on its way from one castle to another. "Will you be staying with the court in Nantes?" he asked tentatively. "Or do you mean to follow your lands to the convent?"

"I haven't decided on that yet, Lord Tiarnán."

Her eyes were lowered again, turned away from him. He watched her profile, the high forehead and the strong bones of the face, and the line of her throat pale and soft within the gold wings of her veil. "I know that Lord Tiher still hopes that you will marry him, and that Duke Hoel intends to give him land of his own," he told her, waiting for some reaction.

Barely a blink. She had withdrawn into some soft, secretive place of her own where she regarded in slow deliberation the choices available to her. "I suppose you did hear that, didn't you?" she replied quietly. "I haven't decided on that, either, Lord Tiarnán."

"Lady Marie," he began, not sure how much he meant to say, but knowing he must say something, or she might think that she had nothing else to decide about, "when Lord Tiher came to Talensac, the day after I returned there, we agreed that we were rivals. Forgive me if what I say now is unwelcome — but Tiher himself implied that my cause was not entirely without hope. I know that he is an honorable and estimable man, and I know that I am a . . ." He hesitated, fumbling again with those sharp and slippery things, words, that had never expressed for him anything of importance. Her face had turned to him, and her eyes, clear and wide in surprise, but still with no trace of revulsion, gave him the will to struggle on. "I know I am a . . . a man who has proved himself a very poor husband to one wife, and a . . ." He paused again, faced with the brutal frankness of an ugly word which he still found false to himself.

"I know what you are," said Marie quietly, and without a trace of either horror or pity.

He let out a breath raggedly and ploughed on. "It may be that you despise me for that. You said that you understood what Eline felt. If you despise me and do not wish me to trouble you again, tell me now, and I'll do my best to observe that faithfully. But if you can, let my love sit beside Tiher's and Saint Michael's, as something about which you must decide."

Marie's face was burning, and she looked at the ground and chewed her finger. She thought of telling him that he really shouldn't have said this until after his first marriage was annulled — but she knew she wouldn't say any such thing. Eline had injured him more deeply than she'd realized, to make all that confident self-possession of his bow into this humble apology for loving her. She couldn't have struck him on the wound — even if she hadn't been desperate to do nothing to discourage him. She looked up again and found him watching her anxiously.

"Lord Tiarnán," she whispered, "I could feel many things for you, but contempt and horror aren't among them. If I understand what Lady Eline felt, it's only from pity. What she did to you was abominable. For my own part, I . . ." She stopped, not knowing how to finish her sentence.

But it seemed she didn't need to. Tiarnán's face had lit like a bonfire.

Judicaël got to his feet. "My garden needs tending," he said. He picked up a hoe and went down to the far end of it.

Tiarnán looked after him in surprise, then looked back at Marie and smiled his rare full smile. "That was his blessing," he told her. "He won't say more than that, in case it would be interfering." And he slipped across the space between them, took her head lightly between his hands, as he had in her dream, and kissed her. She felt as though her heart were being swept down a waterfall. When he lifted his head away, she smiled into his eyes, and then threw her arms around him, holding the shape and warmth of him close. She cradled the side of his face in her hand, and touched the white line on his chin, and it seemed to fill some deep craving that she'd lived with all her life. When his arms were around her, everything came into balance again, the soul moving with the body like the two ends of the same yoke.

"I love you," she told him, finishing her sentence at last.

AUTHOR'S NOTE

This novel is based on the *Lai de Bisclavret* by the twelfth-century poet Marie de France, a talented woman whose works deserve to be better known. I have set it at the end of the eleventh century, but, as befits a medieval romance, the history is not entirely exact.

The poem on page 188 is my translation of "De ramis cadunt folia," a thirteenth-century Latin love song.